BEYOND THE THRONE

BEYOND
THE
THRONE

RACHEL TERRY

PHARUS PRESS

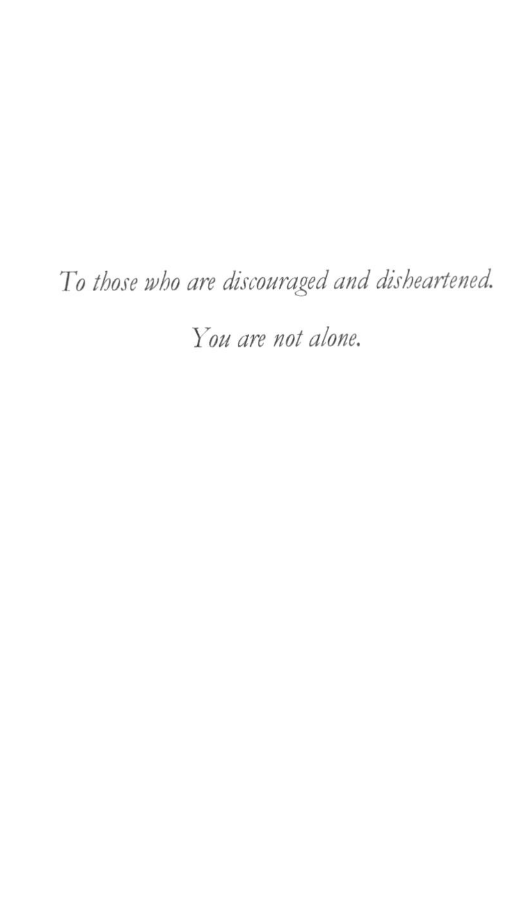

To those who are discouraged and disheartened.

You are not alone.

THE
AKKADIAN
EMPIRE
SOUL STONE MINES
SHEMAR
RIVER CHARNEL
THE BADLANDS
RUINS OF ANARSHA

THE CAPITOL

THE WORKHOUSES

VALDERAN
RAINFOREST

ELATH

PROLOGUE

The kingdom of Anarsha was ready to fall.

King Ulric gazed down from one of the many windows of his tower, taking in the devastation that lay below, consumed by a mixture of horror and dread.

The Badlands. The desolate, barren land that he had once hoped would keep Anarsha's enemies at bay now played host to a graveyard of scattered bodies, picked clean to bones, and mangled iron corpses. Flesh and machine alike had met their end here.

He sighed. The Akkadian Empire was relentless. He should have known better than to think they would be deterred. Their leader was nothing if not patient. They could afford to wait, while Anarsha could do so no longer.

There were no allies now to come to Anarsha's aid. The Empire had marched across the known world, conquering all within. The time to act was well behind them. Shemar and Elath were nothing more than vassal states. Anarsha stood alone for her defiance, cut off and friendless.

The food stores were running out, the army weakened. And now the Empire's machines of war had come for them, like their neighbors before.

Ulric inhaled deeply, imagining he could smell the acrid smoke in the air, thick and choking. The tang of blood.

Feel the heat of the flame, the ground trembling beneath his feet as the enemy approached.

A sudden surge of anger, borne of impotence, seized him. What good was he, what kind of ruler, if he could not even protect his own people? Surrender was not an option; Ulric had too much pride for that. He loved this kingdom more fiercely than life itself—and that was why he had made the bargain that he had, saints forgive him.

The knowledge weighed heavily on his chest, but the cost was one he could bear. It would all be worth it, in the end. It had to be.

Ulric closed his eyes for a moment, allowing himself to imagine the scenes that would play out if Akkadia breached the city walls and flooded the streets.

The Empire would destroy and pillage as they wished and Ulric's people would cry out in despair that he had failed them. They would call out for the saints to save them, but there would be no one.

The saints were gone. Only their legacy remained.

Foolishly, Ulric had turned a blind eye to the plight of Shemar and Elath, assuming Akkadia would leave Anarsha alone, believing that his own kingdom was large and powerful enough to endure. That they would be spared.

What a fool he'd been. While he tarried, the Empire had grown into a force too large now to be stopped.

Unless…

Saints forgive me. But even as he considered what he was about to do, he could see no other way. He had debated with himself long into the nights and found no other answers. The Akkadians were coming and would surely destroy them otherwise.

There was one ally yet who could help. Who could ensure victory, who could make the Akkadian's tremble with fear.

As though summoned by his thoughts, he could feel a presence stir within the room, ancient, malevolent, and powerful. It lurked just beneath the surface, eager and willing.

Waiting to be unleashed.

PART I:

THE

CAPITOL

PART I:

I

Water sloshed around Skye's boots as she ducked into another tunnel in the sewers. The others' footsteps had already faded into the distance behind her. Yet again, she had managed to slip away without them noticing, melding into the shadows like a wraith. She allowed herself a small smile.

"You really shouldn't wander off like that," a crackly voice sounded in her left ear. "You're going to get into trouble someday."

"Only if the Empire catches me," she replied, her voice echoing softly in the metallic tunnels, slightly muffled by the cloth that concealed her nose and mouth. It did little to help the virulent smell, but she'd long since grown accustomed to it.

"And they very well might," Anyah retorted, her voice distorted by the many leagues separating them. "You're too reckless by half."

Skye reached up to adjust the earpiece. "That's why I have you to look out for me."

Anyah's reply was drowned out by static.

Dammit. Skye resisted the urge to slap the comm device. "Didn't get that, Anyah. The signal is terrible down here." *It always is, but we need to get this fixed.*

"I know. That's why *you* should be on your way to District VII right now."

Skye ignored her. Anyah knew she was more than capable of completing her official mission and whatever detour she chose to make. She knew how important this was. Otherwise, one day, Anyah wouldn't be able to warn them at all until it was too late.

A different voice crackled over the line, much clearer since it wasn't being broadcasted all the way from Anarsha. "Looks like we lost the Rat again."

Tiachren. Skye recognized his voice and the amusement in it. He'd been the one to partly challenge her to her second mission that night and she didn't intend to disappoint.

Jonathan, their squad leader, spoke up then. "Skye? Where are you? Come in. This is no time for games."

Skye remained silent and continued on her way. The sooner she could be free of this place, the better. Though the stench of excrement and death no longer phased her, that didn't mean she enjoyed it.

She passed a rose that had been graffitied onto the sewer wall and trailed her fingers over it. The Resistance's calling card. She checked the knives at her belt, one in the front and one in the back, part of her hoping she would have no cause this night to use them.

The other half itched to kill.

A rusted ladder, leading up to a sewer grate, loomed before her. Skye made a quick check of the rest of her weapons. Two hand crossbows at her hips, straps of spare bolts belted to her thighs, and the smaller throwing knives. Her large, two-handed crossbow was a weight on her back.

The smaller crossbows were far easier to wield and to reload, but they wouldn't punch through armor. Not like her Ironsight.

Satisfied, she took a deep breath and gripped the first rungs of the ladder, pulling herself up.

"Anyone up there?" she asked Anyah, grateful that the hacker could speak only to her if she wished, so that their words did not have to be overheard by everyone.

There was a moment of silence as Anyah checked her screens back at headquarters. "Nope, but you've got a patrol at the end of the street, to the south."

"That's fine," Skye replied as she reached up to grasp the grate. "I'm not going that way."

She gave it a sharp twist and lifted it up, gritting her teeth with the effort. In seconds, she had shimmied up the remainder of the ladder and climbed out onto the cobblestone street, glancing around.

Anyah had hacked into the Empire's network, allowing her to see the location of each of their patrols and automatons, but it wasn't foolproof and Skye trusted no one more than she trusted her own eyes. Anyah was right; the coast was clear.

A sigh sounded in her ear. "So what did Tiachren dare you to steal this time?"

Skye knew Anyah thought it was foolish, along with Jonathan, but she didn't really understand. Anyah always remained at the base, her skills different from theirs, though no less valuable. Still, she didn't know what it was to venture inside the Capitol, onto enemy ground, risking her life.

The challenges were a way of mocking death, Skye supposed, of testing fate and proving to herself that everything she'd gone through up until that point had meant something. She'd made it through and was still breathing. It was a way of spitting in the eye of the Empire and Skye relished it.

"A soul stone," she answered, a slight chill prickling her skin.

She had stolen a lot of things throughout the years—signet rings, plenty of books, a gentleman's robe that Tiachren still liked to wear, and even a necklace from around a sleeping noblewoman's throat—but never one of the mysterious crystals that powered the mechs.

Skye frowned. She didn't really know if they powered the automatons or not, but they were always implanted in the iron monsters' chests, so they must have a purpose.

They must.

"The Furnaces, then," Anyah remarked. It was a good guess, but she was also tracking Skye's movement on her screens, so she knew where she was in relation to any enemy patrols.

The Furnaces were a series of massive scrapyards located in District I, where broken mechs and unwanted bits of machinery were melted down so they could be reused.

"Right you are." Skye could see them up ahead, the furnaces' orange glow visible against the night's darkness. "Going silent."

She was too close now to risk open communication unless it was an emergency. Anyah and the others could still speak to her and only she would hear, but she couldn't risk speaking herself.

Skye moved quickly, keeping to the shadows of the ugly stone buildings with their metal roofs. Metal walkways were suspended above the furnaces and Skye glanced up at them as she neared. She could see guards patrolling, as expected, but they were too far away to notice her.

And if they did happen to see her and attempt to raise the alarm… She shrugged her shoulders, feeling them brush against her Ironsight.

Skye wasn't interested in the walkways. What she had come for lay below. She needed to be swift if she wanted to catch up with the others in District VII. Part of her felt like chiding herself for indulging in this little dare. District VII was high and the closer you came to the palace, in District X, the more dangerous it became.

But District VII was where the electronic goods were made and stored and they needed it to keep their communications functional. It was a miracle Anyah had managed to rig it up at all and only spoke to her skill.

In the angry light from the smelting furnaces, Skye could see the heaps of metal that lay piled, as if she wandered into an automaton graveyard. She stepped lightly, rats scurrying away as she approached. Even with the Empire's restrictions on animals, there was no keeping the rats out.

There were no dogs patrolling this scrapyard, like there had once been, well before her lifetime, so she didn't have to worry about being scented.

No, there were no dogs. But these yards were patrolled by something far worse. Her flesh crawled as she eyed the dragon automatons. They couldn't smell her, but they did seem to be able to hear, and they had sensors that could detect movement and body heat.

There were human guards nearby, on the ground, too. She could hear them talking amongst themselves.

"District VI is breathing down the back of our necks to get this stuff melted down and shipped off."

"We can only process so much at one time," another grumbled. "If they weren't so cheap and hired more workers, they wouldn't have to wait so long."

"Come on, talk sense. You and I both know that'll never happen."

"I don't know what the big deal is, either. Some of this stuff has been reused so many times, the armor is like a tin can. Could crush it in your fist."

"Speaking of crushed…you see the one that came back from the patrol earlier this morning?"

"No, why?"

"Looked like a giant took it by the neck and squeezed it in his fist. Its chest was shredded. Metal, ripped like paper."

"Don't be ridiculous. Giants aren't real."

No, Skye thought to herself as she picked her way through the heaps of metal, heading away from the gossiping guards. *But dragons are.*

She had glimpsed them while out on patrol a few times, always from a distance. She had hardly dared believe what she was seeing the very first time. They looked exactly like their iron counterparts in the Capitol, only they had wings. The mechs were far too heavy to fly.

Perhaps the weaker, thinner iron plating was intentional. If they lightened the automata, they might be able to take to the air. *That's all we need. Flying mechs.* Their raids would be impossible then. The beasts could simply fly over the city, using their scanners. And when they picked up a human signature without a government-issued tracker, they'd know who they were.

Skye shook her head and turned back to the matter at hand. The body of one of the dragon mechs lay sprawled before her, its lamp-like eyes dark and lifeless. The red soul stone in its chest had yet to be removed, glimmering in the light like a palm-sized ruby.

But how was she to get it out?

As she stared at it, the familiar anger sparked, burning through her reservations and crowding out all other thought.

She could still feel tons of earth pressing down on her, the ever-present darkness crowding in.

Clenching the hilt of one of her daggers, Skye ripped it free, the long, curved blade glinting cruelly, and set about trying to pry the gem free of the dead beast's chest. It was difficult work, and she worried the blade might snap from the leverage as she viciously hacked and pried at the soul stone. But at last, the stone popped free, shooting out at her so quickly, she scrabbled to catch it and nearly didn't succeed.

She sighed, studying her prize briefly. There was not a mark on it for all her desperate stabbing. She could hack at the stone all she liked, but her blade, strong as it was, would break before she ever made so much as a scratch.

When it came to soul stones, the damn things were indestructible, that much she knew.

She slipped it into one of her many pockets. *Take that, Tiachren.*

Hurrying now, Skye left the Furnaces behind and raced up the ramp that would take her to District II, making her way toward VII. Curfew had fallen and so the streets were empty. Anyone she encountered this time of night would not be friendly.

"I see you're moving again," Anyah spoke up, her voice startlingly loud after the silence. "Did you get what you came for?"

"Affirmative."

"Great. Well, there's a patrol about to round that corner so you don't want to go that way."

It took her longer to reach District VII than if she'd been able to cut a straight path, but in the end, she made it without disaster, cursing the Capitol's design the whole way.

The massive city was composed of ten concentric districts, each one smaller than the one below. Each district was walled and separate from its neighbors aside from the ramps that connected them. Nestled into the mountains, the Capitol was a veritable fortress.

Tiachren had once compared its circular, walled design to the world's ugliest wedding cake and Skye had been unable to see it any other way since.

"Where are the others?" she asked Anyah.

Anyah directed her to a warehouse and Skye slipped in the window that her team had pried open. She spoke into her comm to avoid startling them. She'd learned that lesson the hard way once when Jonathan had nearly run her through.

"I'm here," she said, once she was inside, landing lithely on the floor, dust motes swirling around her in the moonlight that streamed through the windows.

"Ah, the Rat returns," Tiachren said, turning to her with a grin. "Did you get it?"

Skye brandished the soul stone.

Fae, a short young woman who stood beside Tiachren, let out a gasp. "It's a beauty! I can't wait to get back and study it. Maybe then we can find out what its purpose is."

"*If* we live long enough to get back," Jonathan growled. "Good of you to join us, Rat."

He was the only one who managed to make her nickname sound like an insult. From everyone else, it was a compliment, a testament to how well she navigated the sewers, more intimately familiar with them than the rats who inhabited them.

"You worry too much, Jonathan."

"It's that worry that keeps you all alive. If something happens, I'm the one who will have to explain it to the Triad."

"Don't worry," Skye retorted. "I didn't bring any soldiers with me."

Really, if the Empire wanted to keep rebels out of the city, they should raise the metal ramps that connected the districts, but they couldn't risk cutting off any reinforcements that may be called to a certain area at any given moment.

Jonathan grunted. "Let's finish up and get out of here."

The warehouse was one of many that produced the wiring needed for the automata and to provide electricity, mainly to the upper districts. The foundries constantly belched thick smoke into the air.

Skye knew that the lower districts had access to electricity, but it was intermittent. If something needed more power elsewhere, it was diverted. She'd glimpsed few lit windows on her way there.

"All right, Anyah. You're the expert. What am I looking for?"

"The others already got the wiring I need. All that's left is a new transmission dish. Look around and see if you can find one."

Skye had seen Anyah's current transmission dish, so she knew what it looked like, about the size of a dinner plate and gray. Anyah had rigged it in the highest tower of Anarsha's ruins to get the best signal.

The four of them searched but there was no dish in the warehouse.

"I'll check across the street," Skye volunteered, since she had arrived late.

Glancing around to make sure the coast was clear, she darted across to the warehouse on the other side of the street. With the hilt of one of her blades, she smashed the lock on the door, not caring if she left evidence behind. It wouldn't be discovered until tomorrow morning, when they were long gone.

She smiled as she stepped into the room, rows of dishes lined up along the far wall.

"What size do you want?" she asked Anyah.

"As big as you can manage."

Skye didn't want to get too ambitious, but she selected one of the larger sizes—at least bigger than what Anyah currently had—stuffing it into her pack.

"This ought to improve the signal," she grunted as she hauled the pack onto her shoulders, no longer able to ignore the weight she carried. "Eh, Anyah?"

There was no reply. The signal must have cut out again.

Skye sighed to herself and stepped back outside. A low, metallic growl sounded to her right, almost like an engine purring. She felt cold sweat break out on her skin, heart clenching as she turned, slowly, hoping somehow that it hadn't yet seen her.

The dragon automaton was massive, ten feet of solid iron armor plating, gears and wiring. They possessed few weak spots. The two yellow lamp eyes were one. If she could break them, the sensors would be of no use, but that was easier said than done and Skye didn't relish the idea of getting too close to a metal maw full of sharp teeth.

To make matters worse, the cursed things could breathe fire, just like their real-life counterparts. Or at least, the myths said so. Skye had never seen a real dragon breathe fire and as far as she knew, no one else had either. Most within the Capitol believed the creatures to be extinct.

The guard that accompanied the automaton shouted at her. Skye turned and ran. If he'd been alone, she would have taken him out, with either her crossbow or a well-aimed blade. But with the mech, all she could do was run.

Weapons were useless against them, with the exception of one of Tiachren's grenades.

Behind her, there was a belch of steam, the creaking of joints that weren't quite as well lubricated as they could have been, and then the metallic clanking as the beast gave chase, leaving its human companion behind.

"Mech due north!" Skye yelled into her comm. Hopefully, her team would go the other way and find one of the sewer grates to duck into. It was up to her to lead the beast away. To Anyah, she added, "What the hell?"

"The network cut out for a minute," Anyah exclaimed, then added, almost to herself, "I wonder if they're on to me."

Skye rolled her eyes. Anyah wondered that every time she seemed to lose signal. The Empire hadn't found a way to block her access to their system yet, though, so Skye could only conclude they weren't on to her.

"I don't care!" she cried. "Just keep me posted. I don't want to run into a trap."

Fear made her jumpy—and waspish—her every movement too fast, too jerky. But the mechs brought out a primal fright in her. There was just something about facing down something so soulless, that would cut you down without batting an eye or feeling anything at all.

Something that there was no defending against.

"It's all clear that way," Anyah reassured her.

But it wouldn't be for long. The alarm would be raised and as long as she stayed above ground and remained uncaptured, more automata and guards would converge on her location until she was surrounded.

"We really need to find a way to take down their system," Skye panted as she ran, tearing away the cloth that hid her face, allowing for more air. She didn't care if they saw her now.

She, like the other Resistance members, no longer had Imperial trackers, like ordinary citizens did, which caused them to show up on the Empire's own tracking network, pinpointing their exact location and movements. But there were still security cameras at various points, especially in the lower districts, keeping an eye on the rabble.

"Where are you guys?" she asked her team.

Fae replied, "In the tunnels."

Despite the fear coursing through her veins, Skye felt a flicker of relief. Her team was safe. Now she needed to join them.

She could hear the mech gaining on her, its long stride closing the distance. A sewer grate lay ahead, impossibly far and seeming to grow no closer. Skye increased her pace, racing toward it, ignoring the pain forming in her ribs.

The leather soles of her knee-high boots prevented her from slipping on the cobbles as she halted beside the grate. With a wild yell, she heaved it up, dragging it back into place as she climbed down onto the ladder.

She jumped, landing in the foul water with a splash and a grunt, stumbling to her knees, as the automaton's metallic claws scraped over the grate. For a moment, Skye imagined those claws tearing at her flesh and shuddered.

Unnatural beasts. Tireless, emotionless, unable to feel pain. Yes, they occasionally broke down and needed maintenance, but in every other respect, they were the perfect soldier.

Mindless, unquestioned obedience.

That appealed to the Empire all too well.

"I'm in the tunnels," she told her team, getting to her feet and setting out deeper into the sewers. She would catch up with them later.

After all, she knew those tunnels better than the rats that lived there.

II

The clanging of the clocktower jolted Leo from sleep, each dissonant note reverberating in time with his pounding headache. He moaned and pushed himself up from where he'd been lying face down on the bed. He'd awoken two hours early only to drift off again, a sure herald of a headache to come.

Pale sunlight streamed into the room through the threadbare curtains. The number of chimes from the clock finally penetrated his brain and he jerked up in alarm, cursing to himself. He was late. Geoffrey would have his head. *If he was sober…*

There was no time for breakfast or a shave. Leo had slept in his clothes, now rumpled, but his appearance would have to do. He ran a hand quickly through his disheveled hair, the thick curls sticking up every which way.

Straightening the collar of his jumpsuit, Leo yanked the door open and headed downstairs. He nearly collided with his mother halfway down, who had been on her way to rouse him.

"Here," she said, thrusting a paper bag into his hands. "I made this for you."

There was no time to guess at what was in it. "Thank you," Leo replied, somewhat breathlessly. He planted a kiss on her cheek and hurried out the door.

In the distance, a train whistle sounded and he glanced up in time to see it race across one of the raised bridges, heading into an upper district. If he could afford it, he would have taken a train to work, but it was money they simply could not spare.

Instead, he covered the distance on foot as he did every morning. The soles of his leather boots were growing thin and would have to be replaced soon. He'd already been forced to acquire a new pair of laces two weeks ago.

Despite the warm morning light, the Capitol looked colorless as always. If one wanted color, one had to venture into the upper districts, where there were trees and green spaces. In the lower districts, every spare inch of space was given over to practicality.

District III was no different. The buildings were packed closely together, but at least they weren't all but on top of each other, like in the first two districts. They may have been stained the color of soot and in desperate need of a new coat of paint, but they were mostly dry.

The wallpaper had worn off in some places, but Leo took pride in the fact that they had their little house all to themselves. His family didn't have to live in a crowded boarding house where the walls were thin and as many as seven families could be crammed into one room, making privacy a distant dream.

The streets were crowded with people bustling to work or going about their daily business. By evening, the market stalls would be picked over or closed. Carts and wagons pulled by horse automatons rumbled past, the metal creatures hissing steam, bronze coats gleaming.

What a real horse looked like, Leo didn't know, aside from pictures. No animals were allowed inside the Capitol walls except those that were to be slaughtered for food. The slaughterhouses were in District I, the smell occasionally wafting up to the higher levels.

Leo slowed as he approached a statue. There were two in each district, one to the west and one to the east. It stood twenty feet high, carved painstakingly out of stone. They were all identical, each one presenting an image of the first emperor, who had led Akkadia to victory against Anarsha nearly a thousand years ago.

There were a few commoners already gathered at the base of the statue, kneeling with heads bowed. Two Imperial guards stood watch, the lower half of their faces obscured by their skeletal half-masks, ensuring that none passed by without paying obeisance first.

Leo always hated this part of his morning routine. He supposed on the one hand, an emperor deserved respect from his subjects, but the ritual always felt more like humiliation to him. Still, he had seen what became of those who refused to bow.

It was not worth a beating, especially when he was already late. It would cost him precious moments, but better that than bruises.

Stopping before the statue, Leo peered up at the stone face, if it could be called such. The first emperor had worn a mask, though no one could quite agree as to the reason why. Some said he'd been horribly disfigured during the battle against Anarsha. Others claimed he did it to hide the fact that he wasn't entirely human.

Whatever the reason, every emperor that came after had also donned the mask, out of respect for the man who had delivered the last of Akkadia's enemies.

Leo knelt down on the cobblestones, lowering his gaze, counting the seconds. He knew precisely how long he was required to remain, but he always added a few seconds more just to be safe. Then he was free to go on his way, the guards giving him no trouble.

He was panting for breath by the time he arrived, feeling his heart galloping in his chest. He pushed open the door to the workshop and stepped inside, bracing himself for the tongue-lashing he was sure to receive.

"D'Lynn!" a voice snapped and Leo flinched as if he'd already been struck.

Geoffrey strode into view, his tweed suit struggling to cover his large frame. His jowls swung with every step, his tread heavy, his face a mottled red.

The man rarely ventured onto the factory floor and when he did, it wasn't for anything good. He sold the items that were produced here, but he had no hand in making them.

His fingers, thick as sausage links, would never have been able to maneuver the tiny, delicate parts.

Leo snapped his eyes up as his boss reached him, realizing he'd been staring at those very fingers.

"That's the second time this month you've been late," Geoffrey added, breathing heavily. He mopped at the sweat dripping down his face with a handkerchief.

"Apologies, sir," Leo murmured. He did not promise that it wouldn't happen again. He had no idea what might happen from one moment to the next.

He wouldn't have been late at all if not for the recent surge in demand. He'd been sleeping poorly for weeks, worked off his feet. One of the mansions on the upper levels had been bombed a few weeks ago, during a dinner party, resulting in great loss of life and limb.

Geoffrey's factory's main line of work was assembling the mechanical components of artificial limbs. It was painstaking work that required deft fingers and an eye for detail. Leo possessed both, which was the only reason he could think of to explain why he hadn't been fired yet.

As a result of the explosion, "doll makers", as Leo and his coworkers were sometimes disparagingly called, were in higher demand than usual. Such complex mechanical devices fetched a pretty penny and Leo could guess where much of it went, eyeing Geoffrey's suit. He couldn't recall ever seeing that particular one before.

Someone should have told him not to bother. The unflattering green shade only seemed to emphasize the redness of Geoffrey's face.

The man scowled. "You'll work overtime this evening. And you'll keep doing so until you decide to be punctual. Now about your business."

"Sir."

Geoffrey stalked off and Leo let out a breath. How he was ever going to catch up on lost sleep when he had to work late into the night, he had no idea. To make matters worse, such arrangements also came with the unspoken understanding that he would not be paid for the extra work.

Still, he'd been lucky to escape a beating. That much was something. There had been times in the past when he'd had to explain to his mother how he'd come by a black eye.

He punched his timecard and headed over to his locker, placing his lunch inside and fetching his goggles. As he made his way over to one of the worktables, a young woman looked up, meeting his eye and giving him a small smile.

Tanner, one of the few workers who bothered to be friendly.

"Long night?" she asked.

"And even longer days."

"I feel you."

Leo set to work, unboxing the latest shipment of parts they'd received. As he worked, he fervently hoped the Resistance was through bombing buildings, at least for a good long while.

Though the Resistance had made no official communication to the Empire, taking credit for the explosion, everyone placed the blame at their door. The Empire would prefer not to mention the incident at all.

No subsequent attack had followed in the weeks since, but tensions remained high, a sense of apprehension thick in the air. Any whisper of the Resistance's name was dangerous.

Now was the time to keep one's head down and not draw any attention to oneself. Leo was good at that. He threw himself into his work, as he usually did, falling back into the familiar route of working with his hands, assembling, making something out of nothing.

The workroom was large, the only source of light coming through the skylights and narrow strip of windows at the tops of the two longest walls. Leo was dimly aware of the sound of the others working around him, but mostly paid his surroundings little mind.

His thoughts were elsewhere, even as his fingers moved with the ease of long practice. Silently, he cursed Geoffrey, and the Resistance both, for landing him in this mess.

His friend, Fitz, had wanted to meet him that night at the pub and would be expecting him, but Leo wouldn't be able to make it now.

Sometimes he felt like he was back at the Academy, where such punishments were dealt out frequently to less attentive students.

The thought was like a bitter twist in his stomach.

A hand tapped him on the shoulder, once, then again, harder, when he failed to notice. Leo looked up from where he'd just finished placing a gear in the mechanical arm he was working on. He pushed up the magnifying lenses on his goggles, the distorted shape in front of him taking on the form of Tanner.

"Boss has an announcement," she muttered, jerking her head.

Leo stood, pushing his goggles onto his forehead. Geoffrey stood in the middle of the factory floor, hands on hips, as he called a halt to the work.

"I've just been informed," he called, "that an execution's taking place this afternoon."

Leo felt his stomach churn. They were all obligated to watch the public display and though it wouldn't be the first time, it never got any easier.

Tanner leaned close. "I wonder if they've caught the bomber."

Leo shrugged to show he'd heard. Had he known about this? He racked his brain, but could not remember hearing news of any execution. A recent development, then.

Geoffrey's lips thinned to practically nothing. "Come on. Let's get this over with."

Chairs scraped as they were pushed back, workers getting to their feet, their projects temporarily abandoned. Leo stood as well, stretching. Normally he'd be glad for a break, but not if it came at such a cost.

Following Geoffrey, they filed out of the warehouse and into the streets, which were gradually filling, becoming more congested the closer they got to the district square. Leo stuck close to Tanner, scanning the faces in the crowd. Most simply looked resigned.

When the crowd came to a halt, packed as closely together as possible, Leo saw that his group were only a few rows from the gallows that had been erected. He grimaced. They'd have a decent view, Geoffrey not wanting to miss the chance to be seen, the picture of a model citizen.

Near the gallows, at the head of the crowd, stood several dragon automatons, steam hissing softly. Leo felt a knot in his stomach, the sight of the mechs conjuring the same mixture of fear, awe and envy.

How different his life could have been, if fate had been kinder.

Immediately, he chastised himself, quashing the thoughts before they could grow. At least he was far more fortunate than the poor soul whose fate they had all come to witness. Leo could see the man now, being escorted toward the gallows by a pair of guards. They were practically dragging him, as if the man could no longer walk on his own.

He probably couldn't, knowing what they'd done to him. Leo glanced to his right, toward the higher districts, but of course, he could not see Krylok prison from there.

His gaze landed on a familiar figure in the crowd. Fitz stared back at him. There was a certain amusement to the set of his mouth, but his eyes were grim. Leo wanted to reach him, to explain that he would be unable to meet with him later, as planned.

But they were too far away to speak, not that they would dare to do so.

Leo wrenched his gaze away, back to the platform. He could see the bruises and lacerations on the condemned man now, the way he held his hands in front of him, the fingers bent, bloody and ragged.

One of the guards stepped forward, unrolling a piece of parchment and began listing off the crimes of the accused. The man made no sound, no attempt to protest his innocence and Leo wondered if he were really guilty or if they'd done something to discourage him speaking out.

The man had been found in possession of seditious materials, which was a charge so vague, it could have meant anything at all.

Beside him, Tanner sucked in a sharp breath as her earlier musings proved true. This man was responsible for the bombing—or so they claimed. He would make a nice scapegoat, regardless, his death one step closer to restoring order and reassuring the public.

When the charges had all been read, another guard reached for the rope, placing it around the man's head. He looked half-dead already, his clothes torn and filthy, his head shaved, his posture stooped, unable to hold himself upright.

Leo tensed, bracing himself for what was to come. The Empire's justice and a reminder to those who would oppose it. He knew better than to look away, no matter how much he might want to. There were other guards stationed around the edges of the crowd, along with other automatons, taking note of who watched and who did not.

And so Leo watched as the trapdoor yawned open, the body plummeting, the rope snapping taut. A hand reached out, clasping Leo's own and he knew without looking that it was Tanner. Briefly, he considered shaking her off, unsure of what the guards would make of such a gesture.

Instead, he gripped harder, giving her hand a small squeeze as the prisoner's neck snapped. Leo let out a breath. A quick death, at least. He'd witnessed others who hadn't been so lucky.

The crowd began to disperse as soon as the order was given and he followed after the others in a daze as they slowly made their way back to the workshop.

The rest of the day passed slowly. Each time Leo's mind wandered, he saw the moment the trapdoor opened and the man plunged to his death. He heard the snap of bone, perhaps more imagined than real, though he couldn't recall.

He didn't know why it bothered him so much. He'd seen other traitors put to death, their end neither so swift or merciful. He supposed it wasn't an easy thing to witness another's death, no matter the circumstances.

At last, the sky beyond darkened, the others released, free to go to their homes. Most of the lights of the factory were turned off, spotlighting only Leo's table as he was left alone, the last of the footsteps receding.

Tanner cast a sympathetic glance at him over her shoulder as she left, but it wasn't the work Leo minded. He rather liked being left alone, with no boss breathing over his shoulder. Left with only his thoughts and his work, he could focus.

He wondered if Fitz was still at the pub, waiting for him, or whether he'd given up and headed home. Perhaps, without Leo there to keep him on the straight and narrow, he'd found himself back at the gaming tables.

Leo sighed, massaging his fingers, which ached after a long day manipulating small mechanical parts.

He regretted not being there for Fitz, letting his friend down. He regretted not being able to be at home. His thoughts turned to Geoffrey, who, of course, had not stayed behind to supervise him.

The man would be at home right now, having enjoyed a nice hot meal and likely already asleep in a warm bed. Leo felt a sudden stab of anger, which he quickly tamped down.

He had a good life. He must remember that. He could provide for his family, at least, and keep them safe, warm and dry. This job, no matter how painstaking or frustrating, kept his sister fed and his mother from having to toil away.

And that was more priceless than gold.

III

To Skye's relief, Jonathan waited until they had returned to the ruins before approaching her. By then, his anger, which had always run hot, had cooled somewhat. It had been a lengthy journey through the Valderan rainforest, their team leader setting a brutal pace. The distance was one of the reasons why they didn't venture into the Capitol very often, but Skye knew they would need to return, inevitable as always.

Such trips were not without risk, but there was simply no getting around that.

The Badlands were the worst to cross—dry, arid wastelands with no shade or cover, aside from what shade was cast by the rocky outcroppings. Despite the distance between the Badlands and the Capitol, Skye was always wary to traverse them, to leave the cover of the forest behind and venture out into the open. There was nowhere to hide.

Scraps of armor, both mech and human, lay scattered across the seared ground. It had long since been picked over, anything of use salvaged, leaving what remained to the elements—all that was left of the army that had come to grief here.

Fortune seemed to favor their small band; they encountered neither dragon or Imperial patrol on their way through the forest, arriving at the ruins tired and dirty, but otherwise unharmed.

Skye let out a breath of relief as they reached the heavy fog on the other side of the Badlands. And then it cleared, revealing a strip of forest once more and there—looming ahead of them, unfathomably massive—the great ruined wall of Anarsha.

Tiachren and Fae went to get themselves cleaned up, but Jonathan reached out with one hand, barring Skye's way. "A word."

Jonathan waited until the others were out of earshot, glowering at her, arms crossed. He was in his late thirties, a little more than a decade older than her, and powerfully built, the muscles in his chest and arms always straining against his shirt.

"You're too reckless by half," he began.

"How was I supposed to know that there was a mech coming down the street right outside? The signal cut out. Now that we have what we came for, Anyah can set up a better connection and it won't happen again."

"That's not what I mean."

Skye crossed her own arms, mimicking his stance. "I can take care of myself."

"I know you can. But we can't do this without you. What are we supposed to do if something happens to you?"

"Nothing did," Skye pushed back. "And nothing ever will."

No one knew how to guide raiding parties in and out of the city like she did. From her very first mission, the moment she set foot in the sewers, she had studied them, memorizing their pathways with a single-mindedness that bordered on obsession.

Jonathan sighed. "I know you want to feel like you're making a difference. I know why you take the risks you do."

No, you don't. Skye felt heat creep beneath the surface of her skin and gripped her arms more tightly, hard enough to bruise.

"But I'm your team leader," he went on. "I trust you not to take unnecessary risks and to follow orders when I give them. You're a member of my team and that means I care about you. We have the same goal, Skye."

That, at least, was true, though they both had different ideas about what it took to get there and what they were each willing to do.

"It's one thing if you want to put yourself at risk, but not the others. This isn't a one-woman operation." His voice softened. "You can't take down the Empire all by yourself, no matter how much you might want to."

Skye closed her eyes briefly, knowing the truth of his words, however much she hated it. If will alone was enough, the Empire would be nothing but ash.

Still, no matter what he might say to her or any threats he might make, she knew she would not be taken off the raids. There was no one to replace her.

And she also knew how unlikely her previous words were—sooner or later something would happen to her, to all of them. The odds were not in their favor. The Empire had lived for a thousand years and it intended to outlive all of them, too, no matter what they might have to say about it.

"Understood," she muttered.

Jonathan nodded and jerked his head toward the ruins. "Go on. See if Anyah needs any help rigging that new system of hers."

Skye was happy to get away, taking her pack full of wiring and the transmission dish. She found the stairway and slipped underground, suppressing a shiver as she felt the earth close over her head, blotting out the sun.

The Resistance made its home in the vast network of caverns beneath the ruins of what was once the kingdom of Anarsha. It functioned as both home and base and everything in between.

Cool, dry air surrounded her as she descended, the ground eventually leveling out. The caverns were lit by torches and the occasional electric light, powered by the water that lay deeper in the caves.

They illuminated her path as she sought out Anyah, finding her where she usually was, in what she had fondly dubbed the war room. It was a small, hollowed out corner of the cavern, away from the others.

Several large screens had been anchored to the wall, giving off bright light. One displayed an aerial layout of the Capitol with thousands of orange dots moving around. Another screen was completely identical, except here the dots were red or yellow and there were far fewer of them. There were screens monitoring every district as well. Skye didn't know how Anyah kept track of them all.

She sat in front of the screens, leaning back in her swivel chair, wearing the headset that allowed her to communicate with operatives in the field. Even when there were no current missions active, she always seemed to wear it.

Anyah turned as Skye appeared in the doorway and leapt to her feet. "You're back!"

"And I come bearing gifts," Skye said, handing her the pack. "Should all be there."

She watched as Anyah rummaged through it, checking the contents, and muttering excitedly to herself. "You're a life saver." She gave another screen, much smaller than the others, one last glance. "No patrols nearby." She pulled down her headset, her unruly brown curls springing back up. "Let's go. I want to get this installed before dark."

Skye followed her through the caverns, past the portcullis at the entrance and into the catacombs, coming out in one of the crypts.

She kept a close eye on her friend. She was no stranger to the ruins, but Anyah rarely ventured above the surface. The ruined kingdom was dangerous, its walls and buildings threatening to collapse at any moment. Skye shuddered at the idea of being crushed beneath tons of stone, as if she didn't live with such a threat hanging over her head every day.

But there were other things lurking within the ruined city besides just rebels.

They had only encountered a dragon mech in the ruins once. Tiachren had wanted to blow the thing sky high before it found the entrance to their base, but in the end, they were forced to leave it alone. Interfering with it would only have told the Empire the very thing the rebels could not afford for them to know.

You may as well have held up a sign that said 'Here I am! Come get me!'

Anyah picked her way through the rubble, heading for the tallest tower where her current transmission dish was set up. The late afternoon sunlight shone on her dark skin as they climbed the stairs that would take them to the top.

Skye had never hated heights. Far better to be as high as possible, in her mind, than deep underground. She knew the tower was weak. Untrustworthy. It could give way beneath their feet at any moment. And yet, she wasn't afraid to climb ever higher. It had stood for over a thousand years. Surely it would stand a little longer.

The windows had long since been broken out, leaving empty archways. Skye stood in one, pressing one hand against the side of the wall. Even if she had abhorred heights, she thought she would have risked it for the view alone.

Stretching impossibly high, the tower overlooked even the great wall itself. She could see the small woods that separated the Anarshan ruins from the Badlands and beyond, and the Badlands themselves.

Past that lay the Valderan rainforest, massive in size, stretching away as far as the eye could see, mist hanging over the canopy. The greenery was startling in comparison to the Badlands. Had the trees not been there, Skye wondered if she would have been able to see all the way to the Capitol.

"Hand me the red wires," Anyah said, breaking into her thoughts. "If you can bother to tear yourself away." Her voice was thick with amusement.

While Skye had marveled at the view, she'd already disconnected the old dish.

Skye handed her the wires, having no idea what Anyah was doing. This wasn't her wheelhouse. Far too complicated, threading the wiring all the way up here, devising a way to protect them from the elements and knowing what connected to what.

Skye would rather stab something.

She watched as Anyah worked, her long, slender fingers guiding the wires where she needed them to go. At last, she came to the dish itself, setting it in the middle of the tower, facing north, toward the Capitol. She tilted it at a forty-five-degree angle and stepped back, surveying her work.

"Not bad."

"How will we know if it works?"

"If we go back and the screens are still active."

All of the screens were still lit up when they returned, the colored dots moving around.

"Well," Anyah announced. "It works. Only time will tell if there will be less interruptions, but I have a good feeling about this one."

"Let's hope so." Skye didn't relish the idea of stepping into the Capitol blind.

She both loved and hated the prickling awareness she got each time she squeezed up through one of the sewer grates. There was something unnerving and electrifying all at once about being in enemy territory, surrounded on all sides by people that wanted you dead.

Though the Capitol was the most difficult of the Empire's cities to sneak into, it could be done.

Raiding parties were one thing, born of necessity. There were certain items, only to be found in the cities, that the Resistance could not forage or make for themselves. Items that were worth risking life and limb for—like the transmission dish. Having a better signal might one day save all their lives.

Sneaking into the city to meet with informants was another matter entirely and Skye knew the next time she set foot in the Capitol, it would be for such a purpose.

At such meetings, she never knew who to trust, whether one of the commoners assembled was really an Imperial spy, whether a raid was bearing down on them at that very moment—although Anyah would hopefully be able to detect that.

If they were discovered, they would die, along with any potential recruits who had gathered to listen to them.

There was no denying the risk. But to be a Resistance member, Skye knew, was to live a life of risk.

Death hung over them all, a constant companion, never far away. But death did not concern her. She knew what would happen if they failed. It was what would happen if they *succeeded* that kept her awake at night.

That fragile dream, precious beyond measure.

No risk, no reward, and everything stays the same.

IV

The day after Geoffrey made him stay late, Leo was on time the next morning and got to leave with the other employees, stopping short at the sight of a familiar figure waiting for him.

Fitz stood outside the workshop, hands in his pockets. He wore a white collared shirt with a vest over it, his long brown hair gathered and tied at the nape of his neck.

Leo let out a breath, relieved to see him, though he would have preferred heading home to change out of his work jumpsuit first. After he'd let Fitz down the previous night with no explanation, he knew his friend would insist they head directly for the pub, not letting Leo out of his sight.

Fitz saw Leo and spread his hands. "Geoffrey again?"

"Of course."

"Well, I think I might know a way for you to make it up to me." Fitz clapped him on the shoulder and set off down the street, Leo following.

With curfew looming ever nearer, there was no time to lose.

District I, where they were headed, was the lowliest and grimiest district of all, where the poorest members of the Empire lived and slaved away for coppers. There the ramshackle buildings leaned against each other like drunkards seeking support. Soot covered nearly everything and ashes from the incessant factories drifted down like snow, laying in heaps where they had been discarded.

Leo trailed after Fitz toward the section of the district known as the Underground, even though it wasn't underground at all. It was a pleasure district, of sorts, where one could find any sort of cheap entertainment one's heart desired. The two of them passed brothels and bawdy houses, bars and gambling dens.

Fitz glanced over his shoulder as they reached the doorway of the pub. "Finally going to try your luck?"

"Not this time," Leo demurred.

Fitz shook his head. "You work too hard. Surely you've got a little extra stored away? Could be your ticket to a better life."

Like a lot of people, Fitz subscribed to the belief that gambling would provide him with a better future—he only needed to get lucky once. Though to Leo's way of thinking, Fitz was hardly in need of a better life. He worked as a butcher, the man he worked for far kinder than Geoffrey.

But regardless, the tables hadn't seen fit to bless Fitz, though his friend always insisted that victory was just one roll away.

Leo thought that if he had lived alone, he might have taken the risk. But he had his mother and sister to think of. He might win a small fortune or he might lose everything and then where would they be?

No, better to play it safe.

Together, they entered the pub. The building had a low ceiling, the bar at the back. In the middle of the room, just visible in the dim lighting, was a pit with a metal fence ringed around the top. Patrons gathered around, cheering and shouting as they watched the small automata fight below.

Mech fighting was just as popular as street brawling, the only difference being that one was legal and the other was not. Leo came not to participate, but to watch. Fitz liked betting on the mech fights. He may not yet have won his weight in gold, but there was no denying that he won more than he lost and that was one of the reasons he liked having Leo along.

Aside from his company, Fitz brought Leo for his expertise. He had an eye for the automata and could, more often than not, predict which one had the best chance of winning.

Sometimes, it nearly convinced Leo that he should try his hand at betting himself, since he had such an advantage. Nearly, but not quite. Fitz sharing some of his spoils was enough.

The air was heavy with the smell of smoke and cheap alcohol. There was also a certain wariness to the place, the laughter too jittery. Everyone knew they could be raided at any moment, the threat hanging over them like an axe.

Sometimes Imperial guards frequented such establishments, particularly the brothels, but other times they did so in disguise. No one was as they seemed and you never knew who to trust. The person standing right next to you, cheering on the mech fights, might very well be an Imperial informant, keeping an eye on the masses, and an ear out for dissention.

That thought made Leo think of the condemned man, whose execution he had witnessed only the day before.

He swallowed, pushing the thought away, and watched the fights progress, money changing hands, listening to snatches of conversation, and offering advice when Fitz asked for it. He'd already amassed a decent amount of winnings and Leo advised him to quit while he was ahead. Sometimes Fitz listened, sometimes he didn't.

This was one of the rare nights he did.

He sidled over to where Leo sat, nursing the lone drink he allowed himself, stuffing the money in his pocket. "Not a bad night!" he proclaimed, taking a swig of whatever concoction he'd ordered for himself. "Not bad at all."

"We should be going. It'll be curfew soon."

Fitz nodded. "In a minute." He glanced around the room and then lowered his voice, though it was hardly needed. "I saw you at the hanging yesterday."

Leo grimaced. Why did everything keep coming back to that? Why couldn't he put this one out of his mind, the way he had before?

He sighed. "Hardly surprising. We all had to be there."

"Did you hear what he was charged with?"

"Possession of seditious materials."

Fitz snorted. "Right. Resistance pamphlets, more specifically."

"How do you know that?"

Fitz shrugged. "They try to keep things quiet, but word gets around."

Leo grunted. "They also said he was responsible for the bombing. Do you believe that?"

"I doubt it. Surely they would have made more of an example out of him, if he was guilty. No, whoever is responsible, if the Empire's caught them, they're in Krylok right now. And may the saints have mercy on any poor bastard who ends up in there."

Leo shuddered, both at the mention of Krylok and the saints. That ancient Anarshan religion was more of a catchphrase now than anything, spoken without thought— but not without danger. Leo had caught himself slipping more than once.

He glanced around the room. He doubted anyone could hear them, but still… "We shouldn't be talking about this."

Fitz's green eyes narrowed, but he didn't argue. "Fair enough."

Eager to change the subject, Leo waved a hand at the pit, where matches were still taking place. "So, did all the coin I won for you make up for me abandoning you last night?"

Fitz laughed. "Funny you should ask. I meant what I said earlier. There's a way for you to make it up to me."

"I'm listening…" Leo said, wary.

"There's somewhere I'd like you to go with me. I can't tell you when—the date's not been set yet. But I'd like you to be there."

"What is this? Some sort of gambling party with your friends?"

"I'll tell you more when I have the details. But it's with friends, yes."

Leo sighed, resigned. Spending an evening at some gambling party with Fitz's friends while they all encouraged him to part with money he couldn't afford to lose was not time well spent, in his mind.

But he had let Fitz down and if he was inviting Leo to whatever this upcoming event was, it was because he wanted him to be there. Leo supposed he should feel flattered, and he did, slightly, even though such entertainment didn't appeal to him.

"All right," he agreed. "I suppose I can tamp down my curiosity until then."

Fitz grinned. "Excellent." He knocked back the last of his drink. "Now I think you're right. We should get going."

They left the pub together, but parted ways soon after. Leo had just reached the ramp that led to District III when the first curfew siren rang out, long and low, over the city.

The sirens rang for five minutes and by the time they fell silent, everyone had to be off the streets and back home. Anyone caught out risked imprisonment.

Leo broke into a run, heart thudding in his chest. He couldn't say why, but there was something about the curfew sirens that struck fear into him, as they were undoubtedly meant to. Once they stopped ringing, the dragon mechs would be out prowling the streets and he did not want to encounter one of those.

He reached home with a minute to spare and shut the door behind him, bolting it.

"You're cutting it fine."

Leo turned to see his mother standing behind him in their small kitchen, a shawl wrapped around her shoulders. Her hair, so blonde it was nearly white, was pinned up in a bun, stray strands hanging loose around her face.

The two of them couldn't have looked more different—Leo taking after his father—but they shared the same nose.

"Fitz," he said, by way of explanation. "I felt bad for the other night. Wanted to make it up to him."

She turned to the stove. "I heated some stew for you."

"You didn't have to wait up."

But he knew she would, hearing the curfew sirens and fretting that he wasn't yet home, wondering if this time, he would return at all.

The kitchen was warm, comforting, and Leo's eyelids drooped as he sat down at the kitchen table. He wanted nothing more than to go upstairs and climb into bed, but he was also hungry, having eaten nothing since the sandwich she had made him for lunch.

He knew better than to turn down his mother's cooking.

She set a bowl of stew in front of him, still steaming. With haste, Leo dug in, huffing as the hot liquid burned his mouth. But saints, was it good.

So good, in fact, that it took a few moments for him to notice his mother's eyes on him, the pained look on her face.

He swallowed. "Is everything all right?"

"There was a raid down the street earlier today," she answered.

Leo frowned. Raids weren't unusual. The Empire could demand entry into any home in the Capitol at any time, with or without reason. Just because a raid had taken place didn't mean that they had cause, or that they'd found anything.

His thoughts turned back once again to the executed man. The city was on edge, even more than usual.

As if she could sense his thoughts, she sighed, leaning against one of the counters. "After yesterday, I didn't know whether to expect you—or if he'd make you stay behind again. You know this isn't the life I envisioned for you."

Suddenly, she looked thin and frail, worn down by the years that passed between them, acknowledged but unspoken.

Leo's throat suddenly felt tight.

"You should be finding yourself a nice girl and thinking about a home and family of your own, not wasting your youth taking care of us."

He pushed his bowl of stew away. Much would have been different if fate had been kinder. But fate was not kind.

He looked up, meeting her green eyes, so unlike his own. "It's not the life any of us imagined, but it's what we've got."

There was nothing for it but to make the best of it.

Leo stood, gesturing to the stew. "Thank you."

Before he could bid her goodnight and turn toward the stairs, she had crossed the kitchen and wrapped her arms around him, the strength of her grip belying her small appearance.

He was taller than her now, though not as tall as he should have been. At times, food had been hard to come by and he always made sure she and Ana got their share before taking any for himself—even now.

Sometimes he felt more like the parent, forced into the role of protector and provider before any of them had quite known what had happened.

Leo returned the embrace. The raid had her rattled.

When she stepped back, he summoned a small smile, trying to reassure her that all was well.

She knew better than to detain him further; he got precious little rest as it was. "Goodnight," she murmured.

"Goodnight."

He turned, passing through their small living room, and mounted the stairs, trying to put all thoughts of rebels and raids out of his mind.

Leo paused at the top of the stairs, frowning. A strip of light was just visible beneath his sister's door. It was so faint, he'd nearly missed it, flickering slightly.

He knocked softly, once, and then pushed the door open. "Anastasia, you should be in bed."

"I am in bed," she said primly.

His ten-year-old sister, thirteen years his junior, was sitting up in bed, a textbook propped in her lap. Her hair was blonde, like their mother's, but she shared Leo's dark eyes and curly hair. A lit candle on the nightstand provided barely enough light to see by, burning low.

Candles weren't cheap, but they were cheaper than electricity, which they couldn't afford to always have turned on.

Leo stepped into the room. "What are you doing?"

"Studying. I—I have a test coming up."

Leo smiled. "Ana, you know enough to get into the Academy. That test is no match for you."

"I know, but…will you go over some of it with me? Please?"

He sighed, feeling a bone-deep weariness settle over him, but knowing there wasn't a chance he would refuse her.

"All right," he said, reaching out to move the stuffed lion that always resided on her bed. It had been his once, its fur now matted and well-loved. He settled down onto the bed as she scooted to the side to make room for him. "What are you having trouble with?"

He looked down at the open pages of the textbook, at the diagrams of the automata and their various components. *Hardly a bit of light reading before bed,* he thought wryly. Leo could understand why she was having trouble with this bit. It was no small thing to comprehend, studying the machines that had made Akkadia what it was.

It wasn't called the Empire of Engines for nothing.

He listened to Ana read the passages aloud to him, pausing to ask questions when she was confused about something. He did his best to answer, the uncomfortable reminder lurking in the back of his mind that he had not graduated from the Academy.

It hadn't been from a lack of skill. The event that had upended all their lives had made the choice for him.

He had been sixteen, Ana only three, when their father had died. Leo looked down at the top of his sister's head, wondering what, if anything, she remembered of him.

With every passing year, his own memories seemed to grow fainter. He wondered how that could be. How could the fine edges begin to grow fuzzy? How could he slowly forget the man who had been such a force, a presence, throughout much of his own life?

That reversal of fortunes, a simple accident on the factory floor, had made Leo's choices for him. He'd dropped out of the Academy and gone to work for Geoffrey, providing for his family more important than any lofty goals he might have had of following in his father's footsteps.

But that didn't mean such a future would be denied Ana. She was smart, frighteningly so for one so young, and one day Leo knew she would be the one assembling the mechs, even if she couldn't see it herself. Even if she doubted.

It was a nice thought, in a day filled with too few. Leo let his eyes drift shut, intending to close them for only a moment, Ana's voice both rhythmic and soothing.

Ana trailed off, realizing the question she'd asked had gone unanswered, turning to her brother. He leaned back against her pillows, head slumped slightly to one side, eyes closed.

Softly, so as not to wake him, she shut the textbook. They'd almost finished anyway. She felt a strange sort of sadness as she looked at him. He was always so tired, working so hard.

Usually, she thought he looked far older than her, but at that moment, he looked younger, less careworn, the burden he carried no longer weighing on him quite so heavily.

She knew he tried to hide it from her—what all he did for them, how much it cost—but she noticed. He was her brother, but he also tried to fill the gap of the father figure they were both missing, not quite succeeding at either.

Ana sighed, cuddling against his side. He smelled faintly of grease and motor oil. He may have still viewed her as a child, but she knew things and noticed others. She wanted to take some of that weight from him, if she could. Once she was old enough and knew how.

The rest of the week passed by in a blur of monotony as it always did, while Leo waited for Fitz to explain what it was he wanted him to do. In the end, it took long enough that Leo had nearly forgotten that he'd agreed to accompany his friend.

It was nearly the following weekend before Fitz broached the subject again, waiting for Leo outside of his work.

His friend smiled. "You ready?"

"I still don't know what I'm getting into," Leo pointed out.

"You'll see." Fitz jerked his head. "Come on."

He turned and began walking away, his path no different than the one they would take to the pub. Frowning, Leo followed him.

He remained silent as they reached District I, but Fitz didn't stop, leading him away from the evening crowds that had gathered to enjoy some brief entertainment before curfew fell.

"Where are we going?"

Fitz ducked down an alley that held the rotten tang of garbage and Leo followed after a brief hesitation. His irritation was growing now and he was about to stop altogether and refuse to take another step until Fitz explained what was going on.

But he never got the chance. One minute he was following Fitz down the darkened alley and the next, a hood had been thrown over his head and someone was grabbing at his arms. He squirmed and kicked, feeling a moment's satisfaction as his boot connected with someone's shin and there was a muffled curse.

Something prodded him in the ribs and he heard Fitz's voice. "Calm down. They're not going to hurt you."

What was this? Had Fitz gotten himself in trouble and somehow dragged Leo into it too? He felt a surge of anger and a little bit of fear as whoever had ahold of him began to lead him onward.

He managed to find his voice. "What is this?" The hood was scratchy against his face, the air inside stuffy.

"Quiet," a voice growled in his ear. Leo didn't recognize it, but there was no mistaking the menace in the tone.

Leo stopped struggling and allowed them to lead him, occasionally stumbling over the uneven ground. Better to save his energy for when they let go of him, or finally arrived at their destination, so he could break free and make a run for it.

Whatever Fitz was up to, he no longer wanted to be part of it.

At some point, Leo was guided through a narrow opening and down a ladder, which he scaled with painful slowness, gripping the rungs tightly.

After what seemed like an eternity, they stopped walking, but the hood was not removed. Robbed of his sight, Leo relied on his other senses. He could hear water dripping nearby and running further away. Something scurried; the sound of it made his skin crawl. But the smell was worse still.

He had no idea how far they'd come, but he could guess where they were now, even without ever having been there himself. The smell of excrement and mud filled his nostrils, the hood doing little to diminish it.

We're in the sewers.

Rough hands roamed over him, searching, he assumed, for any weapons or valuables. There were none to be found, but he stiffened anyway, gritting his teeth.

The hood was suddenly whisked away and he sucked in a sharp breath, meeting a pair of cold blue eyes. The woman was as tall as he was, much of her face hidden beneath a black cloth. Only her eyes and black hair, cut into a choppy bob, were visible.

She was dressed entirely in black, her fingers and upper half of her face the only bit of bare skin exposed. His eyes went immediately to the weapons at her belt—two hand crossbows and a single blade—that he could see, at least.

"Who's the new guy?"

Leo turned, recognizing the voice as the one who had spoken before. The young man was gangly, also dressed in black, but he made no effort at hiding his face or red hair.

It was Fitz, standing beside Leo, who replied. "The friend I mentioned."

Leo shot his friend a look, but Fitz appeared not to notice. So Fitz had planned all of this. They weren't about to be robbed—at least not yet.

"Can he be trusted?" the woman asked, glaring at Leo.

"Yes. I've already vouched for him."

"What does he do?"

"Doll maker."

Leo bristled at the term and the way they spoke of him as if he weren't even there.

He'd been right about the sewers at least. A lantern had been set on the floor, its golden glow illuminating the grimy walls around them and the water trickling past.

The man nodded, picking up the lantern. "All right. Let's go."

Leo had no choice but to follow them as they headed deeper into the sewers. He tried to catch Fitz's eye, but his friend studiously ignored him.

I wonder why.

Over the sound of the water sloshing around their feet, he could hear faint voices ahead, growing louder by the moment. Light flickered around the corner from another lantern.

More people were gathered, some of them wearing black like the first two. Others were dressed plainly, in work uniforms like Leo. He could have passed any one of them on the street and not given them a second glance—which he supposed was the point.

The man with the red hair surveyed the assembled group and seemed to find it to his liking. "Right. Everyone's here. Reports."

To Leo's surprise, Fitz spoke up first. "My boss was talking about a rumored collapse at the mine in Shemar. It appears natural."

"Rumor has it that the metal plating they use on some of the mechs is getting thinner and weaker. Fewer metal shipments arrive all the time and they're forced to reuse the same material over and over."

"There have been whispers at the foundry of a soul stone shortage," one of the women murmured. "Management seems more upset by that than anything."

The woman with the blue eyes looked at her sharply, but said nothing.

Leo listened to the reports in a sort of daze, everything from the mine collapse to a labor shortage at the Workhouses.

With a dawning horror, he realized what he was witnessing. He was in the sewers beneath the Capitol, surrounded by rebels and spies. His heart was thudding in his ribcage; he could feel the pulse of it in his throat, behind his ears, pounding at his temples.

He struggled to keep his expression blank, not wanting to betray his fear or mounting anger. If the rebels viewed him as a threat, someone who might rat them out the first chance he got, they likely wouldn't hesitate to kill him on the spot.

An image flashed through his mind of his lifeless body being found in the sewers, if it was ever found at all. What would his mother think when she heard the news? What would she say if she knew what he was doing at that very moment?

The blue-eyed woman kept glancing in his direction, setting him further on edge. He could feel her distrust.

I don't want to be here! he wanted to scream at her. *I didn't ask to be brought here.*

When the reports had finished, the red-haired man asked for supplies and those gathered stepped forward, producing small offerings, everything from candles and folded blankets, to canned food items and money, first-aid kits and even a knife that had allegedly been pilfered from the armory.

Even knowing of the Resistance, somehow they had always seemed more of a myth to him, something distant and insubstantial. But no longer.

And Fitz is one of them!

Little wonder he had been so reluctant to tell Leo where they were going.

The man nodded, hefting the lantern once more. "We'll be in touch."

Leo half expected to be blindfolded again and led out of the sewers, but instead he watched as the little gathering broke up, the others heading their own separate ways through the tunnels.

Fitz touched Leo on the sleeve and he hurried after his friend, back, he presumed, the way they'd come.

He sucked in a deep breath the moment they were back at ground level, Fitz lowering the sewer grate behind them.

"Come on," Fitz said, as if nothing had happened. "We'd better hurry before curfew."

Hang curfew. All of the anger and fear that Leo had suppressed down in the tunnels roared to the surface, each one feeding the other.

He stalked after Fitz, grabbed him by the arm, yanked him around, and shoved him, hard. Fitz's back connected with the wall of the alley.

"*What the hell?*" Leo growled, the words hissing out between clenched teeth. "Are you insane?"

There was privacy in the alley, but one never knew who might be listening, a fact that Leo was doubly aware of after what he'd just witnessed.

"I thought you'd find it interesting." Fitz made it sound like it was nothing more than an afternoon outing at a park or going shopping in one of the upper districts. As if they hadn't just risked their lives.

"Interesting!" Leo exclaimed, struggling to keep a lid on his temper. "We could have been killed. We still might be!"

"Relax. Nothing happened. I'm sorry; I should have prepared you more."

"Is there a problem, gentlemen?"

Leo's heart leapt to his throat as he turned to see an Imperial soldier, clad in black and gold armor and the half skeleton mask, standing at the mouth of the alley. How much had she heard?

"No," he forced himself to say. "There's no problem."

She stared at them for a long moment. Leo forced down the urge to bolt—or vomit. He wasn't sure which was stronger. *We're going to be arrested.*

Then she nodded to them and continued on her way. They listened to the sound of her footsteps receding on the cobblestones and waited for what felt like an eternity.

Thank the saints she didn't have a mech with her.

Leo took a step back, away from Fitz. "You're a Resistance member. How could you think to bring me to that? Why would you involve me?"

"You're already involved. This affects you as much as everyone. The Resistance is fighting for a better way of life. I thought you would understand that, maybe even want to do something about it."

Leo let out a bitter laugh. "*Do* something? Like what, blow up another mansion?" At his own words, even his false mirth faded. "Saints, you didn't have anything to do with that, did you?"

A flash of anger appeared on Fitz's face. "Do you want to live like this for the rest of your life, slaving away and all for what? So Geoffrey can keep beating you? So you can keep working late for no pay? What kind of future is that?"

Leo couldn't tell him that he was wrong. There wasn't much of a future in the Capitol. He knew that, along with everyone else.

The Empire controlled every aspect of its citizens' lives, including what district they would live in, where they could live within the district, and even how many children they could have.

He exhaled heavily. "It's not perfect, but it's all we have. This future is better than no future at all."

Which is what we'll have if we end up dead!

"Think of Ana—"

"I am thinking of her!"

Fitz shook his head, disappointment reflected in his green eyes. "You don't get it, do you? Nothing's going to get better. It's only going to get worse. One of these days, you're going to see something that you won't be able to stay silent about. One of these days, you're going to have to choose. How many more must be killed or live their lives in daily oppression before that day comes?"

"And what is the Resistance going to do about any of that, Fitz? What are you going to do? The Empire has reined for over a thousand years."

"Every empire falls sooner or later."

"Not this one," Leo muttered.

Fitz gave him a querulous look. "Surely you don't think the Akkadian Empire will endure forever? There was a time before the Empire and there will be a time after."

Leo shrugged. "No other empire has lasted this long." *And even if the sun does set on the Empire one day, it will be long after we're gone.*

"If everyone thought the way you do, there wouldn't *be* a Resistance." Fitz smiled, but it didn't reach his eyes. "I just thought maybe you were different." He made as if to walk away.

His disappointment stung and Leo felt a stab of guilt, even though he'd done nothing wrong. He hadn't dragged his friend along to a meeting of rebels, risking his very life. He wasn't the one who should apologize.

And yet...

"Why would the Resistance want me, anyway?" he called, waving his hands helplessly. "I don't have any skills to offer them. I'm just a..." *Doll maker.*

Fitz turned back. "It's enough just to keep your eyes and ears open. See if you can learn anything that might be important. Don't underestimate the value of information."

"How would you know whether or not it's important?"

"If you're not sure, you can always mention it anyway. If you don't want to come to the next meeting, you can tell me and I'll deliver the message."

Leo shook his head. "I'm not going to the next meeting. I appreciate what you're trying to do here, I really do, but I want no part of it."

"Aren't you the least bit curious?"

Leo was, but he would never admit it.

"Curious to find out what it feels like to die? No, I can't say that I am."

Fitz shrugged. "It's your choice, of course."

Anything else that might have been said was cut off by the long, droning curfew siren.

Leo tore his gaze away from Fitz and took off at a run, his friend's words haunting him. He ran as hard as he could, gasping for breath and ignoring the pain in his side, but the sirens had ended by the time he reached his own district.

He slowed, wary now of encountering any patrols. He had to stop more than once and wait in the shadows with bated breath until they moved on. He felt like a wanted criminal, hunted within his own city, as though attending a Resistance meeting had made him one of them.

His pulse didn't stop drumming in his ears until he reached his own front door and shut it behind him.

"Leo." His mother came into the kitchen, hearing the door. "Where have you been?"

He looked at her, saw the fear in her eyes, and summoned a smile. "Fitz got a bit carried away at the tables."

Her lips pursed. "I wish you wouldn't go with him."

He knew she thought Fitz a bad influence. *If she only knew how much!* After tonight, Leo wasn't sure he disagreed with her.

"Someone's got to keep him on the straight and narrow."

"And that someone has to be you?"

"I'm sorry." *For being late. For scaring you. For more than you can know.* "It won't happen again."

That much he could promise.

He declined the offer of dinner, his nerves too on edge to even consider eating, and made his way up the stairs to his room. He paused, one hand on the rail, as he glanced toward Ana's room.

There was no light beneath the door this time. He hadn't been much help to her when she'd asked him to help her study. He'd been so tired he could barely keep his eyes open, unlike tonight, when the lingering fear would likely keep him from resting at all.

Leo sighed. Ana knew almost as much as he did about the mechs and yet one of the automatons she loved so much could crush her in an instant, without a single thought.

She was still so small. Defenseless.

Fitz's words kept ringing in the back of his mind. *One of these days, you're going to see something that you won't be able to stay silent about. One of these days, you're going to have to choose.*

Maybe things could change, but was he willing to risk Ana's life in order to bring it about? Or on the other hand, did he owe it to her and his mother both to try? If the Resistance could make things better, didn't he have a responsibility to try and give his family a better life?

He wondered what his father would have done. Would his father have gone back, to the second Resistance meeting? There was no way to know for sure. His father hadn't been a reckless man, but neither did Leo think he would have stayed away out of fear.

He would have gone if he thought it would bring his family a better life. If he thought things could really change.

Was that not why he'd worked so hard, for better pay and a more satisfying job?

But no matter what his mother might think, Leo knew he was not much like his father. It wasn't merely that his father had been a large man, stronger than Leo was ever likely to be. Or that he had laughed a lot, his laugh deep and infectious.

He had been brave, above all those things, and brave was one thing Leo was not. He was a coward and he knew, loath as he was to admit it, that was why Fitz's disappointment had cut so deep.

I just thought maybe you were different, Fitz had said.

But I'm not, Leo thought. *I'm not who you want me to be.*

VI

The question of the Resistance stayed with Leo long after the meeting had come to an end. He wished there was someone he could go to for advice. Anastasia was far too young; his mother would make the decision for him if she knew where he had been, and no one could consider Fitz unbiased in the matter.

He knew what the only answer could be and tried to put it from his mind, but like the executed man, it kept coming back, consuming his every waking moment, becoming an obsession.

Life went on as it always had, as it always would if something wasn't done. No Imperial soldiers came for him in the middle of the night, breaking down the door to the house as he had once feared.

One morning as he was walking to work and approaching one of the emperor's statues, he saw an older man standing upright, refusing to bow down to it. The two guards who always stood sentinel threatened him, but he would not be moved. He stood there, implacably, as they approached.

Leo watched in bewilderment. He wanted to shout at the man to run, but there was no point. He was far older than the guards, who could chase him down easily. The few others who were gathered, some still kneeling, watched in fascinated horror as the punishment was meted out.

The first blow sent the old man to his knees, the second, a vicious kick to the ribs. Something within urged Leo to intervene, to stop this madness before they beat him to death. It almost seemed as though he could feel every blow as it landed, flinching. He could only imagine the pain it must have caused.

In the end, the old man lay there, alive but barely. Leo knew he should help him, get him to his feet so that he could leave before they decided to finish the job, but he couldn't move.

The old man's eyes rolled, meeting Leo's. Through the pain, defiance still glimmered. The guards turned their attention toward Leo, noticing his interest. He had yet to kneel before the statue himself and now the moment had come to make a choice.

The man's stare settled on his skin like a challenge, goading him not to give in. Leo looked back, both admiring his bravery and thinking him foolish.

Yes, he had stood up for what he believed in and refused to be intimidated, but at what cost? What had it gained him? Had it been worth it?

Leo didn't recognize him from the Resistance meeting and he wondered if this were an ordinary citizen, acting out in the only way he knew how.

Perhaps if he could have asked the man why he had done such a thing, he would have understood.

He looked away, shame heating his face as he knelt before the statue.

His choice to join the Resistance was not so dissimilar, he reflected, waiting as the seconds ticked by. It would cause a great deal of suffering and in the end, accomplish nothing.

There was only one choice to make.

As he walked away, he berated himself for being such a coward. But really, he was useless to the Resistance. They didn't need or want members who were cowards. If he wasn't willing to risk a beating, how could he be expected to risk his life defying the Empire?

Still, he couldn't shake the sense of shame that remained with him, or the memory of the man's face, the look of disappointment in his gaze acutely painful.

Work that day fared little better. A messenger crossed the workshop floor, heading for Leo's table, informing him that Geoffrey wished to see him in his office.

Across the table, Tanner glanced up, meeting his eye. *This is it. He's finally going to fire me.*

Leo stood, leaving the half-finished mechanical arm he'd been assembling. The remaining parts, needed for completion, hadn't come in yet. It would have to be set aside, joining the others he'd been working on all week.

He made his way to the back of the workshop, where Geoffrey's office lay, knocked, and entered when bidden.

The office looked more like a gentleman's lounge. The walls were papered a deep, rich red, the hard floor turning to plush carpet beneath his feet. A fire crackled in the grate.

Geoffrey sat behind an enormous mahogany desk, a decanter resting on a table beside him. There was already a glass in his hand, the other holding a lit cigar, which he gestured with, pointing toward the comm device on the edge of the desk.

"Do you have any idea how many clients I've fielded calls from this week, demanding to know why production has stalled and their orders late?"

Leo swallowed. "No, sir."

"You and I both know it's because the parts haven't come in yet, but I can't tell them that." Geoffrey leaned forward, pointing the glowing cigar tip in Leo's direction. "I've told them that all of my workers are going to be working double shifts to make up for the delay and that they'll have the orders out by the end of the week or they won't be my workers anymore."

Leo went rigid, clenching his jaw to keep from scowling. He knew Geoffrey was likely bluffing, just being bloody and taking out some of his frustration on him. He could smell the alcohol rolling off of him in waves, competing with the pungent cigar.

Never the most pleasant person, the worst aspects of Geoffrey's personality where amplified when he drank. And there was nothing Leo could do. The man held his future, and that of his family, in his hands—and knew it.

Leo inclined his head. "Sir."

Geoffrey waved an airy hand at the door and Leo withdrew, pulling it tight behind him.

He let out a breath. At least he hoped Geoffrey was just being bloody. Demanding that they make something when they had nothing to work with—it wasn't just unreasonable, it was asking the impossible.

Leo didn't know how long he stood there, leaning against the door. He knew he should move. Geoffrey could yank the door open at any moment and he would go sprawling. Nor would it earn him any points in Geoffrey's favor if he found him loitering outside.

Faintly, he heard Geoffrey's voice from within the office. No one else had been inside and Leo surmised he must have answered another transmission on the comm device.

He smiled to himself, enjoying listening to his boss squirm for once, trying to explain to some wealthy client why things weren't getting done.

His smile faded, expecting to hear Geoffrey blame the workers for the delay. Instead, what he heard surprised him.

"It's Elath's fault. No one's been able to get anything out of there anymore—and the prices they're asking!"

There was a brief pause, then, "A shortage, they say. Any old excuse, if you ask me. But the Ministries of Labor and Commerce aren't best pleased, I can tell you that much. They're sending an Inquisitor from the Ministry into Elath at the end of the month to find out what's going on. Not nearly soon enough, in my opinion, but better than nothing. They'd better get their act together by then, if they know what's good for them. I wouldn't want to be on the receiving end of a visit from an Inquisitor, no siree!" Geoffrey chuckled darkly. "But if it gets the ball rolling again, I can hardly wait."

Leo pushed off from the door and hurried away. He'd never so much as seen an Inquisitor before, but he'd heard stories of people being questioned by them, usually as a result of a raid.

They always had plenty of questions and were very good at getting the answers.

He felt a pang of sympathy for whoever was in charge in Elath and would have to explain why their mines were no longer keeping up with demand.

Leo hurried back to his worktable. Tanner looked up.

"So, you escaped the lion's den. What did he want?"

"To complain, mostly, about the delay. He's blaming us, telling his clients that it's our fault, and that we're all going to work double shifts to make up for it."

Tanner stared at him, her shoulders going slack. "Is he serious?"

Leo shrugged, picking up his wrench.

Tanner hissed under her breath, calling Geoffrey a very unflattering name. Leo silently concurred, his mind whirling.

A visit from an Inquisitor was no small matter. He couldn't recall ever hearing of an Inquisitor leaving the Capitol to visit one of the outlying cities. They existed solely within the heart of the Empire.

But surely it had to have happened before, over the course of a thousand years.

Leo absently drummed his fingers on the table. There wasn't much he could do about the parts shortage. The mechanical limbs they assembled were crafted from precious metals, hewn from the mines in the mountains of either Shemar or Elath. Leo and his fellow workers merely assembled the parts, they did not craft them. Not yet anyway—Geoffrey would probably demand that next.

Unbidden, Fitz's words came back to him. *Keep your eyes and ears open. See if you can learn anything that might be important. Don't underestimate the value of information.*

Did the Resistance know that an Inquisitor would be on their way to Elath? Would they even care? Was that information even worth anything?

He thought it might be.

Geoffrey hadn't told him that. He hadn't known that Leo was still just outside, within earshot. He hadn't been meant to hear that and he wondered who Geoffrey had been speaking to.

Leo bit his lip. What would happen if he kept such information to himself? What if it *was* important and something terrible happened because he kept quiet?

What if someone *died?*

That seemed a bit dramatic, but people had been killed for less. Once more, the image of the executed man flickered to the forefront of his mind and Leo closed his eyes, rubbing his hands over his face.

Damn it.

Even as he considered what to do with the information, he already knew the answer. He could do this one thing, pass on the information and then wash his hands of the matter.

After that, he would be done. He would have nothing more to do with the Resistance. Any obligation he had would be fulfilled and he could go about his usual business, free of the guilt that dogged him.

That evening, Fitz was waiting for him outside of work, as usual. Leo had thought he might stop trying after their last conversation and his subsequent refusal to accompany him, but Fitz was nothing if not stubborn.

His expression held no hope, as though he expected to be turned down again, but Leo surprised him.

"This next meeting…" he murmured. "When is it?"

Fitz eyed him. "I don't have a date yet, only a location. Do you want me to fetch you?"

Wordlessly, Leo nodded.

Neither of them had long to wait. Ahead of the meeting, Fitz confided that the location would be a pub and suggested that the two of them be seen around the place ahead of time so their presence wouldn't be remarked upon.

The day of the meeting seemed to slip by at an agonizing pace. Leo couldn't concentrate at work, plagued by second thoughts. It wasn't too late to back out, but even as he considered it, he knew he wouldn't.

He would simply pass on what he knew and leave.

Leo had time after work before he needed to meet Fitz at the pub, so he went home briefly to change out of his work jumpsuit. He shucked it off and onto the floor, glaring at it. He'd always hated the dark teal material, the way it made all of them look the same. There wasn't any difference he could see between its design and that of a prison uniform, but perhaps that was the point. To remind them of their station and not to get any ideas.

He changed into his usual choice of attire for when he wasn't working—a white collared, buttoned shirt, tucked into black trousers, black suspenders, and his boots. Leo rolled his sleeves up to his elbows, exposing the tattoo on the inside of his right forearm of the numeral III. Every Capitol citizen had one, representing the district where they lived.

He frowned and made to turn away, but paused, pivoting back to face the room. A small box lay on his dresser and he reached out, flipping it open.

Inside lay a blue stone, the size of his palm, on a silver chain. Silver wire wrapped around the stone, cradling it. The stone was a lovely, vibrant light blue, the seemingly most valuable thing he possessed, though Leo suspected it had no real value. It merely looked expensive.

He didn't know how long it had been in the family, but rumor had it some distant ancestor who had worked in the soul stone mines in Shemar had discovered it.

Leo doubted it was a real soul stone. Everyone knew they were red, not blue.

But still, it was unlike anything else he'd ever seen. He took it out every now and then to look at. He reached out and picked it up, the stone shockingly cold against his skin.

He didn't want to leave it behind, not with the threat of raids. Imperial guards weren't above pinching things that caught their eye, even if there was nothing seditious to find. Leo didn't much like the idea of parting with it.

Lifting the chain, he draped it over his head, tucking the stone beneath his shirt, where it would be safely hidden. It settled over his heart, its cool presence comforting.

Sighing, Leo hurried down the stairs and out the door before his mother could ask him where he was off to.

Fitz was already there by the time he arrived, seated at a table, a drink in front of him to maintain the illusion. Leo joined him and the waiting game began.

The pub was small, mostly empty, dominated by the tables and chairs. The chair Leo sat in had an uneven leg and rocked slightly if he shifted his weight. The floor was covered in a thin layer of sawdust, to mop up any spilled beer or anything else.

There were stools ringing the bar, behind which a man stood polishing glasses with a dingy cloth. He glanced up whenever the door opened, but his expression never changed.

Slowly, more people trickled in, some that Leo thought he recognized, but couldn't be sure. The dim lighting from the wall sconces made it difficult to see, but he supposed that was the point. The red-haired man who had held the lantern in the sewers he definitely recognized, along with the young woman who had accompanied him.

She no longer hid her face and she carried no weapons he could see. Her sharp blue eyes scanned the room quickly, meeting his briefly.

She and the red-haired man split up, each heading to opposite sides of the room. Gradually, the patrons who had gathered for the meeting went over to join them.

Leo caught a glimpse of small items being handed over, the same as before. Fitz got up and approached the red-haired man's table.

Leo hesitated. No one else seemed nervous to him; there was nothing jerky about their movements and no one seemed eager to leave. But he could sense an underlying tension in the room and it made his pulse quicken.

Just tell them what you know and get out.

He considered following Fitz. The red-haired man looked friendlier and more approachable than the blue-eyed woman, but his table was also more crowded than hers.

He rose to his feet, feeling the stone shift against his skin. As he did so, the woman leapt to her feet, eying the back door. Leo was just beginning to turn when the door was thrown open with a crash, nearly torn from its hinges.

An Imperial soldier strode through the opening, dressed in the black uniform, her armor golden. Her breastplate was embellished with a golden, staring eye. The All-Seeing Eye of the Empire.

Leo's heart thrummed. Only high-ranking officers and Inquisitors bore such a symbol.

Her bright blonde hair, cropped into a pixie-cut, stood out in the darkness of the pub. She surveyed the room only a brief moment before the dragon mech followed her inside, its hulking form making the room seem twice as small as before.

The room erupted. Cries rang out. Tables and chairs were overturned as people scrambled to get away. Someone screamed, their voice rising above the clamor, the single word ringing out, *"Raid!"*

Leo bolted for the door, fear shooting through him. Bodies seemed to press close on all sides, buffeting him, and he narrowly avoided tripping.

And then he was free of the musty air of the pub, out on the darkened street.

A hand snaked out, snatching his collar. He gasped as he was slammed up against the pub's outside wall and found himself staring into a pair of piercing blue eyes.

The rebel girl stood before him, two black knives drawn, one at his throat and the other jabbing him in the kidney.

He felt the cool kiss of metal on his skin as he swallowed, throat bobbing. Never had he seen such intensity of emotion in anyone's gaze as he did in hers. Her lips were peeled back in a snarl, teeth bared, the rage blazing in her eyes unmistakable.

"What are you doing?" someone exclaimed.

Leo glanced to the side to see the red-haired man who had been with her.

"I told you not to trust him!" she hissed. "He was the only new one and look what happened."

They think I tipped off the guards!

"I didn't—" Leo started to say, but the knife at his throat bit deeper, discouraging any further protests.

"He's an informant," she added to her companion. "We should slit his throat and be done with it."

Leo didn't doubt she could easily make good on her threat, leaving him lying in the street, bleeding out. He would be just as dead as if the Imperial patrol caught him. He could still hear the mech, crashing about inside.

Silently, he cursed himself for coming here, for daring to trust them.

"Leave it, Skye," the man argued. "There's no time!"

Leo let out a relieved breath as she withdrew her knives. That relief rapidly vanished as she lunged forward, the pommel of one of her daggers hurtling toward the side of his head.

A flare of pain. A burst of white light. Then nothing.

⚙⚙⚙

Leo forced his eyes open. He lay on his side, one cheek pressed to the cobblestones, in exactly the same place. The pub's wall was still to his back, but he could feel blazing heat, painful in its proximity.

Wincing, he pushed up to his hands and knees, swallowing a cry of pain. Gingerly, he reached up, touching the place she'd struck him. His fingers came away slick and red.

He managed to find his feet and took a few stumbling steps away from the pub, only to fall back to his hands and knees, head spinning. Leo blinked rapidly, trying to clear his blurred vision.

Saints, it felt like she'd cracked his skull open.

Clenching his teeth, he turned to face the pub behind him, engulfed in flames. *The dragon automaton.* As though conjured by his thoughts, the lumbering beast rounded the corner of the building, fixing him with its lifeless yellow stare.

It loomed over him, raising one large hand to crush him.

With a cry, Leo rolled away, the mech's claws slamming harmlessly down onto the cobbles. He shoved himself to his feet and took off at a run, the terror he had felt in the pub returning, lending speed to his flight.

He could hear the beast's tread behind him, the clanking of the gears as its powerful legs propelled its body forward. Leo glanced over his shoulder and felt a stab of alarm at how close it was. He could almost feel the hot steam breathing down the back of his neck.

It's going to jump.

And once it did, it would tackle him to the ground and crush him. The clanking stopped as the mech launched itself into the air. Leo dropped and slid across the stones, watching as the mech sailed harmlessly overhead. Its claws skidded over the stones as it landed, futilely seeking purchase.

Slowly, it turned, a low growl rumbling in its chest, like that of an engine. The sound made the hair on Leo's arms stand on end.

Leo stood, searching for an escape. He could only avoid the automaton for so long, but there was nowhere it wouldn't follow. Nowhere to hide.

The sewers.

Of course. His eyes alighted on the grate only a few feet away. He darted forward and grasped it, straining against its weight. It rose much too slowly, the mech already charging in his direction.

With a yell, Leo heaved the grate up. It fell to the side with a clang and he lowered himself down into the hole just as the mech reached him.

Clinging to the ladder, he peered up through the opening. The mech's jaws opened wide and his eyes widened in horror. Leaping off the ladder, he threw himself to the side as a torrent of flame shot down, directly where he had been a moment before.

He landed awkwardly on his shoulder, the heat searing. Scrambling up, Leo set out down one of the tunnels. He had no idea where he was going, his only goal to put as much distance between him and the mech as possible.

If the Resistance used the sewers to get into the city, there must be a way out. The smell was just as horrible as he remembered and without a lantern, he had to rely on small blue lights attached to the rounded walls, but they were few and far between.

He didn't know how long he'd wandered down there, listening to the rats as they scurried away from his footsteps. The fear had faded, leaving only weariness and the growing suspicion that he was becoming hopelessly lost.

Leo paused, leaning one hand against the wall for support as he listened. He could just hear the sound of running water up ahead. He headed toward it, the sound growing louder as the water picked up speed around his feet.

He rounded the corner. Moonlight shone ahead, through a round opening, gradually growing larger with each step. The current moved swiftly now, tugging at his legs and he fought to keep his balance, but in the end, it was a losing battle. He slipped, the rapid water carrying him toward that opening.

Leo struggled to keep from being washed over the edge, unsure of what awaited below. But there was nothing for him to grab onto and he had no strength to fight the water.

Suddenly, the ground fell out from under him and he was falling, momentarily weightless.

Then the water of the River Charnel rose up to meet him and his breath was nearly snatched away by the bone-jarring impact. A new sort of panic overtook him and he flailed his limbs madly, fighting to break the surface.

He gasped in another breath before going under again. The current here was too strong and living in the city his entire life had provided no opportunity to learn how to swim.

I'm going to drown! His heart seized in fear and he thought it might stop entirely. Then another thought came to him, *Kick your legs.*

Somehow, he managed to struggle to the surface again, but not without swallowing half the river, the disgusting water flowing past his lips. A thick branch drifted past and he made a desperate swipe at it, refusing to let go.

It kept his head above water and he no longer had to waste the energy fighting the current. The river gradually slowed, the current pushing him to the side, where the water was shallower. Leo released his grip on the branch that had saved him and crawled up onto the bank, completely soaked through.

His clothes clung to him, the muscles in his arms shaking from the exertion, hair plastered to his head. He wiped water out of his eyes and then promptly vomited up all the river water he had swallowed.

Gasping for air, Leo collapsed onto the bank, grass tickling his face. Beneath his shirt, hard and cold against his chest, he could feel the soul stone.

He wanted to lay down and sleep for hours, but he knew better. He needed to keep moving. Sitting up, he took off his boots, dumping the water out. His socks were still soaked, but there was nothing for it. Leo shoved his boots back on and stood, surveying his surroundings.

Sprawling before him were tall, thick trees and dense undergrowth. The air felt hot and muggy, the water droplets already evaporating off his skin. Raucous animal cries filtered through the trees, insects swarming in the air.

All at once, with a dawning dismay, he realized where the river had brought him.

I'm in the Valderan rainforest.

VII

Why does the emperor wear a mask?

Fabian's sister, Lydia, had often asked him that and he had no answer to give her, other than the tired tale of the first emperor. It was a sign of respect, honoring the first emperor's legacy. It made little sense to Fabian. Masks seemed uncomfortable to him, and he didn't understand how one could see out of them either.

Whatever the reason, he had never once seen the emperor without his mask, even though he spent the majority of his time in the ruler's presence—or so it felt.

Though most would kill to be so close to Akkadia's leader, it was not a job Fabian relished. With each passing day, it seemed more difficult to bear, though he tried to remind himself that he was perfectly placed to gain the emperor's trust and favor—and to learn his secrets.

Fabian scoffed silently to himself. Desmond was more likely to kill him in one of his fits than ever take him into his confidence.

He looked over at him now, resting his fingers lightly on the lute in his lap, studying Akkadia's emperor as he stood by the window of his personal chambers. The room was always dim, made more so today by the overcast sky.

Gauzy curtains draped over the windows, casting a veil over the outside world.

The emperor was dressed in a long, flowing robe, ebony in color. His long white hair tumbled freely down his back, an uncommon sight in the Capitol, where most men wore their hair short.

Desmond turned, his face concealed beneath the mask. Fabian wondered if the man even slept in it. It wouldn't have surprised him. The mask covered the emperor's features from hairline to chin, a solid piece of flesh-colored metal, aside from the lips and eyes. The mouth never moved when he spoke, which would have been unnerving enough, but it was the eyes Fabian couldn't get past.

The eyes were solid gold pieces, hiding even his gaze from view. One never could be certain where or what the emperor was looking at, or what mood he might be in, the mask rendering his face blank and expressionless.

He must have been able to see through it, somehow, because his movements were never anything but precise. Slow at times, but always deliberate.

"Play me something," Desmond commanded, waving one long-fingered hand, then added, "Peaceful."

Fabian obeyed and began plucking at the strings of his lute. On bad days, the emperor had been known to make him play until his fingers blistered and bled. Fabian hoped today wouldn't be one of those days.

He relaxed slightly as the emperor settled himself on one of the lounges, propping one arm on the armrest. His fingernails were too long and sharp, more like talons.

Fabian had barely finished the first song before his fingers stilled, the lute falling silent, as a sharp knock rapped on the door. He knew that knock.

His sister entered when bidden, her armored boots ringing hollowly on the marble floor. She looked resplendent in her armor, posture perfectly straight, her arms held respectfully behind her. Her green eyes flicked to him and a look of regret passed between them.

She bowed to Desmond, still seated on his lounge. "My liege. I come to report that we carried out a successful raid on a Resistance meeting."

Without seeing Desmond's expression, it was impossible to judge whether he was pleased or not, but Fabian saw no reason for him not to be.

His tone sounded approving enough. "Good. Did you take any prisoners?"

Lydia's mouth tightened. "No, Your Highness. They chose to die by their own hands rather than let themselves be captured."

Fabian flinched. That explained the look his sister had given him, then.

He heard the frown in Desmond's voice. "How… unfortunate."

The emperor spoke with his usual drawl, his voice slow and unhurried, enunciating every word with almost painful distinction.

"A few managed to escape. We're tracking one as we speak. He'll soon be in our custody."

"Make sure you take him alive. I want to see how much he knows."

"As you wish, my lord."

"Unless there was…anything else?"

"No, my lord."

He waved a hand languidly, the light catching on his too-long fingernails. Lydia bowed and turned on her heel, leaving the two men alone once more.

Fabian hated seeing her go, but he would hate for her to stay, and see what was to come, even more.

He clenched the handle of the lute, so hard he feared he might snap it, remaining perfectly still, praying his presence would go unnoticed. It wouldn't be the first time the emperor had forgotten he was there.

Fabian tracked Desmond's movements with a wary eye, refusing to look away, even for a moment. He braced himself for what was to come.

Desmond gripped the window sill with white-knuckled hands. "Did you hear that?"

Fabian knew by now that he was not to respond to any question the emperor posed.

A moment passed by, the emperor releasing his hold on the window sill to tap his nails upon it. The sound grated on Fabian's raw nerves. "They're planning something big. I know they are. I can feel it in the air. A palpable tension, as if a storm is waiting to break."

Fabian listened to what seemed like the emperor having a one-sided conversation with himself, wondering what course it would take and how it would end.

"Yes, yes." Desmond waved a hand impatiently and began to pace.

He reached up, his hand touching the metallic side of his mask. "They're already being dealt with," he added, voice rising the longer he spoke. "I've increased the number of patrols, but I don't know how much longer we can keep this up. I've received word from Elath that the raw materials needed for their armor is running out. We're already recycling what we can, but it's not enough. If the metal is too thin, the mechs are useless. Too many already do not come back or return damaged. Do you think they're on to us?"

Fabian's brow furrowed. What did the emperor mean too many mechs didn't come back? Come back from where? And why were they returning damaged? What could possibly damage a mech, aside from another mech?

"Yes," the emperor murmured. "We must get rid of them."

He halted abruptly, his masked face swiveling to pin Fabian with its eerie stare. "Are you still here? Get out."

Fabian gripped his lute and scrambled to his feet, but he didn't move fast enough. Moving with viper-like speed, the emperor lunged forward, one hand raised. Fabian flinched as the blow struck his cheek.

"I said get out!"

Fabian ducked, scurrying for the door. He did not stop running until he reached the quarters he shared with his sister, located in a far wing of the palace. It wasn't much, compared to some, but he knew it was far more than they had any right to expect, with both of them being little more than glorified servants, each in their own way.

He sighed, reaching up to touch his bruised cheek. The emperor's moods were getting worse.

Her brother was waiting for her when Lydia retired for the night, her feet sore from long hours of patrolling, eyes tired from staring at screens.

So far there were no leads on the escaped rebel—nothing solid anyway. It was only a matter of time. They would hunt him down and drag him back to the Capitol, the first rebel to be taken alive. Her heart leapt to think what sort of useful information they could wring out of him.

Still, she wished she'd had good news to present to the emperor. She didn't like leaving Fabian alone with him, much less when his mood was more likely to be volatile.

If only he could have been a soldier, like her. She had no doubt he would have risen through the ranks, clever as he was. But cleverness was no substitute for stamina and physical strength, both of which Fabian lacked.

He was lying on the divan when she arrived, but he pushed himself into a sitting position. He had the same blond hair and green eyes as she did. Their hair was a similar length, Fabian only slightly taller than her. It would have been nearly impossible to tell them apart, were it not for her slightly more feminine features.

"I sent to the kitchens for some food, if you'd like," he said.

Lydia was hungry, but her appetite curdled as she took in the purpling bruise on his cheek.

"He hit you," she said, voice flat.

Fabian waved her concern away. "It's nothing. I can handle it."

"You don't need to be dealing with this among everything else," Lydia growled, stalking further into the room.

The walls were black, with gold accents, the corners of the rooms supported by thick pillars. The floor was made of marble, but covered in plush rugs and carpets.

Incense burned in one corner; Lydia could see the smoke curling lazily into the air. She'd always hated the smell, but Fabian claimed it helped calm him, and she would not begrudge him that. Saints knew he had a difficult enough time as it was.

Lydia eyed the low table in the middle of the room. A ceramic bowl held fresh oranges, the same as they had the day before. They were Fabian's favorite. But whether these were the same fruit as yesterday, or more had been brought up, they hadn't been touched.

She scowled. "I'd have a talk with him," she added, "if I thought it'd do any good."

I'd punch his teeth out, if I thought I could get away with it.

"Don't," Fabian warned.

She looked at him, knowing what he must be thinking. He knew better than most how unpredictable the emperor could be, how violent his moods.

"You're too important."

"And you're not?" Lydia challenged.

He gave her a sad smile. "Not to the Empire."

"You are to me," she shot back and then turned, stalking off down the hallway, eager to be rid of her heavy armor.

She was glad when the wall hid her from Fabian's view, blinking back the hot sting of tears. It wasn't fair. This was the one thing she couldn't beat, couldn't force into submission. Neither of them could.

If it were possible, she would have found a way. She couldn't even protect her brother from the emperor. What good was she? What good was her rank? She could rise to the very top and still lose the thing that meant the most.

But she went on, day after day, going where she was sent, carrying out orders. She would do whatever the Empire asked of her in order to keep him safe.

People like Fabian did not have much use in the Akkadian Empire, which placed little value on such things as music or art. Her service kept him safe and so she would make herself invaluable.

She paused, glancing into her mirror, fingers on the strap of her breastplate. Her hair was short and her frame large, made to look even more so by her armor. But her face was narrow, with sharp cheekbones and dark, long eyelashes.

Her fingers stilled and she turned, striding back the way she'd come, an idea striking her. There was one more thing she could try.

Fabian looked up as she came back into the room. "Where are you going?"

"Out. I shouldn't be long, but don't wait up."

Lydia latched the door behind her and marched forward, her stride fast and long, footsteps ringing on the marble floors, heralding her arrival. No one she passed spoke to her or tried to interrupt.

She moved with a purpose and few would wish to draw the attention of one of the Empire's Eyes.

She slowed as she approached the palace scriptorium, on a lower level and another wing entirely, where the clerks and scribes worked to record the day's events to be later stored in the archives.

Lydia didn't know who would bother to read or even consult half the rubbish that was written down, but for once, it wasn't present events that concerned her.

The room smelled of ink and parchment, mostly empty this late in the day. A solitary figure glanced up at the sound of her approach, hunched over a desk, surrounded by lit candles.

Lydia shook her head. Only Zakarias would choose to work by candlelight when he had the modern marvels of electricity at his disposal.

He nodded his head in her direction, setting his quill aside and capping the pot of ink on his desk. "Captain. What can I do for you?"

The air was cool and slightly musty, below ground level. Lydia rarely ventured anywhere below ground, but it was on her brother's behalf that she did so now. He knew Zak far better.

She relaxed her posture; she had the tendency to put people on edge, regardless of whether that was her intention or not. Though she didn't know the scribe as well as her brother, they were not strangers and this was not a formal visit.

"It's Fabian," she said simply.

Zak's gaze darkened. "How is he?"

"No improvement." Lydia shook her head. "He's getting worse. Slowly, but I see it."

"I'm sorry," Zak said simply.

He was dressed plainly, in a basic robe, almost like what the ancient Anarshan monks wore—or so the rumor went. Lydia, of course, had never seen an Anarshan. No one living had.

But it was the Anarshans that had made her seek the scribe.

"I was hoping you might be able to help."

"Me?" His brows rose.

"It's a long shot, I know, but…I'm worried about him, Zak. I don't mind admitting that."

"We all are."

"He assures me that he's fine, but…" Lydia broke off, looking down.

"What is it that you think I might be able to do? I'm a scribe, not a healer."

"Precisely. No one knows what's wrong with him. No one in the Capitol, anyway. I was wondering if there might be something in the old archives. The Anarshans were rumored to be good healers."

She glanced up at him, feeling foolish now that she'd spoken the thought aloud. It sounded stupid, an impossible hope that would lead nowhere but to more disappointment.

"They weren't simply good. They were unparalleled. Yes…" Zak said slowly. "I could take a look."

Lydia let out a breath. She was so desperate, she would look anywhere, accept anything, even dusty records from a thousand years ago.

"Thank you," she told him sincerely, then added hastily, "Just so long as it's not any of that saint crap. I need facts, something solid, something real, that will help."

The Anarshans had believed in saints—individuals who had wielded some sort of magical power or something along those lines. Lydia hadn't paid much attention to the details—it clearly wasn't true. Just more proof that people would believe anything.

No saint was going to heal her brother.

Zak nodded, getting to his feet. "I understand. I can't make any promises, of course, but if the Anarshans don't know of any cure or explanation, no one does."

PART II:

THE

DRAGON

PART II:

VIII

Leo stared at his surroundings, the night sky hidden from view by the thick canopy of leaves. He had never set foot outside the city walls before, much less in the forest. He took a few steps forward, away from the river, beneath the cover of the trees.

How far away from the city had the river taken him? He was surrounded on all sides by dense woodland, far as the eye could see. It must have carried him past the Workhouses, the farms and fields that lay outside the city.

It didn't matter. He couldn't go back. Even if he'd had a way to get back into the sewers again, how could he go home? He had been seen at a Resistance meeting.

The full realization of what he'd done struck him and Leo sank down onto the forest floor, his back against a tree. He was out in the middle of nowhere, alone, in a forest that could hold unknown terrors. He had nothing with him other than the clothes on his back and—

He reached up, feeling the chain around his neck, the soul stone still hidden beneath his shirt. Leo sighed. For some reason, the stone's presence comforted him, although it was of little use out here.

He had no food or water, no knowledge of what food might be safe to eat out here or even how to find it. The only water he had managed to find was the River Charnel and it wasn't clean, with the Capitol dumping its waste into it.

Leo couldn't go back and worse still—he had abandoned his family, leaving them to fend for themselves, with no clue as to what had happened to him or where he'd gone. What was happening to them at that very moment?

He closed his eyes, imagining his mother still awake, nearly sick with worry, her eyes flicking to the door, wondering why he hadn't returned.

Or had the Empire turned to them for information about his whereabouts and recent activities? Would they be punished for his actions?

Of course they will. You know how this works.

What if they were killed, all because he had decided to go back to another meeting? To brave the risk to pass on information that didn't seem all that important now.

Leo ran his fingers through his hair. *Fool. I'm such a fool.*

He'd ruined everything and for what? He'd known the risks. Why had he gone back? He'd believed every argument he'd given Fitz that night after the first meeting. So what had changed?

And Fitz… Had he managed to make it out of the pub or was he in custody even now?

Poor brave, idealistic Fitz, whose naivety and discontent had led them both down the road to ruin.

Leo buried his head in his hands, at the absurdity and futility of it all, but he couldn't summon the energy for either tears or fury. He was too tired and what good would it do?

He had escaped, for now, and had only two options left. He could lay down and die here, if he believed he had nothing left to lose. Or he could try and get back at the Empire for letting it all come to this. Fitz had been right about that much. If the Empire treated people less harshly, there wouldn't be such discontent that led to the kind of events that had taken place that night.

Leo looked up, listening to the sounds of insects around him. It was so *loud*. For some reason, he'd always imagined a forest would be quieter than this.

Briefly, he wondered if he should try and get some sleep, if it would be better to climb a tree or remain on the ground.

His clothes were still wet and clinging to him, an uncomfortable feeling. Between that, the incessant noise, and the fear of what might be lurking out there, Leo doubted he would be able to sleep at all. And though he wanted to put as much distance between him and the Capitol as possible, there was little point in wandering in the dark. He could barely see a few feet in front of him.

In the end, his decision was made for him. Leo froze as the forest sounds dimmed around him, every sense snapping taut as a bowstring. His straining ears could just make out the sound of something moving through the underbrush. He sat up straighter, eyes searching the dark. The Empire wouldn't have sent a patrol after him, would they?

He couldn't see anything, but he could still hear whatever it was, moving closer and making no attempt to be quiet. Dread crept over him, the undeniable suspicion that he shouldn't linger.

Leo heaved himself to his feet and started walking. He was still too tired from fighting the river to move any faster and in the dark, he risked falling and breaking his neck. Slowly, the rustling sounds faded behind him and he relaxed slightly.

Walking helped take his mind off the consequences of what he'd done and instead focus on a solution. He couldn't spend the rest of his life living in the forest and he couldn't return to the Capitol. He supposed he could try to eke out a living in either Elath or Shemar, but if he was truly a fugitive from the Empire, sooner or later, he would be found out.

That left only the Resistance. One way or another, he needed to find them and convince them to let him join their ranks. He might as well commit fully, given the circumstances.

Easier said than done. Leo shook the doubts away. He needed to find them first before he could gain their trust and he wasn't sure which of the two tasks would be more difficult.

He was so absorbed in his thoughts that he didn't know how far he'd gone when he heard the rustling again, as if something was following him through the brush. Leo slowed and then stopped, glancing around.

There was a loud *snap* as a branch cracked in two and he spun around, blood turning to ice. A pair of glowing green eyes watched him from the undergrowth.

As he watched, a face emerged from the trees. It was not a nice face—with an elongated muzzle full of teeth and eyes that watched him hungrily.

Leo stared, dumbstruck, hardly daring to believe what he was seeing. It was a face he'd seen many times before. They were present in every district in the Capitol. It had been his dream to help build them once.

But this dragon wasn't made of iron or steel. It was a living, breathing creature, no gears, circuitry or steam to be found.

Impossible.

The creature was so black, he could barely see it in the darkness. But there was no mistaking the moonlight that glinted off its claws as it took a step forward.

Leo's shock vanished, replaced by another surge of terror. Dimly, he wondered how many times a person could find themselves in mortal peril in the span of one night before their heart simply gave out.

This dragon might not be one of the Capitol's metallic monstrosities, but it was just as dangerous.

He whirled and charged deeper into the forest, heedless of the vines or roots that could trip him up. He heard leaves rattle behind him as the beast burst out of the undergrowth and dashed after him. He risked a glance over his shoulder but all he could see were branches.

Something lashed around his boot, wrenching his foot, and Leo cried out as he fell, catching himself on his arms, pain lancing through his ankle. He turned to see the leaves part, the large black beast approaching.

He could see it more clearly now. From his position on the ground, the creature appeared enormous, the long claws glinting in the moonlight. Unlike the mechs, it had wings, folded at its sides.

The dragon's teeth were bared in a horrid semblance of a grin, its vibrant green eyes glowing slightly in the darkness, the pupils mere slits. The dragon mech's eyes had no pupils. They were solid yellow, lamp-like and lifeless. Leo wasn't sure which were more terrifying.

He dragged himself away from it and got painfully to his feet, limping as fast as he was able. In the darkness, he hadn't realized that the ground ended abruptly in a ledge, just ahead, and he nearly toppled over it, dirt falling away under his feet. The trees below blocked his view of what lay beneath, but he could imagine.

Clenching his teeth against the pain in his ankle, he turned back to face the beast, which had been slowly slinking toward him, movements unhurried, as if it knew he wasn't going anywhere.

It stopped, eyeing him. And then, to his utter astonishment, it spoke.

"Took a wrong turn, did we?"

Her voice—for it was undeniably female—was shrewd and mocking.

Leo stared at her dumbly. Dragons weren't supposed to exist, much less speak.

"What's the matter? Empire cut out your tongue? Well, you won't have to worry about that much longer."

He sensed the menace beneath her growl, saw the muscles gather in her haunches as she prepared to spring.

Oh, saints.

Desperate, he turned to face the drop behind him and considered throwing himself over the edge. It would probably be a quicker, less painful death than waiting to be mauled.

He hesitated.

Jump!

A sudden surety came over Leo that if he jumped, he would not die. But if he stayed here, he surely would.

The dragon sprang and Leo leapt off the ledge. Branches collided painfully against his body, scraping and tearing at him, and then he had broken free of the canopy, air rushing past his face.

For the second time that night, he hit the water, the impact nearly taking his breath away. It was less terrifying, perhaps because he'd done it once before, or because the dragon he had left behind was more frightening still. He scrambled to the surface, spying a rock glistening in the middle of the stream, and clung to it.

By some force of will, he managed to drag himself to shore, the current not nearly as strong as it had been in the river. He looked up, half expecting to see the dragon waiting for him, but the forest canopy had concealed him from her view.

Leo shook water droplets off of himself, thinking he would never be dry again. Ignoring the pain in his ankle, he set off once more, wanting to get as far away from the black beast as possible.

I've nearly died too many times tonight.

Skye stared moodily back in the direction of the Capitol, eyes scanning the darkened forest. The black cloth that she often used to hide her face while in the city hung loosely around her neck. She longed for some light to see by, but it wasn't cold enough for a fire and the light would only attract the wrong kind of attention.

It had been several years since a Resistance patrol had been attacked by a dragon, but it did happen.

"Stop looking," Tiachren scolded gently. "We got away. No one's coming after us."

"You don't know that," Skye retorted, but she turned her gaze away from the woods and faced him instead. "Someone betrayed us, Tiachren."

"We don't know that," he said, echoing her earlier words. "It could have been random. Nothing more than a bit of bad luck. You know how the Empire is with raids."

"You don't believe that any more than I do."

She knew what he said could be true, but she also knew that he simply didn't want to accept that they had lost people tonight. It was a mark of failure. They should have been more careful. *We should have vetted people better.*

"You should have let me kill him," she muttered.

She could still see the informant's face in her mind. The terror in his eyes had been real enough, but that didn't prove anything one way or the other.

Tiachren sighed. "Fitz brought him in. He usually knows what he's doing. He said we could trust him and I believed him. We have no proof that he's to blame."

There was no point in arguing with him, especially without proof. She turned away again, taking a dried strip of meat from her pack and gnawing on it.

Because they had been discovered in the city, they would have to move far more quickly through the forest, putting as much distance between them and the Capitol. If the Empire did send out patrols—unlikely since all Resistance members no longer had government-issued trackers—they needed to move and move fast.

It would be a fool's errand, but the Empire was desperate to snuff the Resistance out. They had been a thorn in Akkadia's side for far too long.

Skye laid down on her bedroll and tried to concentrate on falling asleep. Tiachren would take first watch. She gripped the hilt of one of her daggers, feeling its familiar weight and cool steel at her side.

He shouldn't have stopped me from using them when I had the chance.

IX

As dawn rose over the Valderan rainforest, so did the heat. By midmorning, Leo was covered in sweat, his clothes once more sticking unpleasantly to his skin. His lips were starting to crack from lack of water and the stifling heat. The air was muggy and close, clinging to him and making it harder to breathe.

He had gotten little to no sleep last night, every sound setting his nerves on edge. His body, aching and exhausted, cried out for sleep, but his nerves were too frayed to allow him to relax.

His forearms were covered in itchy red welts where the forest insects had feasted on him. The heat made it worse, the itch nearly unbearable. His ankle protested every step he took and he feared what he would see when he took his boot off. But nothing quite compared to the throbbing in his head, where the rebel had struck him.

Leo's stomach growled, reminding him that he hadn't eaten since yesterday's lunch. He hadn't returned home for dinner, mistakenly believing he would have time after the meeting. Instead, he'd been forced to flee for his life.

He gazed longingly at berries he passed, some bright red and others black. He knew they might very well be edible, but dared not take the risk.

Birds flitted through the trees and he saw various other creatures he only recognized from manuals he'd studied. Monkeys, some sort of small pig, and snakes. He wondered if any of the creatures might be edible, but even if they were, he had no way of catching them.

As he walked, he kept listening for the sounds of running water. Moving water would be cleaner than stagnant, which he had already encountered several times. But no source of drinking water revealed itself to him.

Near noon, the sun directly overhead, he stopped to rest. The canopy provided some shade, but it was little comfort. His mouth was so dry, despite the humidity in the air, that his tongue stuck to the roof of his mouth. The humidity had made his curls droop slightly, sticking to his forehead, and he pushed them out of his face.

Leo closed his eyes. Who was he kidding? He was never going to reach the Resistance, wherever they were. There was nothing out there but forest and he was going to die if he didn't find water.

The next thing he knew, his eyes were flying open, his body jerking upright, as something large crashed through the trees. He hadn't realized he'd drifted off, but now adrenaline returned once more, bringing him to his senses, temporarily erasing all signs of weariness.

Wincing at the pain in his ankle, he hurried in the opposite direction, careful not to make too much noise. Despite the thick foliage, there was nowhere to hide, unless he could scale one of the towering trees.

The mech broke free of the trees, gears clanking, steam hissing from its nostrils, sunlight glancing off its iron plating. Leo expected it to run him down, pinning him beneath one of its massive hands, but instead, its long strides ran past him, turning to block his path forward.

Leo turned and ran in the other direction, knowing it was pointless, but there was nothing else he could do.

The soldiers, lagging behind the mech, stepped clear of the undergrowth. Leo slowed, barely avoiding colliding with one of them, panting hard.

They wore no armor, but had no need of it. He had no weapons and the mech was protection enough. He eyed their black and gold uniforms in dismay. The Imperial patrol had found him.

Wordlessly, the guard he'd nearly run into reached for him.

If they catch you, they'll kill you.

Baring his teeth, Leo struggled to break free of the soldier's grasp and run—all the while knowing it was pointless. The automaton was still behind him.

But that didn't stop him from kicking and lashing out, flailing desperately. There were too many of them and he was quickly overwhelmed, rough hands grabbing him. A hand tangled in his hair and he was forced to his knees, then pressed flat against the ground, arms wrenched painfully behind his back.

"Going somewhere?"

Leo glanced up at the soldier who had spoken, standing by impassively while the others did all the work. He seemed to be the leader, judging from the rank proudly displayed on the sleeve of his uniform.

"Get him up," the soldier, a lieutenant, barked.

The others roughly hauled Leo to his feet, keeping a firm grip on his arms.

"Search him."

He had no weapons on him, but the soldiers searched anyway. He tensed as they withdrew the chain from beneath his shirt. One of the soldiers arched an eyebrow at the sight of the blue stone, but let it fall back down without comment.

The lieutenant stepped forward, eyeing the tattoo on Leo's forearm. "District III, eh? Another one of you low-level rats causing trouble."

One of the female soldiers curled her lip. "What do you expect from the lower orders?"

"If you're going to kill me, get it over with," Leo growled, his voice raspy.

He wasn't sure where the confidence to say such a thing came from, but he was hot, tired, and thirsty and that fed his frustration.

"And let you miss your appointment back in the Capitol? I don't think so. I'm sure one of the Inquisitors will be wanting to see you."

Leo's courage faltered, realizing the soldiers thought he knew something about the Resistance and that he could tell them important information.

They intended to torture him until he confessed what he knew, but he knew nothing—nothing that was of any use, at least.

"I don't know anything," he protested, trying to struggle free again, but there was no breaking free of their grasp.

"That's what they all say. You'll be singing a different tune soon enough." The lieutenant nodded to the guards holding him. "Bind him and let's go."

The soldiers holding him tied his wrists together none too kindly, the ropes biting into his skin.

Wordlessly, Leo fell into line as they moved, the automaton in the lead. He gazed at it in a mixture of admiration and revulsion. He should have been working on one right now instead of all this. Leo watched the way it moved, fascinated by its fluid grace, as if it had been real.

He looked away, keeping his eyes averted, not wanting to draw the attention of any of the soldiers and invite more trouble. For a time, it seemed to work. None of them spoke to him or paid him any mind. But as time wore on, the sun's heat oppressive even through the canopy, he began to falter, lack of food and water taking its toll. His head continued to pound, nearly obliterating all thought, and it was all he could do to put one foot in front of the other.

It came as no surprise when one of the guards shoved him when he stumbled. Leo lost his footing and fell, landing awkwardly on his forearms, unable to catch himself properly with his wrists bound in front of him.

"Come on, get up," the guard growled, nudging him with a boot. "Get up!"

Leo struggled to rise, movements sluggish. The pain in his ankle was worse than ever. When he didn't move fast enough, the soldier delivered a vicious kick to his ribs and Leo yelped.

The lieutenant turned, his brow furrowed with impatience. "Drag him behind the mech if you have to."

Leo glared at the man and pushed himself to his feet just as the forest exploded.

A snarl rang out and the lieutenant whirled around as something large came crashing through the trees. Leo had time to see a black beast collide with the dragon mech before he was shoved back to the ground by one of the guards. He grunted as he once more landed on his forearms, scraping the skin. He felt the silver chain slide around his neck, the blue stone dangling forward, free of his shirt.

He looked up, through the hair that had fallen in his eyes, and saw the black dragon wrestling with the automaton, snarling, a mess of flashing claws and teeth. He could hear the Imperial soldiers yelling, a few screams ringing out.

The black dragon clamped her teeth onto the mech's neck and gooseflesh erupted over his skin as the metal screeched, crumpling beneath the force as if it were made of paper.

Gritting his teeth, he turned and began to drag himself away, shuffling awkwardly on his arms, hands still bound in front of him. He hadn't managed to make it very far when the forest fell eerily silent.

Slowly, dreading what he would see, Leo rolled over onto his back and sat up.

The metal husk of the mech lay on its side, motionless, gently steaming. The yellow light had faded from its eyes. The bodies of the patrol were scattered around it, the grass stained crimson with gore. Leo stared in horror at the way their bodies had been rent open.

A snort snatched his attention away from the dead, eyes landing on the black beast standing before him. He swallowed, knowing there was no point in playing dead. This wasn't some unintelligent predator that could be fooled by such tricks.

Knowing that she could speak, he looked up into her emerald eyes and said, "Make it quick."

She approached him, steps unhurried, and Leo found himself physically shaking. She raised one hand and he flinched, bracing himself for the pain.

Instead, she slipped one long claw beneath the ropes binding his wrists and sliced through them as easily as butter. Leo stared at her as she retreated a slight distance, settling back on her haunches.

He rubbed his wrists where they'd been nearly chafed raw. "Why did you do that?" He hoped she didn't expect him to run in some perverse game of predator and prey, toying with him before the end.

She cocked her head to one side. "I'm curious." She nodded toward the dead soldiers. "What did you do to make them so angry with you? Steal a moldy piece of bread?"

Startled by her sudden change toward him and not a little bit wary, Leo sighed. "I'm afraid it's much worse than that." He glanced down, stuffing the soul stone back into his shirt, concealing it from view. Despite the heat, it remained cool against his skin, never warming.

"What, then?"

He got to his feet and limped over to one of the bodies, the dragon's keen eyes tracking his every movement. Leo knelt down, trying to ignore the wounds the soldier had suffered and the coppery tang of blood. He unhooked the canteen from the soldier's belt, feeling the welcome weight of the liquid within.

He unscrewed the lid and gulped down several swallows, the water running down his chin in his haste. He lowered the canteen, wiping his mouth with the back of his hand. "I'm a rebel sympathizer."

"Really? Could have fooled me. You look half-dead already. The Resistance must be desperate to recruit the likes of you."

He glared at her. "I didn't ask for any of this." He rooted around, tugging the soldier's pack off their shoulders.

The dragon made a huffing sound. "Looting the dead."

"It's not going to do them much good." He rummaged inside the pack and withdrew a packet of meat strips, tearing a chunk off with his teeth.

Wanting to get away from the corpses, Leo moved closer to the dragon. "Why didn't you kill me?"

"You're not grateful?"

"Of course I am. But you tried to kill me just last night so what changed?"

She unfurled her wings slightly and moved them in what he realized was a semblance of a shrug. "I thought, last night, that you were a member of one of those patrols and had gotten separated from your group. Obviously not, or they wouldn't have treated you the way they did. Of course, it's always possible you're a deserter. But you don't have a uniform and so I have to conclude otherwise."

"What patrols?"

Her green eyes narrowed and he noticed that they were surrounded by a darker, black area that outlined them, perhaps to help with glare.

"You don't know? The Empire sends mechs into the forest all the time. To kill dragons like me."

"There are more like you?"

She looked away. "Not as many as there once was…"

"Why? Why would the Empire do that?"

"I have my suspicions. Suffice to say the emperor views us as a threat. You'll have to satisfy yourself with that."

Leo studied the dragon sitting before him, a creature he had believed to be a myth. Her front feet were more akin to hands—in fact, exactly like human hands, with four fingers and a thumb, only the claws were far longer than human nails. Just one was as long as his entire hand. And *her* hands were as big as his torso.

She was covered, from the tip of her muzzle to tail, in scales black as midnight. They shimmered slightly as the light struck them, showing hints of blue or green. Thick plates of armor ran down her neck, over her belly and beneath her tail. Frills ran from the middle of her forehead to nearly the tip of her tail.

She had two horns, long and ever so slightly curving, extending backward behind her head. Her face was narrow, more pointed than rounded, and there were five frills on either side of her face, behind her jaw. Her hind feet had four toes and a dewclaw instead of a thumb.

Leo took in every detail hungrily, comparing her in his mind's eye to the mechs that he had so long been fascinated by and hoped to build. Here was the real thing.

He could see how the emperor would view her as a threat.

The dragon rose to her feet and Leo did as well, his head barely reaching her shoulder. Her legs were long, her body lithe and muscular.

"Well, that was diverting. You're welcome for the rescue." She began walking away.

"Wait!" Leo cried. "Where are you going?"

She glanced over her shoulder. "Back to what I was doing before I was so rudely interrupted—sunning myself on a rock."

"Do you know how to find the Resistance?" he blurted.

Unlikely that a dragon would know, but she had to be more familiar with the forest than him.

"Why?"

"I need to find them. I can't go back to the Capitol and I can't stay here." He gestured to the trees around them. "I don't know what's safe to eat or where to find fresh water."

Her lip curled, as if in amusement, revealing sharp white teeth. "You're right about that. You wouldn't last a day out here."

"Can you take me to the Resistance?"

She seemed to consider. "I don't know *exactly* where they are. Only an educated guess."

"That's good enough," Leo assured her. It was better than what he'd had a moment ago.

"What makes you think they'll trust you?"

"I don't know. I have to get there first."

"Fine. I'll take you there and then we won't have to tolerate each other any longer."

She began walking once more and Leo followed, stuffing the canteen into the pack he'd found, and hooking it over one shoulder. "I'm Leo, by the way."

"Why tell me that?"

"Well…if we're going to be traveling together, I just thought we ought to know what to call each other."

She didn't reply right away and for a moment, Leo feared she wouldn't answer him. Then, "Sheboleth."

"Sheboleth," he repeated, testing the syllables on his tongue.

"So, *Leo*, how does one become a rebel sympathizer?"

"It's a long story," he sighed.

"It's a long journey."

And so he told her, describing the living conditions within the city walls for her benefit, since, as a dragon, she probably had no idea.

Sheboleth didn't comment when he'd finished. An interlude of silence passed and then she asked, "What do those markings on your arm mean?"

Leo glanced down at the tattoo. He'd had it for as long as he could remember, but he suddenly hated the sight of it.

"It's the district where I live." *Lived.*

"I see."

Leo turned to her. "So what's your story?"

"Not much to tell."

"Come on. I answered your questions. It's only fair you answer mine."

She whirled on him. "Such knowledge comes with trust. You obviously trust me—you don't have much choice. But *I* don't trust *you*."

"Why not?"

"Because you're a *human*," Sheboleth said, spitting the word out as if it left a nasty taste in her mouth.

"I'm not an Imperial soldier," he protested, thinking back to what she'd said about patrols being sent to kill dragons. "I'm not like them either. You saw that for yourself. If I was one of them, they wouldn't be hunting me."

She grunted. "Not yet, maybe. But your kind has a propensity for cruelty. I've seen it. You've seen it. You'll probably see a great deal more before the end."

Leo thought of the executed man, dangling from the gallows, or the old man, beaten by the guards. "Not everyone is like that."

"Maybe not, but you all *could* be."

"I could do a lot of things," Leo shot back, snapping off a branch that threatened to poke him in the eye. "I could throw this stick at you or eat those berries—" he gestured with the stick at a cluster of bright red berries hanging from a vine. "But that doesn't mean I will."

She didn't seem convinced. "All the humans I've met have disappointed me, in that regard. Why should you be any different?"

"You're very blunt," Leo remarked, slightly stung that she had so little faith in him when they'd only just met.

"Get used to it."

"How many humans have you met, exactly?"

She moved her wings in a sort of shrug again. "Enough."

"I thought you were going to say you'd only ever met soldiers. Patrols like the one back there." He jerked his head in the direction they'd come.

"Since you have an idealistic way of looking at things, can a soldier not have a conscience?"

"You said humans are all cruel."

"I know what I said. I'm playing devil's advocate, challenging your way of thinking. What if the soldier is only doing such terrible things because it's the only way he can feed his family? Is it still wrong?"

Leo considered it. "Yes."

"Why?"

"Because the road to hell is paved with good intentions," he replied, somewhat bitterly, as he thought about his own situation. He'd had nothing but good intentions and he'd managed to do anything but good.

"It's never right to do wrong in order to do right."

The look she gave him reminded him of a person raising one eyebrow, which of course she did not have, but the effect was the same. She said nothing, but he thought she seemed pleased with his answer.

The two of them lapsed into silence and Leo sensed that Sheboleth no longer wanted to talk. To distract himself from his throbbing ankle, he focused on the forest around them.

Everywhere he looked, there was green. The trees were tall, with thin, white trunks, the thick forest canopy helping to shield them from the sun. Colorful birds gathered in the branches above them, squawking and arguing amongst themselves. Monkeys nimbly scaled the trees, plucking various fruit from the branches.

As they traveled, Leo ate the rest of the meat from the guard's pack. It hadn't lasted long and he would need to find something else. He eyed another cluster of the red berries.

"I wouldn't if I were you," Sheboleth remarked, seeing his interest. "You'll be dead in five minutes. Unless you're very unlucky. Then you might linger for a while."

Leo swallowed and took a step away from the berries.

Much like the meat, the water in the canteen did not last. Leo doubted he could remember what it felt like to not sweat so much. He was constantly forced to sip water to keep from becoming dehydrated, but Sheboleth didn't seem the least bit affected.

At last, when the water ran out, he was forced to speak again. "You don't know where there's fresh water, do you?" Everything he had managed to find had been brown, stained from rotting leaves.

Sheboleth gave him a look and changed direction. Leo dutifully followed.

"If it's fresh water you want," she said, pushing aside some bushes, "you can't do better than this."

Ahead of them stretched a small pool, surrounded by trees. The water was crystal clear, revealing the sand at the bottom and small fish. Bubbles rose to the surface, glinting as the sunlight caught them like chips of diamond. The water itself was a light blue color.

Leo stared at it a moment, marveling at just how clear it was. Sheboleth had already bent down, lapping at the water with a long, pink tongue. Leo cupped his hands beneath the water, but quickly gave that up and stuck his head under, mouth open, savoring the feel of the cool water as it flowed over his cracked lips and parched tongue, cooling his heated skin.

He pulled back, wiping his mouth with one hand, and caught Sheboleth watching him with what he took to be an amused expression. Sometimes, it was so hard to guess what she was thinking and others, her mannerisms seemed strangely human-like.

They traveled until nightfall. As the sun began to sink below the horizon and the air finally cooled, Sheboleth lowered herself to the ground with a huff and Leo joined her, relieved to get off his aching feet.

"Is it always this hot?" he asked. His shirt was soaked with perspiration and he had never felt more disgusting in his life. *I'd kill for a bath right about now.*

At least his headache had faded some once he'd had something to drink.

"Pretty much."

He sighed and turned toward the pile of fruit she had gathered for dinner. Selecting one, Leo took the knife out of the soldier's pack and set about peeling it. Sheboleth gnawed on hers—some sort of large melon—swallowing chunks with the rind still attached. The piece Leo had selected was surprisingly sweet, staining his fingers with a sticky, maroon juice.

"I'd have thought you ate meat," Leo remarked, "with teeth like that." He watched her long, sharp teeth make quick work of the fruit.

"I do. Dragons will eat just about anything."

The meal finished, Leo came to the task he had been dreading all day, but could no longer avoid. He unlaced his boot and tugged it over his injured ankle, hissing in pain. Sheboleth watched as he peeled his sock off, revealing the mottled, swollen skin of his ankle. Seeing it somehow made the pain worse and he grimaced.

Even the dragon curled a lip. "Looks nasty."

"Yeah, well, it wouldn't have happened if you hadn't tried to kill me."

"Am I supposed to feel guilty for that?"

Leo doubted she felt guilty about much of anything. He sighed again and leaned his head back against the tree trunk, propping his ankle up on a stone protruding from the ground. If he could keep it elevated, the swelling might go down, but it probably wouldn't do much good. He had already walked on it far too much when he should have been resting and tomorrow would be no different.

He swatted at a mosquito as it whined past his face. His arms were still covered in welts from the blasted little creatures and he scratched at them miserably. Sheboleth's eyes watched him. They shone in the dark, giving off a green glow.

"I have something that can help with that," she said, rising to her feet. "Wait here."

Leo was so stiff and sore from walking all day, he doubted he could move even if he wanted to. He waited for her to return and when she didn't, he feared she had changed her mind about acting as his guide and abandoned him.

He tensed as he heard something rustling through the undergrowth, hoping it was her, but wary all the same. They had passed large snakes that afternoon, along with leopards, and while he knew they wouldn't try anything while Sheboleth was with him, alone, he was vulnerable.

Sheboleth stepped into view, her black scales hard to make out in the gathering darkness. She was walking awkwardly, limping forward on three legs, and for a moment, he feared she had been injured somehow. Then he saw that she carried something in one of her hands, dropping a pile of leaves at his feet.

"For the bites," she explained, once more laying down. "You chew them up and smear the paste on them, but I figured you'd rather do that yourself."

"Thank you…" Leo said hesitatingly. He picked up one of the leaves. "Are you sure this is safe?"

"It's safe," Sheboleth said, a hint of weariness in her voice.

Leo sighed. He wasn't thrilled about the idea of smearing leaf paste that had been mixed with his own spit all over his arms, but he figured it couldn't have been much worse than anything else that had happened to him thus far. And the itching was so intense, he was willing to try anything.

He popped the first leaves into his mouth and began to chew. "How do you know so much about humans?"

Covered in scales, Sheboleth was immune to the buzzing, whining insects of the forest, and so he wasn't sure how or why she'd need to know such information.

"Who says I do?"

"You warned me about the berries earlier. Now this."

"If you must know, I spy on the Workhouses. The workers never see me, but I can watch them."

As soon as the paste touched his skin, the itch faded. There was nothing the dragon could do for the state of his ankle, but at least one problem had been solved. As the last of the light faded, Leo looked back in the direction of the Capitol and couldn't help but wonder what his family was doing at that moment.

If they're even still alive.

He pushed the thought away and tried to imagine what they were doing. Had his mother had to explain to Anastasia that he wasn't coming back home? Did they think he was dead? They didn't even know what had happened to him, where he'd been, or why he failed to return.

And now, if they were still alive, they would be forced to find some way to provide for themselves. A wave of guilt washed over him. How would they afford food or keep the intermittent electricity on?

I'm sorry. He wished he could take back what he had done, but there was no going back.

"What are you thinking about?" Sheboleth asked softly.

"My family," Leo replied and then added, after a pause, "I'll probably never see them again." Saying the words out loud somehow made them more real and the hurt bit deeper. "Not if the Empire punishes them for what I did."

"If you cared so much, why did you put them at risk?"

He turned to face her, catching the judgmental undertone. "I took the risk *because* I cared. Because I wanted them to have a chance at a better life."

Despite scoffing at Fitz, he had allowed himself to wonder, to believe that something better might be possible. It was a dangerous hope and it had cost him dearly.

Sheboleth snorted. "Greed, then. Typical human. Not satisfied with what you have."

Anger speared through him. "You don't know anything about me, other than what I've told you." Her judgement stung, mostly because he knew she was right.

He had been greedy, no longer satisfied with the way things were, and wanting more. He'd known the risks and allowed himself to fall victim anyway.

Whatever happened to his family—whether they lost their lives or had to endure even more hardship because he was no longer there to provide for them—it was his fault.

His father would have been so disappointed.

Leo shifted onto his side, facing away from Sheboleth.

He could lie to himself, but the dragon wasn't going to.

X

Lydia stared at the dots on the screen, each one representing a single soldier and the automaton that had accompanied them, willing them to move. But they hadn't moved for hours, ever since contact had been lost.

When the summons had come to report to headquarters, from the Minister of Defense himself, she had felt a swell of pride. She was certain her patrol must have captured the rebel who had escaped. Perhaps they were already back in the city even now, extracting information from him.

It wasn't possible to get a promotion out of it—unlike the lieutenant who had been sent to lead the patrol. Lydia was already one of the Empire's Eyes, as high and powerful as an Inquisitor.

As she had mounted the steps to the massive, mansion-like building, Lydia had been directed into the main room by a servant. The place was a hive of activity, uniformed soldiers hurrying about their business. Others sat at desks, monitoring screens and speaking into comm devices. This was the heart of the web of communication that spread across the entire city—and even beyond.

The Minister was seated in front of his desk, eyes watching the screens before him. There were so many of them, it had taken Lydia years to keep them all straight.

There was a screen for each district, orange, red and yellow dots spread out among the streets. But the one that had snared his attention was of the forest.

As the Minister had informed her of the news, her earlier sense of triumph vanished like mist before the rising sun.

He played the feedback on a loop, so she could see what had happened. The red dot that was her automaton and the yellow, representing her soldiers, had left the city and entered the rainforest. The solitary orange dot—the escaped rebel—had kept moving, managing to evade them for a while, until the two converged.

They began to return to the city, but their progress suddenly halted. Signal with the mech was lost around two in the afternoon, according to the time the last location was beamed out.

The red and yellow spots remained where they were, while the orange rebel continued on his way, moving deeper into the forest.

"Impossible," Lydia whispered as the loop began to once more repeat itself. But even as she spoke, she knew all too well that it was very possible.

This was not the first patrol she had sent into the forest that had failed to return.

But why would it leave him alive?

The rebel must have managed to escape somehow while the beast attacked her soldiers. Fleeing like the craven he was.

She could feel the Minister's eyes on her, the room heavy with his disapproval. He was a tall man, broad in the shoulder, and beneath his uniform, she knew he had arms that looked like they could snap trees. He had been the former instructor at the Academy before being promoted to this position and she had trained under him briefly during his last year.

No doubt he saw her as little more than a pupil still, and one that had failed.

Lydia steeled herself, standing at her full height. "No matter. We'll send only mechs this time and track him down. He's on foot and the terrain is treacherous. If he's not dead by the time the automatons reach him, we'll bring him in."

She wouldn't make the mistake of risking human lives this time. Not when an iron mech could do the job faster.

"See that you do. I want them sent out immediately, before you report to the emperor. He's keen to hear of our progress."

Lydia felt a muscle twitch in her jaw. The Minister was only concerned about how this blunder would reflect on him. *He'd much rather I take the blame.* But two could play at that game and if the emperor was displeased by the news she was about to tell him, she could always attempt to deflect blame.

She was, after all, still an underling. It wasn't her head that would ultimately roll if it came to that.

The Minister turned his attention back to the screens. "Dismissed."

Lydia nodded to him and went on her way, happy to leave the place behind. All of the department headquarters were located in District IX, as high as one could climb with the exception of the final, unassailable hurdle.

She dispatched a message to District VI, where the barracks and warehouses that stored the automatons were located.

One of the attendants there would relay her orders, programing them into the mechs' central control panel. With the exception of any repairs that needed to be made, or being refueled with the coal that they burned, the mechs were completely free of the need for human guidance.

Three of the automata ought to be enough. She would have sent more if they hadn't had the tracking at their disposal, but they would hone in on the rebel's location easier than a hound tailing a scent.

The emperor was in the throne room, when she arrived, instead of his personal quarters. Lydia cast a quick glance around and was relieved to see her brother nowhere in sight.

Her armored boots rang hollowly on the marble floor as she approached the dais at the far end. The floor was made of black marble, the walls equally dark, giving the room a heavy, oppressive air.

Desmond was seated on a solitary throne, clad in an ebony robe. The throne itself looked as though it had been crafted out of black marble, veins of gold running through it. Behind the throne, emblazoned on the wall, was the All-Seeing Eye of the Empire.

The amber eye stared, lidless, its pupil a slit instead of round.

At the feet of the throne lay two mechanical hounds, their muzzles long and ears pointed. Lydia eyed them with distaste as she approached, one hand caressing the hilt of the sword at her hip, though it would do little good against creatures with flesh made of metal.

For some reason, the dogs had always unnerved her. She could have understood such sentiment if they had been real animals. Real animals were unpredictable, much like people.

She was used to being around machines. Why the dogs should bother her so puzzled her. Perhaps it was less the dogs themselves and more the man seated behind them. With his unpredictable whims and moods, there was no telling what he might order them to do.

Lydia steeled herself. She commanded dragons. She would not be cowed by mongrels, mechanized or otherwise.

She knelt before the throne. "My liege."

Desmond stared at her from behind his blank mask. "Have you caught the rebel?"

Lydia swallowed. "Not yet, my lord. We lost contact with the first patrol so I can only conclude they must have encountered one of the dragons. I've already ordered more mechs sent. We'll soon have him."

The words tumbled from her in a rush, desperate to explain herself and make him understand. She hoped she didn't sound as nervous as she felt.

She wished he would send those dogs away.

The emperor rubbed his forefinger along the edge of his throne. "Unfortunate."

Now was her chance. "The Minister suggested sending out only one patrol initially, my lord. I encouraged him to send more, to ere on the side of caution, but he refused, saying we couldn't expend the resources. No doubt he believed one patrol was more than sufficient to deal with one rebel."

"But it wasn't."

"No. And now we must rethink our strategy."

"Yes…" Desmond said slowly. "You were right to send more. I eagerly await the results. Report to me immediately should you learn anything more."

"Of course, my lord." Lydia bowed once more and retreated, even more relieved to be rid of the throne room than she had of the defense headquarters.

Desmond felt a rush of panic once the Eye had given her report and left. He had dismissed his minstrel earlier to wait in another room until he was wanted and summoned again. Desmond summoned him now, thinking the music might help calm his frayed nerves.

The boy entered, but Desmond hardly glanced at him. "Play something, boy. Anything. Just play something."

The minstrel began to plunk out a melody on his lute.

Desmond's hands were shaking and he clasped them tightly together to hide it, fingers pulling at the skin on the back of his hand.

"How is it possible?" he demanded. "How could one boy have defeated an entire patrol and one of our mechs?"

He felt a third presence stir within the room and a voice sounded in his mind, deep and resonant.

"*He must have had help, my lord,*" the voice answered, as the emperor knew he would. "*It's the only explanation.*"

"Yes, but help from who? His fellow rebels? Yes, it must have been them."

The Eye had told him her suspicions. She believed a dragon had attacked this particular patrol, as they had so many others.

But Desmond did not want to believe it. The threat of the dragons grew all the time, looming larger in his mind. He was grasping at straws, at any other possibility, and he wanted the voice to reassure him.

"*You know from whom.*"

"No! That's not possible. Why would a dragon help a human?"

"I intend to find out. But you've no cause to worry, my lord. One rebel is no threat to you and all that you've accomplished."

"Yes," Desmond whispered. "We conquered Anarsha. They were fools, clever fools, but they were destroyed in the end. It bought them a little time, but it was so much easier than I could have anticipated. Walking right into the city square with so little resistance."

"And what is a single rebel compared to a kingdom?"

Desmond tightened his hand into a fist. Yes, he was powerful. How could he forget that, even for a moment? The things he had done and seen. It no longer felt as though it had merely been yesterday. Sometimes, it didn't seem as though he had really done any of those things at all. And yet, he was here.

"Do you think he's trying to return to the Resistance?"

"Undoubtedly. And if he manages to reach them before our patrols arrive, so much the better. We will have finally uncovered their location and it will only be a matter of time."

Desmond looked up sharply as his minstrel missed a note. He hadn't realized the boy was still there. He was doing that more and more often now and it worried him. How much had the boy heard? He could never be sure when he replied to the voice out loud or only within his own mind.

"You! That's enough. Leave me."

The minstrel scurried away, the song abruptly forgotten, as though he feared Desmond would throw something at him again.

The emperor chuckled at the thought. But if the boy ever guessed at the truth, he might have to take more drastic measures. It had been a long time since he'd last killed someone with his own hands, but he thought he could do it.

Of course you can.

He closed his eyes, remembering how it had felt. It had been so easy to plunge his sword into the heart of the first emperor. The man hadn't expected it and why should he?

Betrayal never came from one's enemies.

Lifting his lantern, Zak scanned the rows of scrolls and tomes arrayed before him. Within the archives, open flames were forbidden and so his candle had to be shuttered behind glass. Why no one had bothered to have the place electrified, he had no idea.

But then, no one seemed to have much interest in the past anymore. It was late, the room dark and quiet, about the only time he had to search after work had ended for the day. But even on the rare occasions he had ducked inside during daylight hours, the archives had been empty.

Here, in the oldest section, was even less frequently visited. He was searching for records from before the time of the Empire, something that was hard to fathom after more than a thousand years.

But Anarsha had existed before Akkadia became an Empire, and so had Shemar and Elath. Zak ignored any records from the smaller kingdoms. He had promised Lydia he would see if the Anarshans had possessed any knowledge of the mysterious ailment that afflicted Fabian.

The first few scrolls and books he selected were quickly put back, having nothing to do with healing or medicine. Zak sighed, staring up at the huge vaulted ceiling stretching above his head. The shelves rose into the gloom. He would need a ladder to reach most of their materials.

This was a task that could take years to properly research, searching only by himself, and that was time Fabian might not have.

Zak suppressed a yawn and kept searching. He would endure frequent sleepless nights for the rest of his life if it meant finding a cure for his friend.

The air smelled heavily of parchment, slightly musty from disuse. The paper was so old and brittle, he had to handle it with the utmost care.

These were priceless records of a kingdom and time that no longer existed, all that remained of the history that had forged their current world. They were more precious to him than all the soul stones in Shemar.

Some of the records hadn't been translated and were written in ancient Anarshan. Zak sent a silent thought of gratitude toward his tutor, who had insisted he learn the language. He'd hated it at the time, finding Anarshan a thick, unruly language, written in runes. Spoken, it had harsh consonants, nothing like the smooth, elegant Akkadian everyone spoke now.

He carried an armful of tomes over to the nearest table and set the lantern down, his arm aching from holding it up, trying to cast its feeble light high enough to read the spines of books—those that had writing on them, anyway.

Zak settled down, savoring the feel of the paper beneath his fingers, squinting at the faint ink. His Anarshan was rusty, with little cause to call upon it in his day-to-day life.

Mostly, he and the other scribes fetched records of court cases, rulings made by previous emperors, or conversations that had been recorded, searching for the *exact* way someone had phrased something and could no longer recall.

Nothing remotely like this, he thought as his eyes roved over the page. Rusty though his Anarshan might be, it returned quickly enough, and he soon realized that what he was reading would be of no use to Fabian at all.

He was about to shut it and keep looking, but his eyes kept traveling down the page, fascinated by the text that unfurled before him.

It was an account of Anarsha's fall, written by the Anarshans themselves. How rare that such a document survived! Zak had only ever read the Empire's own accounts, the history as portrayed by the victor.

And immediately he noticed something never mentioned in the Empire's telling. Zak leaned forward.

The Anarshans hadn't simply met Akkadia on the battlefield, their foot soldiers facing off against the mechs. At that time, the automatons hadn't been autonomous at all, but required the guidance of a human pilot, shielded within the mech's armor.

Zak, like all Capitol citizens, had been taught that Anarsha's defeat had been swift and brutal, their infantry no match for the Empire of Engines.

But this tome told a different story.

The Anarshans had successfully defended their kingdom, defeating and driving back the Akkadians. They hadn't only fought on foot against the mechs.

The Anarshans had fought beside dragons.

XI

It had been eleven years since Skye had felt so relieved to see the ruins of Anarsha come into view. She'd been twelve, stumbling from exhaustion and lack of food, covered in blood, clutching a bloodied dagger as if it were a lifeline. From the moment she had snatched that knife, she'd never let it out of her sight. She carried it with her even now, hidden within one of her boots.

She and Tiachren picked their way through the rubble, dirty and tired from traipsing through the forest at such a punishing pace. They squeezed through the crypt entrance and received nods from the guards standing outside the portcullis. She wanted nothing more than to retreat to one of the springs and clean up, but fate had other plans.

Jonathan was waiting for them and upon seeing their defeated expressions, he asked, "What happened?"

Skye slung her pack off, handing him the items the rebels within the city had gathered.

He cracked it open and peered within. "So much less than we expected. What happened?"

There was no point in denying it and they would find out eventually anyway. "The meeting was cut short," Skye said flatly. "We were raided. One of the new recruits must have sold us out."

She noticed Tiachren made no attempt to contradict her. Perhaps he'd had plenty of time to think it over during the return journey and come to the same inescapable conclusion she had.

Jonathan's face darkened. "You'll have to report this to the Triad."

They followed him further into the caverns, to where a large purple tapestry had been draped from ropes near the ceiling, blocking the tunnel and creating a wall, of sorts. Other such tapestries hung in separate parts of the caverns, marking out rooms for people to stay in. They lacked privacy—they couldn't afford the luxury of giving everyone their own room—but it was better than nothing.

Two guards stood watch outside the tapestry and pulled the two sides apart. Jonathan ducked inside and Skye and Tiachren followed. The narrow tunnel branched out into four different rooms, one for each member of the Triad, and one where they could all gather together.

"Wait here," Jonathan instructed and then disappeared into the room straight ahead. Each entrance was covered with purple cloth.

Skye shifted her weight nervously as she waited. She had only met with the Resistance leaders a handful of times, when she had first come to the Resistance, and to make her reports to them directly after important missions, usually ending in the death of an important government figure.

Otherwise, the only reason anyone found themselves summoned by the Triad was if they had done something wrong.

Skye picked at her fingernails, a nervous habit she despised and tried desperately to break, to no avail. She could ignore the urge until her nerves frayed—and they were fraying now. Sometimes, she went too far and ended up taking more of the nail than she intended, exposing the tender skin beneath and making them bleed.

Luckily, Jonathan returned before she got to that point, and ushered them into the fourth room, where the Triad waited. As she stepped inside, eyes adjusting to the dim light, Skye looked at each leader in turn.

Rhaven was an older man, his thick hair the color of pepper. A pair of spectacles perched on the end of his nose. Long past the age of leading missions himself, he gave the orders rather than carry them out.

Jemma, the second member, was a woman in her mid-forties, with long black hair that hung loosely. One strand, near her temple, was shockingly white. Gruff, with a demanding presence, she *could* lead missions if she wanted to.

The man in the center was Tristan, the youngest member of the Triad. He was dark-skinned, well-muscled, with broad shoulders. His long black hair was fashioned into many thin braids. He wore a sleeveless tunic, exposing honed biceps.

Jemma spoke first. "Jonathan tells us there's been a bit of trouble."

Tiachren answered. "Yes. One of our new recruits appears to have betrayed us to the Empire. We were raided and lost a good many of those gathered. How many escaped, I do not know."

"Let us hope none of them were taken alive," Rhaven muttered, his voice more a rasp.

It seemed, on the surface, a callous thing to say, but Skye knew that if they were captured by the Empire, they would be tortured for information until they wished for death. But that wish would not be granted until they either succumbed to the Empire's demands or the effects of the interrogation itself.

Tiachren bowed his head. "I take full responsibility. I should have vetted the newcomer more thoroughly."

"We both should have," Skye spoke up. "The newcomer was vouched for by one of our trusted agents, but…"

"But Imperial informants are not so easily identified for what they are," Jemma said.

Tristan scowled. "We were lucky this time. Anyah reported to me that something was wrong when she saw the majority of the tracker signals did not leave the pub where you were gathered."

Skye drew in a breath. She hadn't considered that, but Anyah would have been able to see on the screens how many left the bar and how many remained. She'd certainly seen the raid coming—at least to give Skye a brief warning.

"How many escaped?"

"Only three."

The words rang in her head like death knolls. She and Tiachren had escaped. Who the third was and where they were now, there was no telling.

"We were lucky," Tristan said again. "None of our members were taken in for questioning. Our secrets are safe."

For now.

Skye breathed out a sigh of relief. If they had been in some way compromised, they would have to pack up all their belongings and move out as quickly as possible. She didn't know where they would go. She could think of no better place than here.

"You're dismissed. Go get yourselves cleaned up."

"And rest," Jemma added, unusually charitable. "You've been through a lot."

We got off lightly, Skye thought to herself as she followed Jonathan back out into the main cavern.

She and Tiachren parted ways, Skye heading for the springs. It was blessedly empty this time of day and she stripped off her filthy clothes, slipping into the warm water. It was heated, but not enough to burn. There were other springs in the caverns that provided drinking water.

Clean and dressed in fresh clothes, Skye went to find Fae, her hair still damp. A makeshift laboratory had been set up in one of the alcoves, for Fae to utilize. The same had been done for Tiachren and his explosives.

Skye knew better than to poke her head in there. She'd nearly had her eyebrows singed off when she'd interrupted Tiachren in one of his experiments and startled him. He still had the burn scar to prove it.

Fae was seated at her worktable, where all manner of instruments were spread out. They looked more appropriate for a dissection than whatever she used them for. Goggles and picks, needles and forceps, scalpels, hammers, and beakers full of liquid. A microscope stood on one side, the red soul stone Skye had stolen beneath the lens.

"Make any progress?" Skye asked, nodding to the stone casually.

Fae looked up from what she was writing and sighed, pulling the goggles off her head. "No. Beneath the microscope, it's just an ordinary gem. I can't figure out what's so special about it, other than it seems to be indestructible. I've tried heating it up, hot as it would go, dissolving it in acid, even a good, old-fashioned smash with a hammer. Nothing. Not so much as a crack."

Skye tried to hide her disappointment. "Maybe the Empire should start making the mechs out of these things, then."

Fae made a wry face. "Let's be glad they haven't." She stood, picked up the stone, and ducked through an opening in the wall, into the room beyond.

Skye followed her. Within, held up by suspended wires, stood a dragon automaton. It was missing one of its limbs, several pieces of iron plating, and other bits and pieces. Skye could see where something was missing, but had no idea precisely what component fit there.

That was for Fae to determine. She'd been working on reassembling one, trying to figure out how they work, by collecting salvaged parts and forging the rest. If they could only get one to work, she said, they could build a whole army of them and use the Empire's most powerful weapon against them.

It was a nice idea, but so far, the mech had failed to come to life, and Skye doubted it ever would. Fae was the most mechanically gifted person she knew, but she hadn't gone to the Academy to learn how to build the metal monsters. And with something so complex, there was only so much one could teach oneself.

Fae walked up to the small slot in the dragon's chest plate, inserting the soul stone. It fit perfectly; there was no denying that it was meant to go there.

But nothing changed. The dragon didn't suddenly emit a hiss of steam breath, or its eyes flicker to life.

Fae shrugged. "If this is the answer, I can't see how. There has to be a use for them, but hell if I know what it is."

Skye ran her fingers over the stone. They had to be important. Why else would the Empire embed them into the dragons' chests? Why were they such a valued commodity? Why did they ruin and waste so many people's lives in the relentless pursuit of drawing ever more soul stones from the earth?

"I'll keep trying," Fae assured her.

"I know you will. I appreciate it."

Skye turned and left, swallowing her disappointment. Why did the Empire want those stones so badly? It was a question that had haunted her for as long as she could remember. There had to be a reason the Empire coveted them, beyond mere greed.

Without realizing it, her feet had taken her to the armory. It was a massive series of interconnected rooms, some with dummies and targets and weapon racks lined along the walls.

But it was the forges that she was drawn toward. Instinct and muscle memory took over, honed from long years of practice. Skye fetched her leather apron and gloves, went about lighting her forge and rifled through the collection of metal pieces, until she found one that would make a nice blade.

She popped it in the forge and waited for it to come to temperature before grasping it in a pair of tongs, carrying it over to the anvil, and channeling the frustration she felt through every hammer blow, drawing it out into the desired shape and length.

Ever since she had learned how, she made every single one of her blades herself and even some for other Resistance members. There were times when hers needed repairs or sharpened. Sometimes they broke or were lost altogether during a mission. And Skye wanted to be able to handle all of it herself, rather than wait on someone else.

The forge gave her a way to focus her anger. And there was something immensely satisfying about creating a sharp, beautiful weapon from a hunk of metal.

She could make a blade in a handful of hours, but she wanted to take her time, usually crafting her creations over the course of days or weeks. They needed to last, not merely look good.

Skye looked up, wiping sweat from her brow, as Anyah stepped into the room.

"Thought I'd find you here. I heard you were back."

Skye shut the forge down and pulled her gloves off. "Fae hasn't made any progress with the soul stone."

Anyah didn't need to ask why it meant so much to her, just like she didn't need to ask how the meeting in the Capitol had gone. She already knew, one of the few people privy to such information.

"If anyone can figure it out, she can."

"Maybe there really is no point," Skye said. "Maybe the soul stones have no use after all."

"You don't really believe that. Why would they want them so badly, if they were useless?"

"Maybe they make us mine them as a twisted form of punishment. To remind us, always, just how lowly we are. That they can make us do whatever they want and there's not a damn thing we can do about it." Skye clenched her hands into fists, the white bone of her knuckles visible against her pale skin, straining to break free. "To remind us that they can make us crawl."

"They have other ways of doing that," Anyah said softly. "Much less expensive, I might add."

Skye sighed, then looked at her. "Tristan said that only one other person besides me and Tiachren escaped."

"About that," Anyah said, perking up suddenly. "That's why I came to see you. I want to show you something."

Intrigued, Skye accompanied her, back the way she'd come, and through the partition that housed Anyah's war room. The screens bathed the stone walls with light, as always.

"I wasn't sure at first," Anyah said, sitting down at her desk. "The signal is really bad out there and it's hard to track, but…" She turned one of the smaller screens toward Skye, pointing at a single orange spot in the middle of the Valderan rainforest.

"What is that?" Skye asked, not sure what she was looking at. It didn't make any sort of sense.

"*That*," Anyah said, "is the other person who escaped. Whoever they are, they ran into the forest and have been moving in our direction ever since."

A spike of panic bolted through Skye. When they recruited someone within the Capitol, the goal was that they remain there, not attempt to find and join the Resistance itself. They were to wait within the city for further instruction and infiltrate it from within.

But I didn't do that.

She had left the mines of Shemar and wandered the forest herself until she had stumbled upon the Resistance. It had been her only hope of survival, of finding someone who would take her in and teach her to fend for herself. To be dangerous. She had been willing to do whatever they asked of her in order to gain their trust and prove herself. And she had.

Part of her felt pity for the unknown person the signal belonged to. Perhaps they felt the same way she had. Unable to return to or remain in the Capitol, they had chosen to seek out the Resistance.

But on the other hand, the orange spot signified that they still had their tracker and they couldn't be allowed to reach the Resistance as long as the Empire could still track them.

"We have to find them before they get too close. The Empire will be looking for them."

This is one they have a chance to take alive.

"That might be a bit of a problem," Anyah said. "I can't pinpoint their exact location until they get closer. And if they go deeper into the forest, I could lose the signal altogether. It's pretty spotty as it is."

As she spoke, the orange dot flickered and vanished. It reappeared a few seconds later, but there was no telling how long it would remain.

XII

Sheboleth didn't apologize for what she'd said about Leo or his family and he didn't expect her to. He woke early, dawn creeping over the forest, surprised that he'd managed to sleep at all, but his body must have been simply too exhausted to resist any longer.

He sat up and looked over at the dragon. The sun filtered through the leaves, landing on her black scales. She was motionless, her front legs crossed, head resting upon them. Her eyes were closed, but that didn't mean she was sleeping.

Leo got to his feet, stretching out the kinks in his muscles. There were a few more insect bites to add to his collection, but not as bad as before. The paste on his arms had hardened and dried, flaking off as he moved. He sighed, wondering how much further they had to go and how long he would be forced to sleep in the woods.

The swelling in his ankle was no worse than before, but it was still painful as he tugged his boots back on. He limped away from their makeshift camp, needing to relieve himself. The air was already muggy at such an early hour, promising another day of misery. He was just about to head back when a branch snapped behind him.

Leo jumped, startled, and spun around. Sheboleth was behind him. "Don't do that!" he exclaimed. She was far too quiet for a creature of that size.

"*Quiet*," Sheboleth hissed, raising her head and looking around, nostrils flaring.

Leo froze, listening, but could hear nothing over the wind and the sound of bird calls.

"Get down," the dragon whispered.

"What?"

"I said *get down*." She reached over with one massive hand and pushed him down onto the grass.

And then Leo heard it. The unmistakable sound of clanking metal. One of the mechs was coming. Every muscle tensed as he scanned the forest for any sign of it, but he couldn't see through the dense foliage. He wanted to run, but Sheboleth had insisted he stay down, and he knew better than to question her.

The undergrowth parted as the metallic creature burst into view. Leo forced himself to stay completely still, hoping it wouldn't see him, but all it noticed was Sheboleth, standing over him.

With a snarl, she sprang at it, but her body weight wasn't enough to knock the mech over and it absorbed the blow. Her claws scraped over the metal, searching for any gaps in its armor. Leo watched in horrified fascination as the two struggled, one made of flesh and bone, the other of metal and wires. He flinched as the automaton raked its claws over Sheboleth's forearm.

It lunged for her neck, but she ducked and with a final, massive effort, wrenched the mech's iron breastplate away, exposing the wiring beneath. A quick swipe severed the connection. The mech's eyes flickered once and then went out completely, the lifeless body thudding to the ground.

Leo got to his feet, glancing at the discarded iron plate, a red soul stone embedded in the center. The metal around it was scratched and rent, but the stone was pristine, untouched by Sheboleth's claws.

"Are you all right?" he asked, noticing she was panting.

"Fine."

He saw blood where the mech had scratched her, tearing the scales away. She glanced down, following his gaze. "They'll grow back."

Both of them tensed at the sound of more heavy treads trampling through the forest, growing closer. There were at least two of them, approaching from different directions, maybe more.

Sheboleth let out a hiss. "Move!"

She took off, darting through the forest, her long legs eating up the ground. Leo followed, gasping as pain shot through his ankle, but he knew at once that he could not catch her. Even if he'd been uninjured, he doubted he could have kept up.

He gritted his teeth and pushed harder, but Sheboleth drew ever ahead, while the mechs behind grew louder. She stopped, glancing back at him.

Leo slowed to a halt. "I can't."

She came back to where he was. "Climb on."

"What? Can't you fight them?"

"I appreciate the vote of confidence," she said dryly. "But not even I can fight two mechs at once. Get on." She laid down, allowing him to clamber onto her back. Sensing his hesitation, she added, "It's the only way to lose them."

He knew she was right. As magnificent as the automatons were, there was one thing that set them apart from real dragons—flight.

It's either this or wait here to be mauled to death.

"Fine."

Leo awkwardly heaved himself up onto her back, between her shoulder blades, grabbing ahold of the frills that ran from her forehead down to her tail. He could hear the mechs crashing through the trees behind, nearly upon them, heedless of anything in their way.

"If it makes you feel any better," Sheboleth growled, "I'm as thrilled about this as you. I suggest you hold on."

The first mech broke through the trees. Sheboleth gathered her legs under her and leapt, launching herself into the air. In the same moment, her massive wings snapped down, generating enough force to lift them a bit higher. Her wings beat furiously, until they were high enough that she could unfurl them all the way.

The mech sprang at them, but they were already out of reach. As they neared the forest canopy, Leo hunched down, trying to stay as close to Sheboleth as possible, gripping her sides with his thighs. He could feel her powerful muscles working to get them clear of the trees and he screwed his eyes shut, pressing his cheek against her scales, smooth and hot against his skin.

All at once, the shade fell away and unfiltered sunlight landed on his face. He could feel the wind threading through his hair. The movement of her wings stopped and they hung steady in the air.

"You can look now," she called.

Cautiously, Leo opened one eye, then the other, and sat up in disbelief. They had risen above the forest and below, the trees rolled out for miles. Sheboleth's wings were stationary, gliding along the current. He could see where the forest was split by a massive river. Glancing over his shoulder, he could see the silhouette of the Capitol, ever fading into the distance.

"You know you're probably the first human to do this in a thousand years," Sheboleth shouted over her shoulder. "How does it feel?"

I could fall and plunge to my death.

"Terrifying. Amazing."

The dragon turned to face forward again, but not before he caught a glimpse of a wicked grin on her face.

"If you think that's amazing…"

She folded her wings suddenly, plunging toward the ground. Leo let out a scream of pure terror, his heart surging into his throat, but the wind tore his voice away as he clung to her neck desperately.

Her wings snapped out suddenly, breaking the fall, and beat several times, slowing the descent until her feet touched the ground, back legs first, then front. The landing was so gentle, it was almost as if she had floated down.

Shakily, Leo slid off her back, wincing as his ankle hit the ground. His arms ached, trembling, from holding onto her so tightly, and his legs were suddenly wobbly.

They had landed in a small clearing.

He turned on her. "Saints, you're insane! Are you trying to kill me?"

"Not very successfully, if I am. Don't tell me you didn't enjoy it."

Leo held his hands out in front of him, watching them tremble. His heartbeat was still racing, the adrenaline not yet fading, but he was still alive. He hadn't died.

And strangely, there was some part of him that wanted to laugh. He had ridden a dragon! Not that he would ever admit it to her.

He lowered his hands. "You're crazy." He sighed. "Why not just fly all the way there? You'd be rid of my company quicker."

"So eager for the journey to be over?" She snorted. "Do you want food or not?"

His stomach growled. "Yes, please."

They hadn't had a chance to eat breakfast.

"Come on, then."

Sheboleth set off for where she knew the river narrowed nearby into a slower stream, perfect for catching fish. She glanced at her traveling companion, brooding over the question he had asked her.

What he said was true—she could fly him to the ruins in only a matter of hours instead of days. But the idea of returning, of laying eyes on the ruins, of seeing what they had become, filled her with dread.

And if she were honest, she was intrigued by this human and what he had done to deserve having multiple mechs sent to hunt him down.

He was lagging behind slightly and so she moderated her pace. He limped heavily now, having further injured his ankle when he dismounted. She could tell it was hurting him a great deal, from the lines of pain on his face to the grimaces when he thought she wasn't looking.

But he never complained. She silently marveled at his ability to tolerate pain—or perhaps it was merely sheer bloody-mindedness.

His thick, curling hair had been disheveled by the wind and his clothes were dirty and clinging to him, his skin gleaming with a sheen of sweat. She felt a flash of guilt at the remarks she had said to him last night. His family could very well be dead, and while one could argue whether or not it was hist fault, he hadn't deserved her derision.

To distract him, she asked suddenly, "Your family. What are they like? Are they like you?"

"And what am I like?" he panted as he struggled to keep up.

When Sheboleth didn't have an answer, he went on, "They don't look like me, if that's what you're asking. My mother has light blonde hair, nearly white, and green eyes. She's kind, but…there's a sadness to her. My sister, Ana, looks just like her, but she has our father's curly hair, like me. She likes to hear stories, her favorite food is fresh blackberries, if we can get them, and she's scared of storms."

"They sound nice," said Sheboleth, in a rare attempt at being as genial as possible.

"They are. I miss them. They're all I have left…if they're still alive."

"You have me." Sheboleth didn't know where the words came from. He looked at her in surprise and she amended, "For now."

Where was this soft-heartedness coming from? She knew better than to get attached.

"For now," he repeated. "What about you? Do you have a family?"

Don't answer. Tell him to mind his own business. She'd already said more than she wanted to, but she replied, "No. Not anymore."

He was smart enough not to ask any further questions, for which she was grateful. The constant reminder of their destination was painful enough.

"Here we are," she announced, as the trees parted to reveal the river, shallow, and surrounded by large stones. "You can sit on one of those rocks while you wait."

Looking relieved, Leo sank down onto one of the stones, propping up his bad ankle. Sheboleth waded out into the water. It wasn't as clear as it could have been, but she could easily make out the bodies of fish flitting beneath the surface, sunlight winking off their scales.

Slowly lowering her head toward the water, she waited. Fish were neither the most patient or the most intelligent of creatures and it wasn't long before one made the mistake of swimming beneath her muzzle. In a flash of black scales and teeth, she had snapped her jaws down and stood up, a large flopping fish clamped in her mouth.

Leo applauded. "Well done."

She dashed its head against one of the rocks and its squirming ceased. One fish that large ought to be enough for him, but she hesitated. He was so thin, perhaps she should catch more. She waded back out into the water and caught three more fish for herself, dragging them up past the rocks.

She pushed one over to him. "There you go."

His earlier enthusiasm vanished.

"What?"

"Um, humans typically cook fish before they eat it."

Sheboleth had already dug into hers, ripping off a chunk of meat and swallowing it whole. Her teeth were best suited to puncturing and tearing, not chewing. Leo looked slightly green as he watched her.

"*Cook* it?"

She knew that already, but thought it best to act as though she didn't. Perceptive as he was, he'd already noted that her knowledge of his kind was more than it should have been.

He smirked. "So you don't know everything about humans. We'll need a fire. You…can breathe fire, right?"

In answer, she huffed a small burst of flame at his feet, causing him to dance back.

"Well, that answers that."

As he set about gathering firewood, Sheboleth finished her first fish, keeping an eye on Leo all the while. Once he had arranged the sticks, she obligingly lit them. With the knife he'd taken from the Imperial soldier, he set about removing the scales and bones from the fish—a task that looked painstaking and needlessly difficult to Sheboleth.

At last, after sharpening a stick, he speared the pieces of meat with it and set about roasting them over the fire. Only once it had cooked did he go about eating it.

Sheboleth had already finished. "You humans," she said, shaking her head. "Is it to your liking?"

"It's good. Fresh fish was always expensive in the Capitol so we didn't get to enjoy it very often."

"Sounds like you didn't get to enjoy much of anything."

"We didn't. That's why I went to the Resistance meeting."

Sheboleth glanced in the direction of the ruins, unseen, but out there. "Well, I hope this Resistance is everything you want it to be."

"So do I."

Thick clouds had gathered in the sky as they enjoyed their meal, threatening rain. They managed to make it to the shelter of the trees before the skies opened up completely, drenching them. The forest canopy did little to shield them.

Sheboleth didn't mind; she had no fur or hair to be matted down by the water. But Leo looked utterly miserable, his hair plastered to his head, clothes once more clinging to him.

There was no telling how long it would last. The rain came down in sheets, making visibility poor. Sheboleth laid down, stretching out one wing above and around Leo, shielding him from the rain.

Thunder rumbled overhead.

"You said your sister was scared of storms?"

"Yes," he answered. "If it's storming in the Capitol, she's probably hiding right now." He smiled, but it vanished all too quickly.

With the sky overcast, it was hard to tell what time of day it was. Hours rolled past, but the rain showed no sign of letting up.

At last, Sheboleth sighed and stood. "All right. Let's go."

"But it's still raining."

"And it might keep raining for a week or more. This is a rainforest, after all. You want to wait that long?"

"No," said Leo reluctantly, rising to his feet.

Sheboleth shouted a warning, but it was too late. The rain and thunder had drowned out the sound of its approach.

The second mech had found them. It crashed into her, clawing at her wings. She hissed and knocked it back with a swing from her tail.

She had fought countless mechs that had wandered into the forest, intent on killing dragons. First, they had targeted her, and then she had actively sought them out. It was what had led her to the one that had been part of the patrol that had captured Leo.

She knew from experience how to fight them, but she needed to be careful. They were much heavier than her, made of iron and steel, while her bones were hollow like a bird's. It was what allowed her to take flight, while the mechs were confined to the ground.

The rain lashed her eyes, making it hard to see and she blinked furiously. The mech's armor was rain-slicked and hard to grab onto, the metal gleaming with moisture.

Her first few attempts failed, the footing treacherous as the forest floor turned to mud, but she eventually managed to clamp her jaws down on its neck, biting down with all her strength, feeling the metal crumple beneath her teeth. Their metal armor had been getting thinner lately, a weakness she was happy to exploit.

She only let go when the automaton no longer moved, its weight slumping to the side.

"How do these things keep finding you?" she demanded.

"I don't know," Leo replied.

She believed him, but she didn't want to push her luck. If the Empire wanted him badly enough to send this many mechs, they'd keep sending more and more until they achieved their goal. Sheboleth knew it would only be a matter of time before they were simply overwhelmed or she made a mistake during a fight.

"Let's move. There's at least one of these things still out here and I don't fancy fighting it in the dark or the rain."

Maybe if she led him deeper into the forest, they wouldn't be able to follow—or lose whatever scent they were tracking.

Sheboleth didn't know how it worked, but she knew it was no coincidence that the mechs knew exactly where to find them.

The rain finally stopped as they stepped out of the forest, at the edge of the Badlands. It was no less hot here, only now there was no forest canopy to shield them from the sun's oppressive heat. Leo stared out at the vast expanse of dry, rolling land.

"What is this place?"

"The Badlands," Sheboleth replied.

They set out across the dusty, scorched earth, the dry air burning Sheboleth's nostrils, dust stinging her eyes. Leo fared little better, but once again refrained from complaint, surprising the dragon with his resilience.

The further they went, they began to see evidence of the battle that had raged there, long ago. Scattered pieces of armor—both human and mech—bones, discarded weapons, and the rusted husks of automatons.

"What happened here?" Leo murmured.

"A great battle," Sheboleth answered. "Well, more than one, really. Anarsha and Akkadia clashed on this plain."

"More than one?" he repeated.

"Over the course of years."

"I thought the Empire defeated Anarsha during a single campaign."

"Don't believe everything they tell you."

He glanced at the lifeless mechs as they passed. They were barely recognizable for what they had once been, scoured over the past thousand years and long since stripped of anything valuable. There were no soul stones in the old models.

Nor had they been autonomous, each requiring a human pilot. Still, even those crude, primitive designs had been better than anything Anarsha may have had, in terms of weaponry. Alliances were a different matter.

Sheboleth glanced down at the ground beneath her feet, still blackened in some places, forever marred by what had happened here. The Badlands were a testament to the losses the Empire had suffered, but they had still won in the end.

Suddenly, she became aware that Leo was no longer with her. She paused, peering over her shoulder. He had stopped, bent over, one hand reaching down to touch his wounded ankle.

"What's the matter?" Sheboleth called, though she thought she already knew.

"I can't," he gasped. "I can't walk any further."

He had put up with it for too long and could bear it no longer.

She turned back. "I expected you'd say something ages ago."

"I tried to go as far as I could."

She knelt down with a sigh, once more making a concession she never thought she'd make. "Get on, then."

Leo didn't protest as he clambered up and she didn't imagine the look of relief as he was able to take the weight off his ankle. "Thank you."

"Yeah, well," Sheboleth said gruffly. "Don't get used to it."

She wondered if the heat and dusty air was rotting her brain. What was she thinking? There had been a time, not so long ago, when she'd firmly believed that the only good human was a dead one.

He'll be no different, she reminded herself. He, too, would find a way to disappoint her. Time was all that mattered.

But the doubt had begun to seep in and it would be hard to shake it free.

The signal for the surviving rebel had vanished once more, reappeared briefly deeper in the forest, and disappeared again. It did not return.

Skye had gone out briefly, searching for whoever it was, but found no sign of them. She hadn't thought it likely, not willing to venture far from the ruins and the trees surrounding them.

But she had wanted to find them before the signal was lost entirely or they came too close to the base. In the end, it had been pointless. She had begged Anyah to try and restore the signal, to do anything in her power to strengthen it, but nothing had worked.

There was only so much she could take, being cooped up inside those caverns, before she began to feel mad. She needed the fresh air, the sun on her skin, and the wind in her hair. There was no sun to be found that morning, the sky overcast, threatening more rain. Skye loved the rain, but loathed being out in it. Even worse, a mist had descended, making it difficult to see.

One day was much like the next. Skye occupied her time with weapons training, hunting patrols, helping out where she was needed, forging or repairing weapons, waiting for her next assignment. Waiting for the day when she could return to the Capitol or one of the neighboring cities.

She knelt down, checking the snares she had set early that morning, but they were empty. Prey had been scarce so far that day. She slung her crossbow off her back and set out further into the trees. If she were lucky, she might catch a glimpse of a deer. A prize that big would provide a lot of food and then the pelt could be used for a rug or a blanket.

The mist made it hard to see, but it also dampened her footsteps. She jerked to a halt. As if conjured by her thoughts, a deer melted out of the fog. Its head was down, grazing, its tawny coat standing out starkly against the surrounding green.

Slowly, Skye raised her Ironsight. She wasn't as good with it as she was with her knives, but she could hardly hope to bring down a deer with a blade. Hunting helped improve her aim, knowing she may one day need to bring down a human target. The training dummies were all well and good, but there was something about a living target that made it seem all the more real, lending a sense of urgency.

This mattered.

The deer's head shot up and it bounded off into the mist just as Skye pulled the trigger. She cursed, watching the bolt sail into the fog. She'd have to retrieve it. They weren't easy to come by.

Returning the crossbow to her back, Skye set off after the bolt. The deer must have scented her; she'd made sure not to make a sound.

Seeing the metal amid the grass, she knelt down, freezing as her fingers brushed against the bolt. Something was rustling through the trees.

For a moment, she thought it might be the deer. But it sounded too big. Warning bells shrieked in her mind and Skye jerked back from the bolt, reaching for her daggers just as the mech appeared in front of her, coalescing out of the mist.

She let out a cry, staggering back as it swiped at her. The metal raked down the front of her thigh, slicing through the leather and into the skin beneath.

Skye fell back onto the ground, staring up at the metallic beast. What was it doing here? They rarely ventured so far. Why did one have to be here now, at the same time as her?

She clenched her daggers. They would do no good against the creature's metallic hide, but if she were going to die, she wanted to die with her faithful daggers in her hands.

A growl rumbling in its chest, it lowered its head closer, jaws parting. Waves of heat rolled over her skin and Skye blinked furiously, fighting back enraged tears.

No! A voice inside her screamed, furious at her own impotence. *It can't end like this! It can't!* She had so much more to do.

When she had escaped that damned mine, and was wandering half-dead through the forest, she had vowed to herself that she would not die until she saw the Empire fall.

No mech could take that away from her.

She rolled to the side, avoiding its jaws as they clamped down. It whirled on her and she wondered how long she could realistically delay the inevitable. The mech's head suddenly snapped to the side and Skye looked up to see what had caught its attention.

A black dragon was charging toward them, long legs covering the distance swiftly.

Oh, saints. Dying was one thing, but at least mechs didn't eat people.

The real dragon let out a roar and launched itself, crashing into its steel counterpart. Skye watched as the two of them writhed, fighting to gain the upper hand. For a second, she feared the mech would prove victorious. And then it was over as quickly as it had begun, the automaton falling to the ground with a heavy thud and creaking of metal.

The real dragon turned to her but made no attempt to come closer. And then a disheveled-looking young man limped out of the fog and Skye's eyes widened. She barely recognized him, dirty and unkempt as he was, with wild hair and stubble on his face. But the eyes were the same dark chocolate brown that had peered into hers that night in the Capitol.

The night everything had gone wrong.

"*You*," she snarled as he reached her, slashing out with one of her daggers.

He was the rebel who had escaped. Escaped because the Empire had never intended to kill him at all. And now he was here, nearly on the Resistance's doorstep. He had led the mech here. He would lead the entire Empire straight to them.

With a growl, the dragon stepped between them. Skye's dagger glanced harmlessly off the scales on her forearm.

"You bastard," Skye spat. "You dare show your face here after you betrayed us."

"What?" he exclaimed. "I didn't—"

If the dragon moved enough to give her a clear shot, she would take it and hurl a dagger right into his black heart. "You sold us out. That's why we were raided."

"No, I didn't. I swear—"

"You expect me to believe you? Imperial informants are good at their jobs."

They gained your trust, pretended to be someone just like you, who understood the struggle. They weren't even above inflicting injuries upon themselves to make it look as if the Empire had attacked them, too, and so they couldn't possibly be one of them.

"I'm not—"

"Look," the dragon snapped. "We can argue about this later. Unless you'd rather do it now, as you're bleeding out all over the grass."

Skye stared at the dragon in shock for a moment and then looked down at her leg, wincing. The sight of blood didn't bother her—unless it was her own.

Reluctantly sheathing her daggers, she reached into her pack and pulled out strips of bandage. But even as she went about binding the wound, she knew it would only help slow the bleeding at best. It needed to be stitched or cauterized, neither of which she could do herself, or she would bleed to death.

"We can help you," the young man said. "Skye, isn't it?"

She looked at him sharply, hating that he knew her name, but he went on before she could speak, "I had to flee the Capitol and I've been trying to find the Resistance. Just tell us where to go and we can take you there."

Skye snorted, both furious and amused, a combination she hadn't thought possible. "As if I'd ever take you to the Resistance after what you've done."

"I'm not an informant!" he shouted, angry now too. "Do you think an Imperial informant would travel with a dragon?"

The dragon flicked her tail. "He has a point. I met him when an Imperial patrol captured him in the forest. I don't think physically beating and trussing him up like a pig is how they treat one of their own."

Skye had to admit that the dragon's presence gave her pause. She had never known a dragon to associate with *any* human, much less one working as an Empire spy, but that didn't mean she could do as they wished.

There was no chance she could make it back to the ruins on her own, but to accept their help meant betraying the Resistance and she would never do that.

But the alternative was even less appealing. She would not lay there and accept the death she had narrowly escaped. She clenched her teeth. *You cannot take me.*

There were rendezvous sites she could take them to, where members out on patrol went if they were separated. Someone would come for her and then they could deal with him. The Triad would decide his fate.

Better they capture an Imperial spy than let him go free. They could always see how much he knew.

"Fine," she huffed. "There's a rendezvous point nearby. You can help me there and someone will meet us. *But*," she added, "I'm not taking you a step further until we get that tracker out."

This would be a test. If he was an informant, he would either protest hotly or submit without complaint. If he was a spy, he'd likely have other trackers embedded beneath his skin anyway, for just such a scenario.

"What?"

"Your tracker. The Empire uses it to know your location and track your movements."

"That would explain how they were able to find us so easily!" the dragon exclaimed.

"No, it doesn't," he insisted. "I've never heard of any tracker."

"They're inserted at birth," Skye explained. "So you wouldn't know about it unless someone told you—which I am right now." She held out one hand. "Give me your arm."

"How do you remove it?"

"It has to be cut out."

"What? No!" he cried, clutching his arm protectively as he eyed the knives at her belt.

Skye's eyes narrowed. He'd grabbed the wrong arm—the one with the tattoo. Trackers were always implanted in the opposite arm. Had he done that on purpose or was he truly ignorant?

She let out an impatient sigh. "Then I don't take you anywhere. It's the only way. The tracker's just under the skin. It's not like it's in the muscle or anything."

"Surely we're out of range by now," he argued, grasping at straws.

"I'm not risking it," Skye insisted, in a tone that brooked no argument. "I'm not taking you anywhere near the Resistance with a tracker in your arm. Now what will it be?"

He hesitated, but she could see that she'd already won. His desire to gain her trust, or at least her approval, won out over his fear.

He sighed, kneeling down next to her. "Do it."

Skye unsheathed one of the daggers at her hip, one of the twin black-bladed ones that curved slightly. She reached out for his left arm, his sleeve already rolled up to the elbow.

"I can't promise that it will be painless, but it *will* be quick."

She kept her daggers sharper than a razor's edge, particularly her black blades. They would make quick work of slicing through his flesh.

Her fingers brushed against his skin, warm beneath her touch. She was aware of the blood rushing beneath the surface, how close her blade was, hovering above.

It would be so easy to kill him, quick as a viper, burying that blade in his unguarded heart. There would be a moment of pain, perhaps a flicker of surprise at what she had done, and then…oblivion.

Her eyes flicked to the dragon who stood just beyond, watching with her piercing green eyes. The dragon, Skye could do nothing about, and she doubted the creature would stand idly by. She would not make Skye's own end so quick.

Her story did not, would not, end here, this way.

"Don't worry," she murmured. "I've done this before."

She had been lucky enough to know about the trackers and had cut out her own, when she'd fled the mines at twelve. She'd had only the knife she had stolen and still had the scar to prove it. She'd been terrified, but she knew that as long as she had the tracker, the Empire could take her back. She'd rather die.

He flinched as the dagger touched his skin.

"What's your name?" she asked suddenly.

It didn't matter, but she thought if she were about to perform minor surgery on someone, she should probably know their name first.

"Leo." The reply was breathless. Then he added, "D'Lynn. And this is Sheboleth."

She hoped he wouldn't faint on her.

"I'm Skye," she replied. "Hunter." Though he'd already known her first name. She didn't mind giving it to him now, since he would shortly be in Resistance custody.

Her knife made quick work of the task, peeling through the outer layer of his skin and revealing the small tracker, the size of the tip of her pinky finger. In one quick movement, it was out, leaving behind a small wound.

She didn't have to go rooting around for it the way she had eleven years ago.

"There you go," she said, wrapping some of the bandages she had around the wound. "You may have a scar, but it'll be small."

"Small price to pay for being free of the Empire," he said and strangely, she thought he meant it.

"All right," Skye said, wiping her blade clean on the grass. "I'll take you to the rendezvous site."

Leo had a bad ankle—or pretended to—and so he couldn't help bear her weight. She was forced to climb up onto the dragon's back, already regretting her decision. She gave them directions, Leo limping along beside the dragon.

The site was at the base of one of the smaller towers among the ruins. As they walked, the trees began to thin and the mist parted, revealing Anarsha's great wall.

Leo let out a gasp, eyes going wide. His mouth even fell open slightly, as the stone ruins towered above them, impossibly high.

"It's magnificent," he whispered.

The dragon—Sheboleth—stared up at the wall. "Should have seen it before the fall."

Leo didn't react, but Skye thought there was something mournful in the dragon's tone.

He helped Skye down from the dragon's back and she sat with her back to the stone tower. "Someone will come along shortly. We just have to wait."

She hoped her leg would last that long. She shifted it into a more comfortable position, grimacing slightly. Blood had already begun to seep through the bandages.

As they waited, she glanced over at her companions. She had never seen a dragon up close before and she was a bit overawed. Sheboleth's claws looked as though they could slice her to ribbons with one quick strike. It was probably best, if at all possible, to remain on her good side.

Skye turned her attention to Leo. He had a narrow face, with a sharp jaw and cheekbones, thick eyebrows and a mass of curly brown hair. There was something resigned about his expression, now that the wonder of the ruins had worn off. He wore a white button-up shirt, black trousers tucked into worn leather boots, and black suspenders. She glanced at the tattoo on his right arm, the numeral III.

"District III, huh?" she asked, nodding to the tattoo. "What did you do there?"

He glanced distractedly down at the tattoo. "I was a mechanic, of sorts."

She studied his hands, dangling in the air, his arms propped on his knees. He had the long, nimble fingers suited to assembling parts, the veins on his hands and arms slightly raised.

Come on, Tiachren. Where are you?

The fog began to disperse, leaving them more exposed. Skye hated waiting out in the ruins. Encountering danger here wasn't certain, but it had happened before and she was useless in her current state.

At least they had a dragon with them. She doubted anything would happen as long as Sheboleth was there.

Finally, Tiachren appeared, calling for her.

"I'm here!" she answered.

He stopped, taking in the sight before him, the dragon most of all. "Saints! What happened?"

"A mech." She gestured to her leg. "We have a…situation. Get Anyah and tell her to bring one of the wands. Fetch Jonathan, too. He'll know what to do."

Tiachren pursed his lips. Skye could tell that he recognized Leo from the meeting and knew as well as she did what his presence meant. He nodded and hurried off, returning with Jonathan and Anyah, who held a long, rectangular scanner in one hand.

"What is that?" Leo asked as she approached him.

"A scanner," Anyah replied. "Just to make sure there aren't any more trackers we don't know about."

Ordinary citizens were issued only the one tracker, but if Skye's suspicions were right and Leo was an informant, the Empire would have fitted him with more than one. She watched as Anyah waved the scanner over every inch of his body, waiting to hear the telltale alert that it had sensed something, but it remained silent.

She raised an eyebrow at that. What game was the Empire playing?

"All right," Anyah stepped back. "You're clean."

Tiachren helped Skye to her feet, her arm wrapped around his neck, careful to keep her weight off her injured leg.

Jonathan stepped forward, searching Leo for weapons, which Skye would have already done if she hadn't been incapacitated. He had only a small knife on him, which Jonathan took. Sheboleth watched impassively all the while, her sharp green eyes missing nothing.

Jonathan lifted a chain out of Leo's shirt, a blue gem dangling at the end of it. "What's this?"

"Family heirloom," Leo replied. "Nothing important."

Skye thought it likely of great importance to him, but didn't say so. It was unusual, almost like a soul stone, but the color was wrong. The silver wire that wrapped around it and secured it to the chain was tapered at the bottom to a point. She supposed it could be used as a weapon if nothing else was to hand.

Jonathan didn't seem to find issue with it. He grunted and let the chain fall. Leo stuffed the gem back into his shirt.

Jonathan reached a hand into his pocket and withdrew a pair of manacles. "I'm afraid, for the sake of caution, you'll have to wear these until the Triad have made their determination."

Sheboleth let out a growl.

"It's all right," Leo told her, holding out his wrists as Jonathan snapped the shackles into place. "If this is what it takes to prove myself, then…" He shrugged, as if acknowledging that he was in no position to argue.

"Then I'm coming with you," she replied.

"You don't have to do that."

"I know I don't. But I'm doing it anyway."

"I'm afraid I can't allow—" Jonathan began. One Imperial spy they could deal with, but a dragon was unpredictable and could easily kill half of the Resistance before they managed to bring her down—if they managed it.

Sheboleth thrust her muzzle into his face, teeth bared. "The hell you can't."

Jonathan scowled, clearly displeased by this development, but there was nothing he could do about it. In this instance, his hands were just as bound as Leo's.

"Fine," he said curtly. "Let's go."

Limping, Skye allowed Tiachren to help her as they moved deeper into the ruins. With Sheboleth in tow, they would have to use an alternate entrance. The dragon was far too large to enter through the crypt.

But she didn't care, her main focus on getting her leg looked at. Leo D'Lynn, and what became of him, was no longer her concern.

XIV

It defied explanation. Three mechs sent, four total destroyed, and several good soldiers with them. Lydia stared at the screen uncomprehending. Three mechs should have been more than enough to bring one escaped rebel to justice. Instead, she found herself looking at the red dots that marked their last known locations, where they had beamed out one final signal before losing all contact.

The Minister of Defense had once again sent her to report to the emperor. She braced herself for the unpleasant conversation to come. No matter what, this must not reflect badly on her.

She could blame the Minister for his restraint in sending out only one patrol the last time, but she had overseen the three mechs herself. She had thought they would be enough—they should have been enough! Whatever they were up against must either be a powerful enemy or they had been extremely unlucky. There was no chance the rebel could have destroyed them all on his own.

Lydia mounted the steps to the palace and made her way to the emperor's personal quarters, trying to practice what she would say to him. There really was no point; she wouldn't know what to say until he spoke and she would have to modify her responses based on that—but it didn't stop her from doing it.

"Tell me you have good news," the emperor said once she had arrived and knelt before him.

"I'm afraid not, my lord. The three mechs that were sent out have lost signal and we've been unable to reestablish a connection."

Desmond went very still. "That's four that have been lost so far. Why is this happening?"

"I don't know, my lord, but if I had to guess, I'd say the dragons are to blame."

"The dragons," the emperor said flatly.

"Yes."

"And what does the Minister have to say about it?"

"He sends his deepest apologies and said that patrols will be doubled."

Lydia knew she was playing a dangerous game, speaking for the Minister, relaying words he hadn't said. In truth, they were her words, but she feared what the emperor might do if he knew that. She might not walk out of here again.

He studied her through the solid eyes of his mask. "And you think more should be done?" He had caught the edge of disapproval and doubt in her voice, as she had intended him to.

Lydia almost nodded before catching herself. The emperor never liked a wordless answer. "Yes, my lord."

"What would you have done differently?"

She took a deep breath. This was it. "I think our automata are far too weak, my lord. The metal for their armor has been reused too many times and it is not as strong as it should be. I believe that is one of the reasons we are losing so many. They were built to hunt down and kill dragons and yet the dragons are destroying them. How long can this continue before the people lose their fear of the mechs that patrol the streets after nightfall? How long until the people begin targeting the mechs? Once they learn how weak they are, there will be no stopping them."

"Yes…there's been a shortage in Elath. I'm sending an Inquisitor to get to the bottom of it, but perhaps I should send the Minister of Commerce as well. Perhaps you're right. We don't need to send more mechs, we need to send better ones. If they are as weak as you say, then it won't matter how many we send regardless."

Lydia breathed out a sigh of relief. She had appealed to his fear of the people rising up against him and it appeared to have worked. It was one of the reasons the mechs had been created, not only to serve on the fields of battle, but to control the masses at home. They were extremely effective in instilling fear and ensuring the people obeyed. Their strength, enough to challenge a dragon, was what made them so intimidating and powerful. If they could kill dragons, there was nothing the people could do against them—and they knew it.

The situation in Elath wasn't for her to solve, thankfully. The Inquisitor could go and put the fear of the saints into the regional leadership there, but if there was no more ore to be mined from the earth, Lydia didn't see what they could do about it.

Such was the problem with the Empire. It had forged its identity through conquering, only now there was nothing in the known world left to conquer.

The Empire's insatiable appetite for raw materials would eventually run out of food to feed it.

"Have you told the Minister this?" Desmond asked.

"Yes. He insists it would take too long—time we don't have—to wait for another batch of automata to be made."

The emperor had been looking out the window. Now he turned back to her. "You think you would make a better Minister than he, don't you?"

With an effort, Lydia schooled her expression, refusing to show the surprise she felt. But she felt a slight heat rise to her cheeks all the same.

"I sense an ambition in you, Lydia."

She didn't bother denying it. "If I happen to be the better person for the job, it is because of fact, not because I simply wish it to be so."

Does that sound suitably humble?

The emperor chuckled. "We shall see. Go. Tell the Minister to increase the number of patrols, for now. These dragons are getting to be more dangerous than the rebels. The Inquisitor will straighten things out in Elath and then more automata can be made."

Lydia bowed. "Thank you, my lord."

If she played this right, losing four mechs in the pursuit of one rebel might just turn out to be the opportunity of a lifetime.

Desmond waited until Lydia's footsteps had faded and the door swung slowly closed before speaking. The minstrel wasn't there to overhear him; he'd made certain of that this time.

"Why does this keep happening? Is what she said true about the mechs being weaker than they should be?"

"Yes, but I'm not telling you anything you don't already know. It's not possible for one rebel to destroy so many mechs on his own."

"What is it, then? What have you seen?"

"He has allied himself with one of the dragons. For reasons unknown, she is helping him."

"So it's the same dragon…" Desmond muttered to himself, then, speaking louder, "A dragon allying with a rebel? Why would it do such a thing?"

"I have my suspicions, but they are of no use to us now."

"They must both be stopped!" Desmond felt panic rise within him, constricting his chest, breaths coming quick and shallow.

Both of his strongest enemies, allied against him. Despite the power he wielded and the passage of time, he was not so foolish as to think himself untouchable. He knew better than most how vulnerable any empire could be.

"Calm yourself," the voice rumbled. *"He has reached the Resistance. They are both beyond your grasp now."*

"Where *is* the Resistance?" Desmond demanded. "Can't you see where they've gone?"

"No. You know my sight is limited."

Desmond let out a growl. The voice had explained to him, more than once, on previous occasions that he could see only those whom he viewed through a soul stone, but could see nothing of their surroundings, and was privy only to the information they gave him, however unwittingly.

"A lot of good you are."

"And whose fault is that?" the voice growled, a true hint of menace creeping into his tone.

"Apologies," Desmond said quickly, his fear shifting from the dragons and the rebels to the presence in the room with him.

He didn't know why he should be afraid. He held all the cards here. The voice couldn't hurt him. But that didn't stop him from fearing it with a visceral, almost animalistic terror.

Perhaps that was because he knew the truth of it. Its origins, its power. He had seen what it could do. If he thought too long and hard about his counselor's identity, it was enough to make him want to flee. As if he could run for his life and succeed.

The voice had been with him for so long, it was easy to forget what he was truly dealing with. And one did that at one's own peril. *You'd do well to remember that.*

Desmond wasn't sure if the thought was his own or the voice whispering to him.

The emperor hadn't sent for him, much to Fabian's relief, so he risked sneaking down to the archives. He'd poked his head into the scriptorium, looking for Zak, but the scribe hadn't been there, and the archives were the next best place to look.

He needed to be quick; there was no telling when he would be sent for and he didn't want to risk Desmond's wrath.

The archives were all but empty, Fabian's footsteps echoing over-loud in the silence. Zak was seated at one of the long tables, pouring over an old document that Fabian couldn't read, brown and worn with age. The moths had gotten to it, nibbling at the corners. It looked like it might crumble at the merest touch.

The scribe looked up at his approach. "What brings you below ground?"

"I wanted to see you. I checked in the scriptorium, but you weren't there."

Zak shook his head. "I spend most of my days here, if I can."

His eyes squinted slightly. Fabian didn't know how he could stand being down here, in the musty chamber with its dim light. It was not a place he would have ever sought out willingly.

"Why?"

"Something I'm looking into for your sister. Well, for you, more accurately."

Fabian frowned. "This isn't about…my condition, is it?"

Zak tapped a single finger on the table. "I may have told her I'd look into it."

Fabian let out a sigh. "You don't need to do that. I'm sure you have more than enough work already. Besides, I'm fine."

"Are you?" Zak challenged, his sharp brown eyes meeting Fabian's green gaze.

Fabian looked at his friend, dressed in his simple robe, his hair shorn close to his scalp. He could hide it, pretend all was fine for his sister's sake. She had a far more difficult job than either of them, walking the delicate line between the Ministers and the emperor himself. She had more than enough to worry about.

But, he supposed, it wouldn't hurt to finally confide in someone. To admit the truth.

"No," he murmured.

The word felt like a stone had been lifted slightly off of him. It wasn't gone completely; it still hovered just above him, waiting to settle back down. But for now, in this moment, he could breathe.

He could deny the truth to the others, but there was no point lying to himself. There was no denying the weight that he kept losing, no matter how much he ate—when he felt like eating anything at all. The constant absence of any energy, his limbs feeling as though they were made out of lead. Some days, all he wanted was to sleep and possibly never wake up again, so resigned was he to the fact that this was his new reality. One that would never change. Never get better.

"But there's no point," he added, gesturing to the documents in front of Zak. "We've tried everything. There's nothing that can be done."

"I doubt you've consulted the source I'm looking into," Zak said.

Fabian's brow furrowed as he looked down at the writing scrawled across the fragile pages. "What is that?"

"Ancient Anarshan."

He smirked. "Are you going to ask the saints to heal me?"

"Contrary to popular belief, there was more to the Anarshans than just their saints," Zak retorted. "They were renowned healers. And while their kingdom may be lost, their knowledge isn't." He gestured to the stacks of papers.

Fabian held up his hands. "All right, all right. So have you found anything?"

Zak's mouth twisted into a frown. "Nothing that will help your cause. Not yet, anyway. But I did find something interesting, though. About the fall of Anarsha. Our records always describe the battle as swift and brutal, but according to the Anarshan accounts, that's not what happened at all."

"Well, of course they wouldn't say that, would they? Who would want to admit they were thrashed so badly?"

Zak grinned. "Well, the accounts can't both be right. And from what I'm reading, the Anarshans were the ones doing the thrashing."

"How can that be? We conquered them."

"Eventually, yes. I haven't yet gotten to that part. But the Empire suffered quite a few setbacks in the beginning."

"What chance would the Anarshans have had on foot, against our mechs?"

"They weren't all on foot," Zak said, leaning closer.

He even lowered his voice, though there was no one around to hear. Fabian could tell he was enjoying this immensely, as though he were divulging some great secret, and he humored him.

"They fought beside dragons."

"Funny you should mention dragons," Fabian muttered. "The emperor has been rather preoccupied with them lately."

Zak sobered at once, his contagious excitement dulling. "He didn't throw you out again, did he?"

The scribe was well aware of the emperor's moods and his treatment toward Fabian.

"No, but he's getting worse. He's paranoid about something. Something to do with the dragons. He talks to himself, Zak. More now than ever."

"What leaders don't speak to themselves? He's the most powerful person on earth and the most important, at least in his own eyes. Who better to talk to?"

Fabian cracked a smile at that. "I suppose so, but you haven't heard him. It's like he's talking to someone who isn't there. If he's having a conversation with himself, I'm only hearing half of it."

"Who can know? He is the emperor; he's not like us. And I'm sure he has a great burden to bear, running an entire Empire."

"You don't think such a burden could drive someone mad, do you?"

Zak looked at him levelly. "It's that serious?"

Fabian shrugged. Whether the emperor's violent mood swings and half-spoken conversations were a sign of madness or merely an outpouring of ego, he couldn't say.

"Never mind. Forget I said anything."

He'd already said too much and didn't want to risk getting Zak in trouble. Questioning the sanity of the emperor, doubting that he was fit to rule, ventured into treacherous waters and Fabian didn't want either of them to drown.

Zak pursed his lips. "Be careful around him all the same, all right?"

"I will," Fabian promised. He was never anything less than careful when it came to the emperor.

The scribe nodded decisively at his manuscripts. "And I'll keep looking."

PART III: ❖

THE

RESISTANCE

XV

The ruins of Anarsha were massive, sprawling monuments of stone and rubble. Leo gazed up at them in awe as he picked his way through them, following the others. With his bad ankle and the shackles on his wrist keeping his arms together, he took extra care not to lose his footing.

It felt surreal, staring up at what remained of the once-mighty kingdom of Anarsha. Finally, the place he had heard so much about was made real.

The massive, crumbling wall separated the rest of the ruins from the trees, the last line of defense for the city. Towers and spires rose above the rest of the buildings, the empty arches where windows had once been staring back at them like sightless eyes. The stone was worn and weathered, scoured by the elements over a millennium.

A thousand years was a long time. Too long for him to look at the ruins spread out before him and imagine what it must have once looked like. It must have been beautiful, a sight to behold. There was a beauty to it now, but it was faded and somehow sad.

Anarsha's fate had not been a happy one.

Their pace was slow, held up by Skye's injury, and Sheboleth's presence meant they had to find an alternative entrance. Leo glanced at Skye, struggling along silently.

After her reaction in the Capitol, he shouldn't have been surprised that she would be less than welcoming, but it still stung. She had accused him of ratting the Resistance out to the Empire and now he would have to somehow prove his innocence.

It wasn't exactly the reception he had imagined.

The man called Jonathan stepped forward suddenly, to where a sheet of ivy hung down over the stone ruins. He pulled the vines aside, revealing a yawning opening and wide stone steps disappearing down into the earth.

"In you go."

Swallowing his trepidation, Leo followed the others inside, feeling the weight of tons of stone close over his head, the temperature lowering the further they went. The air was dark, cold, and still, after so many years.

Water dripped from somewhere. It would have been completely dark and impossible to see if not for the torches that had been lit along the walls at regular intervals, no doubt maintained by the guards that were also spaced there.

Sheboleth's claws clacked on the stone as she moved. Her eyes glowed in the darkness, giving off green light.

The ground gradually leveled out and they were no longer descending. They reached a great iron portcullis, embedded into the stone walls, with guards posted. The sentinels hesitated when they saw the dragon, but at a nod from Jonathan, they raised the iron structure.

It lowered once more after they had passed through, settling onto the ground with a heavy *thunk*, effectively sealing them in. For some reason, Leo felt more like a prisoner now than he had when they'd put him in chains.

The corridor continued straight for a little way and then opened up suddenly into a huge cavern, lit with torches and braziers. A few electric lights were interspersed between them and Leo wondered how they were powered. Red banners hung from the ceiling, plain aside from the symbol of a red rose. Other banners hung nearer to the floor, separating the cavern into rooms.

Despite the fact that they were deep underground, Leo marveled at how the caverns resembled a small city. People hurried about their tasks, some of them mending clothing, others cooking out of sight—the smell of food drifting through the air. He could hear the clacking of machinery, also unseen, coming from somewhere. Weapons were sharpened, supplies sorted and transported.

For a moment, everyone stopped what they were doing and stared at Sheboleth. If that made the dragon uncomfortable, she gave no sign of it.

"Carry on," Jonathan shouted.

Tiachren led Skye away, to wherever the rebels received medical attention. The dark-skinned girl, Anyah, glanced at Leo and gave him a small smile before hurrying away on her own task.

Jonathan gripped his arm. "Come on. The Triad will be waiting."

As Leo was led away, Sheboleth made to follow, but Jonathan told her she would have to wait outside. The dragon snorted, preparing to argue, but Leo held out one hand, a difficult thing to do when they were shackled together, signaling that he would be all right without her.

At least, he hoped he would.

He had caught a glimpse of bars set into the stone of a far wall and the cells that had been carved out of the rock. They were unoccupied, but he supposed the rebels would have to have a way to deal with any members that turned into dissenters. *Or Imperial spies.*

If he failed to convince them, would they put him in one of those cells or just kill him outright? He didn't think Sheboleth would stand for that, but what could she really do?

Jonathan led him down a separate corridor, the rooms at the end veiled by purple tapestries.

"Wait here," he ordered, stepping into the room at the very end of the hall, leaving Leo behind.

He waited impatiently for Jonathan to return, his anxiety growing with each passing moment. Jonathan clearly wanted to speak to the Triad before Leo went in and he wondered what the man could be telling them. He strained to hear anything, but could make out only the low murmur of voices beyond.

At last, Jonathan returned, and this time they entered the room together, where three people waited.

This must be the Triad. He thought it was interesting that the Resistance should be governed by three leaders instead of just one, like the Empire, but he supposed that was just one more thing that set them apart. He studied each of them in turn, but his eyes focused most of all on the tall man with dark skin, since he spoke first.

"What is your name?"

Leo swallowed, but did his best not to appear nervous. He didn't want to give any impression that he might be guilty of what they suspected. "Leo."

"There are some very serious charges against you, Leo. You stand accused of reporting the Resistance and its members in the Capitol to the Empire, and the raid that followed. How do you plead?"

He felt as though he were on trial. He'd heard of trials in the Capitol, rare affairs, but they did happen. One wasn't likely to be given a fair hearing there, if the Empire was determined to find one guilty, and he suddenly wondered if this would be no different.

"I am not guilty."

The woman spoke up. "How, then, do you explain what happened that night?"

Leo made a helpless gesture. "I don't know, ma'am. If the raid was my fault, it was unintentional. I didn't know about the tracker until Skye cut it out. The Imperial patrols might have seen my tracker's signal at the pub and thought it unusual. A friend of mine, who was also a Resistance member, told me to go to the pub several days in a row beforehand, so that my presence would not be remarked upon, but it might not have made a difference. The raids are random. It could all have simply been bad luck."

"You expect us to believe that bad luck was to blame, when on the other hand, we have a new member who just happens to join shortly before we are raided?"

"I'm not a spy," Leo protested, suddenly aware of how he must look.

His clothes were dirty from days spent in the forest and he was in desperate need of a shave. His hair was in disarray. He felt filthy and probably looked and smelled it too.

"Do you have anything to offer as proof of your claims?"

"I have no explanation to give other than the truth," he added helplessly, then remembered overhearing Geoffrey's conversation in his office, about the Inquisitor's upcoming visit to Elath.

It felt like a lifetime ago, the very information he had risked all to bring to the Resistance's attention. Here, at last, he was provided with the chance. He only hoped it would prove to be worth something.

"I…have information that may be useful to you."

He hoped they didn't already know. It didn't seem like the sort of thing the Empire would wish to be common knowledge, giving Elath time to prepare.

He also fervently hoped Geoffrey could be relied upon. He was putting an awful lot of trust in his old drunken employer.

"What information?" the other man asked, older, with a thick head of hair.

Leo took a deep breath. "There's been a shortage of raw materials from Elath. An Inquisitor is scheduled to visit the city at the end of the month."

The three leaders exchanged a look. *They hadn't known.*

"This changes things," the older man said.

"It changes nothing," the woman argued. "He could easily be lying. Our intel has heard no such rumors."

"What kind of spy willingly gives up such information, knowing what might happen?"

"One who's playing a very clever and dangerous game," said the dark-skinned man. "One that hopes to lead us into a trap. Do you know how the Inquisitor intends to travel to Elath?"

"No," Leo admitted.

"It will most likely be by train," said the woman. "But we'll need to know the time."

"I thought he was lying," the older man said wryly.

"He could still be, but the information can be verified easily enough."

"And even if it is a trap," said the dark-skinned man, "it's an opportunity we simply can't afford to pass up." He turned his attention to Leo. "We shall soon see whether or not you're telling the truth. If this is a trap, and it goes badly for us, it will go even less well for you, since you'll be going along."

"Is that wise?" asked the woman.

"A test of loyalty. He'll be given the most dangerous task on the mission. I can think of no better way to prove himself. In the meantime," he addressed Leo once more, "I suppose you're trustworthy enough. There's nowhere you can go." He signaled to Jonathan to remove the shackles. "Feel free to explore. We'll give you more details and further instruction when the time comes. But understand, should you try to flee or contact anyone from the Capitol, we will not be so lenient."

The shackles clicked as they were unlocked and Leo resisted the urge to rub his wrists.

The man raised one hand, gesturing back the way Leo and Jonathan had come. "You may go."

Leo hesitated, glancing back at them, still uncertain about his fate, and left the room. Sheboleth rose to her feet the moment Leo pushed the tapestry aside and stepped out into the main cavern.

She glanced at his wrists. "I see you passed muster."

"Of a sort." He didn't really want to discuss what had happened with her yet, still trying to make sense of it himself. He was saved from having to elaborate further by the arrival of Skye.

A pair of crutches were propped under her arms, her leg bandaged. Otherwise, she looked much the same as she had the night of the meeting. Her eyes were just as blue and intense as ever, ringed by dark lashes. She was dressed entirely in black. He could see two daggers at her hips, and more attached to straps around her thighs. Her black hair was still styled in a choppy bob.

"So, they've decided you're to be trusted, have they?" she asked, stopping in front of him.

"For now," Leo answered. "Are you all right?" He gestured to her injury.

"I'm to stay off of it, but I'll be fine."

Leo wanted to ask if there was someone to look at the arm she'd cut the tracker from, but there was something even more pressing on his mind. "Would it be possible for me to clean up before anything else? I'd feel a lot better after a bath."

"So would everyone else," she agreed. "I'll take you to the springs."

Slowly, her steps halting on the crutches, Skye led him deeper into the caverns. Leo followed, uncomfortably aware of the stares he was receiving. Though the Triad had cleared him for the time being, it hadn't eliminated the hostility towards an outsider.

There were people of all ages, including some children running around and he realized that entire families must live here, the Resistance's numbers always growing from within. One day, if they had not yet achieved their goal, the children would grow up to become rebels themselves. They didn't have to directly take in outsiders to bolster their ranks.

"How many members are there?" he asked as they walked.

"A few thousand."

It was more than he had expected and yet pitifully few with which to take on the Empire.

They ducked down a passage covered with blue tapestries. "Here we are."

Leo could hear water up ahead and soon the stone floor dropped off, giving way to a gently bubbling spring.

"It's heated, but not too hot that it will burn," Skye explained. "This is one of the springs we use for bathing. There are others for drinking." She glanced at him. "I'll leave you to it."

"Thank you."

He watched her leave, then, tired of feeling filthy, Leo stripped off his clothes and gratefully sank down into the water, letting out a contented sigh. He even carefully unwound the bandages on his arm and washed the wound. He would have someone take a look at it immediately after.

It felt good to scrub the sweat off his skin and the dirt from beneath his nails. The beard would have to go next. It itched. He dunked his head below the surface, savoring the warmth of the water.

The soul stone still hung around his neck. He hadn't bothered to remove it; the water would do it no harm. It was still cold against his chest, warming to neither his body heat, nor the water.

Leo resurfaced with a sigh. He'd have to figure out what to do next, what the Triad expected of him, and how he would fit in here. But for now, he just wanted to enjoy a moment to himself. He hadn't realized how very tired he was, the stress of the past couple days catching up with him. Adrenaline and the need to keep moving had kept it at bay, but no longer.

He leaned against the side of the pool and closed his eyes.

For a moment, Sheboleth feared he'd fallen asleep, but his eyes snapped open at the sound of her approach, claws clicking on stone. He had been leaning back, resting his elbows against the stone that ringed the water. But his relaxed posture changed the moment he saw her, moving to cover himself.

"What are you doing here?"

Humans and their modesty.

"Relax, Leo," she said dryly, keeping her gaze focused on the ground. "I don't care how well-endowed you are.

You're not my type. I came here because it's private and I need to talk to you."

She laid down at the water's edge with her back to him, facing the blue curtains that blocked the entrance.

"Less private than one might think," he retorted.

She'd managed to embarrass and annoy him all at once, which, she reflected, really wasn't so hard.

She heard him sigh behind her. "I thought you were going to leave once you'd brought me here. Something about not having to tolerate each other any longer, wasn't it?"

"Something like that. Things change."

The truth was that she'd been rather horrified by the Resistance's treatment of him. Not that she'd expected them to welcome him with open arms, but this seemed harsh even by their standards. They may not have physically beaten him like the Imperial soldiers had, but otherwise, his treatment had been little better.

I didn't bring you all the way here only for them to decide to kill you.

Sheboleth risked a glance at him, over her shoulder, but he wasn't looking at her and so he didn't notice. He seemed thinner than a human male his age should be. *Bony,* she thought.

Her eyes went to the chain around his neck, the blue stone hanging down over his breastbone, half-submerged beneath the water. It pleased her to see that he kept it close.

"How did you manage to convince the Triad?" she asked, turning back around.

"I had information that they wanted." She listened as he told her what had happened and what he knew of the Inquisitor's visit.

"What do you think they want you to do?" she mused, shifting her weight.

"They neglected to say."

"You must have some idea, at least. Do you think they expect you to kill the Inquisitor?"

Somehow, she didn't think the Resistance would leave an important government official alive and if they intended to give Leo the most dangerous job, she could think of little more dangerous than the role of assassin. But would they really leave that task in the hands of someone untrained and very likely incapable of carrying it out?

"I don't know. I wouldn't have thought so—I'm no assassin."

"But if they wanted you to, would you?" Sheboleth pressed.

"Oh, I don't know," Leo snapped. Her question must have struck a nerve. "There's no point in speculating or trying to decide what to do until I know what they want."

Sheboleth frowned, but he couldn't see. The man she had first met, out in the rainforest, would have refused to play assassin. His words came back to her. *It's never right to do wrong in order to do right.*

But what choice did he have? If he wanted to be trusted and accepted by the Resistance, didn't he have to do what they said? What would they do to him if he refused?

The thought made her feel bitter. To a certain degree, he was right. There was no point in speculating until they knew for certain. But she wished he had taken a stand then and there.

You shouldn't be surprised if he compromises, she told herself. She knew all too well how humans were.

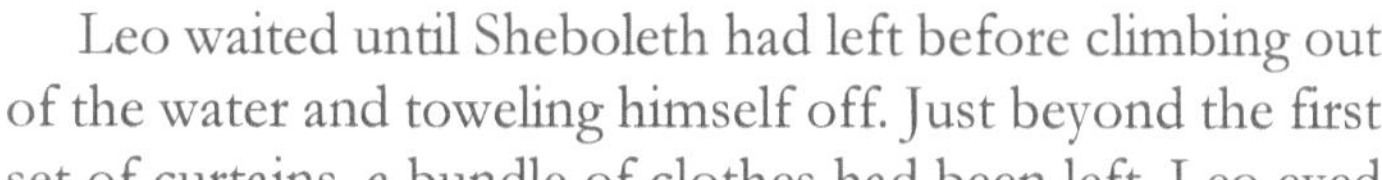

Leo waited until Sheboleth had left before climbing out of the water and toweling himself off. Just beyond the first set of curtains, a bundle of clothes had been left. Leo eyed them, wondering who had gone to the trouble, but he was hardly going to wear his old clothes, filthy as they were.

The new outfit wasn't dissimilar to what he'd worn before: a collared, button-up shirt and trousers, both black. The new pair of black leather boots were a bit too small, pinching slightly, but that could be fixed easily enough. Everything else fit surprisingly well; the waistband on the pants was a little loose, so he fetched his suspenders.

"You look like an entirely different person," Sheboleth remarked, after he had shaved and stepped back out.

I feel *like a different person.*

He'd been bothered by her questions, already having considered the possibility himself, but it made it somehow more real to hear her say it. He was too tired to think about it now.

He left the springs behind and went to find Skye. He didn't have to look long; she'd obviously been waiting for him and he wondered if she had brought the clothes.

"All done?"

"Do you know if someone could take a look at this?" He held out the arm she had cut the tracker from.

"Follow me."

She still didn't seem particularly approving of his presence, but at least she was no longer trying to kill him.

The infirmary was a separate wing of the caverns, concealed from view by white sheets that had been hung at the entrance and also between the cots, to give patients some form of privacy.

Skye waited for him at the entrance while one of the medics expertly bandaged his arm again. When she removed his boot and saw the state of his ankle, she scolded him roundly for walking on it and gave him a brace for it, instructing him, now that he was here, to stay off of it as much as possible.

The brace helped ease some of the discomfort, but he knew there was no substitute for rest.

"Better?" Skye asked when he reemerged.

"Much. Is there anything else I need to do? I'd like to rest, if that's all right."

Now that he was finally here, some of the tension and anxiety had eased, leaving behind only weariness. He'd nearly fallen asleep in the springs—as embarrassing as that was—and probably would have, if Sheboleth hadn't interrupted him.

"Just one, for now. Anyah needs to see you."

"Why?" he asked, following her once more.

"Because if you're going to stay here and eventually become one of us, you need to be equipped with a Resistance tracker."

Leo slowed to a halt. "Another tracker?"

Skye sighed. "It's necessary, trust me. It helps us keep tabs on you, make sure none of our operatives decide to go rogue, and it helps keep you safe if you go on any missions. Anyah can tell you more, I'm sure."

You don't have any choice, Leo reminded himself. He wanted—needed—to gain their trust and if that was what they asked of him, he would do it. They really weren't asking anything major, he supposed.

Not yet, anyway.

Skye stopped before more of the cloth room dividers. "She'll be in there."

Leo parted the curtains and ducked inside, revealing a single room occupied by numerous screens, their light harsh and glaring in the otherwise dim light. The dark-skinned girl that had checked him for more trackers was seated in a chair in front of the monitors, but she rose as he entered.

She wore a dark purple tank top with olive green cargo pants and sturdy boots. Her hair was thick, dark and curling, framing her face. She had large brown eyes and a friendly smile, a nice change from most of the people he had met.

"You're the new guy."

"Yes. I'm Leo."

"Anyah," she said, shaking his hand. She glanced at his tattoo. "Skye says you're a mechanic."

Leo frowned. "Doll maker, more like."

She shrugged. "Doesn't matter to me. You know anything about the mechs?"

"I studied them. Briefly. At the Academy." *Emphasis on briefly.* "I'd hoped to be able to build them one day, but that fell through."

She nodded, her curls bouncing. "I'll have to introduce you to Fae, then. She'll be eager to pick your brain. You here for a tracker?"

"Yes. Skye said you could explain it all to me." He turned to face the monitors. "What is all this?"

Anyah's eyes lit up, thrilled to have someone new to explain her role to. "This is my war room. I've hacked into the Capitol's network." She gestured to an intricate map that Leo recognized as a layout of the city. "This allows me to see the location of every patrolling soldier, citizen, and automaton. The orange dots are civilians, yellow are human soldiers on patrol, and red are the mechs. See?"

She swiveled to face another large screen. "This one displays all of the rebels' locations in blue. I can cross-reference this map with one of whatever town or city we're infiltrating and compare our operatives' locations with that of the patrols, allowing me to give them an early warning and alert them to what's coming. That's why the trackers are so important."

"It's impressive," Leo said honestly. "How did you manage to hack into the Capitol's system from all the way out here?"

Anyah sighed. "It wasn't easy, let me tell you. I had to put the transmission dishes up in some of the towers in order to get a high enough altitude."

"I'm not thrilled by the idea of having to get another tracker, to be honest. Not when I just got free of one."

"It was never supposed to be this way. In your case, I mean. All of the people that we recruit in the Capitol are never supposed to come to us. They're to stay put, observe and report, so there's no need to remove their trackers. You're a unique case. Even if they did leave the city, they'd have no way of finding us." She paused, considering him. "So how did you?"

"Sheboleth," he sighed. "The dragon."

She grinned. "You'll have to introduce us. Don't worry, though. It doesn't hurt much. Nothing like taking one out, anyway. And it was the only way for me to keep an eye on our operatives. They don't appear in the Capitol's network because they don't have government-issued trackers. If they did, it would be disastrous. The Capitol could just track their location back here to the base."

"Isn't there a chance they could already do that? If you hacked into their network, couldn't they somehow trace the signal back here?"

"Yes, it's definitely a risk. Every time one of the operatives contacts me or vice versa, there's a chance that the Empire could intercept the transmission. They could reverse trace it and know our exact location. I have several security measures already in place and it hasn't happened yet, but it's only a matter of time. That's why we need to make our move sooner rather than later."

"Seems dangerous."

"It is, but the alternative is to shut down the network and all communication, which would leave our people all alone out there, with no way for me to warn them of approaching danger. That was the way it used to be, in the past. Worked about as well as you'd expect." Anyah tapped one of the monitors. "Besides, this allows me to make sure our agents don't go anywhere they're not supposed to."

"Get a lot of that, do you?"

Leo was appalled, though not surprised, at the idea of the Resistance being betrayed by one of its own. It was one thing for them to think him a spy for the Empire, quite another to actually be ratted out by one of your own.

"Thankfully not, but you never know. Someone might lose faith in our mission and think they could get immunity if they spill their guts. The Empire would promise and do whatever it took to get the information they wanted, and then, once the traitor told all they knew, their guts really would spill, if you know what I mean."

Leo grimaced. He could well imagine.

"Sorry," she said, glancing away. "I talk too much. It's just that not many people are interested enough in what I do for me to really explain it. And I don't go out on missions with the others. This is my contribution, such as it is."

"It's a very important contribution."

She smiled and it lit up her expression. "I'll get your tracker."

Anyah disappeared briefly and returned with what looked like a small syringe. She took his right arm gently, the one with the tattoo, and inserted the needle beneath the skin, placing the tracker.

She glanced at one of the screens, where a new blue dot flickered to life. "All right, you're in the system."

"Thank you," Leo said, eyes on the blue spot that represented him.

He wasn't sure how he felt about his every movement being tracked, even if the Resistance was far more benevolent than the Empire. His movements had been tracked his entire life, but he simply hadn't known.

Still, for the first time in his life, the Empire had no eyes on him. Anything was better than that.

"Is there anything else you need?"

"A place to lie down would be nice," he confessed. "I feel dead on my feet."

"Oh! Of course."

Anyah took him to another small alcove of the caverns, also blocked off by the red rose tapestries. The "room" was lined with cots, each with a small dresser with a candle on top. There were already a few men inside resting and those that weren't glared in his direction.

"You know where to find me if you need anything," Anyah murmured. "Or if you want to pop in and say hello. Don't be a stranger."

Despite the unfriendly looks shot his way, Leo smiled. He tried to ignore the others and picked out an unused cot at the end of the row, so there would be only one other bed beside his, the stone wall on the other side. He laid down with his back to the room, glad to be off his feet. The cot was hard and lumpy, but after days of sleeping on the forest floor, it felt like heaven.

There were sudden indrawn breaths and low murmurs from the other men and Leo glanced over his shoulder to see Sheboleth duck inside the room, her size instantly making it look and feel smaller than it really was. She laid down between his cot and the one next to him.

He sighed, and without rolling over, murmured to her, "I don't need you to stay with me, Sheboleth."

He was more concerned about the others thinking him weak, as if he couldn't bear to be alone.

"I know," she rumbled. "Old habits." She had stayed with him during all the nights spent in the forest. "Besides, I don't know anyone else here."

Leo hadn't considered that she might be just as lonely and lost here as he was, surrounded by strangers, not all of them friendly. *Most of them unfriendly,* he corrected himself. Anyah seemed a rare exception.

"And anyway," she muttered, "I don't want these idiots getting any ideas about shanking you in your sleep."

In spite of himself, Leo chuckled at the absurdity. "Shanking? How do you even know what that means?"

"I told you—I spied on the Workhouses," she said, a note of pride in her voice. "A lot."

XVI

Leo awoke to the smell of food. He sat up, blinking in the dim light. The small room with its cots was empty aside from Sheboleth, who sat in the middle of the aisle between the beds. A small tray had been wheeled over, with two bowls resting on it. One was of average size and contained some sort of soup within. The other was quite large and empty.

He swung his legs over the side of the bed. "How long was I out?"

"Long enough," Sheboleth replied.

"What's this?"

"Dinner. You missed it. Anyah brought us some. Should still be warm; she just left a few minutes ago."

"That was nice of her," Leo murmured, reaching for the smaller bowl.

"Mm," said Sheboleth noncommittally. "You might change your mind once you've had a taste. I already ate mine. Wasn't very good."

"Doesn't matter. I'm starving."

The soup consisted of a thin broth, with bits of stringy meat floating in it. The broth was salty enough to conceal the taste of the meat, but not the texture.

After only a few bites, Leo set it back down on the tray. "You're right. It's terrible."

"You're not going to eat it?"

He shook his head. "I hope all Resistance food isn't this bad."

"No wonder you're so scrawny," Sheboleth muttered, bending to finish what he'd left.

"I'm not scrawny," Leo protested. "I'm just on the thinner side. There's a difference."

"Not much of one."

"If it's so terrible, why are you eating it?"

"I'm a dragon. I'm sure she was well-intentioned, sending a bigger bowl, but I need more food than you do."

The next day, Leo tried to make himself useful, but he didn't know where to start. He didn't consider himself to be very good at anything that the Resistance required. There was no point in attempting weapons training. He didn't have a weapon and doubted they would let him have one at that point either.

In the end, he and Sheboleth assisted with moving supplies. It was slow going, with his ankle still healing, but he was grateful to have something to do. After the meals were over, Leo made his way into the kitchens. The cooks wouldn't let him assist in the preparation of the food, probably because they feared he would somehow contrive to poison them all, but they welcomed his help when it came to washing the dishes.

Part of him suspected that because he was new and eager to prove himself, they gave him more work than was strictly meant for one person to take on. But he didn't mind much, used to working long hours and there was no other way to gain their approval and trust until it came time for the Elath mission.

Besides, the lengthy days kept his mind off of the Capitol and the family he left behind and for that, he was grateful.

Days went by with no further word on what the mission might consist of. Whenever he thought about it, it left a gnawing dread in his stomach. He tried not to think about it much.

Eating in the dining hall wasn't required and Leo was tempted not to, disliking the open stares he received. But Sheboleth insisted he needed to be seen. Most members that weren't busy at tasks they couldn't afford to step away from gathered in the dining hall, sitting along long benches. Leo found himself sitting alone. He knew no one here aside from Skye and Anyah and he didn't think Skye would welcome his presence.

She was sitting with the man named Tiachren and a freckled girl.

Sheboleth sometimes joined him, but her size and the fact that she wasn't human made it difficult. She preferred to stay closer to the kitchens, praising the cooks in the hope of being given more morsels. The Resistance already had thousands of people to feed and they weren't prepared to handle the appetites of a dragon as well. Sheboleth had muttered something to Leo earlier in the day about joining the hunting patrols.

"Is this seat taken?"

Leo looked up from where he'd been picking at that day's dinner. It wasn't nearly as bad as the soup, with venison, wild onions, and some canned baked beans smuggled from the Capitol.

Anyah stood in front of him, holding her own tray.

"No," he said quickly, gesturing for her to join him. "Please."

"Thanks." She sat across from him. "I usually eat in the war room. I don't get out much." She made a face. "But someone needs to keep an eye on the screens at all times."

"But there aren't any missions currently underway, are there?"

If there were agents sneaking into a city right that very moment, he could understand the urgency. But if not…

Anyah hesitated, looking at him uncertainly.

Leo felt himself flush. "Sorry." He looked away, forcing himself to smile, but it was self-deprecating. "That sounds exactly like the kind of thing a spy would ask, doesn't it?"

Now it was Anyah's turn to blush. "I'm sorry."

"It's all right. Everyone else here thinks I'm a spy." *Why wouldn't you?*

"But that's just it. I don't think you're a spy."

"Why not?"

"You have an honest face. That's a good thing, I think, but not something you want in a spy."

"No, I guess not." Leo glanced down at his hands. They were already beginning to turn red and raw from washing so many dishes. "Thank you for what you did the other night. Bringing me and Sheboleth some food."

She shrugged, but he could tell she was pleased. "Wanted to."

When he didn't say anything else, Anyah leaned forward conspiratorially. "So, how did you become acquainted with a dragon?"

He told her, the words spilling out of him, about being forced to flee from the Capitol and ending up in the Valderan rainforest, omitting nothing. He explained how the dragon had tried to kill him when they'd first met, only for her to recognize him later after he'd been captured by the patrol and, curious to know why they had tracked him down, kept him alive and agreed to take him to the Resistance.

"Do you think she'll stay?"

Leo had wondered about that himself. She seemed in no hurry to leave, but then, he hadn't proven himself to the Resistance yet. Maybe she would go after the mission had been completed and he'd either earned their trust or not.

If there was another reason she lingered, he didn't know it.

The Triad sent for Skye a week after her injury. She no longer needed the crutches, but knew better than to overexert herself. It was hard to be patient when she chafed to do something, but she knew from experience that rushing would help no one.

Still walking with a slight limp, she ducked into the hall that led to the leaders' separate rooms, heading for the room at the end of the hall, expecting to find all three of them assembled, but it was only Tristan waiting for her.

She didn't mind. Of all the leaders, she felt most comfortable in his presence. He had been the one that advocated for her after she had first arrived. He had seen her potential, her willingness to learn and do whatever the cause required. Loyalty was valued and rewarded above all.

Tristan wasted no time. "We have a job for you, at the end of the month, if your injury will be sufficiently healed in time."

"It will be," she replied, without hesitation. She would continue to stay off of it as much as possible if that was what it took, but there was not a chance she would miss out on a job.

Not if it's a chance to strike back.

He nodded. "I'm glad to hear it. The mission entails the Inquisitor's upcoming visit to Elath."

Skye listened silently as he laid out the details of the plan.

"I will, of course, speak to the others separately. Jonathan, I've already spoken to, since he will be leading the assignment. I'd like you to speak to Leo. Make sure he knows what we expect of him and introduce him to the others. He needs to know who he'll be working and risking his life with."

"I will," she agreed. "But I make no promises that he'll agree." She still didn't trust him.

In the Capitol, when she confronted him, he had looked just as terrified as she had felt. But was that because he was just as surprised by the raid as she was or because she'd been threatening him with a knife pressed against his throat? Impossible to tell.

"I understand. The decision is his alone, along with whatever consequences follow." Tristan hesitated. "It goes without saying, but should the initial plan fail, it will fall to you to…finish the task." He nodded at the daggers strapped to her hips.

Skye faced him without flinching. "Understood." He knew she had no qualms. She would not hesitate. She would not fail.

He nodded again. "Dismissed."

Skye walked back down the corridor and went in search of Leo. She found him, speaking to the dragon, but whatever they were saying, they broke off as she approached.

Luckily, they were alone. Not many people knew of the upcoming mission and the fewer that were aware, the better.

"I'd like to speak with you," she said, glancing at Sheboleth out of the corner of her eye. "About the mission. I'm sure you're curious to know what your role will be."

"Whatever you have to say, you can say in front of both of us," he replied.

Skye felt a flicker of irritation and suppressed it quickly. What did she care if the dragon overheard? Briefly, she outlined the plan as Tristan had explained it to her.

The Inquisitor would most likely travel to Elath by train, but they had no way of knowing which train or when he would arrive. Any agents they had currently residing in the Capitol would be instructed to keep an open ear, but they couldn't rely on them.

Skye would be stationed in Elath ahead of time, to monitor any incoming trains and watch for the Inquisitor's arrival. Once he stepped off the train, Skye would shadow him as he would most likely meet with the regional leadership in Elath. Any information that was discussed would then be relayed by Skye to Anyah via the comm system.

When the Inquisitor's business was concluded and he boarded the train to return to the Capitol, Leo would take the stage. The Triad had tasked him with placing explosives along the tracks, which would be remotely detonated. They would wait at a safe distance, tracking the train's progress, for the exact moment to blow the charges.

In Skye's opinion, he had the easier job. He listened silently as she explained.

"No," he said firmly once she'd finished.

She sighed. "I thought you'd say that. This is the task the Triad has given to you. You're free to make whatever choice you like, along with accepting the consequences that come of it."

"I don't want to kill anyone."

"You won't be killing anyone. Tiachren will be the one detonating the explosives."

"Yes, but I'm still the one placing them."

She tilted her head to one side, considering him. "This Inquisitor is not a nice man, Leo. You've no idea the things he's done. He deserves to die."

"And you do know, I suppose? How many people has he killed?"

"I've no idea. Perhaps none." She crossed her arms. "But he's part of a system that has killed *thousands* of us. Doesn't that mean anything to you?"

Besides, torturing someone, reducing them to the point that they begged for death, was hardly any better than delivering it outright.

Leo shook his head. "This is wrong. We have to be better than they are."

"We are better," she snarled. "He would order you executed as soon as look at you—or maybe something far worse. How can you defend that?"

"What does the Resistance gain by killing him?"

"Sometimes it's not about our gain so much as the Empire's loss. And any loss they suffer is a gain for us." She looked away. "We send a message, to both the Empire and its people, that the Resistance is a threat to be taken seriously. It gives the people hope that we have a chance to stand up to the Empire and win."

"Can you?" he challenged. "Win? You've been fighting for so long and nothing's changed."

"If you don't believe, why are you here?"

She had him there and they both knew it.

Leo gave her a pleading look. "Skye, I can't do this. I can do something else to prove my loyalty. Just not this."

She glared at him. "Not something violent, you mean? What do you think this is going to be like, Leo? That we can just march up to the Capitol walls and nicely ask the Empire to stop killing and oppressing its people? They don't reason or negotiate. They kill without consequence. So we speak the language they understand. We *become* their consequence."

"I'm in," Sheboleth spoke up. "I have a few ideas on how I can contribute."

Leo whirled on her, his expression a mixture of outraged confusion.

"You do?" Skye asked.

The dragon made a shrugging motion with her shoulders. "Well, for one thing, I imagine it's easier to reach Elath if you can fly there, rather than go on foot."

"I'm sure you'd be more than welcome. But why?" Skye asked. "You don't have a stake in any of this."

"Oh, but I do. I hate the Empire even more than you do."

Some of Skye's feelings, that she tried to keep hidden from others, must have shown through. "I doubt that."

She found it hard, if not impossible, to believe that anyone could possibly hate the Empire more than she did. If they did, she had yet to see it.

Sheboleth leaned down, her eyes glittering, teeth slightly bared. "Don't assume you have the monopoly on hate. You know nothing of it."

Skye could see the truth in the creature's eyes. She smiled grimly. "Then I look forward to working with you." Her gaze flicked to Leo. "I *hope* I get to work with both of you." She stepped closer to him, lowering her voice. "You don't question orders, you obey them. If you're going to be a member of the Resistance, you do what they ask of you, when they ask it." She stepped back, turned on her heel, and walked away.

She had said her piece. Whether he accepted or refused, his fate was his own to choose. She hoped, for his sake, that he hadn't come all this way only to throw it all away now.

But if nothing else, he had brought Sheboleth to them. Having a dragon on their side…it was unheard of. The possibilities were endless.

And if Sheboleth hated the Empire as much as she herself did, Skye could only imagine the utter ruination the two of them could wreak.

Leo rounded on Sheboleth the moment Skye was out of earshot. "You approve of this?"

"I have no love for the Empire. I wouldn't have thought you did either."

"I don't, but—"

"If you want to wait another thousand years for the Empire to peacefully die of natural causes, be my guest. For my part, I intend to hasten its demise."

He glowered at her. "The Inquisitor won't be alone on that train. How many more people are going to die when it goes up?"

"It's your choice to make, Leo, not mine."

"But it isn't, is it? There is no choice. Not for me."

The dragon frowned. "The Empire nearly took everything from you, and it will take still more if given half the chance. This is *your* chance to take something back." She stood and made to walk away. "You must do what you think is right."

Leo watched her go. *I know what I think is right. But how can I do it? How can I do either?*

The Inquisitor might not be innocent, but it felt wrong to adopt the Empire's tactics, even if using them against it. The Resistance had to be better or else how were they any different than the very thing they claimed to hate and fight against?

We'd become the very thing we hate.

But at the same time, Skye was right. The Empire would not be diplomatic with them and listen to what changes they wanted brought about. If they didn't do something drastic, would anything ever change? Wasn't that why he had attended the Resistance meeting in the first place? Because he had believed they could make things change for the better?

If nothing changed, nothing would get better. Countless more families like his would struggle and suffer and for what?

If you have the chance to make a difference, to do something, shouldn't you take it?

If he sat by and did nothing, by refusing to help with this mission, did that make him no different from the Empire? Was complacency just as bad?

It's not as if you have a choice. Not really.

If he refused to do as the Resistance asked, he would be branded a spy and either killed or banished. He doubted they would simply let him go. He knew too much, if only the location of the base. No, they wouldn't eject him from their ranks and let him leave, to go on with his life, somehow, somewhere else.

Would Sheboleth defend him if they tried to kill him? Maybe, but why take the risk?

This was the only future he had left to him. He had burned bridges back in the Capitol and risked his life to come here, in the hope that the Resistance would accept him. He was nearly there, so close to achieving that goal.

All they asked of him was to place a few remotely-detonated explosives.

It would be easy to do. And then it would be over and the stigma against him would be gone. He would finally be accepted.

Besides, Skye is right. It's not like you're the one detonating the bombs. You're not really killing anyone.

Leo tried to take what comfort he could from that, but it felt like he was trying to convince himself.

XVII

Zak rubbed his tired eyes. The text of the parchment, faded at the best of times, seemed to blur before him. He stood with a sigh, gathering up the documents to return to their shelves. It was late, the archives devoid of any other living presence. It was unlikely he would find anything more tonight, if at all, and he knew he would be better served to retire for the night.

His search had been fruitless. He'd found little in the way of healing records, even less that might have dealt with Fabian's mysterious condition. But he couldn't give up. Admitting defeat would be no different than giving up on Fabian and that he could not do.

Zak slid the last of the documents back into its home amongst the shelves and bent to retrieve his lantern from the floor. He hesitated, his eyes drawn deeper into the archives.

Into the restricted section.

He'd never had cause to venture there and would no doubt be reprimanded if he were caught. Hefting the lantern, he glanced back along the corridor, but the archives were silent and empty.

And anyway, he would have been unable to see anyone if they had been there, the lantern light ruining his night vision.

Turning, Zak plunged deeper into the archives, his shoes scuffing along the floor. If possible, here the tomes grew even older—or at least looked it. A fine layer of dust covered the spines and Zak coughed as he dislodged it.

Carrying his newest finds over to the nearest table, he pursued its contents, eyes skimming across the pages, too fast, he knew. He risked missing something important, but there was no time.

Finally, his eyes slowed, his fingers stilling, pulse quickening, as he came across the first mention of an unknown illness. It seemed to have afflicted the prince of Anarsha, though this was the first Zak had read of it. Perhaps few had known of it; he didn't imagine it was the kind of knowledge one wanted spread around.

Vexingly, as he read on, there was no more mention made of the prince's malady, leaving him frustratingly wondering whether it had been cured or left to run its course.

As before, the volume turned to a bigger problem facing Anarsha—the approaching Akkadian army. They had been routed before, forced back by the Anarshan soldiers and the dragons they fought beside.

But the Empire had merely retreated for a time, licking their wounds, regaining their strength, before trying again. Anarsha was too big a prize to simply let go and worse, she had dared challenge Akkadia. For that, she must be punished, her defiance crushed.

In the years that had passed since the last attack, Anarsha had weakened. Cut off from its former allies, Shemar and Elath, with whom it could have traded and imported goods, Anarsha suddenly found itself facing down a food shortage.

Its people were starving, hungry and dissatisfied. Some, who had previously supported the kingdom's resistance toward the encroaching Empire, now denounced Anarsha's leadership, saying they would have been better off to surrender at the time, even if it meant becoming another vassal state for Akkadia. At least then, they argued, they would have been fed.

It was against this backdrop of inner turmoil and unrest that the Akkadian army once more came marching. The weakened Anarshan army was suddenly no longer enough. The tale would only end one way if the Empire reached the city's great wall.

And so King Ulric was faced with a terrible choice. One that would have been—and still was—unthinkable to many.

Zak frowned, growing increasingly puzzled by what he was reading. He hadn't yet read this far into the account of Anarsha's eventual fall. Already it was different from how Akkadia presented its own version of events. This differed even further.

Ulric, in his desperation and his kingdom's darkest hour, had summoned a beast. But what kind of beast? What had it done? What had happened to it?

The questions came fast, rising within Zak's mind, tripping over each other in their haste. But he froze before he could read on.

He listened, straining to hear over the sound of his own heart. For a moment, he thought perhaps he had imagined it, but no—there it came again. The sound of footsteps, scraping on the hard floor.

He was no longer alone.

"Have you any news of the Resistance?" Desmond asked.

Fabian was more tempted than ever to directly ask the emperor who he was speaking to. With each passing day, he grew more convinced that the emperor was mad, either speaking to himself or a voice that only he could hear.

Lydia had come and gone, hours ago, reporting that there was nothing more. They had lost the escaped rebel's trail and they still had no idea where the Resistance operated from, their location just as much of a mystery as it had always been.

But the emperor had been unable to let it go, pacing around the room as the night grew long, and still he had yet to dismiss Fabian. He stifled another yawn, wanting nothing more than to return to his own quarters.

Instead, he was forced to stay here, listening to the ravings of a madman.

"How is that possible?" the emperor breathed suddenly.

If Fabian had been a braver man, or perhaps a stupider one, he might have worked up the courage to ask. But he didn't. Desmond didn't seem to notice he was there, once more forgetting his presence, both a blessing and a curse, in this case.

Fabian didn't want to draw attention to himself and have something thrown at him again. But neither was Desmond likely to dismiss him if he had forgotten he was even there. Fabian kept his eyes open with a will. Falling asleep in the emperor's presence was perhaps the most dangerous thing he could do.

The melody he'd been asked to play had long since trailed off and he lowered his fingers from the lute, focusing instead on the emperor and his words.

"That is not reassuring," Desmond said slowly, then sighed, "I suppose it matters not. Let them come."

He reached up, his long fingers gripping the edge of his mask. Fabian sucked in a quiet breath and held it as Desmond lifted the covering away. Fabian had never seen the emperor without the mask in place—and to the best of his knowledge, neither had anyone else.

Some instinct screamed at him to get out, to flee, that he was looking at something he had no right to, something private that was not meant for another's eyes.

But he did not look away.

The emperor's face was smooth, his pale skin mostly free of lines, which immediately struck Fabian as odd. He had been on the throne for fifty years, but the man before him appeared no older than forty. His hair was white as snow, but it tumbled past his shoulders and down his back in thick waves. Time had yet to ravage him in any discernable way.

But what most gave him pause was the eyes. Desmond's irises were a glittering, liquid gold, as if made of metal that had been melted down and poured—an unnatural color.

The emperor was still holding the mask a few inches from his face. "I've always loathed this thing."

Fabian couldn't tell if Desmond was talking to him or to himself.

"I believe you have an admirer."

Desmond froze, his muscles tensing, as he slowly turned his gaze on the minstrel in the corner. He had forgotten about the boy entirely and made the one mistake he always wished to, but never allowed.

He had removed his mask and allowed the boy to look at him. The minstrel was still looking now, his face bleached of color. The fascination that had been there a moment ago was gone, replaced by fear.

"Kill him."

"No," Desmond replied, setting his mask on the window sill. "Not yet."

He lunged forward, moving with surprising speed, and grabbed Fabian, slamming him back against the wall, his fingers gripping the boy's cheeks, long fingernails digging into his skin.

"He won't tell anyone what he's seen. Will you?"

The minstrel was breathing hard, chest rapidly rising and falling as he gasped. Desmond relished the fear in his eyes, pleased to know he could still inflict it after so many lifetimes. He hadn't lost his touch; he'd only adjusted his methods.

He could feel the minstrel's fine bones beneath his fingers and a great strength rose up within him, not entirely his own, yearning to crush them.

The boy gave the slightest shake of his head.

"We asked you a question," Desmond hissed, gripping harder.

The boy winced. "N—no."

"Good." He released the boy as quickly as he'd grabbed him. "Now get out." He crossed the room and replaced his mask, the metal settling over his features as easily as if they were his own.

Fabian ran from the room, his heart jackrabbiting in his chest. *What the hell was that?*

The emperor had thrown things at him many times, even physically struck him, but he had never threatened him in this way before. Fabian reached up to touch where the emperor's claw-like nails had dug into his cheeks, his fingers coming away red.

He shouldn't have looked. Why hadn't he left the room when he had the chance? Would it have mattered?

He's insane. He's completely insane. The emperor wasn't losing his mind—he'd already lost it. Talking to voices that only he could hear and flying into a rage at any given moment.

Fabian slowed, coming to a stop, and found he was trembling. He was afraid of Desmond.

He continued on, his steps taking him toward the archives. He wanted to confide in Zak, but the scribe wasn't likely to still be there this time of night. It was far too late.

But that didn't deter Fabian. The archives would be empty, at least, and that suited him just fine.

As he walked, he couldn't help casting nervous glances over his shoulder. He had dared look upon something forbidden. Would Desmond send for him again or would he simply send someone to murder him in his sleep?

He shuddered, already dreading his next meeting with the emperor.

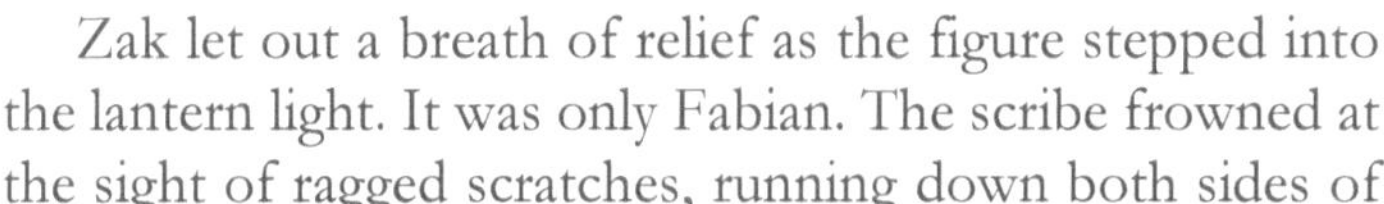

Zak let out a breath of relief as the figure stepped into the lantern light. It was only Fabian. The scribe frowned at the sight of ragged scratches, running down both sides of Fabian's face.

"Dare I even ask?"

"The emperor," Fabian confirmed, sitting down across from him.

"What did you do this time?" Zak asked, returning his gaze to the manuscript before him.

Fabian swallowed audibly. "I saw him without his mask."

Zak looked up, manuscript forgotten. "You what?"

"He took his mask off. I saw his face. I think he forgot I was even there. Zak, he has golden eyes."

Zak's frown etched deeper, but he could think of nothing to say, no explanation to give.

"You read more than anyone I know. Have you *ever* come across anything like that?"

"No," Zak admitted.

"He's insane." Fabian shook his head. "I don't want to think about it anymore." He nodded to the manuscripts. "Have you found anything?"

"Something that might be promising. I was hoping this document would go into more detail, but it seems to be more interested in the conflict between Anarsha and Akkadia."

Fabian let out a mock groan. "Not that again. What now, more dragons?"

"Not exactly. This record claims that King Ulric summoned some sort of beast to help Anarsha fight the Empire."

"Beast?" Fabian's brow furrowed. "What sort of beast?"

"I don't know. I haven't gotten that far."

"Well, let me know what you find out. It sounds interesting, if nothing else."

Zak could tell his friend didn't think there was any truth in the Anarshan's account. But if dragons were real, why not this beast?

Whatever it was, from what little Zak had managed to read, it seemed to have frightened Ulric badly. But what could have terrified him more than the approaching Akkadian Empire?

XVIII

Skye's words continued to haunt Leo, as the days slipped by and the mission in Elath drew ever nearer. He no longer ate in the dining hall, preferring to slip away with Anyah to her war room where he was free from judgmental glares. She didn't seem to mind. In fact, she seemed pleased by his company.

She had covered the hard stone floor with blankets and old cushions she had managed to find. Bathed in the glow from the many screens and cut off from the outside world, the room was positively cozy.

Leo worried she might get in trouble for associating with him. After all, if he really were a spy, she would be one of the best people to falsely befriend in order to extract information from.

But Anyah had waved his worries away.

Leo set his tray aside, finished with it. Before long, the meal would be over and the dining hall would empty. He would have to make his way back to the kitchen and help clean up for the night.

"What's wrong?" she asked.

They were seated on the floor, their backs to the far wall, facing the sheets that concealed the entrance to the room. Every now and then, Anyah would glance up at her many monitors, which still seemed to defy explanation for Leo.

He had already told her about his dilemma. "I just don't know what to do."

"I don't think it's right of them to make you do this. Proving loyalty is one thing, but can't you do that without going against what you think is right?"

"Apparently not. They must think this is a perfect test to see whose side I'm really on."

"Maybe you could talk to the Triad?"

He shook his head. "This was their idea. I doubt they'll change their minds. Besides, they'll look at it not as a moral issue, but that I'm looking for any excuse to get out of it, like an Imperial spy would. Skye was right. They give an order and you either follow it or don't."

Anyah's brow furrowed. "Well, she would say that."

Leo glanced at her, wondering what she meant, but she didn't elaborate. Her gaze flicked to the screens again, but she apparently didn't see anything alarming.

"Do you always have to watch them?" Leo asked, glad for a change in topic.

"More or less. Sometimes others will pitch in, but I prefer to do it myself."

"What about when you sleep?"

"I have an alarm system that will let me know if anything's wrong." She sighed, drawing her knees to her chest and wrapping her arms around them. "Sometimes I wish I could go out on missions, if only to get out of these caves. They're so gloomy, don't you think? There's a disturbing lack of anything green and growing."

"I know what you mean." Leo hadn't been there all that long and already he missed the sun.

By now he knew that Anyah had been with the Resistance all her life. Her parents were dead, but they'd died when she was so small, she didn't remember them. It had been her grandmother that had taught her all she knew of the screens and the system of tracking. Her grandmother had once worked in the Capitol itself, on their network, before defecting and coming here.

When she had asked about his own family, he'd given some vague answer, the subject still too painful to think about.

"What's the story with your necklace?" Anyah asked. "I see you fiddling with it sometimes. Was it your mother's?"

Leo looked at her, surprised that she'd noticed. He rarely ever brought it out into the open and so she must have been watching him closely. The thought brought a slight flush to his face.

"No, just a family heirloom." He wished now that it had been his mother's. It would have been nice to have a piece of her with him still.

He lifted the chain, pulling the blue stone out from under his shirt.

"Can I see it?"

He handed it to her, still keeping the chain around his neck, and she scooted over to look at it. "It looks just like a soul stone. Except everyone knows soul stones are red."

"Yeah," Leo said as she handed it back. He stuffed it back inside his shirt. "It's probably worthless."

"But it means a lot to you," she pointed out.

It was true, though he couldn't have said quite why. But he never parted with it. It remained around his neck at all times, the only part of his family and old life he had left.

The thought was acutely painful and he felt a twinge in his chest as the cold stone settled against his skin.

Leo took both of their trays back to the kitchen, leaving Anyah to her work. Skye was waiting for him. There would be no washing dishes for him that night.

She led him deeper into the caverns. "Have you made up your mind about the mission?"

Leo had, though he didn't much like it. From the moment he'd been handed the ultimatum, even before Sheboleth had thrown her support behind it, Leo knew there was only one decision he could make.

"I'll do it, but I don't have much choice."

He would do this one thing and that would be it. He would prove his loyalty and need not do it again—or so he hoped.

She nodded. "Then I'll introduce you to the others—officially. You should know who you'll be risking your life beside."

Jonathan, he had already met, a taciturn man who would oversee the mission and ensure, so far as he could, that nothing went wrong.

Skye led him into what looked like a laboratory, crammed full of clutter, from microscopes and burning beakers of colorful liquid, to sticks of dynamite laying around in open crates.

"Tiachren will be in charge of making and detonating the explosives you'll place," she explained over her shoulder. "His flaming hair might not be an asset when it comes to stealth, but where explosives are concerned, there's no one better." Raising her voice, she called, "Tia!"

From a doorway further in came the red-haired man Leo recognized from the meetings.

"I wish you wouldn't call me that," he grumbled, tossing a rag over his shoulder. His gaze fell on Leo. "Don't get many new faces. Aside from the babies that are born here and they take forever to grow up. You know what I mean." He waved a hand and drew in a breath. "So, you're the Imperial spy."

"I'm *not* an Imperial spy," Leo bit out.

"Mustn't be, to convince the Triad."

A young woman followed him through the open doorway. She was short, with a smattering of freckles across her cheeks, her brown hair shaved quite short.

"Is it true you brought a dragon with you? Can I meet her? Please, can I?"

Her youthful exuberance reminded Leo of Ana. Quickly, he pushed the familiar pain away.

Skye introduced her. "This is Fae, our resident expert in all things mechanical. I'm sure the three of you will have plenty of chances to work together, but for now—" She steered Leo back out of the room. "—you're needed elsewhere."

He followed her, feeling dazed. Everything felt like it was happening too fast.

"Is there someone else I need to meet?"

"No," she said brusquely. "Now keep up."

She took him to the armory, the far wall still lined with training dummies. Off to one side, in a circle, sawdust and sand had been spread over the floor where combatants could spar.

Leo looked around. "What are we doing here?"

"Do you know how to fight?" Skye asked. He'd had only a small knife on him the day they'd met, but whether he could use it or not was another matter entirely.

"Never really had cause to learn," he replied, a hint of irony in his voice. "Capitol citizens aren't allowed weapons. Only the soldiers."

Skye knew that. For someone like Leo, his only weapon would be his fists and judging by how thin he was, she didn't think him likely to win.

She suppressed a sigh. No matter. They could work with that. She'd been even thinner when she'd first come to the Resistance. Now she was wiry, all corded muscle, honed from hours spent training and at her forge, swinging a hammer.

She reached down, taking out one of the knives she always kept in her boot. She handed it to him, handle first. "Here."

He looked at it in surprise. "You're…trusting me with this?"

"Only if you promise not to trip and fall on it."

To her surprise, he smiled wryly and took it from her. "I thought I was a spy."

"I still don't trust you. Not yet. But I'm not letting you go on this mission unarmed. I wouldn't do that to anyone. Everyone has the right to defend themselves and for that, you need to know how, so…"

She raised her fists, settling into a fighting stance.

Leo eyed her. "What are you doing?"

"You need to know how to fight with the weapons you have. You can't run until you know how to walk and there's no guarantee you'll always have a blade."

She herself had learned hand to hand combat when she'd arrived and now it was his turn. He didn't have long to learn—they only had until the end of the month before the Inquisitor arrived in Elath—but that only made Skye more eager to get started.

Reluctantly, Leo raised his fists, trying to mirror her stance. "This is stupid."

She dropped her stance and moved closer, adjusting his form. "Thumbs on the outside of your fists or you'll break them."

He flushed, embarrassed by her ministrations or critiques, she wasn't sure. Probably both.

"And it isn't stupid," she said, assuming her own pose once more. "It might just save your life."

Over the next several hours, she demonstrated proper form and technique on the training dummies and practice bags. She informed him of where to strike, how to strike, what to watch out for, the subtle changes in your opponent's posture that signaled their attacks.

She had debated what sort of weapon, if any, to give him. With little to no training, the knife wouldn't do him much good, but it was better than nothing. Her crossbow would prevent him from needing to get up close and personal with an enemy, but it needed training as well and she wasn't giving him the opportunity to shoot her from a distance. If he was a spy, as she believed, he would have received some form of training, no matter what he claimed.

She had plenty of throwing knives, but they required even more practice in order to be any good.

Each night was more of the same, Skye fetching him after dinner when the armory was usually empty. She taught him how to use his body as a weapon and how to absorb blows. Every night, when the session had ended, she sent him to bed aching, with fresh bruises.

But to her surprise, he never complained. She corrected him without judgment and complimented without reservation. In only a week's time, she watched his confidence grow.

She showed him the proper way to hold the knife she had given him, grip neither too tight or loose, how to slash and stab, demonstrating with the straw dummies, and where on the body to aim. She watched his technique, following the instructions she had given.

One thing was clear, despite his growing confidence—either he was a damn good actor or he had received no training at all.

Skye wasn't sure what to think.

Leo sighed suddenly, lowering the dagger. "How are you so…okay with all of this?" He gestured to the knife in his hand and the savaged straw dummies.

Was she okay with it? She certainly wasn't *not* all right with it. Her first kill had been one of desperation, which had made it easy. They had all come easy after that, fueled by undimming rage.

If ever she had any doubts, she made herself remember her mother's face, filled with terror, or her father's lifeless eyes. She remembered the guard who had leered at her and steeled her resolve.

No, violence didn't bother her.

"I don't regret the lives I take," she replied. "I don't regret what I do."

He slipped the dagger into the sheath she had given him, attached to a belt that he slipped around his hips. Gone were the suspenders. Between the training and three meals a day, he'd begun to fill out.

"This isn't easy for me."

He may not have had cause to kill before, but he did now. "If it helps, think of it this way: we are at war with the Empire. People die in war all the time. People kill in war."

"But not innocent people. They're not supposed to die."

And yet, they're the ones who suffer most.

"They're not innocent," Skye snapped, feeling that familiar rage rise.

Were the guards that had stood by innocent? They had stood while the rebels were overpowered. The men, they had beaten within an inch of their lives, but the women…they took their time with them.

"Why do you hate the Empire so much?" Leo whispered.

"You don't?" Skye retorted. "Why did you join the Resistance, then?"

"Because I thought you could make things better."

"We can, but that doesn't mean it's going to be easy. This is the price. Is the promise of a better future not worth paying for?"

He leaned against the wall, observing her with those dark eyes. Her gaze traveled over the dark hair on his arms, the veins on the backs of his hands.

"You want to tear down the Empire. But how can you guarantee that what you replace it with won't be just as bad if not worse?"

Skye scoffed. "It can't be worse."

"It can *always* be worse."

"Because we have good intentions." Skye was quickly tiring of the conversation. "We're trying to do good, unlike the Empire." No one could look at the Empire now and say that of them.

"Nothing starts out bad."

I'm pretty sure the Empire did.

"What is your point?" she demanded.

He fidgeted uncomfortably. "I just think we need to be careful, is all. We can't become like them or else nothing will get better."

"We *aren't* like them, Leo. You see enough of the Empire's ugliness, the things they do, and you'll realize that." She stalked away, done for the night. "If you're having second thoughts, I suggest you bury them."

Before they bury you.

Every night, Leo went to bed sore, tired, and stiff, but he didn't mind. He could feel his body changing, growing stronger, and knew he would need every one of Skye's lessons for the day of the mission.

He might not come back from it. All of them might not.

But the more he got to know the others, he found himself trusting them, in a way he'd never trusted anyone before. And knowing they'd have a dragon with them didn't hurt matters any.

He met Tiachren in his lab to go over the explosives—how they worked, how to place them and where.

"Don't touch anything," Tiachren warned. "It might explode." And then, seeing the look of concern on Leo's face, added with a laugh, "I'm kidding."

Even so, Leo didn't touch anything.

Tiachren showed him the explosives he'd been working on, each one about the size of Leo's palm, that would be attached to the train tracks. They were surrounded by tiny red lights that would glow once the bombs were placed and activated, ready for detonation.

Leo watched carefully as Tiachren demonstrated how to set them. It seemed simple enough. *Almost too easy.*

The young woman called Fae would not be going on the mission, but Leo spent a good portion of the day working with her. She, too, had a laboratory of sorts, but hers was filled with metal scrap and tools instead of explosives.

"Anyah tells me you're a mechanic," she said excitedly, shaking his hand the first day.

"Well, not exactly."

"Do you know anything about the dragon mechs?"

"I studied them. Not for very long, but I remember what I did manage to learn."

"Well, it's better than nothing and I'm sure it's more than I know." She stepped through the curtains into a separate room where the hull of a dragon automaton stood, suspended from the ceiling. "I can't tell you how nice it will be to finally have someone to work with on this."

Leo walked closer, eyeing it.

"I've been assembling it for so long, but I didn't have all the parts, and honestly, I don't know where some parts even go," Fae confessed. "I salvaged some from the mech that attacked Skye—the one your dragon friend destroyed."

"Impressive. What do you plan on doing with it?"

"Ideally, reassembling it and finding out how they work. If I can program it somehow, we might be able to use it against the Empire. I'd like to make a whole army of them—crazy as that sounds, I know—but that will have to wait. I have to get this one working first. I was hoping you might be able to help me."

Leo stared up at the lifeless mech, resisting the urge to reach out and touch it. This was what he had wanted to do nearly all his life, finally coming true, albeit in the most unlikely circumstances he could have imagined.

"I'd be happy to help." It would give him something to contribute to, other than working his hands raw from washing dishes.

Fae clasped her hands together. "Great!"

Leo smiled; her enthusiasm was infectious. Together, they set to work, sifting through parts, taking stock of what they had and what they didn't.

They had just attached one of the wrist joints when Fae asked, "You don't happen to know what the soul stones are for, do you?"

Leo glanced at the empty socket in the beast's chest. "No. They didn't cover that at the Academy." *At least not in the classes I took.*

"Ah, well, no matter. We'll work it out together."

She led him back into the main room, where a red stone rested in a silver clamp, the narrow fingers holding it up. It was a perfect soul stone, deep red in color, without a flaw.

"Skye stole this from one of the mechs in the Capitol's scrapyard, but I haven't been able to figure out their purpose. They must have one, though, or else why would the Empire bother with them?"

The stone reflected the light, shining like a large ruby. Other than a pretty bauble, Leo couldn't think of any use for it just by looking.

They left the stone then and began the painstaking task of separating the parts Fae had salvaged from the mech that had attacked Skye. Some pieces were harder to identify than others, they had been so badly mangled.

Sheboleth really did a number on this thing.

Some of them would need dents beaten out of them and others Leo feared were damaged beyond repair, torn and crushed, with holes punctured through.

The armor, which should have been thick and heavy iron, felt more like aluminum in his hands.

XIX

Fabian had no intention of telling Lydia about his latest encounter with the emperor, but the cuts on his cheeks were impossible to hide. She looked up as he stepped through the door of their quarters, her eyes narrowing.

She shot to her feet. "What did he do to you?"

"It's nothing," Fabian said quickly.

"He's gone too far."

"You said so yourself—staying close to him is the safest place for me." Fabian grimaced even as he said it, hating the words but knowing their truth.

There were few places in Akkadian society for someone like him, too weak to pull their own weight. He could not become a soldier, his body too fragile for manual labor. His options were slim.

"Until he kills you."

He sighed. "It was my fault. I saw him, Lydia. Without the mask."

Her green eyes widened and she sank back down into one of the chairs. "What?"

"He didn't realize I was still there or that I'd seen. That's why he…" He trailed off, gesturing to his face, then hurriedly carried on before she could interject again. "He's been on the throne for fifty years, but the man I saw, behind the mask, couldn't be a day over forty."

Lydia frowned. "You think he wears the mask to hide the fact that he's not as old as he claims?"

"I don't know. All the emperors wore masks."

She stood again, a certain purpose to her movements now. "I'm going out." She paused as she passed him in the doorway, lifting one hand to touch his face. "You should put something on that."

Zak spent every spare moment buried in the archives, searching for more references to the mysterious 'beast', somewhat to his chagrin. He had promised Lydia he would look for a cure, or at least an explanation for what ailed Fabian, and here he was, getting lost in the past.

But, he consoled himself, Fabian had asked him to look into this, too, even going so far as wishing to be kept informed. Perhaps he was just as curious as Zak.

The battles between Anarsha and the Empire were well-documented, but there were fewer mentions of any beast. Zak searched obsessively. He needed to at least have something to tell Fabian when he next visited.

His days passed by in a state of muddled confusion. It was a wonder he could function at all, as little sleep as he was getting. But in the archives each night, he came alive, filled with renewed vigor and purpose. He was close—*so* close—he could feel it.

At last, nearly buried behind another manuscript, he sought what he was searching for and as he sat down to read it, Zak could scarcely believe what he held in his own two hands.

This was an account of the conflict and what followed, written by the hand of King Ulric himself. Zak's hands trembled slightly as he flipped through it, knowing how priceless something like this was. He hardly dared read it, almost afraid of what he might find, even as his eyes raced ahead, eager to get to the conclusion before he was quite ready.

King Ulric's handwriting unfolded before him, elegant and flowing, but there was something unsteady about it as well—from age or fear, Zak couldn't say.

Greedily, he read:

Of myself and my advisors that summoned the Beast, few now remain. When I die, he will gain his freedom and I fear that day more than I ever feared the Akkadians. I wonder now how I could have been so foolish.

Zak let out a hiss. Much to his annoyance, part of the parchment was missing, torn or cut out. He skipped ahead to the next part he could make out.

I would have done it myself, but while I fear to keep it, I fear to be without it more. I will pass it on to my son. Through his leadership, Anarsha will stand firm. She is now all that stands in opposition to the Empire.

I pray to the saints that this will be enough, that they will not try again. But the saints no longer seem to hear me, after what I have done.

Zak's brow furrowed. He still was no closer to understanding what the beast was. What had Ulric done? What had he unleashed upon his enemies?

He scrambled among the papers, searching frantically, until he had his answer.

If the saints do not come to our aid, perhaps a demon shall. Some of my advisors balk at the notion. They warn me that I am tampering with forces I cannot control and do not understand.

Believe me, I comprehend the absurdity of these words even as I pen them, but what other choice do we have? Perhaps my advisors are right, but I see no other way, and when I ask them for one, they are silent.

Our army cannot stand against the might of the Akkadian Empire. Not any longer. If we are to avoid the fate that befell Shemar and Elath, this is the only way. We can no longer tarry. While we bicker among ourselves, the Akkadians march on our borders.

The Beast assures me that victory is certain. He alone can destroy Anarsha's enemies and bring the Empire to her knees. He alone can deliver us from this evil. He awaits my orders.

The Akkadians have long ago forsaken their belief and instead put their trust in the power of steel. But not even the Empire of Engines can stand against this foe.

This deliverance will not come without a cost, I know, but I can pay any price, so long as I know my beloved Anarsha and her people are safe.

As surely as the Beast reaps the Empire's army, so too will I reap the consequences.

It is done.

Zak blinked and read the passage again just to be sure, struggling to comprehend it. The beast was not a dragon at all, but a *demon.*

He let out a slow breath. It was all too much to believe. Akkadians—and he was no exception—did not believe in the supernatural, be they demon or saint. Certainly, Zak had never encountered one, nor had he met or read of anyone who had—until now.

But King Ulric was an Anarshan to his bones, a pagan, who believed in such nonsense. Dragons, Zak could believe in. There had to be some truth to them, the real-life inspiration for the automatons.

He could even believe that the dragons had been instrumental to defending Anarsha against the invading Akkadian forces. But a demon?

He tapped one finger against the table. It all sounded like the ramblings of a mad, desperate king, facing down the end of his own empire and clutching at anything, no matter how delusional, that might save them.

Sad, really.

Still, he would keep this to himself for the time being. It wouldn't help Fabian and likely only disappoint him. Whatever they had thought the beast was, whatever they had hoped for, this was not it.

Zak sighed. Perhaps he had been wrong to search for a cure among the old Anarshan documents. Renowned healers they may be, he could no longer separate them from their pagan beliefs.

Maybe there was nothing to find after all.

He stiffened, glancing up at the sound of footsteps, the stride too fast to be Fabian's. Whoever they were, they made no attempt at stealth, their heels ringing on the hard floor.

Zak found himself holding his breath—right up until the moment Lydia stepped around the nearest bookshelf, into the light of his lantern.

"Hell, it's dark in here," she muttered. "How can you possibly see anything?"

He let out a silent exhale. "Practice."

Her eyes skimmed over the papers assembled in front of him. "Have you found anything?"

Zak began to gather them up, as though to hide them from her view, even though he was certain she couldn't read the Anarshan runes. It felt like he had stumbled upon something illicit, something secret, that he didn't want anyone else to see.

"No. I found a passing mention of the Anarshan prince. It's possible he and Fabian may have shared the same condition, but if so, I haven't been able to ferret out any more about it."

She nodded, looking away.

"I'll keep looking, of course. But I'm starting to suspect that there might not be anything to find."

"You're doing your best. That's all anyone can ask."

Zak glanced away, feeling his face heat with shame. He wasn't doing his best; he was letting himself get distracted—by tales of demons, of all things. It felt so stupid to think of now, he couldn't even imagine saying it out loud and he was glad of his decision not to tell anyone.

"You will let me know the moment you find something?" Lydia asked.

"Of course."

Silently, Zak vowed to begin his search early the next morning. This time, he would not allow himself to get sidetracked. He'd satisfied himself as to the beast's origin, even though that had ultimately led nowhere.

He would seek out more about the prince, so far his only possible lead. He would find something to tell Fabian. Anything. Even if it was only to confirm what they all feared—that there was no hope. At least then they would have an answer, an end to the endless wondering.

If he had to scour the archives and read every dusty old document in order to give them an answer, then so be it.

XX

The day that Leo had been dreading ever since he arrived at the Resistance drew ever nearer. The very next morning, Skye would depart to scout ahead in Elath, in preparation for the Inquisitor's expected arrival. And yet, even knowing what awaited her, and that she would depart early, she still insisted on giving him one last training session before she left.

The whole time, Leo's focus was off, thinking of the mission that lay ahead and his upcoming part in it. He stopped, breathing hard after running through a sequence of quick knife attacks on the dummy in front of him. Skye said his movements were getting faster, but he knew he still wasn't anywhere near good enough. Not like her, her movements fluid and viper-like.

Skye glanced at him. "What is it?"

Leo pushed hair out of his eyes. "The information I heard when I was in the Capitol—I overheard my employer talking about it. What if he was wrong? What if things have changed since then?"

Those questions had been bothering him over the past few days. What if Geoffrey had been mistaken? What if he didn't know what he was talking about? Leo had no idea who had been on the other end of the comm device, but it could have been nothing more than drunken blustering.

Skye shrugged. "Then the information is wrong. It's still worth treating it seriously, though. Not every day an Inquisitor visits one of the outer cities."

He nodded.

She crossed her arms. "I've been meaning to ask….that mech Fae's been working on. Do you think you can reassemble it?"

Leo glanced up at her. "I don't know. It won't be easy."

"What about the soul stones? Have you figured out a use for them?"

He shook his head again, watching her. Skye's posture remained as nonchalant as ever, but he could see the disappointment in her eyes. She had hoped that he would know, being a mechanic from the Capitol.

"Ah, well," she murmured, beginning to walk away. "Better luck next time."

Skye had never ridden on the back of a dragon before. She didn't like how much trust she was putting in Sheboleth, but the dragon was right about one thing— flying to Elath was much faster than traveling there on foot.

The two of them set out early, before dawn had crested over the horizon, the sunlight alighting on the top of the ruins before slowly making its way down. Skye wore her black leathers, the cloth she used to hide her face wrapped around her neck. She wore a black cloak and carried a satchel of supplies, theoretically anything she would need to wait out the Inquisitor.

Sheboleth dropped her off at the edge of the forest, being unable to fly all the way in, and Skye made the rest of the way on foot. A comm device was tucked into one ear, allowing her to contact Anyah the moment a train pulled in.

The city of Elath was still quiet when Skye arrived, moving quickly, flitting between shadows like a wraith. It wasn't her first time in the city.

Elath was nestled at the foot of a mountain range, with a large, sprawling lake. Skye circled around the water as she entered town. The air this close to the mountains had a bite to it, which was just as well; Skye was certain the smell of fish would only be worse in the heat.

Taking a rope from her pack, Skye clambered up onto the top of one of the buildings. The rooftops were steep and gabled, covered with dark tiles, which would help her blend in. She took care not to slip as she moved about, but the soles of her boots gripped firmly.

The vantage point she had chosen allowed her a clear view of the station where the train would arrive and from here, she could eavesdrop, catching snatches of conversation that would be inaudible from within the room of an inn.

She pulled the cloth up to hide her face, drew her cloak around her, and settled against the side of the chimney, the bricks giving off a pleasant warmth.

And then she waited, observing the city, watching as it came to life.

Half of Elath was built upon the lake, the buildings rising up from the docks, some of which were interconnected, while others could only be reached by boat. She could see the crafts bobbing in the water below, long and narrow, filled with nets.

Elath's main source of trade came from its fishing industry, along with the raw materials mined from its mountains. The very raw materials that now necessitated a visit from an Imperial Inquisitor.

The buildings were tall, multiple stories high. Space was a premium when one lived on the water, so they had built up instead of out.

The distance between Elath and the Capitol was not a small one and Skye resigned herself to wait, watching the townsfolk as they emerged from their homes and went about their business, all the while unaware that they were being watched.

Their clothes were dark and worn and they moved briskly through the cold, keeping their heads down, never lingering in one place for long. There was little finery to be found here.

As the sun moved across the sky and began to set, Elath really came into its own. The many windows up on the watchtower on the cliffs on the other side of the lake, and the buildings themselves, took on a warm glow. A lamplighter moved about, lighting the hanging lanterns that marked the water's edge where the docks ended.

A few of the houses had balconies and Skye eyed them warily, shifting her position slightly. She had moved around the chimney throughout the day, always remaining in its shadow, but she was cramped after so long curled up, presenting the smallest target.

There was no guarantee that someone would raise the alarm if they spotted her—they had no way of knowing that she belonged to the Resistance—but ordinary people didn't loiter on rooftops. More likely, they'd think her a thief, about to break in.

Or an assassin. She'd taken a turn playing at that, too, once. The rooftops of Elath were an assassin's dream.

As night fell and the lights winked out, one by one, Skye remained awake, on the alert. She doubted the Inquisitor would arrive in the middle of the night, but she was reluctant to finally close her eyes and get some sleep herself, resting in short bursts, relying on the sound of a train whistle to alert her.

But none came until the next morning, sounding far off in the distance.

Skye stretched, wincing at her stiff muscles. One leg had gone numb. She could just make out the steam the train gave off, though she had yet to see the machine itself.

Finally, it emerged, slowing to a halt on the outskirts, unable to pull too far in because of the lake. If it had been heading to the mines, it would have bypassed the city altogether and headed up into the hills.

From a glance, she could see that the train was relatively short compared to those that were used to transport cargo. Its doors were marked with the Empire's symbol, the unblinking amber eye with its slitted pupil.

It was impossible to determine how many people were on board. Skye watched, motionless, as the doors opened, her fingers itching to grab her crossbow. But the Inquisitor and all aboard were slated for a fiery death and not at her hands—not this time.

She stiffened as the Inquisitor themself stepped out. She couldn't say with any certainty whether they were a man or a woman. They weren't broad enough for most men, but taller than most women.

A mask, not dissimilar to the one the emperor wore, covered every inch of their face. No hair or skin was visible, not even on their fingers, hiding every trace of human features.

Inquisitors were meant to be anonymous and eerie, something not even human. This one wore black robes, embroidered in gold. The Empire's eye stared out from the middle of their chest. Gold rings adorned the end of each finger, fashioned into claws, and Skye wondered if they were functional.

They weren't meant to be soldiers; their weapons were psychological. And that made it somehow worse.

Skye reached up to tap her comm device, but stopped as a second figure stepped out behind the Inquisitor. This man was much larger, the fabric of his tunic straining against the swell of his stomach. He was clean-shaven, with a ruddy, jowly face that spoke of a love for wine. His clothes were made of fine gray silk, signifying his status as a Minister.

The situation in Elath must have been dire indeed to send a Minister and an Inquisitor both.

She fingered her daggers, wanting nothing more than to hurl them downward, their blades seeking hearts, but that wasn't the plan.

A small group had gathered to greet the emissaries from the Capitol. One stepped forward to greet them, bowing low. He was a thin man, with a trimmed beard, and more finely dressed than anyone else in Elath. Skye concluded that must be the governor, Elath's appointed regional leadership.

An ornate boat was being rowed out toward them across the lake, much larger than the fishing vessels, a dragon-like figurehead slicing through the water.

The wind picked up, becoming sharp, and Skye shivered at its chill, but it carried the sound of voices to her.

The Minister eyed the approaching boat with distaste. "Are there no other means of transportation?"

"I'm afraid not," the governor replied apologetically, all smarm. "But we'll be at the hall shortly and I trust you'll find it more to your tastes."

The Minister grunted. "Well, it's not for long, thank goodness. We're only here for forty-eight hours…unless we should need to stay longer. But I trust that will be more than enough time to come to a satisfactory resolution."

The Inquisitor remained silent throughout the exchange, hands clasped in front of them. But despite their silence, their presence seemed to loom large, impossible to ignore.

The governor's gaze flicked to them, his face blanching of all color. "Yes, of course. More than enough time. Shall we get started right away?" He gestured to the boat, which had arrived.

The wind lessened and Skye could no longer make out anything that might have been said, but she was no longer listening anyway.

She reached up, tapping her ear piece, activating the mic. "The Inquisitor has arrived. And a *Minister* came with them. They're both here for forty-eight hours."

It was Jonathan's voice that replied, crackling slightly. "Excellent. We'll be on our way."

Skye would have liked nothing more than to join the others wherever they would be making camp in the forest, but they couldn't afford to leave Elath unobserved. Anything might happen while she was away. The Minister could finish up early and leave ahead of schedule, or there might be some unforeseen delay that she would have to make the others aware of.

She sighed, settling back against the roof, peering up at the sky, waiting until she could climb down and trail them as surreptitiously as possible. The Minister didn't worry her, but if anyone would notice her, it was the Inquisitor.

She would bide her time, sticking to the rooftops and the shadows. So long as it didn't rain, it wasn't all that bad. And even if it did, she'd endured worse. She could endure anything for the cause.

Whenever her muscles protested or the cold began to seep in, she consoled herself with the image of her daggers plunging into the Minister's chest. It would be so easy to sneak into his quarters and finish it there, but that wasn't what the others had decided.

And besides, it gave Leo no opportunity to prove himself. If her suspicions about him were right, the whole thing would be a trap. She needed to be ready.

But Skye couldn't help the smile spreading across her lips. An Inquisitor and a Minister in the same place, at the same time, taken out with a single strike.

It was the chance to finally deal a meaningful blow to the Empire.

The moment Skye's message came through, Leo went to see Anyah. He'd taken the chain from around his neck and now the stone sat in his palm, cold and heavy.

She swiveled in her chair as he stepped into the room. "You'll be off, then."

"Yes. I have a favor to ask. Would you keep this for me?" He held the stone out, offering it to her. "In case things go bad."

At least if the worst happened and he never returned from the mission, the part of his family that remained would not also be lost.

Suddenly, he felt foolishly vulnerable, holding it out to her, wondering what she would make of the request. He didn't know why he cared so much. Perhaps he should just keep it with him.

Anyah smiled, taking the stone reverently. "I'll keep it safe," she promised, looping it around her own neck. "But don't worry. It won't go bad." She gestured to the screens. "I'll be watching out for you."

Leo smiled in return at that, pleased by the idea. "I know you will."

She handed him a small ear piece that he would use to communicate with the others while they were split up. Once he had it on, she handed him a larger one, with a long mic attached. "I modified this for your dragon friend."

They wouldn't be able to track Sheboleth, but she still needed a way to communicate with them over long distances.

The dragon let out a huff when Leo approached her with the idea, tolerating his ministrations as he attached the device, looping its bendable wire around one of her horns.

"This is ridiculous," she complained.

Once it was attached, there was nothing for Leo to do but collect his supplies and meet Jonathan and Tiachren. All three of them clambered onto Sheboleth's back, the dragon bearing the weight without comment.

Leo's stomach seized at the idea of taking to the air again, but there was nothing for it, and he wasn't going to show the slightest bit of weakness in front of the others. Not on the mission where so much depended on him.

He would get this one chance to prove himself. There would not be another.

He glanced over his shoulder as Sheboleth took off, the ruins of Anarsha growing distant behind them, eventually fading out of view altogether.

Sheboleth descended in the forest, where they would make camp slightly north of Elath. Skye would eventually rendezvous with them there, once the Inquisitor and the Minister departed the city.

Leo swallowed at the thought. A Minister, too. Suddenly, it felt like this mission carried twice the weight.

Peering through the trees, he could just make out the train tracks as they ran along the forest's border, connecting Elath with the Capitol.

If everything went according to plan, he would be expected to place Tiachren's explosives along those tracks. He settled back to wait, trying not to think about it.

But until the two of them left the city, he had plenty of time to think.

The light dimmed as the sun slipped below the horizon. Once more, the sounds of the rainforest surrounded Leo as he lay on his back, peering up through the canopy. There was no fire. They were too close to Elath to risk it.

Sheboleth lay off to one side and he wondered what she was thinking. She seemed to be the only one of them that wasn't affected by nerves.

Tiachren kept taking the explosives out of his pack and sorting them, making sure that he had them all and that they weren't damaged in any way. Leo wished he would stop and it seemed Jonathan felt the same, for their leader finally snapped at Tiachren to put them away.

Leo rolled over onto his side, knowing he should try and get some sleep, but he was too nervous to even shut his eyes. He was acutely aware of the stone's absence around his neck. He hadn't parted with it since leaving the Capitol that fateful night and now it felt like a piece of him was missing.

He glanced at the others out of the corner of his eye. He knew they didn't want him to wander off on his own— they still wouldn't trust him until those bombs were planted and detonated, but he managed to use the excuse of needing to relieve himself to slip away. He needed to move, to do something. Anything but continue to lay there, waiting.

Leo didn't wander far, not wanting to get lost. The mosquitoes were just as bad as he remembered. That alone would keep him from staying away for too long. At least back at the camp, the little parasites had Jonathan and Tiachren to choose from besides just him.

"Leo," Anyah's voice sounded softly in his ear, so clear she might have been right beside him. "Everything all right? I saw your tracker move."

He knew she would be awake, diligently watching those monitors. He imagined her sitting in her chair, feet propped up, knees drawn to her chest, a mug in her hands, and smiled. "Yes, just needed to stretch my legs."

"Everything will be fine. Don't worry," she said, as if she could sense how restless he was.

"Is Skye all right?" he asked. Jonathan had kept glancing in the direction of the city and Leo thought he worried for her.

"Yes. I've been checking in on her every now and then."

"Must be lonely, waiting on top of a roof for something to happen."

"You'd think so, but she doesn't seem to mind."

"I should head back to the others," Leo said reluctantly, not wanting the conversation to end. But if he took too long, his excuse would no longer hold up and they might come looking for him.

"All right. Goodnight, Leo."

"Goodnight."

He rejoined the others, sinking down into his bedroll and pulling the blanket completely over himself to discourage the bugs.

For a moment, before Anyah had spoken to him, with the forest stretching out in all directions, he had considered simply running away. Vanishing into the trees and leaving the Resistance behind. It was an irrational thought, there one moment and chased away the next. But then he wouldn't have to place the explosives that would take more than one life.

It would solve one of his problems and create countless others.

There was no place for him to go. Sheboleth seemed strangely dedicated to this course of action and he couldn't expect her to come with him. He would be all on his own.

It was the cowardly thing to do and Leo was sick to death of being a coward.

Anyah's voice had reminded him that the Resistance was tracking his every move. If he ran, he would only prove them right in their minds and they would hunt him down. He would much rather have them as allies than enemies.

The job was almost over. He had a small role in it, but an important one. All he had to do was place the explosives the way Tiachren had shown him and it would all be over. He would finally earn their trust.

His last thoughts, as he drifted off to sleep, were of Skye, perched on her roof.

The next thing he knew, someone was nudging him awake. Leo pushed the blanket back and sat up, momentarily confused as to where he was. The forest was still dark, the sky just beginning to lighten with the first hints of dawn.

Sheboleth stood over him, her eyes luminous. "It's time."

"But it hasn't been forty-eight hours," Leo protested, getting to his feet.

"Change of plans. They're getting ready to leave now."

Adrenaline shot through his veins, quick as lightning, chasing away any lingering effects of sleep. *This is it. It's really happening.*

Skye's voice came over the comm, apparently having been listening in. "Things must have gone better in Elath than expected. Whatever the case, they're heading for the train right now. Get moving."

Leo frowned. How did one fix a shortage of raw materials—and so quickly? That seemed beyond the skill of even an Imperial Inquisitor. His stomach churned to think of what had transpired in the city that night. If the governor had been unable to appease them…he didn't want to think about what might have happened to the man.

"Here." Tiachren handed him the pack of explosives and Leo took it delicately, even though he knew they wouldn't explode until remotely detonated. Probably.

He glanced at the train tracks, hardly visible through the darkness. *Saints*. Before he could allow himself to think and lose his nerve, he darted out from the cover of the trees and into the open, feeling vulnerable and exposed.

Suddenly, he was aware of Sheboleth beside him, matching his stride easily. Her eyes glowed in the darkness, giving off green light.

"You don't have to come," he said, secretly grateful for her presence.

"I know I don't," she retorted, repeating the words she'd spoken the day they'd arrived at the Resistance. "But I'm doing it anyway."

And then the tracks were stretching out before them. Leo knelt beside them and reached into the pack, pulling out the first explosive. Sheboleth leaned close, lending him some light, but it was still nearly too dark to see.

He had gone through the process so many times with Tiachren, he could probably do it with his eyes closed, from touch alone. But his heart hammered in his chest, his hands shaking.

He spaced the bombs out, estimating the distance to the best of his ability. A train whistle sounded in the distance and Leo cursed as his fingers slipped.

"Hurry it up." Tiachren's voice crackled in his ear.

Leo reached back into the satchel, fingers brushing only empty air. All of the explosives were in position, each one blinking a faint red to show that they were armed. Leo snatched the pack up and hurried back for the safety of the trees, Sheboleth following.

Skye had reached the camp in the time it had taken him to place the bombs. She nodded to him before laying down with the others, their stomachs pressed to the ground, presenting as small a target as possible, peering through the trees at the tracks.

Leo joined them, taking deep breaths to try and still his racing heart. He had done it. He had done his part and now was helpless to watch the fruits of his efforts unfold. There would be no stopping it now, even as his chest gave a small twinge of regret that this was how it had to be.

Tiachren gripped a small cylinder, a red button at the top. His thumb hovered over it, ready to press down at precisely the right moment.

How strange it must feel, holding someone's life in your hands, Leo thought and stared at the tracks.

Waiting once more.

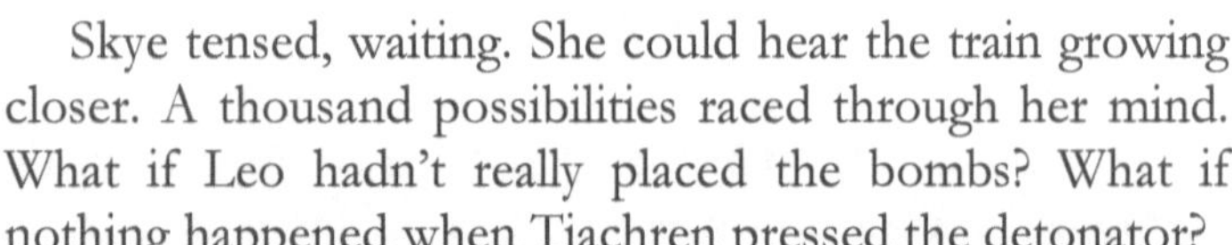

Skye tensed, waiting. She could hear the train growing closer. A thousand possibilities raced through her mind. What if Leo hadn't really placed the bombs? What if nothing happened when Tiachren pressed the detonator?

The one thing she was certain of was that the Inquisitor and Minister both were on board. She had watched them, along with their contingent of guards, step into the train. She had waited until it had begun to pull away before leaping down from the roof and sprinting for the forest, no longer caring who saw her.

Without even realizing it, she'd begun to pick and tear at her nails. Leo watched her silently and she forced her hands apart, clenching them into fists. Let him judge her. What did she care?

She squeezed her eyes shut, only opening them when the rumble of the train grew quite loud, the earth shaking beneath her. Glancing to her right, she could see it, charging in their direction, belching smoke into the air.

It was moving at a decent clip. Tiachren would need to be not only quick, but his timing perfect. Such was the risk of using remotely detonated explosives, instead of ones that would go off when the train rolled over them. But they hadn't wanted to risk blowing up the wrong train.

Skye held her breath as the engine rolled over where the explosives had been placed. Tiachren's thumb jammed down on the button and an orange ball of flame erupted beneath the center of the train. Skye flinched from the heat and the noise, metal screeching as it was torn apart.

Part of the track itself was ripped from the ground. The train cars were lifted off the tracks, the force of the blast rending them apart. Some of them tilted onto their sides, metal grating as they were dragged along to a slow halt. Part of the train combusted into flames, the fire spreading rapidly.

Skye sprang to her feet as Tiachren let out a whoop. They needed to confirm the kills and get out of there as fast as possible. The people in Elath would hear the explosion and come investigate.

"Be careful," Tiachren warned. "It's possible that not all the explosives detonated. There could be a delayed reaction."

His voice sounded distant and Skye realized her ears were ringing slightly. She heard his words but doubted them. Mistakes could always be made, but she knew how meticulous he was with his bombs.

The only sound from the train was the roar of the spreading flames. Skye reached the train first, everything bathed in a furious orange glow. She peered into the open windows and any openings that had been torn through the cars. All the glass had been broken out.

She paused, gaze falling on the lifeless body of the Inquisitor. Their mask was gone, revealing the face of a young woman, eyes sightless and unseeing, half of her face blown off.

The Minister lay only a few feet away, his neck bent at an odd angle, silk clothes torn, skin bloodied, limbs mangled.

Skye stepped back with a grim sense of satisfaction. "They're dead. Torch it."

The train would likely need little help with that, but this would speed things along. Sheboleth sent forth a torrent of flame, consuming the nearest car, the metal warping in the heat.

"Watch out!"

Skye gasped as she was flattened to the ground, someone's weight on top of her, pressing her down. She heard something whizz overhead, the sound of metal striking the side of the train car.

Leo lay on top of her, his body shielding hers. Skye whirled around to see a solitary guard, her uniform singed and torn. She was bloody, but somehow, she had managed to survive the explosion. She must have crawled out of the wreckage on the other side and circled around.

The guard gripped a crossbow in her hands, the fired bolt embedded in the train car above them. Her hands shook as she struggled to reload.

Skye scrambled to her feet, yanking one of her throwing knives from the belt around her thigh, and hurled it at the guard. The blade flew true, glinting in the firelight. It took the guard in the throat, blood blossoming in the air. The crossbow fell from her hands. She sank to her knees, one hand at her neck, but she was already dead when she hit the ground.

Skye stared at her, breathing hard. She hadn't thought. She'd simply thrown, like she'd been trained to. *She could have killed me.* Skye glanced up at the bolt fired from the crossbow. If she'd still been standing, it would have been about level with her heart.

She would *have killed me.*

Leo was still lying on the ground. Skye looked down at him in stunned silence, taking in his messy curls, the streak of dirt on his sleeve from when he'd tackled her.

The man she had accused of being a spy had saved her life.

She let out a breath, stirring the hair that had fallen in her face, as shame surged through her. She shoved it away, offering him a hand.

He grasped it, letting her help him to his feet.

"I suppose you disapprove," she said, nodding toward the guard's corpse. Her voice held a harder edge than she'd intended, but it was too late to take it back.

Something in Leo's expression shuttered and he dropped her hand. "It was self-defense. I know the difference."

He stalked away, leaving Skye standing there, a burning train at her back, feeling like a fool. She walked over to the fallen guard and savagely ripped her blade free.

XXI

The sense of victory that Skye expected to feel at the conclusion of a successful mission was nowhere to be found on the journey back to the ruins, through the rainforest and across the arid Badlands. Leo didn't say a word to her and he didn't acknowledge her presence whenever she glanced at him.

She wasn't used to being wrong or admitting to it, and the feeling made her uncomfortable. Her reaction had been inappropriate and she knew that he'd been disappointed by it. She owed him an apology—never an easy thing—and possibly an explanation as well. She wondered which would prove to be the harder. She looked forward to neither.

Sheboleth caught a large stag before they left the forest and dragged it with her, one of its antlers firmly between her teeth. It would do well for the celebration that would no doubt begin upon their arrival.

Once there, they were greeted by cheers and swarmed with questions. Casks of ale were even dragged out to commemorate the occasion.

Tiachren basked in the attention, perfectly at ease, surrounded on all sides, enthralling his captive audience with recollections of the explosion.

Skye sighed, pushing away her mug of ale. She had never cared for it, not even when celebrating the successful assassination of two important government officials. It was a great victory for the Resistance and yet, she couldn't bring herself to feel happy.

Perhaps because she knew it wouldn't make a difference in the grand scheme of things, though she dared not speak this thought aloud. It would be demoralizing. But she knew it was true.

A new Minister would simply be appointed, another Inquisitor trained, rising through the ranks. What they had done that day wouldn't bring the Empire to its knees, it wouldn't stop innocent people from being killed. Perhaps some of those very innocents would be punished for what they had done.

Still, she imagined that the news of the explosion was on its way to the Capitol that very moment. She consoled herself by imagining the look on the emperor's face when he heard.

She stood from her table. The dining hall was crowded, everyone gathering to enjoy a meal of roast venison, the alcohol flowing freely. Leaving her untouched glass behind, she made for the exit, wanting to feel fresh air on her face. Now was not the time to be underground.

Skye took the crypt entrance, a narrow flight of stairs looping up to the surface where they ended in a hollowed-out stone casket. She pushed the lid aside and stepped out into a small mausoleum set into the ruins.

Dawn had long since arrived and she blinked in the sudden sunlight. It was always hard, down in the caverns, to remember what time it was. The light down there never changed.

Leo sat on a fallen pillar, the slight breeze stirring his curls. Wordlessly, she went over to join him, sitting a few feet away.

"You're missing the feast," she said, when it became clear he wasn't going to break the silence.

"So are you. Worried I might run away?"

"No," Skye answered, her mouth suddenly dry. "Not anymore."

He turned and looked at her then, the silver chain around his neck once more, visible just beneath his collar.

She braced herself, the words tumbling out in somewhat of a rush. "I'm sorry. I was wrong. You're not a spy. No spy would have done what you did."

He waved her words away. "Forget it. I forgive you."

She had treated him badly—tried to kill him, even—and he forgave her, simple as that. She narrowed her eyes at him, wondering how he could be so understanding.

"I wouldn't have forgiven you, if the roles had been reversed."

Leo glanced at her, but said nothing. He pulled the knife from his belt that she had given him and offered it to her, hilt first.

"Keep it. You've proven yourself now; I expect you might need it again." *For future missions.*

His mouth twisted into a grimace. "So long as it doesn't involve killing anyone else."

Skye exhaled heavily. "You're not still hung up about that, are you?"

"I helped blow someone to pieces. No matter what the cause…it doesn't feel right."

Skye had been glad that he'd gone through with it. At least he was no longer in a place to lecture her about morality.

She tugged at a patch of grass. "You said you thought the Resistance could make things better."

"This wasn't what I had in mind."

"Sometimes you have to tear down before you can rebuild."

Leo sighed. "I still don't see what's to be gained by killing a Minister and an Inquisitor."

"They're bad people, Leo. They deserved to die. Even if they're not directly responsible for anyone's death, they're still complacent. They could have stood up to the Empire, but they didn't."

"They would have been killed," Leo said bitterly. "Like my family. That's what happens to those who oppose the Empire."

"Your family?"

"My mother and younger sister. I don't even know if they're still alive, but I doubt it. And it's my fault."

Skye felt a chill spear through her. Most likely, they were already dead. Dead, at the hands of an Imperial Inquisitor, like the one they had blown up. Perhaps even the very same.

But she didn't point that out. It wouldn't make him feel any better.

"It's not your fault," she said instead. "It's the Empire's. If they weren't the way they are, there would be no Resistance. There would be no need."

He picked up a small pebble and tossed it. "Maybe they did deserve to die. But who gets to decide that?"

Skye gave him a hard look, suddenly annoyed again. "Doesn't it make you angry? What the Empire did to your family?"

He turned his dark eyes on her, probing and perceptive. "Is that what happened to yours?" he asked softly.

Skye took a deep, steadying breath. "I've never told anyone about my family, except for the Triad, Tiachren, Fae, and Anyah."

"You don't have to tell me. You don't owe me anything."

"No," she agreed. "But I'm going to tell you, because I want you to understand why I do the things I do." *Why I hate the Empire more than anything.*

He waited. With the sun behind him, his eyes looked black.

She looked away. "I grew up in Shemar, in the soul stone mines. My parents were both workers. It's hard work, long hours, but they give you food and housing, so you don't have to worry about that. The guards can be harsh if you don't meet your quota—or if you're late coming back."

She paused. She could feel the past trying to drag her back, the pain and anger rising with it, and fought to tamp it all down, twisting the handle of one of her knives in her hand. The metal grounded her.

"The guards aren't supposed to bother the workers, but they take liberties anyway. It's mostly the women they're interested in, but no one is safe. Not even the children.

"They took an interest in my mother and my father took exception. He fought back—and he wasn't alone."

Her father had gathered some of the other disgruntled workers and led a rebellion against the mine's overseers. A rebellion that was as short-lived as it was ill-conceived. It could have only ever ended one way.

"The mine's overseers didn't want to lose the workers, but an example had to be made. They put down the rebellion…and made the others watch. There was no one to protect my mother and the other women then."

Skye closed her eyes. "They killed my father and the other rebels, but my mother's death was slower. They took their time and each guard who wanted a turn got one. Her body couldn't take it. She died shortly afterward and she wasn't the only one.

"I was only twelve at the time, so afraid they would turn on me next that I kept out of the way. I never drew attention to myself. I stuck to the shadows, kept my head down. And it worked, for a while. No one ever paid me any mind. Sometimes, it almost felt like I was invisible, that they couldn't see me at all.

"Until one day I was late coming back. They were having us dig deeper to find more stones and I got lost in the tunnels. By the time I found my way out, I knew it was after curfew. I thought maybe no one would notice me in the dark, but one of the guards saw me."

Skye gripped the dagger harder, the metal pressing into the skin of her palm. "I could tell he was drunk. He told me that if I agreed to be a good girl and play along, he wouldn't tell the overseers that I was late. The next thing I knew, he had pushed me to the ground and was on top of me. I knew what came next because I'd seen it."

His drunken fingers had fumbled with his belt, buying her time.

"I don't know if the fact that he was drunk gave me courage or if I just decided I would rather die. But I grabbed the knife at his belt, yanked it from its sheath, and buried it in the side of his neck."

She could see the scene playing in her mind, as vividly as if it had been yesterday, and yet it was the sensations from that night that she remembered the most.

The darkness of the tunnels closing in, frightened that she might never find her way out. That she would die down there, without the sun on her face, her bones discovered by the next unfortunate miner. The reek of alcohol on the guard's breath. The fear coursing through her, so strong she thought it might be the thing to kill her. And then the splatter of warm blood across her face.

"He was my first kill. I knew I had to leave. I was covered in blood and if they found I had killed a guard, no matter the reason, they would kill me, too. So I took the knife with me and fled, running into the forest, until I eventually found the Resistance."

Skye pulled the other blade from her boot, light winking off of it as she held it up. "I still have that knife. I keep it with me to remind me of how far I've come, how far I still have to go, and who I'm fighting for."

She had vowed that night that she would *never* feel that helpless again, and as long as she had a knife at her side, she never would.

She replaced the blade. "Now you know. *That's* why I hate them. They deserve to die, all of them. They deserve to suffer. And that's why I want to know about the soul stones. I want to know what they're for. I want to know why the Empire wants them so badly. But most of all, I want to know what my family suffered for."

Leo watched her, brows drawn. "I'm so sorry."

"I didn't tell you this so you'd feel sorry for me. If we're going to work together as allies, then we need to understand each other."

He nodded slowly. "I think I do, now."

Skye stared out across the ruins. "I suppose I have to believe there's a heaven. I have to believe I'll see my family again, or at the very least, that they're in a better place now where no one can touch them. But I do believe in hell."

A place where evil would be punished and those guilty of it would suffer and keep suffering for what they had done.

She stood, looking down at him, feeling as though she had given him a vulnerable piece of herself, and yet, strangely, she did not wish to take it back.

"I'm sorry about your family. But don't let their sacrifice be for nothing. Make the Empire pay." She turned to head back inside, speaking over her shoulder as she went. "Saints know they deserve it."

XXII

Lydia stood before the emperor, heart in her throat, awaiting his orders. He kept her in suspense, choosing his words with care.

She already knew some of why she'd been summoned, the situation most upsetting. The Minister of Commerce had been killed, along with an Imperial Inquisitor, in a train explosion. Evidence at the scene suggested the act had been deliberate.

Lydia knew this would not reflect well on either her or the Minister of Defense. They were charged with protecting law-abiding citizens and that included the Minister of Commerce. They were supposed to root out Resistance threats, learn of their plans, and put a stop to them before something like that happened. They had succeeded in the past, but not this time.

Lydia could only hope that her criticism of the Minister of Defense, the seeds of doubt that she had so carefully planted, would shield her from the worst of the emperor's wrath. Perhaps most of the blame for this failure would fall on her superior.

Desmond reached down, stroking the head of one of his metallic dogs. "Send word to the Minister of Defense. I wish to speak with him at his earliest convenience."

Lydia let out a breath, but her relief was short-lived.

"You're to accompany him."

She closed her eyes. So punishment was to be meted out on both of them. Her thoughts darted to Fabian. How would this reflect on him? She could not allow him to suffer for this.

Trying to hide her fear, she bowed, and went to carry out the orders.

When Lydia returned with the Minister, Desmond gave neither of them the chance to speak, to offer up explanations. Enough time had been wasted already.

He spoke directly to his Minister. "I confess to being disappointed."

The man had the audacity to look puzzled. "My lord?"

"The attack in Elath is unacceptable. First you fail to bring me a single rebel and now this. The Resistance has attacked and killed two government officials."

"My lord, I—"

"*You* are tasked with eliminating the rebel threat. A single serpent may be harmless enough, but left to its own devices, it will seek out others of its kind. And when they have grown in number, they will strike." Desmond paused. "The Resistance is bad enough, but there was evidence at the scene of the explosion that suggests a dragon was involved."

"A dragon, my lord?"

"There were tracks found near the scene, and the train had been set on fire, burning far more quickly and hotter than it should have. The dragons are yet another threat I have entrusted to you, but the mechs you send out never return."

"Their armor is weakened—"

"Yes. I sent the Minister of Commerce to Elath to address that issue. And he's dead now."

The Minister of Defense had fallen silent, offering no more excuses, as if he could sense the mounting tension in the room.

Desmond savored it. The Minister was an imposing man, having risen through the ranks of the military once, as Lydia had. Medals adorned his jacket. But in this moment, there was little imposing about him. They were both at his mercy—and knew it.

"In light of the loss of the Minister of Commerce," Desmond went on, "I am loath to lose another Minister. But this cannot stand. I must put my faith in someone else."

The Minister's eyes widened and he sank onto one knee. "Your Majesty, please."

Desmond waved the fingers of one hand. His mechanical hounds sprang to their feet and surged forward, swarming over the Minister.

The throne room rang with the man's cries as the beasts tore into him, their iron teeth rending through cloth, skin and even bone. Desmond watched from behind his mask.

Lydia had gone quite pale, one hand instinctively reaching for her sword, but to his approval, she didn't look away either.

He waited until the man fell silent, the last of his screams rebounding around the room, and the dogs returned to his side, before addressing her.

She turned to face him, breathing hard, braced for whatever might come next.

"I find myself short an Inquisitor and two Ministers. While I have no doubt that you would make a fine Inquisitor, you studied under one of the latter. I do believe a promotion is in order. I pray you do not disappoint me as your predecessor did."

The look of surprise on her face was well worth it.

But she bowed to him; there was nothing else she could do. "I shall endeavor to carry out your orders and serve the Empire to the best of my ability."

"I'm pleased to hear it. To that end, we must respond to the Resistance. I want an increase in raids. Track down any rebel spies you can locate and bring them in alive at all costs. I want to know what they know. Send some of your men to the lower districts. See what they're saying about the Resistance and if any of them praise their actions. Round up a few of them and if there are none, bring some in anyway. I want them executed in the town square as a public example."

She nodded to him. "As you wish, my lord. It shall be done."

She walked out of the throne room as quickly as she could without running, no doubt eager to be away from the dogs.

Desmond shifted on his throne. He didn't doubt Lydia's ability. He had sensed the ambition in her, ambition he had once shared.

The voice, which had been a silent presence in the back of his mind, stirred. *"Do you think this wise?"*

"Why wouldn't it be?" Desmond snapped. If there was one thing he despised, it was having his judgment questioned.

He reached into the collar of his robes and withdrew the stone, glaring down at it as though it contained all the answers to his every question. The amber surface of the stone felt warm against his skin and he shivered. He was always cold.

"You want the people to fear you."

"It's the only way to keep them in line."

Few Resistance attacks were so brazen. There was the bombing of one of the upper district mansions, of course, but no government official had been killed. Just a few simpering elites and their servants and the world could always do with fewer of them.

But this…this attack had targeted him, if indirectly. It was an attempt to weaken the government and his leadership—or at least make them appear weak in the eyes of the people.

He did not need some desperate commoners using this as inspiration to mount attacks of their own. So long as they were afraid, they wouldn't dare.

"*That's not as true as you would like to think,*" the voice countered. Desmond wasn't sure if he was merely replying to what he'd last said, or if the voice could read his mind. Sometimes, he could well believe it possible.

"*Fear works, but only to a point. Only until their anger and hope becomes stronger than their fear. You can only push them so far before they decide that the risk of rebellion is better than waiting to die in some other fashion.*"

"Then I ask you this," Desmond ceded. "How far is too far?"

"Your sister has been given a promotion."

The emperor had spoken as soon as Fabian stepped into the room, wasting no time. He shut the door behind him slowly.

They were in the emperor's personal chambers, an opulent platter of food resting on the table. Grapes nearly overflowing their bowl, a bottle of rich wine, waiting to be poured, fresh bread from the ovens, still steaming and smeared with butter, roasted potatoes seasoned with herbs, and chicken, smothered with sauce.

There was more than one person could eat, and Fabian's mouth watered to look at it. Of course, on one of the few instances he had an appetite, he wasn't allowed to touch any of it.

And neither would the emperor. He often had food summoned and proceeded to simply look at it, as he did now, rubbing the fingers of one hand together.

Fabian had never seen the man eat. He supposed that would require taking his mask off, which he never did, until recently. Or maybe he never ate. Perhaps he did not need to, in order to survive. Just another of his odd quirks, like his unusually youthful appearance.

"I thought you should know," the emperor added, breaking Fabian out of his musings.

He approached warily. "Would you like me to play for you, my lord?"

"No need. I only wished to inform you of the new development. She's the Minister of Defense now." Desmond's hand reached up, absently fiddling with the chain around his neck.

Fabian's eyes tracked the movement. He'd never seen the necklace before—the long silver chain and amber gem that dangled over the emperor's chest.

Desmond stroked the gem, mindful of the sharp-looking silver that surrounded it. "I hope she doesn't disappoint me."

Fabian glanced at the food on the table and then to the door. The emperor usually did not address him so directly or even acknowledge his presence. He hated when Desmond seemed to forget he was even there, wondering when he would remember and how violent his reaction would be, as though he blamed Fabian for his lapse.

But this was somehow worse. Fabian wished the emperor would go back to ignoring him, unsure what the man wanted or why he'd been summoned in the first place. Desmond had delivered his news and if he didn't want Fabian to play for him, there was no need for him to stay.

Fabian risked a glance back at the emperor and froze. Desmond had ceased fiddling with the gem and now held it perfectly still in his hand, the stone facing Fabian.

As he watched, its amber surface seemed to *stir*, moving like liquid, eventually parting to reveal an eye. It peered back at him from within the gem, rich amber in color, and unblinking. The pupil, slitted like a cat's, stared, and Fabian had no doubt that it could see him.

He sucked in a sharp breath, thinking at once of the eye downstairs in the throne room. The eye that graced the breastplate of his sister's armor. The eye that he saw everywhere, that symbolized the Empire itself, now stared back at him.

Terror seized him, goosebumps creeping over his arms, muscles frozen in fear. He wanted to move, to look away, but he couldn't.

And then the eye blinked once and vanished as if it had never been there at all. The spell was broken. The unspeakable terror faded and Fabian found he could move again, though the memory was not so easily banished.

Desmond seemed not to have noticed anything amiss. "That was all. You may go."

Fabian had never been more grateful to flee from the emperor in his life. He could still feel the eye's gaze on him, even though he knew that was impossible.

What was that thing? What had he seen?

He raced back to his quarters, wanting to share what he'd seen with Lydia, and discuss her new promotion, but there was no response when he called for her. No doubt she was over at the Ministry building, trying to get things sorted.

Not wanting to be alone with the memory of what he had seen and let his thoughts spiral out of control, Fabian made his way to the archives, eyes adjusting to the darkness as he went.

Zak was in his usual spot, nearly buried beneath the mountain of papers surrounding him. How he found any enjoyment in such an activity, Fabian would never understand.

Zak looked up. "What news? Has the emperor finally cracked?"

No, but I think I might have. Suddenly, the idea of telling anyone what he'd seen seemed absurd. Who would believe him?

But he wasn't crazy. He hadn't imagined it. He knew that what he'd seen was real.

He just didn't have an explanation for it.

"I…saw something odd today. Something I've never seen before. Or, well…I have seen it. You have, too. Probably every day."

"What are you talking about?"

"The Eye of the Empire," Fabian said, taking a seat. "I think I know where it came from."

Zak said nothing, but set aside the document immediately in front of him. Fabian knew he had the scribe's attention.

"The emperor was wearing a necklace when he summoned me. I've never seen it before." Fabian did his best to describe its appearance—ordinary, until it wasn't. "It kind of reminds me of a soul stone. I looked away for a moment and then, when I looked back, there was an eye, peering back at me. The same eye that we see everywhere."

"The All-Seeing Eye of the Empire."

"Yes," Fabian nodded. "Exactly."

"What did the emperor say about it?"

"Nothing. I don't think he even knew that I'd noticed it. I know it sounds crazy, but…"

"Not as crazy as you might think."

In the dim light from the lantern, Fabian could see his friend had paled considerably—no small feat, considering how little sun he got.

Fabian felt his stomach drop. "You've found something, haven't you?"

This was it. The moment had finally come when his friend would tell him that there was nothing to be found on his condition. Or that he'd found a name, an explanation, for what it was and that there was nothing to be done. The end result would be the same either way.

"Yes. I've discovered the identity of the beast King Ulric summoned. I wasn't going to tell you because it sounded ridiculous, but now…"

Fabian stared at the scribe, feeling like he was many floors up, in Desmond's chambers again, staring into that eye.

Zak sighed. "King Ulric summoned a demon and unleashed it against Anarsha's enemies. If one knows anything about the history of Anarsha and its beliefs, then that should tell you how desperate Ulric was."

"A demon?"

"I don't know the details, but such arrangements always come at a cost. Given that Akkadia ultimately defeated Anarsha, and what you've just told me, I think we know what happened to the demon Ulric summoned."

Fabian's heart beat slowly, each thud felt throughout his whole body. "You mean the eye I saw belongs to a demon. The demon summoned by the king of Anarsha and now inside a necklace owned by our emperor."

He knew of the old stories, that Anarshans believed that humans once shared the world with demons. Demons who were eventually banished by heroes—the saints.

But they were just that: stories. Pagan superstition and nothing more. But if Zak was right and Fabian had seen a demon, then they were mere stories no longer.

"I told you," Zak said. "I don't have all the details. I only know what I've read. If you have a better explanation, I'd love to hear it."

Fabian had no explanation at all.

"*That was a thousand years ago!*" he cried.

Zak held up his hands. "It explains what you saw. And that's not the only thing. It also explains why you think the emperor is going mad. Every time he seems to speak to himself, I believe he's really talking to that demon. I think he hears its voice inside his head. Ulric spoke to the demon, too. I know that much from what I've read."

Fabian blinked, looking down at the papers scattered across the table, as he absorbed his friend's words. "*Saints.*"

Zak smirked. "You have no idea."

"Well…what do we do?"

"I'm not sure. Yet. But don't tell anyone else. I doubt they would believe it."

"I'm not sure I do," Fabian shot back, but he knew. In his heart, he knew there was no other explanation for what he'd seen.

"I didn't believe it either, until what you told me just now."

Fabian made to stand. "I need to go."

Despite what Zak said, he needed to tell Lydia. He did not want to face the emperor again and she would know what to do. As dangerous as they thought Desmond to be, he was even more so if a demon was whispering in his ear.

And we thought he was mad. This is worse.

Zak reached across the table, clamping his hand down on Fabian's wrist, his grip surprisingly strong.

"Be careful," the scribe warned. "More careful than you've ever been in your life. The emperor may not be mad, but he's being led by something far worse."

A chill darted down Fabian's spine and he pulled away, racing back up the stairs.

Lydia was seated on the sofa in their quarters, feet tucked up beneath her, enjoying a glass of wine, when Fabian burst in, slamming the door behind him as if Desmond's mechanical hounds were on his heels.

She wasn't sure if the promotion was a blessing or a curse, but it was what it was, and she intended to enjoy it, for however long it lasted. She'd shed her uniform—perhaps for the last time, if she were expected to wear the gray silk of a Minister—and decided to indulge in a rare glass of wine, music playing softly from another room.

Her brother turned to her as she looked up. "I heard about your promotion. The emperor told me."

Lydia made a wry face. "I didn't ask for it, if that's what you think."

In truth, she wasn't sure what she wanted. She had long wished to be in charge, answerable only to the emperor himself, but she also knew the dangers of leadership. She was under no illusion as to what would happen should she fail.

Fabian moved further into the room and sat down on the other end of the sofa. "I need to talk to you."

She quirked one eyebrow.

"Zak found something. Not about me," he hastened to add. "Something worse."

"Worse?"

"Something about the emperor."

"I'm listening," Lydia said warily.

"He's not going mad. When he summoned me to tell me about your promotion, he was wearing a necklace I've never seen before. Almost like a soul stone. I looked away for a moment and when I glanced back, there was an eye staring out of the stone at me. It...terrified me to look at it. I don't think Desmond knew I'd seen it. Or if he did, he gave no sign. I mentioned it to Zak. Going through the old Anarshan records, he's found accounts of the battles between Anarsha and Akkadia—and let's just say it didn't play out the way we've all been led to believe."

"How so?"

"For starters, Akkadia didn't defeat Anarsha at the beginning and it certainly wasn't without resistance. The Anarshans fought beside dragons. That's how they were able to resist the mechs. But over time, Anarsha weakened from lack of food. They were all alone, cut off from former allies. Their army wouldn't be able to withstand another assault, dragons or no."

Lydia eyed Fabian without comment, wondering where all of this was going. But something had disturbed him greatly and so she would hear him out.

"You remember the old stories about what Anarshans believed? About how the world used to be filled with demons, who were banished by the saints?"

"Superstition," Lydia said dismissively. "Nothing more. There's no such thing."

"I thought so, too. But the records Zak read claim that King Ulric, in desperation, summoned a demon to our world. A great beast, who destroyed Akkadia's army. I don't understand it all myself, but somehow, Zak thinks the eye I saw belongs to that demon. It's...contained inside Desmond's necklace somehow. And what's more, Ulric supposedly spoke to the demon he summoned. Zak thinks that's what Desmond is doing whenever he appears to be talking to himself. It sounds insane, but I don't have any other explanation for what I saw."

Lydia frowned, fingering her wine glass. It certainly sounded insane, far-fetched, the ramblings of a madman. The old Anarshan records were hardly reliable. Of course they would paint a different picture of how events had unfolded over a thousand years ago, inventing some elaborate fairytale to make their ultimate defeat seem less humiliating.

Though why, if they hated demons so much, they would claim their king summoned one puzzled her. It was a stain on Ulric's name. Perhaps he hadn't been a very popular king and at the end, facing defeat and being conquered, the people turned on him, blaming him for their trouble. Bringing doom upon them, as surely as if he had summoned one of their greatest enemies.

Still, she knew better than to dismiss it all outright. Even the most fanciful stories often held a glimmer of truth. And while she doubted the accuracy of the Anarshan accounts, she did not doubt Fabian and what he had seen.

She could offer no explanation for the eye he had seen or the terror it had instilled.

Her brother was watching her, waiting to see what she would say.

"Demon or not, this proves what we've long suspected. The emperor is too unstable and his instability is a threat to the entire Empire." She drained the rest of her wine and stood. "I'll see what Zak has to say about it."

Zak clutched the leather satchel tighter to his side, glancing fearfully over his shoulder. He needed to get back to the archives before anyone noticed he was missing or what he had done.

The palace shrank behind him as he descended into the lower districts, feeling far too conspicuous in his scribe's robes. What he was doing was rash and he hadn't given it as much thought as he would have liked, but there was no time. If he'd had time to stop and think about it, he would likely have been paralyzed by fear and in the end, done nothing.

He had to act. He knew the truth, which had quite literally stared Fabian in the face. Every moment was precious. It might already be too late.

There was still much he didn't understand, that the record did not reveal to him. But he knew enough to understand the magnitude of the danger they were in. This could spell the end of the Empire as they knew it. The end of everything.

And to think, we would never have known—no one would have known—if not for Fabian's condition.

His search for a cure had set him down a dark path. Strange, how the events of a thousand years ago could still have such an impact on the present—and the future.

This was far bigger than any of them, and Zak could only hope that if he got the information into the right hands, they would know what to do with it. He could think of no one else who could.

The Resistance needed to know what they were dealing with. If all that he read was true, not only did a demon have a hand in defeating the Empire all those centuries ago, but that demon was still here, threatening the very existence of the Empire and the lives of all who lived in it.

The fight, the endless struggle, was bigger than any rebel could ever have imagined.

And yet they were the only ones who stood a chance at preventing such calamity from coming to pass.

Zak paused beside a rose garden. He was in District VIII, not nearly as far from the palace as he would have liked, but this was where the contact always met him. He'd been here only a handful of other times, and never to report such important information as this.

Each time, he left with his heart in his throat, wondering if he'd been followed. If this would be the last time. If he would return to his rooms to find an Inquisitor waiting for him.

Zak shuddered at the thought. He lifted the top of the satchel and peered at the stacks of papers within. A few of their corners had been bent, in his frenzied haste, as he shoved them in. But they were readable—or at least, the rapid translations he'd dashed off were, summarizing the ancient records as concisely as possible, while also trying his best to convey their importance.

He took a deep breath, inhaling the scent of roses, and tried to appreciate the beauty of the garden. Only the wealthier districts had space for such things, taking pride in how artfully they were arranged, with an eye to color and presentation. This garden held only roses, but they were all different colors, a polychromatic profusion.

He was aware of how exposed he was, standing on the sidewalk, surrounded on both sides of the street by multiple-storied mansions, blocked off by fences.

Each time someone passed, he forced himself not to flinch. If any of them were here to meet with him, they would make that known. A few glanced in his direction, but he must have looked respectable enough. He held their gaze as they passed by, offering a friendly smile. He would not look away or give any indication that he did not belong and so, he hoped, they would not remember him.

In the gathering dusk, lights began to switch on behind windows, the electricity that the upper districts took for granted. Even the street lamps here were electric.

At last, a young man approached, hands casually in his pockets. He was dressed in a common laborer's clothes, his brown hair gathered and tied at the back of his neck. He could have been anyone's servant, off on a task for his master.

He stopped, admiring the roses. The air was thick with their perfume. "Lovely, aren't they?" he remarked. To anyone passing, the comment would seem innocuous enough.

Zak nodded. "They're my favorite flower."

The young man cocked his head to one side. "And why is that?"

"Because they're both beautiful and dangerous."

The ritual finished, the young man's eyes hardened. "You said you had sensitive information?"

Zak quickly handed the satchel over. "It's all in there. Everything they need to know. Please, make sure it reaches them."

The young man flipped the top of the satchel up and peered briefly inside, rifling through the papers. He had no time to read any of them, but he was apparently satisfied with what he saw, shutting the satchel and looping it over one arm.

"Will do." He glanced up at the sky. "Looks like it could rain. I daresay the roses could do with it, but I'd not like to be caught out."

He departed then, as casually as he had arrived. Zak knew a warning when he heard one and hurried back toward the palace.

To his immense relief, no one remarked on his absence as he ducked back through the passages to the archives.

No one tried to speak to him. It appeared he hadn't been missed.

The archives were just as he had left them—quiet and empty. His single lantern still burned on the table. He had placed the other documents back on the shelves, the most important and damning finding their way into the satchel. All that remained was to retrieve his inkwell and clean up from where he had spilled some in his haste.

He reached out, fingers latching around the handle of his lantern.

"I hear you've been busy."

Zak jumped and spun around. There, at the edge of the lantern light's reach, stood Lydia. She was still in her soldier's uniform, despite her promotion. She leaned against one of the shelves, arms crossed, but straightened as he turned.

He let out a breath. "And I hear congratulations are in order. Fabian told me about your promotion."

She waved the compliment away. "I've just seen him. He told me some very interesting things and I came straight here, but you weren't in."

"Stepped out for a moment. I'm afraid I haven't found out any more about his condition. I'm sorry."

"No, but you've uncovered something interesting all the same. What's this I hear about a demon?"

"What did Fabian tell you?"

He listened as she recounted the information her brother had passed on. Zak felt a flicker of irritation that Fabian had told anyone, after the warning Zak had given him. But he supposed he shouldn't have been surprised that he'd told his sister. Lydia was all right, but he wouldn't want it going any further.

"Then you know all of it, more or less," Zak said, when Lydia had finished.

"Who else knows?"

"Only Fabian—and now you."

"Do you believe it?"

"I think the situation is quite serious, regardless."

She nodded thoughtfully. "Mad or not, the emperor is clearly unfit to rule."

Zak swallowed. To say such things was treason and if anyone overheard… But there was no one. They were still alone.

"What do you intend to do about it?"

The emperor had no heirs and wasn't, so far as Zak knew, in poor health, likely to die any day now. Fabian would have said if he was. More likely, Zak's friend would die before the emperor ever did.

The thought brought a wave of sadness and a pang of fresh guilt that he had found nothing in all his searching to help Fabian.

"First, I'd like to see these documents of yours."

Zak tensed, his knuckles pressing against the edge of the table. He could not produce what he no longer possessed. With any amount of luck, the documents were well on their way to the Resistance as they spoke.

"You wouldn't be able to read them," he hedged, knowing Lydia likely was not fluent in ancient Anarshan.

"You can transcribe them, can't you?"

"It may take some time…"

"Fetch them." She nodded toward the shelves. "I can wait."

Disappointment settled over Zak's shoulders like a heavy woolen cloak. She would not be dissuaded. He did not move.

"Fetch the documents, Zak."

"They're not here," he said finally. She would find out the truth soon enough.

"Not here?"

When he did not answer, her expression hardened, her green eyes like cold emeralds. For some reason, he was reminded of an Inquisitor's mask.

Slowly, she took a step toward him, coming more fully into the light. "Where are the documents, Zakarias?"

Zak found himself shaking. He'd never been afraid of Fabian's sister before. There had never been the need. But he was afraid now.

He knew what he risked by refusing to give her what she wanted, but he dared not. Already, she knew too much and he knew Fabian had made a mistake in telling her.

Zak also knew too much.

He gave her a tight smile, conveying without words what they both knew to be true, but would never acknowledge out loud.

So much more was at stake than any one person and she would never understand that.

He said nothing, even as she drew nearer.

No matter what, he would not talk.

XXIII

Lydia stood outside the cell, leaning against one wall, fingers of one hand tapping against her arm as she waited for the Inquisitor to emerge. It was cold in the corridors of Krylok prison, a place she'd rarely had cause to visit in the past.

The cell behind her was quiet now, the sound of snapping bones and cries of pain fading away. The soft murmur of voices was all that could be heard within, too faint to make out the words.

She swallowed down the bile that threatened to rise in her throat and the guilt that said she should at least have the decency to look, to see what her actions had wrought.

But she was a Minister now. She had to put the good of the Empire above her own feelings. What was one scribe compared to that?

Zak had been a friend of hers, of a sort, though they had never been as close as he was to Fabian. Fabian…the friend he had failed. Rather than searching for a cure as he'd promised, he had gotten lost in tales of the past. Lydia tried to take some comfort from that, some sense of justification.

Zak had gone digging where he shouldn't have and that had sealed his fate.

Finally, able to wait no longer, Lydia pushed off from the wall and swung the cell door open. The Inquisitor looked up as she entered, his expression unreadable behind his mask.

Zak was seated at a low, narrow table, shackles around his wrists, chaining him down. One of his hands was a mangled, pulpy mess and Lydia cringed to look at it. The delicate bones had been snapped like twigs. Very likely he would never write again.

When it became clear Lydia had no intention of interfering, the Inquisitor turned back to his work. It had been a few days since she had taken Zak in and he had managed to hold out thus far, showing a surprising resilience to pain for such a fragile scribe.

He had given them only a vague description of the rebel he had met with. It could have fit half the men in the city that were the proper age.

But the Inquisitors had their ways. If this man could be found, they would find him.

Lydia wasn't surprised that Zak had disposed of the documents—she might have done the same, albeit in a different manner. What did surprise her was that he had met with a rebel, which meant it wasn't the first time. Resistance members were naturally suspicious and wouldn't have agreed to meet with him on such short notice unless they had already done so.

A rebel, right under our nose, this whole time. Lydia couldn't help but wonder how many more might be disloyal that she couldn't even begin to guess at.

However justified the interrogation might be, Lydia would not tell Fabian. Better that she should spare him this pain.

"Let's try this again," the Inquisitor said, his voice deceptively at odds with his nature. He stepped forward, lifting one hand to show Zak a photograph. "Is this the man you gave the papers to?"

Lydia glanced at the photograph, of a young man with longer brown hair and green eyes, his jaw dusted with stubble.

Her eyes snapped back to Zak, but she could detect no obvious difference in his expression. But the Inquisitor must have seen something she did not, for he lowered the picture.

"I thought so."

"No," Zak protested, squirming suddenly against his bonds, even though it was much too late. The game was done. "It's not him."

The Inquisitor tilted his head to one side, the way a curious animal might. "It doesn't matter what you say. It was easy enough to rewind our database footage of the last few days. I could see, clear on the screen, where you were and who you met."

Lydia sucked in a breath. The trackers had given them away. It would have been too easy to identify the number of the tracker for the rebel who had met with Zak and put a name and face to the mysterious figure. Now they knew who to look for.

Zak hung his head for a moment and then turned his attention to Lydia. "Please, you have to stop this. You must believe me. The world will suffer if you don't. It won't matter if Fabian finds a cure or not then."

"Why?" Lydia demanded. She could feel the Inquisitor's disapproving eyes on her, but ignored him. "Why would the world suffer?"

"Because the past can hurt you."

She scoffed. "The past only has power over us if we let it."

It was done, finished. Anarsha lay in ruins, the Empire victorious.

Zak shook his head, the look he gave her one of pity, as though she were the one in chains instead of him.

"Why?" he asked, turning to the Inquisitor. "Why bother interrogating me at all if you could so easily find out what you wanted?"

It was Lydia who answered him. "I wanted to see whether you were honest. Or not, as may be the case."

Regardless of his intentions with the papers and his beliefs about what they contained, he was still a rebel and that was enough.

The Inquisitor handed her the photograph. "We're looking for a man named Michael Fitzwilliam. Answers to 'Fitz', apparently."

Lydia nodded, her gaze sliding over the man's features, memorizing them. She would dispatch some of her men to track down the rebel at once.

The Inquisitor gestured toward the captive scribe with one clawed hand and Zak cringed away. "What are we to do with this one?"

Lydia didn't look at him. "He passed sensitive information on to the Resistance. He's a traitor."

The Inquisitor nodded and Lydia left then, leaving him to carry out the sentence. She had a rebel to find.

At least Zak could comfort himself with the knowledge that when the world came to an end, he wouldn't be there to see it.

Tristan glanced up from the message he'd just been handed. It had been dashed off in a hurry, Anyah's spidery writing darting across the page, short and concise. Across the roundtable, Jemma and Rhaven watched him intently.

"What is it?" Jemma asked impatiently. "Repercussions from our attack on Elath?"

"No, nothing so dire," Tristan answered, handing the paper over. "A contact in Elath received word from a contact in the Capitol and passed it on. The contact in the Capitol has received urgent, sensitive information and wishes to pass it on to us as quickly as possible."

Rhaven frowned. "What kind of information?"

"It doesn't say. I can only assume its nature prevents it from being put into writing."

"It must be urgent indeed," Jemma agreed, "if they want us to retrieve it from the Capitol."

"A trap?" Rhaven mused.

It was exhausting, always assuming or wondering if a trap had been laid. But such a suspicious nature was the only reason the Resistance had survived for as long as they had.

"We must be prepared for such a possibility."

"I don't think we have a choice," Jemma said softly. "If this information really is that important, then it must be retrieved."

"And don't forget," Tristan added, "we have a dragon now. That will make getting in and out far easier than it's ever been."

"True," Rhaven said grudgingly.

"Who do we send to retrieve it?"

"The Rat," Jemma said without hesitation. "There's no one better at getting in and out, even if they won't be using the sewers. And if something should go wrong…"

Tristan nodded. "I agree."

"If the dragon goes, it seems a foregone conclusion that Leo will accompany her," Jemma pointed out. "The two of them are inseparable."

"I'd like him to go," Tristan said.

"I'm surprised," Rhaven admitted. "You weren't keen to trust him before. Such a dangerous assignment is asking a lot of a newer recruit, don't you think?"

"Yes, but he proved himself to my satisfaction during the Elath raid. I heard what he did. Besides, he lived his whole life in the Capitol. His knowledge of its layout will be invaluable, and it's possible he may even know this contact they're to meet with."

"I don't know that I like it," Jemma murmured. "But a dragon is one of the more valuable assets we've ever had at our disposal. If the two of them are a package deal, we need to make sure we act accordingly."

Rhaven raised his hands in a resigned manner. "We are in agreement, then?"

"It would appear so," Tristan said. "I will inform them of the developments and have them leave at once."

Once her soldiers were dispatched, Lydia returned to the Ministry building, remaining in the study where she could keep an eye on the screens that displayed the movement of the entire Capitol's population. She quickly located the tracker that belonged to Fitz and waited for word to come that they had brought him in. She could watch his movements, see where it was he went, and knew that it was only a matter of time.

The report came sooner than even she expected and she went downstairs to speak with the returning patrol. "Do you have him?"

Her greatest fear was that even if they had managed to track him down, the rebel might have somehow contrived to pass on the information to someone else, knowing how dangerous it was to hang on to. Then she would have to start the interrogation process all over again and she wasn't looking forward to that.

And then an even worse possibility crossed her mind— that Fitz had managed to swallow one of the poison pills rebel agents were known to carry with them. It was one of the reasons why they had so far failed to take a Resistance member alive.

Dead, he could tell her nothing.

But her fears were misplaced.

"We traced the tracker's signal," the soldier reported, saluting to her. "But it didn't lead us to him."

Lydia's eyes narrowed. "What do you mean?"

"The tracker had been attached to the bottom of someone's boot. They had no idea it was even there. We brought them in for questioning, but they knew nothing about the rebel or any sensitive information."

Lydia could have sworn. They had been outplayed. The rebel they were dealing with was no fool. He knew they would track him and so he must have cut his own tracker out and attached it to someone else, with none of them any the wiser.

He could now be in any part of the city—or beyond— and they had no way of finding him, aside from legwork. Lydia sighed. As the newly appointed Minister of Defense, she had the entire Capitol guard at her disposal and she would need each of them to find Fitz.

She drew in a deep breath. Fine, she could work with this.

"Summon the commanders of each district's guard. I want them posted at each of the ramps connecting the levels. No one gets through without producing identification. I also want guards posted at each of the sewer entrances."

The rats got in and out of the city somehow and she thought that a pretty good guess as to how.

"And one last thing: if you happen to get eyes on the rebel, do not approach. I want him followed, nothing more. I want eyes on him at all times, but you're not to engage. See if he meets with anyone else. If we're lucky, he might lead us to the whole nest of rats."

Their forces would be spread thin, with only a handful of guards at any one location. They could be easily overwhelmed, but Lydia doubted the Resistance would come with any great force. Their greatest strength lay in stealth, but as soon as they overplayed their hand, the guards would close in and the noose would tighten.

Better spread thin but wide.

"Going back to the Capitol. That must be exciting."

Leo looked over at Skye, the dagger he'd just thrown flying wide of its mark. He didn't have her accuracy.

They were once again in the training rooms, continuing their nightly ritual, even though Leo had proven himself on his first mission. He was still nowhere near being confident in a fight and saw no harm in continuing to hone such skills.

And now, there was another mission on his doorstep.

Since returning from Elath, the hostile glares Leo had come to expect had vanished. Suddenly, the others welcomed him as if he were a hero.

Where once there had been glowers, now there were smiles, people congratulating him and slapping him on the shoulder. And all because he had helped blow up two government officials, though he tried not to think about that.

He tried to welcome their praise and simply bask in the fact that he was accepted. It was what he had wanted, after all.

Still, their praise only made him feel worse about what he had done to achieve it. He didn't deserve to be treated like some sort of hero, because he wasn't one. He hadn't done anything to warrant such treatment. Even though he hadn't been the one to detonate the explosives, there was no getting around the fact that he had helped end someone's life.

The explanation Skye had given him certainly helped him understand her motivations. He found it hard to judge her for it, now that he knew the truth. He couldn't imagine what he would have done in her place, if his family had suffered such a fate. Would he have gone down the same path or found a different road?

And Sheboleth…where did she fit into all this? What reason did she have for hating the Empire? He still didn't know.

"Terrifying, more like," Leo said, in reply to Skye's remark.

The idea of returning to the city that had been his home all his life was both thrilling and frightening in equal measure. He'd never expected to go back, much less so soon. When he next stepped within the city walls, he would do so as an enemy. This was no longer home, a place of relative stability, if not complete safety.

It was enemy territory now.

The contact in the Capitol wanted to meet them in District III, outside a warehouse on the far end. Leo knew he should focus on the task at hand, but he couldn't help but wonder if his family would be just down the street, at home, completely ignorant that he was so close.

It was a foolish hope to believe that they were still alive, but one he couldn't let go of, despite the odds.

If they were still there, he had to bring them back with him, to the Resistance, where they could not only be together again, but safe. There was no other option.

He opened his mouth to broach the subject, to inform Skye of his intention, but stopped, losing his nerve. It hardly seemed the right time.

Leo watched as she drew one arm back and then flicked it forward, the motion fluid, the blade soaring through the air to land, blade-first, in the chest of one of the training dummies.

She was dressed entirely in black, as always, but she wore a sleeveless tunic. Despite the chill of the caverns, they often worked up a sweat during their training sessions and he could see the moisture glistening on her muscled biceps.

She gave a satisfied shake of the head, trying to move the hair out of her eyes. As if feeling his gaze on her, Skye turned, her blue eyes meeting his. "What?"

He looked away, suddenly self-conscious. "Nothing."

Skye walked across the floor, retrieving her dagger. Leo watched her go. She brushed her thumb against the edge of the blade as she walked back, testing its sharpness.

"What's your favorite color?" he asked, apropos of nothing.

She looked up sharply. "What?"

He shrugged. "We've spent all this time together and yet I feel like I barely know you." He hesitated. "I want to get to know you."

She let out a chuckle, but he could hear the nerves in it. "What, sharing my darkest secret with you wasn't enough?"

Leo waited, patiently. She would either tell him or she wouldn't.

"There are more important things to know." She raised the dagger in her hand. "Like learning how to stay alive."

"Maybe," Leo acknowledged. "But the little things…they're important, too."

She looked at him for a long heartbeat and for a moment, Leo thought she wouldn't answer.

"Blue," she said finally. "Like the sky."

The sky that you couldn't see from the caverns or the soul stone mines.

She went about re-sheathing her dagger. "What about you?"

He wondered how many blades she had on her person at any given time.

"Green, like the forest."

"You don't get a lot of that in the Capitol."

The only green in the Capitol seemed to be reserved for the upper districts. Before stumbling into the Valderan rainforest, he had never seen so much color in his life.

Leo frowned, his thoughts returning to the city and what awaited him there.

As if sensing his thoughts, Skye turned, dropping into a fighting stance. "Come on. Let's see if you can actually beat me for once."

He smirked, but humored her, grateful for the distraction. He would have to face the Capitol and its memories soon enough.

XXIV

They left in the morning, wanting to give Sheboleth enough time to reach the Capitol by nightfall. The benefits and risks to entering the city after curfew had been hotly debated. Their presence would be remarked upon if they were seen roaming the streets after curfew. If they arranged the meeting during daylight hours, when other people were about, they would seem instantly less suspicious.

But Sheboleth would fly them in and her black scales were infinitely more suited to the darkness. Her large body would be easier to spot than the rest of them and only nightfall offered the protection they needed.

Once again, the dragon allowed herself to be fitted with a comm device so Skye and Leo could communicate with her. Before they left, Skye had handed Leo a small yellow capsule. She had one of her own, tucked into a pocket in her tunic.

"What is it?" Leo had asked.

"Poison," Skye replied grimly. "All agents are given one when entering the Capitol. Kills almost instantly. In case you get caught."

Leo had looked at the pill as if it were a coiled viper that could strike him. He slipped it into his own pocket but had no intention of needing to use it. The thought of having to take his own life in order to avoid suffering at the hands of the Empire was not a pleasant one.

No wonder the Empire never takes any rebels alive.

When it came time to leave, they followed Sheboleth outside and climbed up onto her back. Skye clambered up without hesitation, before Leo could even ask if she were nervous.

To help take off with the added weight, Sheboleth climbed up onto the ruined wall that had once acted as Anarsha's last defense, launching herself off the top, snapping her enormous wings out. Leo's grip on Skye tightened momentarily in fear, but he relaxed as the dragon rose above the trees and her flight leveled off.

He caught a glance at the main tower and thought he saw Anyah's transmission dish within, but couldn't be sure. They would be relying on her to guide them away from enemy patrols and alert them if anything was coming.

Once they reached the Capitol, she would freeze the security cameras, replacing their live feed with a still image that made it look as though nothing was amiss. It wasn't fool-proof and would only work until the Capitol realized something was off. They would need to be quick, get what they came for, and get out.

Unease settled firmly in Leo's stomach at the thought of his plan to try and find his family. They couldn't afford to waste time, and yet his house was just down the street. *So close, yet so far.* He couldn't ignore the opportunity. Not when they were so near.

Somehow, he would just have to convince Skye to go along with it.

Absently, he reached up with one hand, fingers trailing over his collarbone, but the silver chain was gone. He'd once more given the soul stone to Anyah to safeguard until he returned.

The initial thrill of flight quickly wore off, giving way to monotony and discomfort. Flying straight through all day was tiresome and even though he had strapped leather guards to the insides of his calves, Sheboleth's scales still chafed against his legs.

The dragon carried on, seemingly tireless, using the warm air currents to stay aloft, only requiring an occasional beat of her wings to maintain altitude.

The Valderan rainforest spread out below them, the river that cut through glimmering in the sun like a jewel. Leo tried not to think about what it would be like to fall from such a height—or about his arms wrapped around Skye's waist, her body pressed close to his.

He judged they were about halfway—based on the position of the sun—when Anyah contacted them. "I'm seeing a lot of increased patrol activity. They have at least two soldiers positioned at each of the ramps connecting the districts and more at the sewer entrances."

"Do you think they got wise to the plan?" Skye asked, using the comm to speak to the others since the wind would otherwise snatch her voice away.

"Maybe it's just a precaution after what happened in Elath," Leo suggested, but he could hear the doubt in his own voice.

"The meeting shouldn't take long, but we might need a distraction. Something to make sure the patrols stay away from the warehouse and focus their attention elsewhere."

"You have something in mind?" Anyah asked.

"Leave it to me," Sheboleth growled.

As dusk fell, they could see the Capitol from a distance, lit bronze by the setting sun. Its outer wall, surrounding District I, was the largest, each level slightly smaller than the one below it, surrounded by walls all the way to the top.

The city was surrounded on three of its four sides by mountains, a stone bridge extending outward, slowly sloping down the mountainside until it touched the flat ground that led to the Workhouses and forest beyond. Leo had never seen his city from such an angle before and marveled at how fortress-like it was.

Water poured through bars and grilles set into the outer wall, emptying into the River Charnel. It was the only thing that had allowed Leo to escape without fleeing down the bridge, where he certainly would have been seen.

Darkness descended and the lights of the Capitol winked to life, the windows of homes filled with gold. Circling above, they could hear the curfew sirens as the alarm went up, the sound at once so familiar and foreign after being gone so long that the hair on Leo's arms rose.

Slowly, some of the lights went out as people turned in for the night. They couldn't go out and there was no reason not to go to bed. The lower districts, which always had spotty electricity at best, remained mostly shrouded in darkness.

"There's the warehouse," Leo remarked.

They could see the large building at the far end of District III. There were no lights on within, the building cloaked in shadow, a hulking mass.

"They've got guards along the wall," Sheboleth said. "If I'm going over it, we'll need to take one out."

Leo leaned over to look, but could not make out any people along the wall. He would have to take the dragon's word for it.

The fewer people they encountered, the better. There was always the risk that if they were forced to kill any guards, someone would stumble across the corpse and raise the alarm. But they also couldn't risk one of the guards seeing Sheboleth as she swooped over the wall and trying to bring her down with a ballista. Leo could see the massive siege engines stationed at regular intervals along the wall, the metal tips of their huge arrows glinting in the dim light.

"I've got it," Skye said. "Just stay steady."

Taking her hands off of Sheboleth's spines for a moment, she reached behind and shrugged her crossbow off her back.

Sheboleth remained motionless, her wings stretched wide, soaring around the wall. Once she managed to load a bolt, Skye raised the crossbow, aiming at the guard that was just visible, strolling back and forth.

It was a hard shot to make in the dark, let alone from the back of a dragon, no matter how still she may be. If Skye missed, the bolt might alert the guard and then the whole game would be up before it had even begun.

Leo found that he was holding his breath, waiting.

There was a faint whistle as Skye squeezed the trigger and the bolt shot forward, slicing through the air. Leo couldn't hear the impact, but he saw the guard's body flinch as the bolt hit home. He toppled over the side of the wall and vanished from sight.

Skye quickly slung the strap over her shoulder. "Let's go."

Sheboleth angled her wings, swooping downwards. She cleared the wall with only a few feet to spare and then she was diving downward again toward the ground. With a few rapid, powerful beats of her wings, she landed lithely on the cobblestone street beside some of the unlit houses.

Skye and Leo hastily disembarked. The warehouse was barely a block away.

"I'll see about that distraction," Sheboleth said, spreading her wings as soon as they stepped clear. "Say if you need me."

She launched herself into the air, her body blending into the night sky.

Skye wasted no time, taking off down the street and Leo felt a stab of panic. He needed to act now, before it was too late. Before his chance was lost forever.

"Skye, wait," he hissed.

She turned. "What's the matter?"

He hesitated. Would she go with him? Or would she tell him he was being ridiculous and wasting time? Jeopardizing the mission. Some of the emotion, warring within him, must have shown on his face, because her brows drew together in concern.

"I—I used to live in this district. My house is just down the road." He gestured behind him, in the opposite direction from where they needed to go. "My family could be there. I have to know."

"Leo—" She shook her head, but the unspoken words were clear.

They're dead. Don't do this to yourself.

"Please."

"We don't have time."

"*Please*, Skye." He was pleading with her now, but he didn't care, his pride be damned. "If they are there, we have to take them back with us. Don't tell me you wouldn't do the same, if you had the chance. I'll go by myself if I have to."

He watched her wrestle with the decision and hated himself for manipulating her that way. For bringing up the family she couldn't save, knowing what her answer would be. What she would do.

"Damn it," she muttered and then let out a more colorful curse. "All right. We'll take a look. But we can't linger. And if there's no one there, we go straight to the warehouse."

He could have kissed her. "Thank you."

"You can thank me when this is over," she hissed. "Lead the way."

They hurried down the street, moving behind houses that concealed them from view. If Anyah noticed that they were moving the wrong way, she didn't comment.

Instead, she warned them of a passing patrol and they waited, crouching behind a house, barely breathing. They could hear the heavy, metallic tread of one of the mechs and Leo was grateful their sensors couldn't see through walls.

When the patrol had passed, they continued on. Skye moved so quietly, sticking close to him, that a few times he feared he'd lost her, no longer sensing her presence.

At last, he slowed as they reached his former home.

"No lights on," Skye observed.

"Doesn't mean anything," Leo replied, knowing he was trying to convince himself more than her. "They're probably both asleep."

She shot him a doubtful look he chose to ignore.

They would have to step out into the open in order to reach the door and Leo realized he'd given no thought as to how they were going to get in. If his family were home, the door would be locked.

He voiced the thought aloud. "The door might be locked."

"I can pick it."

Leo glanced at her, this girl of many talents, and felt a wave of gratitude that she was with him. Despite his earlier bluster, he would not have been able to do this alone.

They darted out into the open, up the stairs and onto the small step. Leo's heart hammered in his chest, pounding in the side of his neck. What would he do if his family wasn't there? He refused to accept it. It couldn't be true. This couldn't have all been for nothing.

Skye reached out to try the handle and it moved freely beneath her hand. She glanced at him. It wasn't a good sign.

Leo felt sick as he watched her turn the handle and push the door open. Everything seemed to move far too slowly as the door swung wide and they ducked in, shutting it behind them so that nothing would appear suspicious from the street.

He remained rooted where he stood in the small kitchen. Some of the cabinet doors were open, others torn off entirely, the contents dumped onto the floor. One of the cabinets had even been ripped from the wall, lying broken.

Leo had never witnessed a raid, but he knew what one looked like. His throat tightened and he suddenly couldn't breathe.

Something cool brushed against his hand—Skye's fingers trailing over his own as she stepped past him, further into the house. He forced himself to follow into the living room. This room had not escaped notice either, furniture overturned and broken.

The few photographs that his family had owned still hung on the walls, though some had fallen to the floor and those that remained were crooked. Skye studied them, but Leo didn't need to look and couldn't bring himself to.

He couldn't bring himself to move, too afraid of what he might find, too upset at what he'd already seen. His vision seemed to tunnel, blackening at the edges, breath coming in short, shallow gasps.

Skye had disappeared from view, ducking into the other rooms. She came back, crossing the living room and stopped at the foot of the stairs that led to the bedrooms.

"Leo?"

Her voice brought him back from the edge. Moving as if underwater, he crossed to her and saw what she pointed at. A dark stain at the foot of the stairs. Without a light, it was impossible to be certain, but Leo knew.

He slumped against the wall, the only thing that kept him from sinking to the floor. "Oh, saints," he moaned.

It was one thing to suspect his family's likely fate and another to be confronted with the evidence of his actions. He had done this to them, the night he went to the Resistance meeting, as surely as if he had signed the death warrants himself.

Skye hurried up the stairs. He knew he should follow her, but couldn't. He just stared at the stain and its sinister implications.

Did the blood belong to his mother? Or was it Ana's?

Skye returned a moment later. "Nothing. There's no sign of them."

At least there were no bodies. But then, there wouldn't have been.

"I found this in the hall." She handed him a small stuffed lion.

One of its eyes, made of buttons, was gone. That was new, but its body, which had been sewn and repaired countless times, was not.

Unable to afford a new toy, it had been passed on from Leo to Ana. Leo had been sad to relinquish its company, feeling foolish, but missing the comfort it provided all the same.

He took it from her. It felt like he was trying to swallow a stone, too large and jagged, cutting his throat.

"I'm sorry," Skye whispered. "Is there…is there anything you'd like to take with you?"

"No," Leo said harshly, handing the lion back to her. "We need to get to the warehouse."

A wail sounded outside, loud and jarring. It made both of them jump.

Skye's hands moved to the knives at her belt. "What is that?"

"A fire siren," Leo replied numbly. It was eerily similar to the curfew siren, but not quite.

Understanding dawned in Skye's gaze. "Sheboleth's distraction."

"Oh, saints," Leo breathed. "We need to hurry, before she burns the whole city down."

"Would that be such a bad thing?" Skye muttered, on his heels as they darted for the door.

Leo wished, as they ducked outside, that Sheboleth would burn the house down. There was nothing left but loss and painful memories.

I never should have come here, he thought as Skye shut the door firmly behind them.

The warehouse at the end of the road was massive in scale. Skye had to tilt her head back to look up at it. It had fallen into slight disrepair, some of the windows broken or missing entirely.

Her eyes kept darting around, searching for threats and for any sign of their contact. She couldn't see any guards nearby and Anyah hadn't warned them, so she had to assume that they weren't waiting, just around the corner, to rain arrows down upon them.

She glanced at Leo, who hung back slightly. She'd known it was a mistake to take that detour to his house, even as she'd been unable to deny him. The truth, no matter how unexpected, could still cut deeply and she worried for him. His focus needed to be on the mission ahead of them, not the family he left behind, though Skye knew all too well it was an impossible ask.

The warehouse door moved slightly, opening just enough for a figure to step out of the shadows. Skye made to draw one of her daggers, but stopped when she saw the young man wasn't wearing a uniform.

"The rose gardens used to be so beautiful here," he remarked.

To anyone else, it wouldn't have made much sense. If there had ever been flowers growing where the warehouse now stood, they were long gone.

But Skye knew what it meant. Even though she recognized the man now from past Resistance meetings—Fitz—the ritual still had to play out.

"A pity," she said, stepping forward. "I would have liked to see them. They're my favorite flower."

"Mine as well."

"And why is that?"

"Because they're both beautiful and dangerous."

Skye allowed herself to relax a fraction. "You have what we need?"

He held out a leather satchel. "It's all in there. I can't make heads or tails of it myself, but maybe you'll know what it means. The scribe seemed to think—" He broke off suddenly, staring over her shoulder.

Skye turned. Leo had lingered behind her, more hidden in the shadows, but he had stepped forward.

"Leo?" The young man's face split into a grin and he came closer, clapping Leo on the shoulder in a comradely gesture. "It is you! I thought you were dead."

"You made it out," Leo said. His voice sounded numb from shock and he looked terribly pale in the faint moonlight, no doubt still shaken from the discovery they had made in the house.

"Barely. And a good thing, too." He grinned again, looking Leo up and down. "Look at you, going on raids and everything."

Anyah's voice sounded suddenly in Skye's ear. "The signal just cut out on my end. The screen's frozen."

Skye felt a frisson of fear. "Did anyone follow you?" she demanded of Fitz.

He shook his head. "I cut my tracker out so they couldn't follow me."

"Smart." She looped the satchel over her shoulder. "It's been a touching reunion, but we need to go."

Leo turned to his friend. "You should come with us. If they find out what you've done…"

Fitz opened his mouth to say something, probably to offer some excuse, but he never got the chance. Something metallic whizzed through the air and Fitz flinched from the impact. A crossbow bolt protruded from his chest, fired from behind.

"Skye—!" Anyah warned.

More crossbows fired and Skye cursed, ducking down to present a smaller target. It was hard to tell in the dark, but they seemed to be firing from above, concealed behind the warehouse's broken windows, on the second floor.

Leo stared in horror at Fitz, who had slumped motionless to the ground.

"Move!" Skye cried, taking off down the street, in the opposite direction. They had no other choice with the street ending here at the warehouse. There was nowhere else to go.

Her boots pounded on the cobblestones, air rushing past her face. They had to hurry. The guards would alert the others, each one flocking to their location, and soon they would be surrounded.

She heard footsteps behind her and glanced over her shoulder to see Leo following. She slung her crossbow off her back and loaded it in case they needed to shoot their way out.

Skye drew in a breath to call out to Sheboleth on the comm device when she heard a grunt of pain behind her.

She whirled, slowing to a halt. Leo was lying on the cobblestones. One of the guards must have thrown a bola, for it had wrapped around his legs, tripping and pinning him. He reached down, struggling to free himself.

Skye glanced past him. Several guards rapidly approached. She fired at one of them and they dropped like a stone, but the others kept coming.

She cursed, hastening to reload. The tension on the crossbow was strong and it was no easy feat at the best of times, much less now with her hands shaking. Leo was all but thrashing in his desperation to shake off the restraints.

Suddenly, he broke off his frantic scrabbling at the bola and reached for something in his pocket. She knew at once what he was searching for—the poison pill she had given him earlier.

But it was too late. The guards were on him, pinning his arms and hauling him to his feet. Skye raised the crossbow, once more reloaded. If she could take out one of the guards, he might have a chance to escape, but she couldn't risk possibly hitting him instead.

She hesitated, staring down the iron sight. The guards began to retreat, dragging Leo with them.

Skye turned the crossbow slightly so that it pointed at Leo's chest instead. If he couldn't reach the pill she had given him, this was the next best thing. Quick, if not painless, ending it.

He raised his head, his dark eyes meeting hers, pleading, but for what, she wasn't sure. She wavered, her finger stilling on the trigger.

"Go!" he shouted.

Shoot the guard on the right and take the other out with a throwing knife. She could do it, if she acted quickly enough. The idea was tempting.

"What are you waiting for?" Leo cried. "Skye, go!"

She could feel the satchel's weight on her shoulder. No matter what, those documents had to reach the Resistance. That would never happen if she charged headlong into a trap.

Closing her eyes for a brief second, cursing the world in one breath and offering an apology with the next, she turned her back on Leo and ran. This was no longer about her, or him. The mission must be completed.

"Sheboleth! I need you! *Now.*"

"On my way," came the reply.

A siren rang out, deeper and more droning than the fire siren. Skye could hear footsteps racing in her direction and see guards cutting through side streets as they converged on her location. She took one out at a run with her crossbow and then returned it to her back. She reached down to the belts strapped around her thighs, drawing several of her throwing knives, feeling their weight between her fingers.

A dragon automaton rounded the corner, stepping into the middle of the street, and Skye slid to a halt. Her knives were useless against such an opponent.

Several soldiers accompanied it. She spun in place, met with advancing guards in every direction. With one hand, she reached up to the pocket in her tunic, where her own pill waited. She had never expected to actually need it.

How had it all come to this?

A roar rang out and Skye looked up to see Sheboleth swooping down toward her, enormous wings flapping, claws outstretched. A shout went up from the guards behind Skye as the dragon landed, crushing them. Skye broke into a run toward Sheboleth.

"Get down!" the dragon snarled, her green eyes fixed on something past Skye. *The mech.*

Skye dropped into a slide as Sheboleth's jaws parted and a torrent of bright orange flame shot forward, engulfing the mech and its guards. Skye could feel the heat as she slid beneath them, threatening to singe her eyebrows off, the heat stealing the breath from her lungs.

She waited for the flames to cut out before daring to look back. The guards had been reduced to charred remains, the air filled with the scent of smoking meat. It made Skye want to retch.

The mech had melted, its iron armor warping and distorting like candle wax.

"Get on!"

Skye scrambled to her feet and up onto the dragon's back.

"Where's Leo?" Sheboleth demanded.

Skye didn't reply, the words sticking in her throat. How could she explain that she had failed him, leaving him to the mercy of the Empire? If their places had been reversed, would he have shot her, knowing what was at stake?

The fate that awaited?

The answer came swiftly. *No. He would have tried to save me.*

Sheboleth turned to face her when she didn't answer and Skye felt shame wash over her.

"He didn't make it out."

The dragon's eyes darkened. The pupils, already slits, narrowed even further and Skye caught a glimpse of unbridled rage.

If the Empire hadn't already been alerted to their presence, she thought Sheboleth might have flown straight up to District X and torched the palace to the ground.

But they had already lingered too long. Sheboleth climbed up onto the wall separating District III and II, launching herself off the edge and into the air. Her wings snapped downward; Skye could feel the dragon's muscles working beneath the scales.

As they rose higher, Skye could see the furious orange glow that lit the night sky, flames rising from what looked like the fifth level. *Sheboleth's distraction.*

The air stung her eyes. It felt wrong, leaving the Capitol behind, without Leo seated behind her. She felt his absence like a gaping wound.

She squeezed her eyes shut, trying to hold back sudden tears. Why hadn't she just shot him?

Anyah had tried to warn them that they were walking into an ambush, at the last second. Her signal must have returned, but it had come too late.

Anyah. Skye realized that, if the signal had returned, Anyah already likely knew what had happened. She would see Skye's tracker leaving the city behind, while Leo's was taken further in, and draw her own conclusions.

I never should have let him come with me to the warehouse. She had seen how badly shaken Leo was after seeing what remained of his home. She should have told him to wait somewhere out of the way, in the shadows, while the transaction was completed.

I never should have let him go to the house in the first place.

No doubt the Triad would tell her as much when she was forced to give them an explanation. They would reprimand her severely, and rightfully so. Her actions had condemned Leo to death.

When had she become so damned sentimental? Why had she let him convince her?

But she knew the reason. If her family had possibly still been alive, she would have done the same, in a heartbeat. Even if there was only the smallest chance, she would have taken it. She couldn't have walked away and left them without knowing and it was unfair to ask that of him.

Still, she should have asked it of him. She should have refused to help him, even if he thought her cruel and unfeeling. At least then he would have lived, riding along with her now.

No. He would have gone alone, without you. Skye would have liked to believe that there was nothing she could have done. Perhaps, by going with him, her presence had been of some comfort in those brief moments, no matter how small.

But that did nothing to change what happened.

XXV

Skye and Sheboleth were both swarmed upon their return, everyone wanting to know what was so important that they'd had to travel to the Capitol in the middle of the night to retrieve. Skye didn't know. She hadn't looked.

Few of them seemed to realize that only the two of them had returned. Perhaps they thought Leo was simply out checking snares or hunting for something for dinner, never mind if that wasn't what he usually occupied his time with.

His absence did not go unnoticed by Anyah. She had raced out of her war room, her expression grim. She searched Skye's face, looking for answers. Whatever she found there must have been telling enough because she retreated back into her room.

Skye's mission was not yet finished. She took the leather satchel down the corridor leading to the Triad's rooms and handed it over to Tristan. She needed to speak with them. A report would have to be given.

All three of them gathered in the far room to hear her. Her own emotions about the mission had retreated, locked deep down in some distant part of herself and her tone was almost numb as she explained.

"They were ready for us," she finished, thinking back to Anyah's warning about there being more guards than usual. "I don't know how they found out."

It was probably asking too much of coincidence that the patrols had just happened to increase at the same time they were planning a mission. Someone had talked and it wasn't Leo.

"This loss is regrettable," Tristan remarked, voice soft.

It seemed callous, so few words to sum up the loss of one of their own, but the Resistance could ill afford sentimentality. If someone fell behind, no matter the reason, they were left behind. Skye knew this, but it still hurt.

This had been one of the few missions she had been trusted to lead herself, without Jonathan by her side, and she had failed in the most spectacular way. She closed her eyes briefly, wondering what he would say if he were in the room.

Her duty finished, dismissed from the room, she found herself outside of Anyah's war room, staring up at the cloth hanging over the entrance.

Pushing aside the drapes, Skye stepped inside. Anyah sat on the floor, amid blankets and pillows that had been spread out, knees drawn close to her chest. Her hands clutched a blue stone, surrounded by wicked-looking silver wire.

Skye recognized it at once as the stone Leo always wore around his neck. He must have given it to Anyah before they left, for safe keeping. The silver wire had cut Anyah as she gripped it, blood running down her hand.

"It's my fault," she murmured.

"Nonsense," Skye said briskly, going over to join her. "If I had warned you—"

"The network cut out. There's nothing you could have done."

"The Empire must have realized I had frozen their video feed."

"Probably." There was no predicting when the signal might go out. The distance between the ruins of Anarsha and the Capitol was just too great to be foolproof.

Usually, it was fine. Usually, it was no big deal.

This time, someone had died.

Skye's breath caught in her throat. She was already thinking of Leo as though he had passed on from the world, but she didn't know that. It might not have happened yet.

She wondered if he were still alive, already wishing for death's release.

"I should have saved him," she whispered, staring straight ahead at the stone wall. "Or at least—"

Pulled that trigger.

Anyah swallowed. She reached out, taking Skye's hand, placing the blue stone in her palm. "He asked me to look after this for him. I think you should have it."

Skye looked at her. "Why me?"

Her friend said nothing, simply closing Skye's fingers over the stone. It was surprisingly cold to the touch.

Skye squeezed it hard, knowing it wouldn't break. It was made of something stronger than her.

It was agony to hold it in her hand, the only piece of Leo she had left, the only part of his family he'd had left. Now they were both gone. It felt like a punishment. For leaving him there, for failing him twice over. It was a pain Skye welcomed.

"I told him I'd keep him safe," Anyah said, gesturing to the monitors above them.

"Anyah…"

"That's the problem with being stuck in here. I can never do anything that matters!"

"That's not true."

Skye knew Anyah was speaking out of emotion. How hard it must have been, to watch Leo's tracker signal venture deeper into the Capitol, the two of them separated by hundreds of miles, and Anyah, helpless to do anything but watch.

She put an arm around her friend and Anyah rested her head on her shoulder.

"I hope that whatever the information was, it was worth it."

"So do I," Skye replied, but she couldn't see how anything could be *that* important.

The three Resistance leaders poured over the documents that had been smuggled out of the Capitol, reading them by flickering candlelight until Rhaven grew tired of that and demanded the use of electric lamps. The electricity within the caverns was a limited, precious resource, but Tristan acquiesced. They needed to be able to read the documents clearly and make sure they missed nothing.

They read the remainder of the day, arguing and debating what it meant. Jemma, always a skeptic, was reluctant to believe. Rhaven was unsure what to think.

"If I'd known," Jemma growled, "that this is what we were sending our agents to retrieve, I wouldn't have bothered to send them at all. We lost an operative and for what? Some supernatural drivel."

"But what if it is true?" Rhaven argued. "For the sake of argument, if nothing else. What if the emperor is being manipulated by a demon?"

"*That* is not the part that concerns me," Tristan sighed heavily. "I think we have to act as if this is true. If not, no harm done. But if it is, and we fail to act…"

"No harm done?" Jemma scoffed. "We have limited time to act. If it is false, we will have risked all for nothing."

Tristan glared at her. "Risk rather comes with the territory, don't you think?"

"What, then, do you propose we do?"

"We don't have enough evidence to act," Rhaven said quietly. "And until we do, I don't see how we can condone the aggressive action such an undertaking would require."

"I agree," Jemma said, jabbing one finger into the table. "We have more pressing matters to discuss."

Tristan knew without asking what she referred to.

Their location may well be compromised.

As unfortunate as the loss was, it would have been better for everyone involved if Leo had simply been killed. But he'd been taken alive and now their fate rested upon whether or not he would give them up under torture—a hard ask for anyone.

They would have to make the difficult decision about whether to move the Resistance and where they would go. Such a decision would need to be made quickly.

The Empire might already be on its way.

Leo didn't know how long he had been there, whether it had only been a day or an entire week had slipped by. Time passed differently when you couldn't see the sun. Even within the Capitol's smog-filled, soot-stained walls, he could still see the sun, when it wasn't hidden behind the clouds. But not here.

There were no windows at all in Krylok prison. It was the one place he had always feared the most, the one place he had never wanted to end up, the fear behind every raid.

Those that stepped within its walls never came out again. And yet there he was, despite his best efforts, locked in a cell.

The guards that had captured him had wasted no time, dragging him directly to the prison and entering him into the logs. They had stripped him of his clothes, hosing him down with freezing cold water. He had been given a plain prison jumpsuit that reminded him uncomfortably of his old work uniform. They had even shorn off his thick curls, until it seemed that nothing of his old identity remained.

None of it mattered. He had already resigned himself to the fact that he was going to die within those walls. He only wished he hadn't hesitated and had taken the poison pill, as he'd been instructed to do. Then he would have already been dead and the suffering wouldn't have gone on.

As it was, every inch of him ached, the kind of pain that screamed in agonized protest with the slightest movement. Even the shallowest breath was painful. Several of his ribs were broken, he suspected.

They had beaten and kicked him. His face was bruised and swollen; his nose possibly broken as well. It had certainly bled enough. His wrists ached, the shackles chafing the skin, the chains anchored to the ceiling, forcing his arms taut above his head. His feet barely touched the floor and he grimaced, gripping the chains, trying to take some of the weight off.

But he hadn't talked. He had not given them what they wanted.

Leo had vowed, even before the initial beating, that he would not, no matter what they threatened, no matter what they did to him. His body could only stand up to so much before it simply gave out and then it would all be over. He would die, yes, but if he talked, so many more would share his fate.

He thought of Skye and Anyah, Tiachren and Fae. If he betrayed them, the Empire would descend upon the Anarshan ruins without warning or mercy and kill each and every one. At least this way, only one person had to die. This way, his death could still mean something. But if he gave them away, it would mean nothing.

He thought of Skye most of all. Of her favorite color. *Blue, like the sky.* He pictured every blue item he could think of and tried not to think of the sky that he would likely never see again.

Leo raised his head slightly as the cell door clanged open, revealing the blonde woman again. Her hair was cut short and her green eyes gave nothing away. When he'd last seen her, she had been wearing an Eye's uniform. Now that was gone, replaced with gray silk. *Like a Minister.* Behind her, he could see a handful of guards.

An Inquisitor ducked into the cell behind her. For some reason, the mask that hid his features reminded Leo of the lifeless eyes of the mechs.

The blonde woman remained silent, letting the Inquisitor take the lead.

"I trust you've had time to think over your decision."

The time they had given him was just as bad as the pain. He never knew when they would suddenly stop and vanish, leaving him alone again. He never knew when they would return to begin all over again.

And return they would. It was not possible that they would simply forget him.

The anticipation, the promise of more pain to come, was almost worse. A different kind of torment, inflicted on the mind, one that could not be healed or reached.

The Inquisitor studied him. "Very few rebels have ever been taken alive, an opportunity I intend not to squander. We *will* keep you alive, using whatever means necessary, for as long as it takes. But if you tell us what you know, it need not go on."

Leo sneered at them. "I'm not telling you anything."

He hoped he sounded braver than he felt, though he didn't doubt the Inquisitor meant what he said. However this ended, it would not be quick.

The Inquisitor made a small sound between his teeth and motioned with one hand for the guards to enter the cell. It really was becoming cramped inside with so many people and no place to go.

Leo felt a moment of confusion as the guards unlocked his shackles, freeing his arms. The muscles in his back cried out after so long, but his relief was short-lived.

"Hold him," the Inquisitor instructed.

Two of the guards gripped him roughly, forcing him up against the wall. The one on the right grabbed ahold of his wrist, flattening his palm against the wall, fingers splayed.

The Inquisitor wheeled a cart into the cell, surveying the many instruments arrayed there. Leo sucked in a sharp breath, watching over his shoulder. He knew it had been done intentionally. They wanted him to look.

He would not give them the satisfaction of looking away. He watched as the Inquisitor's long fingers hovered over the various implements, finally choosing one with the utmost care.

It was some sort of saw and Leo didn't have to guess what its purpose was.

"Let's try this again, shall we?"

The Inquisitor drew near, bringing the saw toward Leo's splayed hand.

Oh, saints.

He inhaled sharply as the full realization of what was about to happen hit him.

"We'll see if you talk now."

The cool metal of the blade met his flesh.

Leo thrashed and struggled, but the guards held him fast. He didn't care if they saw his fear. He would never talk.

And so he screamed instead.

Skye tried to return to her daily routine, going about mundane tasks that did not require much thought. During the day, she was all right, but as evening approached, she was reminded of Leo's absence even more strongly.

The training room felt empty without him beside her. She had trained alone for a long time, after Jonathan was satisfied that she'd learned the correct technique and form. She preferred being alone, with only the silence and her own thoughts for company, nothing to break her focus.

When had that changed?

Skye squared her shoulders and went through the motions, but she knew it was a doomed venture before she even began. With each passing second, she became more aware of Leo's absence. Her focus was gone, her technique sloppy.

And she had no one to blame for it but herself.

No, she thought, not just herself. The Empire, that had taken yet another thing from her.

White-hot rage speared through her, lightning-quick and shocking in its intensity. It left her skin burning. She yanked her throwing knives from her belt and sent them hurling toward the nearest training dummy, the unfortunate recipient of her fury.

She threw the blades with such force, barely pausing to aim before the next had left her hand. She threw the knives as if the dummy were the source of all her anger, her frustration, her disappointment and bitterness. As if just one more well-placed dagger would bring the Empire to its knees. As if the perfect aim would somehow bring Leo back.

Her fingers found the last blade and sent it hurtling forward with all her strength behind the throw. It went wide, striking the stone wall beside the dummy instead. The blade shattered.

Skye stared at it for a moment, breathing hard, listening to the *tink* of metal shards hit the floor. Suddenly, her vision blurred until she couldn't see the broken blade at all.

Angrily, she brushed the impotent tears away. She wasn't upset about the broken dagger. She could forge another one. But Leo could not be fixed so easily.

She couldn't put his pieces back together once the Empire had finished breaking him.

Taking a shaky breath, Skye crossed the room and knelt, beginning to gather the scattered shards. She tensed at the sound of claws clacking on stone, trying to slow her uneven breathing.

"Thought I might find you here."

Skye sighed, turning to see Sheboleth, the dragon sitting back on her haunches. "What do you want?"

"To see if you were interested in doing something other than feeling sorry for yourself."

Skye glared at her. "You don't think I wish things had turned out differently? But there's nothing I can do about it." *Not now.*

"No," Sheboleth agreed. "There's nothing you can do. Not on your own. But there might be something *we* can do."

She stared at the dragon, hardly daring to believe what she was hearing. "Like what?"

"We left Leo behind—something I intend to remedy."

Slowly, Skye got to her feet. "You don't mean—"

The dragon nodded once, tersely.

"No. You're insane. Krylok is the most secure prison in the entire Empire. Probably even more so than the palace. No one's ever broken out of it."

"I'm not trying to break *out*. I'm trying to break *in*."

She shook her head. "It's too late."

"There may still be time."

"No one who's gone in there has ever come back out. What you're suggesting is impossible."

"For a human, maybe. But not for a dragon."

Skye looked at her, at the steel glinting in her green eyes. To the best of her knowledge, a dragon had never attempted to break into the prison. She took in the sight of her, her long claws, the muscles beneath the scales. Skye thought of the fangs that were currently hidden and the fire she had witnessed in the Capitol.

If anyone could do it, surely a dragon stood the best chance.

She thought of the destruction she had imagined that the two of them could wreak on the Empire and couldn't deny that she was a little bit tempted. Maybe this was the start of that destruction, that could eventually bring the Empire to its knees.

At any rate, she owed it to Leo to at least try, after leaving him behind. She had failed him before, but that need not be the end of it.

And if it truly was too late, she wouldn't say no to a little vengeance.

"Do you think…" a new voice whispered, "that it's possible?"

Skye glanced past Sheboleth as the dragon stepped to the side. Anyah stood there, eyes wide.

"I'm willing, if you are," Sheboleth said.

"But we don't even know if he's still alive," Skye protested, one final attempt to tamp down her foolish hopes and keep them from rising. It would only hurt more in the end.

"I've been watching the screens," Anyah said. "His tracker signal hasn't moved. If he's dead, they would move him out of the prison."

"They won't kill him," Sheboleth said firmly. "Not as long as there's a chance they can get something out of him."

Skye closed her eyes, warring within herself, knowing she had already lost.

Leo had gone to his family's home, despite knowing the danger. Putting his life at risk was nothing when he did it for the ones he cared about because that's who he was. Skye had been wrong not to see it from the very beginning, but she knew it now.

He had saved her life once and he would have come for her, had their positions been reversed. How could she do any less for him?

But they didn't know what level of the prison Leo was being held on, or which cell. Despite Anyah's assurances, the Empire might have managed to break him already. What if he had told them what they wanted to know and they had killed him? What if he were dying at that very moment, while they debated?

Such thoughts whirled around her mind, logic struggling with emotional impulse, each fighting for dominance.

No, she refused to believe it. Leo was stronger than that.

She reached up, her hand over her heart, feeling the cold outline of the stone beneath her tunic.

"All right," she murmured, hardly knowing what she was agreeing to. "I'm in."

If the Triad knew what they were planning, they would forbid it and never allow her to go. But what they didn't know wouldn't hurt them and if she died in the attempt, then so be it. They could hand out whatever punishment they liked once she had returned, safely, with Leo.

"I'm going with you," Anyah insisted.

"No," Skye said gently. "We need you here. Keeping an eye on the guards will be more important in the prison than ever."

Anyah sighed. "All right. I'll do whatever it takes to get him back."

Sheboleth nodded. "Good. Get whatever you need. We're leaving now, if we're to reach the Capitol by dusk tomorrow."

Another visit to the Capitol, so soon. It took a full day of traveling by air to reach the city and Skye knew Sheboleth must be tired after setting off on such a journey only a little less than thirty-six hours ago. But if so, the dragon gave no sign of it.

If they left now, it would take them another full day to reach the Capitol. Skye hoped Leo could hold on that long. With any amount of luck, at the same time the next day, they would be back and Leo would be with them, the mission a success.

Skye's plans for the evening had not consisted of sneaking out of the caverns to embark on what was likely a suicide mission, but she had no arguments.

Every second mattered. They may already be too late.

XXVI

Sheboleth flew faster with only one person to carry, covering the distance in less time. Skye wanted to call out, to tell the dragon to conserve her energy. Once they actually reached the prison and came to the business of breaking in, she would need all her strength, especially if mechs were brought in. The other part of her wanted to shout at Sheboleth to go *faster*.

Exhaustion began to weigh on Skye the longer they traveled, the effects of the past day and night catching up with her. She had been awake for over thirty-six hours straight and it would be even longer before they returned. She hadn't even considered trying to sleep after the first mission, knowing it would be a pointless effort.

The two of them waited on the edge of the forest for night to fully fall, the moon rising in the sky, before they ventured into the Capitol. Waiting, the minutes passing by, made Skye's nerves stand on end, stretched so taut, they might snap.

Leo had been in the prison ever since she had left the Capitol behind. It felt like an eternity, even though she knew it hadn't really been long at all. What could be done to one person in that amount of time?

Skye shuddered to think, checking over her equipment. She had only her knives, both for throwing and her regular daggers; her crossbow on her back and the two smaller hand crossbows at each hip. In her pack, she carried the wand Anyah had given her to check for trackers.

Neither of them thought it likely that the Empire would have given Leo another tracker. No one who went into that prison was intended to come out again and the last thing they would expect was that the Resistance would come for him. It had never been attempted before, to the best of her knowledge, and it wasn't officially being attempted now.

She had gone rogue. Skye wondered if her absence had been noticed yet, and if so, what the Triad must think.

The Resistance leaders would never have approved it. But she and Sheboleth both knew the risks, that either of them might not come back out again. If they failed, they had no one to blame but themselves and no other losses would be suffered.

But if they did somehow succeed, she would have to explain to the Triad what she had done and why. They would not likely be sympathetic. Their anger would be swift, punishment severe.

It doesn't matter. She was doing this for Leo, not herself.

Anyah had reported to them that the increased patrols from twenty-four hours ago were gone. There were still patrols, of course, but that only served to solidify Skye's suspicions that somehow, the Empire had known to expect them.

Well, they don't know to expect us now.

The walls of the Capitol rose beneath them. As Sheboleth stilled, allowing the wind to carry her, Skye leaned forward, pointing out a large, tower-like building in District VIII.

The dragon snorted. "Why would they put a prison in one of the rich districts? I wouldn't think the elite would like that very much."

"They don't," Skye agreed. "But it's one of the more secure levels and Krylok has such a reputation that it's near impossible anyone could break out and cause trouble for them."

If someone were approaching from ground level—as everyone who didn't have a dragon assisting them would—they would have to avoid the guards' detection and make their way up eight different district levels, just to reach the prison.

No one had counted on an assault from the air.

Sheboleth plunged downward toward the prison, Skye's stomach lurching with the sudden movement. She supposed the building was pleasing enough to the eye, from an architectural point of view. The spire was completely circular, all dark stone and metal. There were five stories that Skye could make out, each with an outside balcony and guards strolling along.

They had discussed before leaving, calling upon Skye's limited knowledge of the prison, which level Leo was most likely being held on. Skye had guessed the third level. She knew the ground floor was only the processing area, where new prisoners were registered, their information taken down. There were no cells there.

The highest level would be for the most dangerous criminals or people deemed a threat to the Empire. Leo, as a Resistance member, would be considered a threat, but they only wanted information out of him, not to contain him indefinitely, so it was unlikely he would be there.

Sheboleth angled for the third level of the prison, her massive wings beating as she slowed herself and alighted on the walkway with surprising stealth for a creature her size. Her black scales blended into the building well, but her green eyes stood out starkly.

Skye drew a dagger. The nearest guard had his back to them, in the process of walking back the other way. She stole up behind him and swiftly drew the blade across his throat, slowing his fall so that he didn't strike the metal too loudly.

A large, solid iron door stood to their right. Sheboleth would have to duck in order to enter, but it was wide enough.

Skye knelt, searching the guard for keys to open the door. It wouldn't be left unlocked. "We need to hurry. The other guard will be back around soon."

But her fingers found no key ring at his belt or in his pockets. If the guards didn't have individual keys, which admittedly was a risk, they would have to knock on the door at the end of their shift in order to be relieved.

There was a slot about halfway up the door that could possibly be slid aside from within, allowing the guards on the inside to see who was on the other side. Knocking wouldn't get them to open the door. As soon as they slid the slot aside and saw Skye with a dragon beside her, they would raise the alarm.

She stood. "No good."

Sheboleth's eyes narrowed. "We need to get the door open."

Skye suddenly felt a prick of doubt creep up on her. What were they doing here? How had they thought that they could possibly pull this off? It was impossible. They had flown all the way here and couldn't even get the outer door open!

Sheboleth stepped forward. "Stand back."

Skye had no choice but to move or be shouldered out of the way. "What are you—no, wait!"

Sheboleth reared up on her hind legs, almost doubling her height. Her head nearly touched the top of the walkway above them. She threw her weight forward, slamming her hands against the door.

With a groan of steel, it careened forward, knocked off its hinges. For a split second, Skye caught a glimpse of the startled faces of the guards within, before they were crushed beneath the falling door, the force of the impact reverberating throughout the corridor. The rest of the hallway was empty—but it wouldn't stay that way for long.

Skye whirled on the dragon. "Great! Now the whole prison knows we're here."

"Good," Sheboleth snarled, her eyes flashing. She strode forward, stepping over the door and the bodies beneath, and into the corridor.

Hissing between her teeth, Skye had no choice but to follow, but she drew both of the curved, black daggers at her hips. Their weight in her hands was comforting and she twirled them slightly.

The hallway curved around the bend of the building and opened up into a massive room, still circular. The lighting here was brighter and yet somehow still dim. There would be no hiding in shadows here.

The corridor continued straight, to a room lined with one-way glass, where the warden would stay, if he were on that level. Skye looked around, taking in her surroundings.

The cells were arranged around the central room in a circle, side-by-side, placed in such a way that the prisoners within could not see each other, but each could be observed simultaneously by the warden.

It was deviously clever. Skye exhaled heavily. They had only a matter of moments to locate Leo, if he was even on this level, before they were spotted and the alarm raised.

"Let's move."

Moving fast, but as silently as possible—the only sound Sheboleth's claws clicking on the metal floor—they circled the cells. A brief glance through the iron grille set into the doors revealed the occupant within. Some were empty and could be skipped even more quickly.

"Stop!"

Skye looked up to see a guard advancing toward them, hand on his sword hilt. She drew one of her throwing knives and sent it flying, sinking into the soft side of his neck.

Anyah had assured them that Leo was still being kept in the prison. She could see his tracker signal on one of her screens. But Skye was about to admit defeat. He must not be on this level after all. She had guessed wrong and wasted valuable time.

She reached up, tapping her comm device. "Anyah! Is the signal still there?"

There was a brief, agonizing pause.

Anyah's voice, when she replied, sounded slightly uncertain. "Yes…it's still in the prison, but not in the same spot anymore."

Skye cursed. They had moved him. That didn't bode well. She was certain they must move the corpses of the prisoners after they killed them, transporting them wherever the bodies were disposed of.

Frantically, she moved to the last few cells on that floor, peering in and then quickly hurrying on.

As it was, when she found him, she nearly moved on, barely recognizing him. He lay on his side on a narrow cot, eyes closed, wearing a prison jumpsuit like all the rest, his familiar curls gone, the hair shaved off.

"Saints," she breathed, spinning around. "Sheboleth— the door!"

She didn't have time to try and pick the lock or hunt down the key.

"Leo," she called out, seeing Sheboleth approach out of the corner of her eye.

He did not respond.

"There are guards closing in on your location," Anyah's voice warned.

"How many are we expecting?"

"At least a dozen."

Skye stepped aside as Sheboleth reached the door, gripping it with both hands, her long claws wrapping around the iron bars. She heaved backward with all her strength, the muscles in her forearms rippling.

With a clang, the cell door gave way and Skye silently marveled at the dragon's strength. Sheboleth carelessly tossed the door to the side and turned back to face the corridor.

"Someone will have heard that."

Almost immediately, a shout came from elsewhere on that level.

Skye stepped into the cell and knelt in front of Leo.

"Leo? Can you hear me?"

His eyes flickered open, fixing on her, and she let out a breath. He wasn't dead, but he didn't look far from it. What skin she could see was mottled with bruises and she could see small nicks on his scalp where someone had been careless with a razor.

"Skye?" he whispered, as though he hardly dared to believe it.

"I'm here."

Gently, she reached out, helping him into a sitting position. His face contorted with pain whenever she touched him and she felt a surge of anger.

And then her gaze fell upon his right arm.

Or rather, where it should have been.

Skye felt her stomach spasm. Where his right arm had once been was now a bandaged stump, ending just above the elbow. The sleeve of his jumpsuit had been cut back to accommodate the shorter length. She could see a hint of blood beginning to seep through the bandaging.

She reached up, her fingers hovering just above his cheek, trembling with barely-suppressed rage.

"Who did this to you?"

Leo didn't answer, his gaze glassy, staring past her to the open cell door and the commotion that was taking place beyond.

Skye left his side briefly and peered out. In the hallway, one of the guards raised his crossbow. Skye heard the bolt release, bouncing harmlessly off of Sheboleth's scales, hard as a soul stone.

The dragon lashed out with one hand, her black claws gleaming as they raked down the guard's torso, ripping him open as easily as if he had been made of paper.

Skye watched, momentarily frozen, as Sheboleth sprang forward, a beast of teeth and claws, rage and ruin, slashing and tearing the guards asunder. Her eyes blazed, gore dripping from her jaws, and yet she did not slow. She had absolutely no regard for the lives of the humans before her, killing without hesitation.

It was pure hatred on display.

She remembered what Sheboleth had said about hating the Empire even more than her. In that moment, Skye believed her. Her fingers itched to take up her daggers and join the dragon, inflicting her rage on those who had hurt Leo or stood by and done nothing.

But he needed her more. He would not be able to make it out of the prison without her help, that much was clear from the state of his injuries.

Shaking herself, she ducked back into Leo's cell.

"What's going on?" he rasped.

"Sheboleth's raising hell," she replied and thought she saw the flicker of a smile on his lips.

"Come on," she added, ducking down to slip his one remaining arm around her shoulders. "We're getting out of here."

Bracing against his weight, she helped him to his feet, calling out to Sheboleth, "I've got him!"

"Good," Sheboleth said and sent a column of flame roaring down the corridor at the guards that still stood in their way. Amazingly, none of the walls caught.

The path down the corridor, back to the walkway outside, seemed to take an eternity. The floor was slick, footing treacherous, and Skye tried not to pay any attention to what she stepped on, the coppery tang of blood thick in the air.

She sucked down a deep breath when they stepped outside. Sheboleth knelt down and Skye helped Leo climb up onto the dragon's back, the task all the more difficult with only one arm.

She scrambled up after him, keeping one arm around his waist to prevent him from falling off.

Sheboleth rushed forward, launching herself off the walkway and into the air. The prison and the alarm began to fade behind them, but Skye glanced over her shoulder at the building, her glare baleful.

"We've got him," she told Anyah, then turned back to the dragon. "Sheboleth, burn this place to the ground."

The dragon growled in agreement, hardly needing any encouragement, and swung back to face the prison, and sent forth a torrent of flame, the heat blistering.

It seemed there was no end to the flame she spewed forth, the fury she rent upon the building. Skye didn't know how much it would burn, being made mostly of stone, but she didn't care. Her eyes watered from the heat by the time Sheboleth finally turned away.

Slowly, her adrenaline ebbed, her fury cooling, and the full realization of what they had done set in. She felt like laughing hysterically with relief. They had done the impossible and spat in the eye of the Empire.

Not so all-seeing now, are you?

But she sobered quickly. Leo's wounds were severe and she knew there was even more under the surface, that she could not see. The amputated arm worried her the most. They needed to get him back to the ruins as quickly as possible.

He leaned into her, his head lolling against her shoulder, and for a moment, she thought he had passed out.

But then he spoke, his voice barely audible over the wind rushing past her face, his breath warm against her skin.

"You came."

"Of course," Skye said simply.

Briefly, his eyes flickered up at her. "I didn't talk. I told them nothing."

She realized just how important those words were to him. "I knew you wouldn't."

All that he had endured and still, they hadn't managed to break him. The Resistance was safe.

Somehow, if such a thing were possible, it almost made the wounds worth it. They had done their worst. They had hurt him, but he had won.

XXVII

They stopped briefly once they were safely within the Valderan rainforest, following the River Charnel. Using the wand Anyah had given her, Skye checked for additional trackers, but found none.

The sun had risen and nearly set again by the time the ruins came into view. At some point along the way, Leo had fallen unconscious, slumped against Skye, and her arm ached from struggling to keep him from falling off of Sheboleth's back.

She worried about him constantly, frequently checking to ensure that he was still with them. His severed arm worried her the most; the Empire had obviously tended to it to some degree, not wishing him dead yet, but it was a serious injury. One that could easily be fatal.

She was exhausted, both mentally and physically, by the time they entered the caverns. Anyah waited for them at the entrance, her eyes lighting up upon seeing them, and then her expression dimmed as she took in the extent of Leo's injuries.

Sheboleth laid down and Skye slid to the ground, helping Leo down. She handed him over to Anyah, who supported his weight with the dragon's help.

"Get him to the infirmary," she instructed. "I have to speak to the Triad."

She wanted nothing more than to go with them, to make sure that Leo would pull through and their efforts of the past day hadn't been in vain. But she knew if she didn't speak to the Triad, they would only summon her and she'd have no choice but to go anyway.

Only one of the two guards that always stood watch outside the Triad's quarters was there when she approached. The other must have ventured within to inform them of her return.

Skye took a deep breath and plunged in. Sure enough, the guard was present in the furthest chamber, giving his report. He broke off sharply as she entered, not bothering to announce herself.

She had acted defiantly by breaking into Krylok prison. There was no point in pretending any different.

The guard nodded to the leaders and retreated, leaving Skye facing three stony expressions.

Tristan finally broke the silence. "Your little escapade has been brought to our attention."

"You're very lucky," Jemma said slowly, "that you're not dead."

"You took a grave risk," Rhaven added. The lines in his face seemed deeper than usual, made harsher by the lighting. "And a foolish one. If you had consulted with us—"

"You wouldn't have let me go," Skye interrupted. They all knew that.

"And for good reason!"

"It was the right course of action to take. I couldn't leave him there. The Resistance does not abandon its own."

"That window of opportunity had already closed," Jemma said.

Skye felt her face grow hot, but her expression remained stony, her chin raised high. If they expected an apology, remorse or contrition, she would not give it to them.

"I opened another one."

"You're lucky you're such a valuable asset to what we're trying to accomplish. But the Resistance has no place for loose cannons. We can't have agents running around, doing whatever they feel like and taking all sorts of unnecessary risks."

"I didn't put anyone else at risk. Only Sheboleth and I went. If we were killed in the process, so be it. Only our lives would have been lost, no others."

"Do you think they would have killed you?" Tristan asked, his voice cold. "They didn't kill Leo. They'd have tortured you for information and, yes, then you would have put everyone else at risk."

"It didn't happen. And it never would have. They wouldn't have taken me alive." She'd have swallowed that poison pill before it ever got to that point. "And Sheboleth was with me." The dragon had proven more than equal to the task.

"What if you had been separated?"

Skye wanted to tear at her hair and scream at them that nothing *had* happened. She was tired and irritable, even though she knew the Triad had to put on a good show of chewing her out, expressing their disappointment in order to save face. She'd been up for the past two days straight and wanted only to check in on Leo, her thoughts straying, winding through the caverns, into the infirmary.

Instead, she found herself picking at the nails of her left hand. She knew she should stop, but couldn't.

Arguing with the Triad would get her nowhere. Perhaps she could bring the unpleasant conversation to an end if she stayed silent and appeared at least a little contrite.

Tristan sighed. "What's done is done. Had you failed, this story would have ended quite differently. But I urge you, Skye, with the strongest possible caution, not to tempt the limits of our patience again. Is that clear?"

"Yes, sir."

"You may go."

Not eager to remain, Skye turned and left. Really, they had been overly generous with her. But then again, she had succeeded. If she had failed, as Tristan pointed out, there was nothing the Triad could do that would be worse than what the Empire would inflict.

Still, she would have to tread carefully. One more mistake and they wouldn't be so compassionate.

Skye wanted nothing more than to find her bunk and crawl into it, feeling as though she could sleep for a week, but she had to check on Leo first. Reassure herself that he was all right—or as all right as he could be.

She made her way to the infirmary, to the cots at the back where the more severe injuries were treated. The curtains had been drawn around the bed, creating a separate room and blocking them off from the other patients. Anyah was already there, sitting in a small chair beside the bed and Sheboleth lay on the floor, flicking her tail restlessly.

The partition sheets had been drawn back further than usual to accommodate the dragon.

The nurse must have already come and gone. Leo was lying in the bed, propped up to help ease his breathing. The prison uniform was gone, replaced with a hospital gown. Skye's gaze trailed over the tubes and wires that had been attached to his remaining arm. The stump of his right arm had been properly rebandaged.

His eyes were closed, his skin pale, looking small and vulnerable, but alive. Skye swallowed past the lump in her throat and stepped closer.

"How is he?" she asked softly.

"The nurse gave him something for the pain," Anyah replied. "And to help him sleep. She said, barring infection setting in, that none of his injuries are life-threatening. Rest is what's most important now."

Skye nodded numbly.

Anyah stood. "Here, you can have my seat. I need to get back to the war room anyway." She hesitated. "Did they punish you? The Triad?"

"No," Skye answered, sinking down into the chair. "Not really."

"Well, that's something," Anyah said and stepped out of the room, the curtains swinging back into place behind her.

Skye closed her eyes and waited.

Leo came to slowly, unsure of where he was. When he opened his eyes, the first thing he saw was a stone ceiling, high above his head. He felt cold and every inch of him seemed to hurt.

He glanced to the side. Skye sat curled up in a chair beside him, asleep. He let out a slow breath as the memory began to return to him. He remembered Skye stepping into his cell, listening to the commotion in the corridor outside, and then the sensation of falling. No, not falling. Floating was more accurate.

And with it, another memory resurfaced, one he'd tried to bury in the dark corners of his mind. Leo glanced to his other side and saw all that remained where his right arm had once been.

His breathing quickened, pulse thrumming. Suddenly, he was no longer in the caverns beneath the ruins, but back within the walls of Krylok prison, his own screams ringing in his ears as the blade of the saw bit through bone.

He cried out, locked within the memory, thrashing in his desperation to be free of the pain, the fear.

And then Skye was there, pinning him down. He railed even harder, his desperation lending him strength, but he was no match for her in his weakened state.

He heard her call out to someone but could not make out the words over the sound of the memory. And then a second person appeared over Skye's shoulder—a woman dressed in some kind of white uniform.

Leo shrank back from her, whimpering. He knew what she wanted. She was there to patch him up, put him back together so the Empire could break him again.

And then Sheboleth was there, too, which gave him pause. Why would Sheboleth be with these people if they wanted to hurt him? Sheboleth would never hurt him.

"Leo." For some reason, he could hear her voice just fine, cutting through the clamor. "You're safe now. You're safe."

Safe?

Dimly, he felt something prick his arm. His struggling began to weaken, his eyelids growing heavy. The last thing he saw was the green of Sheboleth's eyes, but he could feel Skye's hand in his own as he sank back into the dark.

When he next came to, he had no recollection of what had come before. He stirred slightly, taking in his limited surroundings. On one side, Sheboleth lay on the ground, her head lowered, eyes closed. On the other—

"You're awake."

Skye sat up in her chair, leaning forward, her blue eyes wide and anxious as she took him in.

"You came," Leo murmured.

It hadn't all been a dream. She and Sheboleth had come, taking him away from that terrible place where he'd expected to die. It wasn't simply some illusion his mind had conjured up. It was real.

She was real.

"Always."

Suddenly, his eyes stung, though whether that was from the pain or some other feeling, he didn't know.

"Of course we did," Sheboleth said, with some of her usual brusqueness, as she sat up. "What, did you think we were going to leave you there?"

Leo exhaled a small laugh, even though it hurt his ribs. "Thank you."

"How do you feel?" Skye asked tentatively.

His tongue felt thick and his head felt like it had been stuffed full of cotton. Every inch of his body ached, but his arm—or what was left of it—hurt the most. It felt *tight* somehow.

He winced. "I've been better."

He had expected to die in that prison, but his friends had come for him and suddenly, that bleak future had been whisked away. It was all too much to take in and then his eyes really did start watering.

Leo chose to blame whatever drugs they had given him. They dulled his senses and addled his wits.

Skye reached over, taking his hand. She held it gently as one would handle a butterfly, afraid of crushing it. The necklace he had given Anyah hung around her neck, the blue stone visible.

She must have caught him staring, because she glanced down at it. "Oh, Anyah gave it to me. You'll be wanting it back now."

She took it off and handed it to him.

Moving stiffly, Leo managed to drape the chain around his own neck, but he didn't bother to hide the stone beneath his clothes.

Its presence comforted him, strangely. It was a remnant of *before*. That much hadn't changed, at least.

Sheboleth's gaze lingered on the stone for a long moment, her expression darkening.

Leo wanted to ask her what was wrong, but he couldn't seem to put the thought together.

Skye gave his hand a squeeze. "You should get some rest."

He doubted he had much choice in the matter. Already, he could feel his eyelids growing heavy again.

Both of them were asleep when he opened his eyes again, disoriented and wondering how much time had passed.

The pain had lessened slightly. Leo shifted positions awkwardly onto his side, which was more comfortable for his ribs. He stared at the curtains that had been drawn around his room, through a drugged haze.

How long had he been in the prison? How much time had passed between leaving there and waking up here?

It was hard to concentrate. His mind felt numb, as if he were not concerned with anything, did not care about a single thing. That was probably for the best. Thinking required effort.

Thinking was painful.

When the voice spoke, he was neither surprised nor confused. He did not sit up and search wildly for who had spoken. None of his companions stirred.

Your family was still alive, Leo.

Likely wishful thinking induced by the pain killers they had given him. He had seen the state of his house for himself.

Still, he found himself mumbling back, "How do you know?"

The guards were bringing your mother in, to use as leverage against you, since you seemed unmoved by pain. They thought perhaps watching pain be inflicted on someone else would change your mind. Lucky you escaped when you did.

Leo's blood ran cold. "What happened to her? After I escaped?"

Do you really wish to know?

"Tell me."

Very well. I'm afraid she was interrogated in your place, but she, of course, knew nothing. There was nothing she could tell them. That did not save her.

"What does that mean?"

She's dead, Leo. I'm sorry.

He was vaguely aware that the words did not have the effect they should have, his numb mind refusing to fully comprehend.

"And Ana?"

But he must have slipped back into unconsciousness, because the voice did not answer.

XXVIII

Recovery was slow. Leo tried to sleep when he could, but soon tired of that, unable to do anything but lay in bed all day, with nothing to occupy his mind.

His broken ribs, he was told, would heal within eight weeks. Otherwise, there was little that could be done for them, other than to manage the pain and avoid anything that might risk further injuring them.

The bruises faded. The stump of his right arm was the worst. It was kept bandaged to reduce swelling and the bandaging needed to be changed every handful of hours, the nurses and doctors stopping by frequently to check on him and monitor healing.

Leo refused to look at it each time, already knowing what he would see. To look at it would be to acknowledge that it was real. It was a piece of him that was gone and would never be normal again.

Working with his hands was the only thing he knew how to do and do well. It was his life. His long, slender fingers were perfectly made for assembling gears and other machinery. Now, everything he had learned from Skye about self-defense and wielding a knife, everything he had done assisting Fae in reassembling the mech, was no longer possible.

But his body did heal, all the same. Slowly, he relied on the pain killers less and less.

Still, Leo worried about the injuries he *couldn't* see. Even though he hadn't been in the prison that long, how would that time affect him?

Skye came to see him each day, wanting to know how he was doing. He forced himself to smile and lie. How could he ever explain to her what they had done? Some of it she already knew, from his physical injuries, but others could not be spoken of. Somehow, to do so would be to make them real.

He also said nothing, to anyone, of the voice that had spoken to him. Leo still wasn't convinced he hadn't imagined it as well, but he knew the voice had spoke the truth. His family was dead. He had seen the proof of that with his own eyes. How could they not be?

And even if they had still been alive when he'd ventured into the Capitol, they were dead now, as surely as the sun had risen that morning. It would be just like the Empire to keep them alive to serve some future purpose only to use them against him.

He didn't like to dwell on the idea, didn't like to think about what he would have done if faced with the scenario the voice had described. Would he have betrayed the Resistance then? Or would he have let his family suffer?

In the caverns, detached from it all, and considering the dilemma logically, Leo knew that spilling his guts in order to spare his family from further pain was pointless. It wouldn't save them, any of them.

He pushed his thoughts away forcefully and regarded Skye, who seemed to spend a great deal of her time by his side. "I never did thank you for what you and Sheboleth did."

She shrugged, trying to make light of it. "Anyone would have done the same."

"No, they wouldn't have."

Her blue eyes flicked up to meet his and for a moment, he caught a glimmer of the same guilt that tortured him, whenever he thought of his family.

"I should have stopped it from happening in the first place."

"You couldn't have known it would happen."

Anyah had felt much the same way. She had nearly broken down crying on one of her visits, apologizing for not warning them in time.

"We're only human," he added.

The corner of Skye's mouth quirked up. "Except Sheboleth."

"Yes." Leo leaned back against the pillows, closing his eyes, and then opening them again as a sudden thought occurred to him. "What was so important that we had to venture into the Capitol in the middle of the night to retrieve? What was written on those papers?"

He thought of Fitz, picturing him in his mind's eye, and the moment the crossbow bolt had struck him, and winced. Thinking of his friend left him feeling hollow. One moment he had been so alive and relieved to see them, the next, lifeless, callously struck down.

He wondered if Fitz would have gone with them, if he'd had the chance.

"I don't know," she admitted. "I never looked and the Triad haven't said anything about it."

"Odd, don't you think? If it was so important?"

Leo had to admit that he felt a bit cheated. He wanted to know what had been so important, what Fitz had been so desperate to give them. He had died to get that information to the Resistance, whatever it was. Leo himself had been captured and tortured and the Resistance leaders remained silent.

"I don't suppose you could find out?" he asked, glancing at Skye hopefully.

She grimaced. "I can try, but I'm not exactly their favorite agent right now."

"I hope they didn't punish you too badly."

"No." She looked away, fixated on her fingers, picking at the nails absentmindedly. "I'll be all right."

"Stop it," Leo said softly, reaching over to grab her hand.

Skye looked down for a moment, at his one remaining hand in hers, and then gently shook him off. She took a deep breath and stood. "I'll mention it to Sheboleth. Maybe she can convince them."

It was as good a plan as any. Sheboleth wasn't beholden to the Triad the way the rest of them were and he didn't think she would back down from anyone.

Ignoring the guards posted outside the Triad's corridor, Sheboleth ducked inside, her claws clicking softly on the stone. Skye and Leo both must have been just as intrigued by the mysterious documents as she was. It didn't seem right to ask them to risk their lives and then not tell anyone what all the fuss was about.

Well, all that secrecy ended now. She was going to get those papers—never mind that she couldn't read. Leo could read them to her.

Sheboleth ducked into the first room on the right and found the one called Tristan sitting at a desk. He was pouring over what looked like a map—not likely to be one of the papers she had come for.

He looked up sharply. "Can I help you?"

She could tell he was annoyed at being interrupted and she didn't think he liked her very much. She was convenient, there was no denying that, but that didn't mean he cared for it. *Well, he's gonna like me a lot less in a second.*

She sat back on her haunches, indicating she didn't intend to leave until she got what she wanted. "I was hoping I could take a look at the papers I helped retrieve from the Capitol."

He frowned. "I'm afraid that won't be possible."

"Why not?"

"They contain sensitive information."

Sheboleth snorted. "We risked our lives to get you those precious papers. The least you could do is tell us what they say, but you haven't even done that."

"They're no concern of yours."

"I'll be the judge of that."

"The three of us have analyzed them extensively and come to the conclusion that they were of little value. Unfortunate, but there you have it."

"So we put ourselves at risk for nothing, then?"

"That's the long and short of it, yes. Our contact within the city wasn't as discerning as we would have liked."

"I still want to see them. Skye and Leo deserve to know what they risked so much for. At least one agent died to get that information here and another was captured and tortured."

"All the more reason to move on. We have more important issues to turn our attention to. Our location may have been compromised and we will likely have to relocate."

"Nothing's been compromised. Leo didn't betray you. He said nothing."

"So he says, but that doesn't make it true."

"He's not lying—" Sheboleth growled.

"I'm not saying he is. He believes what he says, I've no doubt. But he likely doesn't remember what he might have said in the moment, delirious with pain."

"If he says he didn't talk, then he didn't," Sheboleth hissed, leaning closer. "He was willing to die to protect the Resistance and that includes you. The least you could do is let him see what it was he suffered for."

Tristan hesitated, clearly uncomfortable and—she hoped—starting to get the hint that she wasn't taking no for an answer.

She pressed her advantage. "Let me put it this way, if it makes it easier for you to understand. Either you give me those papers or I walk. You can do this whole revolution thing without me, I don't much care. And, while I'm going, I think I'll tell everyone that there was nothing for us to retrieve in the Capitol. That you sent us there on a fool's errand and set us up."

He licked his lips nervously. "You're bluffing."

She bared her teeth. "Try me."

The two of them glared at each other for a long, breathless moment. Then Tristan let out a sigh and reached into a drawer in his desk. He pulled out a stack of papers, bound together by a piece of twine, and dumped them unceremoniously on his desk.

"There. Maybe you can make some sense of them."

She reached out, wrapping her claws around the pile of documents, and made to walk away before he could change his mind. He wouldn't forgive her for this, adding yet another strike against her no doubt, since she had been the one that enabled Skye to carry out the unsanctioned prison break.

But she paused in the doorway and turned back to say, "I meant what I said about Leo telling the truth. If the

Empire knew where you were, they would have been here by now."

Sheboleth turned and left him then. Just as she reached the main entrance to the corridor, concealed by its purple tapestries, the twine around the papers loosened, some of the parchment slipping from her grasp.

She let out a growl as the papers fluttered to the floor and turned to pick them up, freezing as her gaze landed on the text written there.

She could not read Akkadian, the common tongue that all humans were now united by, but she could read ancient Anarshan and recognized the runes staring back up at her. *Even after all these years...*

The words scrawled across the parchment made her blood freeze. Little wonder Tristan had deemed them to have no value. And yet, these documents were more important than he could have ever imagined.

She shut her eyes briefly, debating what to do. Here was the proof she had waited so long for. She needed to tell Leo, but in his current state, still weakened and recovering, the last thing he needed was for her to dump this on him, even though she knew that was precisely what she should do.

She should push aside her own feelings, her concern for him, and do what must be done, while there was still a chance. None of them knew how much time they had left. Even now, it could be too late.

But no. Even as the thought crossed her mind, she already knew what her answer would be. She would not tell Leo. Not yet. Not with the horrors of Krylok so fresh.

Silently, she gathered up the fallen papers and took them to Leo's old room, stuffing them beneath the mattress. They had waited this long. They could wait a little while longer.

She hoped she was right, that she wasn't making the biggest mistake of her life. Even so, she knew she could only buy Leo, and all the rest of them, so much time.

There the papers remained for two long weeks, until Leo was allowed to leave the infirmary. His hair had started to grow back ever so slightly. The stump of his arm was still bandaged, more, she thought, to conceal it and help prevent irritation.

He and Skye were in the war room with Anyah when she finally fetched the papers, heart heavy in her chest. Would they believe what she was about to reveal to them? What would their reaction be? She had no idea how one was expected to react to the possible ending of the world.

At least the war room would provide a little privacy, where they could pour over the documents together without being interrupted.

Anyah looked up as Sheboleth ducked inside, her eyes going at once to the documents in her hand. "What's that?"

"The papers."

Skye's eyes narrowed. "I thought you weren't able to get them."

Sheboleth hadn't lied—she despised liars more than just about anything—but she had said nothing more about the papers and avoided Skye's questions when she'd asked, letting her think her attempt had been unsuccessful.

She avoided Skye's remark now, saying only, "Tristan wasn't thrilled about the idea of letting me see these."

She set the papers down in the middle of the floor, where they could be easily reached by all three of them, and settled down, waiting as they poured over the documents.

There were translations provided, as she'd suspected, written out in Akkadian. Sometimes they paused to compare notes and debate among themselves what it must mean. She forced herself to remain silent, even though every instinct screamed at her to jump in and explain, to make them understand that they all faced a greater threat than they could have fathomed.

Whatever Leo read, it must have disturbed him, for he had gone quite pale. His dark eyes stared down at the paper as if horrified, but transfixed, unable to look away.

At last, Anyah looked up. "I don't…understand."

Skye set down the sheet in her hand. "What is this?"

"What do you think it is?" Sheboleth asked.

"It seems to be some sort of transcribed record of King Ulric's ramblings. I can see why the Triad didn't say anything about it."

"It says King Ulric summoned some sort of beast and used it to defeat Akkadia…at least initially," Anyah added. "It says he bound the beast in a spirit shard." She stopped abruptly and looked up at Sheboleth again. "What's a spirit shard?"

Sheboleth sighed wearily. "He meant a soul stone."

Skye looked up at her sharply. "A soul stone?"

"I'll explain in a minute. Keep going, Anyah."

She continued, "'I have bound the creature in a spirit shard. I pray that my son will destroy the shard one day, when the creature's assistance is no longer needed. I know I should have done it myself, but, while I fear to keep it, I fear to be without its guidance more.'"

"Its guidance?" Skye repeated. "What does that mean?"

"I think I know," Leo muttered. He had thus far been silent, still pale as a sheet. "These transcriptions weren't written by King Ulric. They're signed by a scribe named Zak, who must have compiled all of this for us."

"What does Zak have to say?" Anyah asked.

"He…makes some rather bold claims, saying that the emperor is consorting with demons and that the beast mentioned in the original documents is the same demon.

He claims that Desmond keeps the demon locked in an amulet around his neck, an amber stone, and that he speaks with it. It speaks to him, offering counsel and guidance, while manipulating him."

"*What?*" Skye exclaimed.

"There's more," Leo said heavily. "Zak attached another page written by the king that expands on what Anyah was reading earlier. He and his advisors somehow bound this beast into a stone of some kind in order to contain him, where he is bound to remain for a thousand years. 'If the thousand years should come to pass and the stone has not been destroyed, the beast will be released from his prison, free to wreak his vengeance upon the world.'"

For a long moment, the four of them sat there silently, absorbing what they had learned.

"So," Skye said at last. "This scribe alleges that the same demon that King Ulric bound is the very one that the current emperor has."

Anyah nodded. "Perhaps the emperor at the time took it when Akkadia conquered Anarsha."

"This can't be true!" Skye exclaimed, throwing her paper down in disgust. "I mean, it's absurd!"

"It's true," Sheboleth said darkly. "Every word."

The three of them turned to look at her.

"I know because I was there."

"You—" She wouldn't have thought it possible but Leo paled even further.

"I was there when Anarsha fell."

"But that would make you over a thousand years old!" Leo cried.

"Yes," Sheboleth said simply. "Dragons and Anarshans fought side by side against the threat of the Empire, but in the end, it wasn't enough. Our forces weakened and their war machines only grew. In desperation, King Ulric turned to a higher power and committed one of the gravest sins of all—he summoned a demon back into the world."

"Back?" Skye asked, at the same time Anyah sputtered, "Demon?"

"The Anarshans believed that this world was once filled with demons, until they were banished by heroes, revered for their bravery and sacrifice."

"The saints," Leo whispered.

Sheboleth nodded. "Whether the stories are true or not, I can't say. It was before my time and both demons and saints had departed from the world by the time Akkadia came marching. But the demon Ulric summoned was real enough, so that leads me to believe at least some of it is true."

"You saw the demon?" Leo asked.

"I saw the demon. I watched him lay waste to Akkadia's armies." She shook her head. "The folly of man, they called it. Ulric sought a power he could not control and we all may yet pay for his mistake."

"What do you mean?" Skye asked.

"In order to strike such a bargain, Ulric would have had to offer the demon something in return. What that was, I can't say. But at some point, Ulric seemed to grow frightened of the thing he had summoned. Once Akkadia's armies were decimated, the terms of the bargain were fulfilled. But though he feared it, Ulric was unwilling to part with having such a creature at his beck and call. So he sealed it in a soul stone. *That* is a soul stone's true purpose: containment."

"Then why does the Empire put them in the automatons?" Skye demanded.

"I'll get to that," Sheboleth promised. "Being sealed in a soul stone was not something the demon intended. Ulric may claim he intended to destroy the stone, but he didn't. The stone was never destroyed. And with each day that passes, we grow closer to the demon inside breaking free. Soul stones don't contain their hosts indefinitely. A thousand years is a long time, but it's not forever."

"So," Anyah said slowly, "if the stone isn't destroyed, the demon inside will break free after a thousand years?"

"Exactly. That's how the saints banished the demons all those years ago. They sealed them inside soul stones and then destroyed them."

"How do you destroy a soul stone?" Skye asked, leaning forward. "They're indestructible. Nothing seems to damage them."

"There's only one way—dragonfire."

"You still haven't explained what the Empire uses them for."

Sheboleth sighed. "The Empire doesn't use them, not really. The demon does. They are how he sees his kingdom, how he knows what's going on. He sees what those mechs see. He controls them. They were once controlled by human pilots, remember? All that changed when Akkadia conquered Anarsha and discovered the soul stone. Then they had the amulet. Then, they had the demon to control the mechs."

"How is that possible?"

"All soul stones—and spirit shards—share a connection. That's how Reaper is able to control the mechs. Without a stone in their chest, they're just lifeless hunks of metal."

"Reaper?" Leo repeated.

Sheboleth grimaced. "The beast. Whatever his real name is, I don't know, if he even has one. Reaper will suffice. It's what he did—and will do again, if given the chance."

Skye held up both hands. "You're saying that the mechs are controlled by a *demon*?"

"Yes. That's why the emperor sends them to hunt down dragons. He doesn't really want us dead. To him, we're not much of a threat. It's Reaper that wants us dead and he's convinced Desmond that the dragons are a threat so he'll try to exterminate us."

"But *why*?"

"So there will be no one to stop him from breaking free! If there are no dragons, the soul stone cannot be destroyed and all he has to do is wait, his freedom assured."

They stared at her in a mixture of disbelief and horror.

"Reaper has been hiding in plain sight, protected by his proximity to the emperor. All he has to do is bide his time until he is set free."

"And if that happens…?" Anyah trailed off, the rest of her question hanging in the air.

"The world will end," Sheboleth said. "Reaper is a demon. He cares for nothing but destruction. The moment he is freed from his prison, he will wreak vengeance upon the world for being sealed away in the first place."

"So how do we stop it?" Skye demanded.

Sheboleth felt a flicker of warmth toward the young woman. There was a steeliness to her blue eyes, a refusal to back down or give in, even facing such odds or an enemy that had single-handedly wiped out Akkadia's armies.

"There are only two ways," she replied gravely. "The first is to destroy the amulet before the thousandth year comes to pass. This should have been done centuries ago, but no one knew what had become of the amulet after Anarsha fell. I had my suspicions, but nothing actionable. No proof. Until now." She looked down at the papers the scribe had provided. "Now we know the amulet is in the emperor's possession."

"So that's why the scribe felt he had to get these documents to us," Anyah said quietly. She had wrapped her arms around her knees. "If Reaper returns, the world comes to an end. Kind of makes the Empire seem small in comparison, doesn't it?"

"The Empire isn't the real enemy," Sheboleth agreed. "Even the strongest empire can be made to fall. But Reaper is an enemy you cannot kill. You can't harm him. Your only hope is to seal him away. He is the true leader of the Empire. Desmond is merely a puppet. But we have to act soon. I don't know how long it's been, exactly, since Ulric sealed Reaper in the soul stone. I don't know how long we have until the thousandth year, but I do know we have less time with every passing moment. We must destroy that amulet."

"But how?" Skye asked. "The emperor has it and we can't just walk into the Capitol and take it from him."

"No," Sheboleth agreed. "Such an endeavor would require careful planning and that takes time."

"Time we don't have," Skye said flatly.

"I don't like it anymore than you do. In fact, I hate it. But better that than rushing in blindly and destroying any chance we do have."

"What's the second way?" Leo asked suddenly.

The two women turned to him.

"You said there were two ways to stop Reaper," he added, addressing Sheboleth. "What's the second?"

She met his gaze evenly. This was the moment she dreaded, more than any other. But she would not lie to him. She would not turn away.

"If we fail to destroy the amulet and Reaper returns, there is still one option. He could be sealed away again, in another soul stone, and then that stone would be destroyed."

"Hardly ideal," Anyah remarked, "but it should be easy enough to get another soul stone."

Sheboleth shook her head. "Not as easy as you'd think."

"What do you mean? There's one in every mech."

"Not exactly. The stones that are mined in Shemar, that are placed in the mechs—it would be more accurate to call them spirit shards. They are similar to soul stones, and share the same connection that allows Reaper to manipulate the automata. But you can't seal anything in them. They can't hold a bound spirit. It says here," Sheboleth gestured to the papers with one claw, "that the emperor's stone is amber. Have you ever seen an amber soul stone?"

"Of course not," Skye said. "They're red, not amber."

The dragon nodded. "Soul stones—true soul stones— only turn amber when they have something bound inside of them."

"All right," Skye said, in a business-like tone. "If we can't bind Reaper to one of the red stones, and soul stones only turn amber after something has been sealed inside, what kind of stone do we need? What color was the amber stone before it was used?"

Sheboleth paused, looking at them each in turn, her gaze lingering the longest on Leo. "Blue."

PART IV:

THE

REAPER

XXIX

Leo made his way outside after leaving the war room. None of the others moved to stop him. He walked through the cavern tunnels, past the portcullis, and emerged into the sunlight, blinking. It never failed to surprise him just how bright the world outside was, after spending days or weeks in the dark.

He stepped over to one of the fallen pillars of stone and sat down with a sigh, letting the breeze brush through the hair that had barely begun to grow out.

Reaching down, he slowly unwound the bandaging around the stump of his arm. The nurses had said that sunlight would be good for him, aiding in the healing process, though it didn't seem that there was much more healing to do.

Leo forced himself to look at what remained of his right arm, knowing it was foolish to pretend any differently. It had healed well, the skin stretched over the severed bone, smoothed out.

The tattoos that had marred him from the day he was born were gone. District III was no longer his home, only a distant memory. The Empire no longer owned him.

It still ached, a cramping sensation that he doubted would ever fully go away. It kept him awake at night sometimes, but that was as much a blessing as a curse.

He was more worried about the injuries he *couldn't* see. He had wondered, when he'd first been brought back to the caverns, how his time spent in the prison would affect him. He hadn't been there that long, but he knew that the wounds weren't the only marks left on him.

That question had since been answered. Once he was discharged from the infirmary, he found his sleep no longer deep and undisturbed, but filled with terror and pain. He relived the interrogations, both real and imagined, and feared closing his eyes at the end of the day.

And now the end of the world. A demon's return. And the only soul stone capable of banishing him again hung around Leo's neck.

The stone felt twice as heavy, freezing cold against his skin.

He didn't doubt what Sheboleth said. Leo gazed at the ruins of the great wall around him. She had been there when Anarsha fell. She had seen this once-great kingdom in all its glory. Before the fall.

Leo sighed again and tipped his head back, letting the sun bathe his skin. He heard her approach but did not open his eyes, wondering how long he had been out there. It felt like hours, but might have been only moments.

At last, he opened his eyes. Sheboleth sat a few feet away, the sunlight glistening on her black scales.

"You knew," he said softly. "You knew of Reaper's existence and his possible return all this time. When, exactly, were you planning on telling us?" *When were you going to tell me?*

She regarded him levelly. "Ideally, never. If we could get to the other amulet and destroy it in time, there would never be a need for any of you to know. But I worry that's not possible."

"How is it that I happen to have one of the few true soul stones in existence in my possession?"

"I don't know. How did you come by it?"

Leo frowned. "It's a family heirloom."

Sheboleth shrugged. "It doesn't really matter where it came from, where it's been all these centuries, or how it was passed down until it came to you. All that matters is that you have it now. And a good thing, too."

He reached up, slipping the chain over his head, holding the stone in his hand, feeling its weight and chill.

"At least this explains why you decided to stay, after everything," he muttered. "I'm not a fool, Sheboleth. I know you saw this stone the day you rescued me from that patrol. That's why you agreed to help me. That's why you stayed, even after we reached the Resistance. You recognized it for what it was. It wasn't me you were staying for, it was the stone."

"That may be how it started," she acknowledged. "But it didn't stay that way."

He looked up at her.

"I didn't break into the most secure prison in the entire Empire for that stone, Leo. It could have remained back here, safely out of the Empire's reach. I came for *you*."

He felt his face heat slightly in shame, unable to deny the truth of her words. "I know."

Her tail flicked briefly. "It pains me to admit this, but I like you."

"Thanks," he said, somewhat wryly.

"Don't let it go to your head." Sheboleth let out a deep breath. "After Anarsha… I spent so long away from humans. Their folly nearly cost us everything and could still cost us a great deal more. And yet…I wanted to believe that there was at least one good person left in the world. When I met you…I hoped it would be you."

Leo swallowed, surprised by her faith in him and a little uncomfortable. "And am I?" It was no small expectation to live up to.

"I think so. You remind me of someone I knew once. A long time ago. Chandra. I think that's the first time I've said her name in nearly a thousand years."

"That's how you knew so much about humans, isn't it? Not spying on the Workhouses, but because of Anarsha."

"Well, it's because of both. But yes, most of what I know of humans came from her."

Leo didn't bother asking what became of Chandra. Whether she survived Anarsha's fall or not, she would be long dead by now. And still Sheboleth lived on. She had witnessed the day Anarsha fell and had been yearning to see the Empire join it ever since.

His throat suddenly felt tight as he considered what a lonely existence such a long life must be.

He closed his fingers over the stone, careful not to cut himself on the silver wire. "So, now that we know what we're up against, what do we do?"

"We'll have to tell the Triad, formulate some sort of plan. Hope they listen. I wish I could offer you something more, but I've never lied to you and I'm not about to start now."

"It's all right," Leo murmured, even though it felt anything but. "There's something else I wanted to ask you…" He hesitated, unsure if he really wanted to know the answer, but he also knew that it would drive him mad until he knew for certain. "In those documents, the scribe said that Reaper speaks to the emperor, that he gives him guidance and counsel. Do you think that's true?"

"I don't doubt it. Or rather, he gives the emperor what Desmond *believes* to be wisdom and guidance. Why do you ask?"

Leo thought of the day he'd heard the voice speak to him, shortly after he'd been rescued. It had been easy at the time to blame it all on the pain killers he'd been given, but now…after reading those papers, he wasn't so sure.

His whole world had been turned upside down in such a short amount of time. Sheboleth had said that all soul stones—and even spirit shards—shared a connection of sorts. And Leo had one hanging around his neck.

Sheboleth fixed him with a hard look when he didn't initially respond. "Leo?"

It was on the tip of his tongue to brush it off and chalk it all up to mere curiosity, but he didn't think she would believe him.

And she was right. She'd never lied to him, even when it would have been the easier path to take. He wouldn't lie to her either.

She'll think you're crazy.

And that's precisely why I have to tell her.

"This…might sound insane, but…I've been hearing voices. Or a voice, I don't really know. I didn't notice it until recently. I thought it was just my own thoughts, and maybe it was, I don't know." This was going terribly. "The only time I *know* it was a voice and not my own thoughts was when I was in the infirmary. It could have been the drugs, but it told me something I couldn't know on my own."

"And what did it tell you?"

His throat tightened again, threatening to choke off the words entirely. He thought if he were speaking to anyone else, he might not be able to get the words out.

"That my family had still been alive when we were in the Capitol to retrieve the papers, but that they'd been killed after I escaped the prison. That the Empire tortured them for information in my place…"

"And after reading the papers, you wondered if the voice you heard was Reaper."

Wordlessly, he nodded.

"It's possible," Sheboleth said, a warning in her voice. "He's probably connected to you through the soul stone you carry, just like he's connected to all the other stones."

"Are we in any danger? Can the Empire figure out where we are through that connection?"

"No, or else we would have been found by now. But whatever you do, *never* attempt to converse with him. Don't believe anything he tells you. Do you understand?"

He nodded. She was beginning to frighten him.

"He is a demon, a creature as old as the world itself, maybe even older. He feeds on the inner darkness that lurks within all of us. He is a deceiver above all."

"Does that mean what he told me was a lie?" Leo asked, hardly daring to hope.

She shook her head. "I can't promise that. Just because he is deceptive above all else doesn't mean every word is a lie. But he only tells the truth if it suits him. I can only assume that he told you that because he meant to hurt you."

Leo bowed his head, slipping the chain back around his neck. He didn't want a demon whispering in his ear and he certainly didn't want the soul stone anymore, family heirloom or not.

What had once been a source of comfort, he now wished he'd never laid eyes on.

"I don't want this, Sheboleth. You should have it."

"It doesn't do me any good. A human has to be the one to seal him away. I can only destroy it after that happens."

"Why does it have to be me? I'm—" *A nobody. A coward. I didn't ask for any of this.*

"Maybe it does. I know this isn't what you want to hear, but you already have a connection to Reaper. He knows you have that stone and trust me, he knows what it is. You've been marked, whether you like it or not."

"You're right," he snapped. "It's not what I want to hear. I didn't ask for any of this. I joined the Resistance to help stop the Empire's oppression, not so I could seal some ancient demon away. I don't want this responsibility!"

"I know. And I'm sorry. If I could take this burden from you, I would. I swear to you, I will do everything in my power to stop Reaper from returning, to ensure that it never comes to this." She nodded at the stone hanging down over his chest. "But if we fail and the worst should come to pass, something must be done. He must be sealed away again. Or else everything ends."

Leo closed his eyes, wishing for a moment that he'd never attended any of the Resistance meetings. That he had kept his head down and gone about his days as he always had, never looking for trouble, never letting himself become dissatisfied. Never allowing himself to dream, even for a moment, that things could be different.

But he knew, even as he wished for such a thing, that it would have changed nothing. Reaper would have still bided his time and when he returned, Leo would have had no idea of the true nature of the stone around his neck.

The world would still end and everyone he had ever cared about would die.

At least this way, he knew what he was dealing with, what weapons he had at his disposal, and could do something about it.

He might still die, but better a fighting chance than none at all.

"I don't feel ready."

He doubted he could ever truly feel ready to face down such an outcome, but his body had barely healed from what he had suffered in Krylok. And there was a small part of him, that he didn't even like to acknowledge, that feared his mind might never heal.

"I put off telling you for as long as I could," Sheboleth said. "You didn't need all of this on top of everything else. And I hate that I even had to tell you now. I wish I could say how much time we have left. Reaper could return in a day, a week, or months from now. I simply don't know. But what I do know is that in this very moment, we're fine. The world hasn't ended yet. And until Reaper returns, we can spend that time however we like. I choose to find some small measure of happiness where I can, sitting with a friend, basking in the sun."

Leo nodded. The sun had begun to set, but its light would linger for a while longer.

He had expected to die in Krylok, but he hadn't. He was still alive, still breathing, his heart still beating. He supposed his current circumstances, no matter how bleak, were an improvement compared to that.

The soul stone still weighed heavily, but in that moment, he no longer noticed it.

The three Resistance leaders sat back, gathering around a circular table, regarding Sheboleth. They had listened without interruption as the truth was laid out before them. Sheboleth waited, with bated breath, to hear what they would say.

She had debated bringing Skye or Leo with her, since they believed, but she had asked enough of them for the moment.

"We wanted to act on the information," Tristan said at last. "But we lacked evidence."

She wasn't sure she believed the explanation for why they had kept the papers to themselves, but it mattered little now.

"*If* this turns out to be true, it can't be ignored," Jemma said. "But in order to reach the amulet and destroy it, we have to get close to the emperor and there is no easy way to do that. Either it would require a small group to infiltrate all the way to the palace and take the amulet from him, or an all-out assault, which would likely mean a siege. And should all of this turn out to be false, we will have risked and possibly wasted a great many lives and resources for nothing."

"It won't be for nothing," Sheboleth said firmly. "I can promise you that. But it *won't* be easy, whatever option we choose."

Rhaven sighed. "I think we must act as it if were true. There are risks to such a plan, yes, but if it is true and we do nothing, the risks of that course of action far outweigh the risks of a siege on the Capitol."

"How much time do we have?" Jemma asked.

Sheboleth shook her head. "I don't know. It could be months, it could be tomorrow. All we can do is act and hope we're not too late. Regardless, any plan we choose will take time."

"Time we don't have. We can't have much time left if the demon was sealed and Anarsha fell a thousand years ago."

"Give or take." The exact amount of time since Anarsha's fall wasn't worth haggling over. They all knew there was far more behind than ahead. "It'll have to do."

"Much as we'd like," Tristan said, "we can't just mount an assault on the Capitol. Not without undermining the

Empire's strength first. We must weaken it further or we'll be crushed before we ever breach the Capitol."

"You could mount a fully-fledged assault with every member of the Resistance and our numbers would still not be enough," Sheboleth said. "We need help."

"And where," Tristan asked, "do you propose we find any?"

She sighed. "I am not the only dragon in the Valderan rainforest. I can summon the others and make them understand what's at stake. They will fight, as they once fought at Anarsha's side. But it will take time."

The dragons had scattered following the old kingdom's fall and many had gone into hiding once the mechs ventured into the forest, intent on hunting them down. Many had been killed.

Sheboleth had no idea how many were even left. She hadn't sought out the company of her own kind in a long time, but they would need every dragon they could get if they were to stand a chance against the Empire's metal army.

"It's…unorthodox," Jemma allowed. "But we share a common enemy. This…demon will destroy all of us if he's not defeated first."

Tristan turned his gaze on Sheboleth. "Do what you can and let us know what you find out. We'll turn our attention to weakening the Empire."

She nodded. It was the best they could hope for and all any of them could ask.

How had it all gone so wrong? Lydia wondered. *And so quickly.* She had gone from being feared and respected for her position as a newly appointed Minister to becoming fearful herself. Each moment that passed by, she feared the summons that she had been dreading would come.

She had exhausted all options, following the assault on Krylok. Her soldiers had fanned out across the city, searching for days on end in every nook and cranny, for the missing prisoner and those who had freed him. They stopped everyone they encountered and questioned them, they conducted more raids than the city had possibly ever seen, and yet no one seemed to know anything—at least not that they would admit to—and the rebels remained nowhere to be found.

Lydia was under no illusion where the blame would come to rest or what would happen to her. The last Minister that she had replaced was punished for less.

None of it would have mattered if she had managed to get the prisoner to talk. But he had resisted the Inquisitor's efforts, which both vexed and impressed her. It hadn't mattered what they had done to him physically. He would not be moved.

She had given the order to bring his family in. They had been moved out of their home after he had first gone missing. Lydia hadn't realized it immediately, but the rebel they had captured was the same who had escaped the Capitol. The same rebel they had wasted so many mechs trying to bring in. Now he was here and she would be a fool to waste such an opportunity.

And yet, she had. Krylok prison, the most secure building in the Empire, was no match for a dragon. She had seen the burned-out husk that remained and knew that would only incense the emperor further.

Not only had she failed to get anything useful from the prisoner and then let him escape, she had lost the entire prison in the process and any other information the prisoners within possessed.

But the summons had never come. She feared that Desmond would take out his anger on Fabian, the one thing that would hurt Lydia more than anything he could ever do to her alone. But each day, Fabian returned to the quarters they shared with nothing to report, as though the emperor had simply forgotten about her. All he said, after the news initially broke, was that the emperor had gone into a frenzy, raving not about her, but the dragons and how they were intent on his destruction.

Lydia had expected to have to plead with Desmond, to give her time to search for the rebels, but she knew it would be hopeless. They would have long since fled the city, likely on the back of the dragon. Clever, that, and terribly inconvenient.

She stood in her living room, debating whether or not to open another bottle of wine, when the summons finally came. She wanted to keep her wits about her at all times, but the wine might help calm her nerves. She hadn't been sleeping well at all since the night of the prison break, jolting wide awake in the middle of the night, fearful that someone would come for her.

And now, at last, the reckoning. Whatever fate awaited her, she would handle it. Better that than the endless waiting.

Some form of punishment was guaranteed, she knew, but what form it would take was another matter entirely. She hoped, fervently, that Desmond wouldn't sic his dogs on her.

Recently promoted to Minister, given the opportunity of a lifetime, and you somehow manage to squander even that.

Her disgust at herself was crowded out only by her apprehension toward whatever course of action the emperor would decide to take.

Desmond was in the throne room when she arrived. She was dressed in a simple tunic, trousers and boots, leaving her Minister's robes behind. It did not seem wise, given the circumstances. She was no longer worthy of it.

The mechanical dogs lay at the base of the throne and Lydia eyed them warily. She would have been wary of them before, but now terror threatened to choke her. Were they simply present because Desmond wished them to be, or were they there for her?

A quick glance around the room confirmed that Fabian was not present. She let out a soft breath at that. Whatever her punishment was to be, at least her brother wouldn't have to witness it.

Desmond waited, studying her implacably from behind that horrid mask.

Lydia drew a deep breath. "We have searched everywhere, my lord." If that wasn't the complete truth, it certainly felt like it. "The rebels have left the city."

"And the prisoner told you nothing?"

"No." He knew this already, but likely only wanted her to repeat it. Acknowledge, once more, her failure.

"You know," he said, rising. "Krylok was never breached under the former Minister. I'm left to wonder if I was perhaps too hasty…"

"I will not fail you again—" Lydia began, realizing too late it was the wrong thing to say.

The emperor held up one hand, the sleeve of his silk robe dangling. "No," he agreed. "You won't."

In one fluid motion, he signaled to his hounds. Lydia took an involuntary step backward as the dogs rose to their feet, teeth bared, growls reverberating like engines in their chests.

They advanced down the steps from the throne and then paused, the air all at once heavy. Lydia froze, staring at the red stones that glimmered in their chests, but the dogs did not move.

For a moment, she thought perhaps the emperor had changed his mind. And then she realized it was *something else.*

The emperor, too, had frozen and he stood with his head cocked to one side, as though listening. Lydia could hear nothing but the pounding of her own heart.

Was he listening to the demon? Was it whispering in his ear? She prayed it would tell him to spare her, though why it would do such a thing, she did not know.

"Perhaps you're right," Desmond murmured at last, even though she hadn't said anything. He sank back down onto his throne. "She could yet be useful to us."

Lydia glanced up, past the emperor, to the large eye staring out from the wall behind him. The eye that Fabian had claimed to see in the amulet. She couldn't tell if the emperor was wearing it now. If he was, it was hidden beneath his clothes.

She fought to slow her racing heart and steady her breathing, not daring to believe she might have escaped.

She could not see the emperor's expression, but she heard the smile in his voice. "You may go. It seems you have friends in high places."

The remark puzzled her, but she didn't care to examine it too closely. Bowing, she turned and bid a hasty retreat.

There could be no more mistakes after this. She would not get another chance, friends or no.

It had to have been the demon after all, influencing Desmond—and the dogs. They had been ready to carry out his orders and rip her to pieces, only to be stayed. Desmond had changed his mind instantly. She might have once chalked it up to his unstable moods, but now she knew better.

But why? Why should the beast help her?

The answer came readily and she knew it as certainly as she knew anything. *Because he knows that I would make a better ruler.*

Lydia paused at the doorway, turning back. Even across the great expanse of the throne room, she could see the amulet now, resting on the outside of Desmond's robes, over his heart.

A single eye stared back at her, unblinking, orange and amber as though lit from within by flames.

XXX

Lydia raced back to her quarters, fearful that at any moment, Desmond might change his mind and send the mechanical hounds after her. But no one came.

She shoved the door open, bursting into the room, and nearly collided with Fabian, who stood just inside the foyer.

"There you are," she gasped, shutting the door and bolting it behind her, as if that would truly keep them safe.

"I just got back."

Lydia eyed him, not asking where he'd been. With each passing day, he looked thinner than before, his eyes sunken and shadowed. She thought of Zak and the cure he was supposed to be looking for and felt a twinge of disappointment.

"Desmond summoned me," she explained, stepping into the living room. The bottle of wine she had laid out still rested on the low coffee table. "When you weren't there, I thought…" She trailed off and picked up the bottle.

No longer would it serve to soothe her nerves. She had escaped unscathed and that was worth celebrating.

"What happened?" Fabian asked. "Or do I not want to know?"

"I'm alive, aren't I?" she said, pouring two glasses and handing him one. "I got off lightly, though…I'm not sure why."

"Do you trust him not to change his mind?" Fabian asked, settling on the sofa.

She shook her head, joining him. "It doesn't really matter anymore."

His green eyes narrowed. "What do you mean?"

She raised the glass to her lips. "Desmond has to die."

"What?" Fabian lowered his own glass. "Lydia, do you even hear yourself?"

"You already knew this," she challenged. "We've both known for some time that it was always going to come to this. The fact that we know the source of his madness doesn't change what it is." She took a sip of wine. "He's unstable. Unfit to rule."

"And you have to be the one who kills him?"

"If we don't, he'll kill one of us sooner or later."

She hadn't forgotten that horrible moment the dogs rose to their feet, moments from springing at her and carrying out Desmond's orders.

She had been spared and she believed this must be the reason why. She had to dispose of Desmond.

Fabian eyed her worriedly from the other end of the couch, but Lydia ignored him, refusing to meet his gaze. She couldn't tell if it was the danger of such a plan that concerned him or the plan itself, but neither were going to stop her.

"I went down to the archives," he said, swirling the wine in his glass but drinking none of it. "Zak wasn't there, nor was he in his quarters. The other scribes haven't seen him and couldn't tell me where he'd gone or when he'd be back. Have you heard anything?"

Lydia sighed. She had managed to deflect any questions about the scribe so far, but knew she'd have to tell him something eventually. He couldn't fail to notice his friend's sudden absence.

"Those documents," she said, choosing her words carefully. "The ancient Anarshan ones he showed you. They're missing."

"Missing? It's not like Zak to leave papers lying around."

"He didn't. He took them and passed them on to a rebel, here within the city."

"What?" Fabian leaned forward, his brow furrowed. "Why would Zak do such a thing?"

"He and this rebel obviously knew each other—"

"No! No, I don't believe it. Zak's no rebel."

Lydia shrugged. "I don't know why he felt it was so important that the Resistance obtain the papers, but he must have felt quite strongly to risk what he did. I'm sorry."

Fabian glowered at her. "How could you turn him in? He was your friend, too."

"I have a duty," she snapped back, "in case you haven't noticed. Or have you forgotten what happened to the last Minister of Defense? My loyalty to the Empire is what keeps us both alive. I don't like a damn thing about it, but if I have to choose between him or you, I choose you. I'll always choose you."

Fabian turned away.

"Besides, he wasn't much of a friend. He wasted all that time, losing himself in old documents that had nothing to do with healing when he was supposed to be searching for a cure for you. And then he stole priceless documents from the archives and passed them on to rebels. Apparently he deemed that more important."

"I'm sure he had his reasons," Fabian muttered.

Don't we all.

Lydia set her glass down on the table and got to her feet. "I did what I had to, to protect you. And that's what I'll keep doing, even if I have to kill the emperor himself."

"Can you protect me from myself?"

Lydia stalked from the room without answering.

Leo's eyes snapped open, the darkness of the caverns barely discernable from the darkness of his dream. His chest heaved, breath coming heavy and fast, the remnants beginning to fade, but still lingering in the corners of his mind.

He winced, sitting up, the chill air of the caves cool against his sweat-dappled skin. The stump of his arm ached, cramping, throbbing in time with his racing heartbeat.

It had hurt in his dream, too, only then, he'd still had both arms. The ceiling of the caverns had collapsed, pinning his arm in place. No matter how hard he shoved against the fallen rubble, it would not budge. Trapped, he'd called out for help, but no one came, leaving him helpless, in the dark, alone.

He'd expected to dream of the prison, but he never did. Instead, each of the nightmares always involved a situation that evoked the same sense of helplessness, knowing no one was coming.

Leo glanced to his right, knowing what he would see. But for a moment, he almost expected to be greeted with the sight of his right arm, there once more, as though nothing had happened.

He'd had both arms in the dream and it had felt *so real*, even the pain. Pain he should no longer be able to feel, in a limb that was no longer there. The rest of it may have been an illusion, but the pain wasn't.

Despite knowing it was only a dream and nothing more, Leo couldn't help the sense of disappointment that crashed over him, greeted with the sight of only a stump.

Why did his mind play such tricks on him? He knew what had happened to him. It was with him every moment of every day, the pain even following him into sleep.

He raked his fingers through his hair, which continued to grow out. It had always grown fast, but he knew it would take several more months before it returned to its previous length.

Leo gazed around his "room". After being discharged from the infirmary, he'd had his belongings moved to a more isolated corner of the caverns, the red cloths draped on all sides to offer a bit of privacy. They wouldn't block sound like actual walls would, but at least this way he stood less of a chance of waking anyone else.

He missed the way Sheboleth had laid beside him when he'd first come to the Resistance. Her presence alone would have helped ease some of his fear, knowing nothing truly bad could happen to him with a dragon by his side.

But she had left over a month ago to rally her kin and he'd had no word of how the search progressed since. He missed her, even though he knew her absence was necessary, if they were to have a fighting chance.

He threw the covers back and swung his legs over the side of the bed, shivering in the cold as he slipped his boots on. He knew better than to try and fall asleep again and wasn't going to simply lay there all night, alone with his thoughts.

By now, the guards stationed at the portcullis were familiar with his routine and let him pass without comment. Where once he had been viewed with suspicion, now they looked upon him with pity, which was almost worse.

They didn't know what to make of him, the rebel they had doubted, who had given more for the cause than most of them ever would.

He stepped out of the tunnel into the ruins, bathed in moonlight. He took in a deep breath, the air warmer than down in the caverns.

The ruins held a sort of haunting beauty, enhanced by the silver light, softening the edges. He debated sitting down for a moment, but decided against it. If he wanted to sit still, he could have easily done that inside. He kept walking, footsteps crunching over fallen stone.

As he rounded the corner of one of the buildings, a dark figure came into view. She whirled around, twin black blades drawn, her blue eyes wide.

"Oh," Skye sighed, lowering the daggers. "It's you."

"Who did you think it was?"

"Silly of me," she said, shaking her head with a little laugh. But she didn't answer the question.

"Couldn't sleep?" he asked.

She shook her head again. "I hardly think I need ask you the same."

"No," Leo agreed, sinking down onto the stone steps. It was impossible to tell what the building might have been, once, but he supposed it was safe enough.

Wandering around the ruins was dangerous, particularly at night. And yet, there they both were, doing just that. He didn't press Skye on what had driven her aboveground. Her secrets were her own.

As he moved to sit, Leo felt the soul stone shift beneath his shirt, cold as ever against his skin. He kept it with him at all times, as always, but now for a completely different reason.

Skye sat beside him, the moonlight turning her black hair silver. "Are you all right?" she asked softly. "I mean…really all right?"

Leo didn't answer, thinking back to earlier that day. Or was it yesterday? He had no idea.

He'd finally approached Fae, hoping to continue their work on the mech, despite his obvious limitations. He refused to believe that there was nothing he could do.

But most of the tools required the use of two hands and lifting some of the larger parts certainly did. In the end, his refusal to accept his new reality had only led to disappointment. He'd settled for handing whatever small parts Fae needed, watching her reassemble the mech.

He had yet to return to his daily training sessions with Skye. She had assured him that he could take all the time he needed before they gave it another go. His body had likely healed enough by now that he could try again, but he put it off, not wanting to be faced with yet more disappointment.

He thought Skye suspected the reason why, but was too polite to say it.

Leo looked up at the night sky stretching above their heads, the stars twinkling, and wondered if Sheboleth could see it from wherever she was, and if her thoughts ever strayed back to him.

"How can this be real, Skye?" he whispered. "How did it all come to this?"

Instead of trying to come up with an answer that both of them knew would fall short, she reached over wordlessly, threading her fingers through his.

Leo tore his gaze from the sky, to their joined hands. His hand was much larger than hers, the fingers longer. Her fingernails were short and ragged where she'd picked at them, her hands covered in a myriad small scars.

In the moonlight, he could see the scars from where she'd been nicked by blades; others, burns from her forge. Her fingers were rough, calloused in his.

She followed his gaze and looked away, lips pursing. "I know."

He looked up at her. "Know what?"

"They're ugly."

It was the furthest thing from his own thoughts that he was momentarily struck speechless.

"Is that what you think?" he murmured, brushing his thumb across her knuckles.

She leaned closer slightly, her eyes searching his. "What do you see when you look at me?"

Leo didn't have to think very long or hard about his answer. "A fighter. A survivor."

Every obstacle life had thrown in her path, she had beaten into submission until it lay at her feet and she could step over it. It had left its marks on her, but it was she who walked away the victor.

Her eyes narrowed slightly and she turned, angling her body toward him. With her free hand, she reached out, cupping his cheek. Leo drew in a sharp breath, her skin warm against the night's chill.

"Why don't you see yourself the same way?"

He swallowed, throat suddenly tight. Why didn't he? Why did he view his own scar as a weakness, something to be ashamed of and hidden?

Leo closed his eyes, leaning into her touch. In that moment, the two of them could have been anywhere, far away from the conflict that had come to define both of their lives.

In his dreams, his mind might be unable to discern between what was real and what wasn't. *But this moment…it's real.* And so was she.

XXXI

Sheboleth was gone just over two months, gathering the others, before she returned. The sight of the ruins made her steps slow, bringing back a fresh wave of memory each time she saw them. Whenever she gazed up at the crumbling wall, it was as though she saw two—one, the wall of her memories, the second as it appeared now— superimposed upon each other.

Dragons lived a long time—she herself was evidence of that—and even when she shared her news, telling the others of the urgency, that the fate that they had waited for and feared for so long was finally on their door, they were still annoyingly slow to act.

Some did not wish to get involved, believing it the fault of humans for bringing Reaper into the world and so the humans should be left to deal with it alone. On the one hand, Sheboleth could understand the sentiment and agree with it, to some extent. But she was no fool and knew that such a fate would not be exclusive to the humans alone.

It would come for them all and none would escape.

Finally, they had agreed to meet on the night of the full moon and Sheboleth raced back to the ruins, to share her news. She knew better than to get her hopes up. They had agreed to a meeting, nothing more. That did not mean they would act.

They must. They have to. She would make them see reason if it came to that, but she would not be denied. Not after everything.

But one thing they had all made clear was their desire to see, for themselves, the human who bore the soul stone. Sheboleth would not be going alone to the meeting. Much as she didn't wish to drag Leo along and invite him into the politics and posturing of her kind, she had no choice. Not if she wanted to convince them.

He did not protest when she told him and together, they set out the night of the full moon. With difficulty, he clambered up onto her back. It would take too long to reach the clearing on foot and they needed to act fast. Sheboleth wanted to arrive before the others so they could watch and see who came and who did not.

The sky was clear, the full moon shining down on the forest below, staining the leaves silver. A faint breeze blew, rattling the tree limbs above their heads as they landed at the edge of the clearing. It was a large space, completely surrounded on all sides by the thick trees of the rainforest.

In the middle of the clearing stood a large, slanted stone. Sheboleth gazed around as Leo slid off her back, but she couldn't see any of the others. She scented nothing on the wind, but that didn't mean that they weren't already there, waiting as she was, not wishing to be the first to step out into the open.

Dragons were solitary creatures by nature and the Empire's attacks over the years had only made them more cautious. The only good thing about being so exposed was that there were no trees to impede them, should they need to suddenly take to the air.

"Where is everyone?" Leo breathed. He had dressed entirely in black, making him harder to see, but his pale skin did nothing to aid that goal.

"Just wait," Sheboleth hissed.

There was sudden movement on the far side of the clearing. Sheboleth held her breath. A blue dragon stepped out into the open, his movement slow but confident. He had likely made this journey many times, even before losing his sight, and he knew the way.

She watched as Koal climbed up to perch atop the stone in the center of the clearing. If any could be considered to be their leader, it was him.

Then there came more movement as the others moved forward. Now they would show themselves.

"Let's go," Sheboleth said softly. "Stay close. None of them are particularly fond of humans and they don't know you. There's no telling how they'll react. And don't show the stone until I say."

"I know," Leo reminded her. "You said."

He was right; it wasn't her first time giving him instructions, but she was worried in spite of herself. At around ten feet tall, she was the average size for a dragon. Some of those assembled were slightly smaller, others bigger, but if more than one of them decided to attack, she wasn't sure she would be able to protect Leo.

Their dislike of humans ran deep, even though few of them were old enough to have fought beside Anarsha or witnessed her fall. The idea of allying themselves with humans again, no matter the cause, was not a popular one.

Sheboleth wondered if Leo's thoughts followed a similar pattern, for he looked paler than normal beneath the moonlight as they stepped forward, pace even and unhurried. He stuck so close to her side, he was practically touching her. When they were halfway across the clearing, he reached out and laid his hand against her shoulder, as if suddenly needing the support—or perhaps he found it reassuring.

She could feel many heads turn in their direction, many sets of eyes on them. Low growls rang out amid the murmuring and general shuffling. She ignored them and kept walking.

There were more of them than she had expected, but fewer than she had managed to hunt down. It was too much to hope for that everyone would come.

Even if every single one had gathered, their numbers would still have been pathetically few, a pale shadow of what they once were. The old, familiar anger kindled to life in Sheboleth's chest. Perhaps she could use that and hope their hatred for the Empire—and their fear of Reaper— was stronger than their distrust of humanity.

She strode into the center of the circle and stopped, but before she could speak, an angry female voice rang out above the others.

"You dare bring one of those devils here? Have you no shame, no honor?"

Sheboleth opened her mouth to tell the other dragon that Leo's presence had been requested by most of the others, but the blue dragon on the stone raised one hand.

"Peace, Widow." He turned his cloudy eyes on Sheboleth and the human at her side.

She sucked in a deep breath, projecting her voice so that it reached the far edges of the clearing. It sounded harsh to her own ears, abrasive in the relative quiet.

"I promise you, I would not have brought a human here except in great need. Most of you wished to see for yourselves the one who holds the soul stone. You know why I've summoned you here. You know what is at stake, what we may soon need that soul stone for." She bent her head to Leo and whispered, "Show them the stone."

Keeping his movements slow and nonthreatening, Leo lifted the stone out of his shirt. He slipped the chain over his head and held it in one hand, lifting it for all to see, the blue stone dangling from the end, reflecting the bright moonlight, cold and clear.

The murmuring redoubled. It was one thing to be told about the existence of a soul stone—not merely a spirit shard—that held the power to prevent Reaper from destroying their world, and another entirely to see it.

Koal reached out with one hand, palm turned upward. "May I see it?"

Reluctantly, at Sheboleth's encouraging nod, Leo stepped forward and placed the stone in the dragon's hand.

Koal curled his silver claws around it. Though he could not see the stone itself, he would know what it was, sense its power and purpose, perhaps in a way that sight alone could not.

His scales were a dark blue, almost navy, with brighter pieces of armor running from his throat to the tip of his tail. Five black horns protruded from the corner of his jaw and four long horns, two on each side of his head, curved upward. Instead of spines of any kind, a mane of thick black hair extended from his forehead to the middle of his back.

"Where did you find this?" he asked at last, deep voice rumbling.

Sheboleth nudged Leo. It was his question to answer and it would help the others to understand why she had brought him.

"It's mine," Leo began, but one of the others shouted at him to speak up and he was forced to start again. "It belonged to my family," he said, louder this time. "It's an heirloom."

"You know what it is, I take it."

"Yes. I do now."

Sheboleth raised her voice again. "Leo is a member of the Resistance, the remnants of Anarsha, who actively oppose the Empire. Only recently were they made aware of Reaper's existence and the threat he poses. We dragons have known about Reaper since he was sealed by the last king of Anarsha, but his amulet was lost after the kingdom fell. Long have we suspected it to be in the possession of the Akkadian emperor, but unable to prove it."

There was an angry hiss from one of the others. "The Empire's symbol is an all-seeing eye. There's no guessing as to what *that* means."

"Now we have proof," Sheboleth went on. "We know that the amulet is, as we suspected, in the emperor's possession. The Resistance plans to siege the Capitol and destroy it to prevent Reaper's return. But they can't do it alone. The question now before you is whether you will aid us. Will you stand with the Resistance, as you once stood with Anarsha? Will you fight once more?"

Her words were met with a moment of silence, and for a moment, Sheboleth dared to hope that they had been moved by her plea.

Those hopes were quickly dashed.

"Why would we ally ourselves with humans? They nearly doomed us all once, and they are the only reason Reaper still poses a threat now!"

"Without our help, the Resistance will fail," Sheboleth retorted, "and Reaper will return."

"I say let Reaper destroy them! It's nothing less than they deserve!"

"They will have brought it on themselves!" someone else shouted. "They summoned him in the first place."

A low growl rumbled in Sheboleth's chest, building, ready to burst forth. But to her surprise, Leo stepped forward, out of her shadow, staring down the gathered dragons.

"You have every right to be angry," he called. "For the things that have been done to you and for what's been taken from you. The Empire has taken things from me, too." Absently, he reached across with his remaining hand and clasped his other arm, just above the stump. "I'd like them to pay for it, but not if it means the whole world coming to an end. I have no doubt Reaper would destroy the Empire if he returns, but he will not stop there. He will rampage and burn until there is nothing left of our world. That is the future that awaits us if we fail."

His voice grew softer, confiding. "A short time ago, I didn't believe in the existence of dragons or demons. Now I find myself in possession of a soul stone that can seal Reaper away, if he should return. I pray to all the saints that it doesn't come to that. But if it does, I will do what must be done."

Sheboleth's gaze flicked around the clearing. Some of the dragons shuffled their weight, looking elsewhere. He had shamed them. A human, willing to face down a demon, while the dragons cowered in their forest.

Koal held out his hand, offering the stone back to Leo. "This belongs to you."

He reached out and took it almost reverently. "Thank you. I'll try to be worthy of this task."

The blue dragon stood, his voice easily carrying out across the clearing. "Reaper is the enemy of all and it is he we must focus our attention on. Should we fail to destroy the amulet, only a human can seal him away again. And even then, only half the task is completed. It will not be finished until a dragon destroys it. We need each other for this task. Whether we like that fact or not makes it no less true."

"I want revenge on the Empire as much as you do," Sheboleth called, slowly turning in a circle, taking them all in individually. "And so does the Resistance. I've seen it. I've helped them do it. Together, we can bring the Empire down and stop Reaper from returning, all at once. I think we've waited long enough."

This time, there were murmurs of assent.

Koal turned to Sheboleth. "Keep us apprised of the Resistance's plans. When the time comes, we will be there."

"Thank you."

She knew that just as not everyone had come to the gathering, not all of those who had appeared tonight would aid the Resistance. She just hoped that when the time came, it would be enough.

The meeting began to break up, some of the others already slipping away. Sheboleth was in no mood to linger. It was already late and she and Leo needed to return.

They didn't speak until they had reached the ruins.

Sheboleth glanced over at Leo. "You did well."

Dragons despised weakness, as a rule, so the fact that he had been bold enough to speak up, addressing them directly, had been a point in his favor.

He sighed. "I said all those things. I hope I really meant them."

"Of course you did."

"It's easy to say one thing when you're facing down dragons. It's another thing to actually do it, when you're facing down an ancient demon."

"You have an odd definition of 'easy'."

He made a face. "You know what I mean. I've had months to think about what I have to do if everything goes wrong. And yet there are times when it still terrifies me and I can't imagine having to do it for real."

"I have faith in you," Sheboleth said bluntly, then jerked her head back the way they'd come. "Certainly more faith than I have in them."

Funny, that she was saying that about a human. What a strange turn her life had taken ever since encountering that patrol in the woods. Never would she have imagined, years ago, that she would one day ally herself with another human, much less advocate on their behalf for an alliance.

And now she found herself staring down the end of the world with one.

Some things never change.

"How many do you think will come?"

"I don't know," she replied. "But I think Reaper has good cause to be worried."

Despite the late hour, Sheboleth went off to speak with the Triad, leaving Leo to make his way to his room, telling him that it was late and she'd kept him up long enough. It was on the tip of his tongue to tell her that he wasn't a child, but he was too tired to argue.

He pushed back the drapes, stepping into the small room he had all to himself, surveying the single bed and dresser, with a basin for water on top. He didn't care how cramped it was, so long as it was private.

No doubt some of the others thought him stuck up or prudish, wanting such privacy to himself, but he didn't care. Their negative opinions of him were far better than them knowing the truth.

He sank onto the bed, doubting sleep would come after the excitement of the meeting, his mind replaying everything that had been said. He wasn't even aware of drifting off until the dreams came for him.

He was standing in the Capitol, only it looked different. Less dirty, and more bright, the sun streaming down the mountains, bathing the city in light. There were no signs of any mechs and Leo knew that they had succeeded. The Empire had fallen and Reaper was no longer a threat.

Ana stood beside him, looking just as she had the last time he'd seen her, blonde curls framing her face.

Leo sighed, taking in the sight of victory. The thing that they had fought so long and hard for was finally a reality, but not all of them were there to see it.

"I wish Mom could have seen," he murmured.

Ana looked up at him. "But she can."

"What do you mean?" he asked. "She's dead."

Ana shook her head. "Not dead, only injured. Come on, I'll take you to her." She held out one hand.

Leo's heart leapt. His mother hadn't been killed in the siege, only wounded. He would see her again. He reached out, but the dream dissolved as his hand touched hers.

For a moment, Leo lay there, motionless in the darkness, the details of the dream already fading. He struggled to hold on to them, knowing even as he did so that there were details already lost, that could never follow him into the waking world.

As with most dreams, it seemed so flat and lifeless when compared to waking reality, so ridiculous that he could have ever believed, even subconsciously, that it was real. But it had felt real in the moment. *So real.*

But how could it be? His mother was dead, his sister along with her, and his stubborn mind refused to believe it, bringing them back to life in his dreams the same way it tried to restore his arm. If only it were that simple.

In the wake of the dream's passing, as confusion cleared, reality set in, and with it, disappointment. A great weight settled on Leo's chest, the pain sudden and sharp, threatening to crack him in two.

His eyes felt wet and as he lay motionless in the dark, he felt a tear slip free, trailing down the side of his face. Whether his dreams accepted the truth or not, his mother was dead and she was never coming back.

And it's all your fault.

He sucked in a breath, the effort painful and not enough. He couldn't breathe. Air. He needed air. Why couldn't he breathe?

Leo sat up, his movements too slow, raking his hand through his hair. What time was it? Without the sun, time passed slowly in the caverns, which were perpetually dim.

But it must have still been night, the usual thrum of the Resistance going about its business absent. The only sound he could hear was a distant clanking, as of machinery, the same as he had heard upon first arriving. He still didn't know its source, but he imagined it must have something to do with the electricity that the Resistance generated.

Briefly, he debated seeking out Skye, though he wasn't sure why and didn't care to examine that motivation too closely. But he didn't want to wake her, and though he wanted the comfort her presence could provide, stronger still was his aversion to the idea of her seeing his weakness.

Instead, he got to his feet. Walking mechanically, hardly knowing where his own feet were taking him, he found himself in front of the portcullis that led outside. *Of course.* All paths led out of the caverns, sooner or later.

The ruins were still bathed in moonlight when he emerged, though the moon had moved to a different position. Now, instead of appearing beautiful, the fallen stone looked strange in the light, eerie and mysterious. And unspeakably sad, a tired shell of what it had once been. People had died here. Lives had been ruined, come crashing down around them. Ultimately, this was a place of sadness.

Leo tried to shake off his mood, but it was no good. His stump was throbbing, aching as if it were still whole, as if the missing part was still there, connected to him somehow.

But it wasn't and never would be again. The Empire had taken something from him he would never get back—something more than just the use of his dominant arm.

He sat down heavily on a fallen chunk of stone. His body would never be whole again and he was starting to think that his mind never would be either.

Leo sighed, thinking back on what he'd said to the dragons at the gathering. So much had happened since he had made the decision to attend the Resistance meetings.

So many people had died.

His family had died. And in the end, it was still his fault.

And what did the Resistance have to show for all their efforts? More people dead, the only difference being that they were Empire instead of Resistance. But the Empire still stood. Someone had likely died in the Capitol or Shemar or Elath that very day, of starvation or torture, of execution or disease. Or perhaps even despair.

The Empire remained. It endured, even after a thousand years. It would still be there tomorrow, when the sun rose, and it would still be there even after all of them had passed on from the world.

Unless Reaper returned and the world came to an end, and then none of it would matter anymore. It would all have been for nothing.

Leo buried his head in his hand, the weight that had descended upon him redoubling, threatening to crush him.

It was too much. It was *all* too much.

A ragged sob crawled up his throat, and he fought to restrain it, but in the end, failed. He wept bitterly, hating himself, the Empire, and the cruelty of the world, the racking sobs sending pain through his ribs.

But most of all, he wept for his mother, whose face even now grew fuzzier, less defined in his mind's eye. And Ana. Her features were clearer, having appeared in his dream, but he knew that in time, she, too, would fade until he could no longer conjure up the sound of her voice or hear her laugh.

He thought of what Skye had said to him once, about wanting to believe in a heaven. That there was a place better than the world they had known, where they would be reunited again.

But in that moment, he was drowning, unable to believe in anything but the hell she had spoken of. He believed in that. Hell was real. He had seen enough of it.

Leo didn't know how long he had sat there. He felt exhausted, scoured out, the grief and the pain giving way to anger, burning in his chest like a white-hot coal, searing. Was this how Skye felt, the loss of her family burned into her like a brand?

Was this what enabled her to do the things she did? He couldn't blame her. He had ceased to blame her a long time ago, ever since she had shared her story with him, but now…he understood.

"You see…they deserve it."

The voice whispered against his ear, slippery as silk.

A shiver speared through Leo and he recoiled from it. "I know what you are!" he growled.

"I should hope you would recognize a friend when you see one."

"You're no friend to me."

"Oh, no? Have I not proven time and time again that I only ever had your best interests at heart?"

Leo hesitated at that. If he was right and some of the things he had mistaken for his own thoughts had really come from Reaper, the demon *had* helped him on more than one occasion. But why? Sheboleth had told him that the demon did nothing that didn't serve his own best interests.

Why would saving my life be in his interest? He'd had the stone with him the entire time. The one stone that could seal Reaper again, should he attain his freedom. Surely it would have been better for the demon if Leo died, the stone lost along with him.

"We are bound together, you and I. Together, we can shape the world."

"You're a demon!" Leo snapped, shaking himself out of his musings. He felt like a fool, speaking aloud to the open air, but the demon could obviously hear him.

"What difference does it make what I am?"

"Stop talking to me." Sheboleth had warned him not to carry on a conversation with Reaper. It was probably best to listen.

The voice ignored him. *"You think my deeds evil."*

"Of course I do! Look at everything the Empire has done. *You're* the Empire. You're the one controlling it from the shadows, not Desmond."

"I am used, just as you are. Do you really think Desmond needs my help to be as wicked as he is?"

Leo had no answer for that. Sheboleth had called Desmond a puppet, and perhaps he now was, but at some point, he must have willingly chosen to ally himself with Reaper, even knowing what he was.

"The world is full of wicked people, Leo. You've seen it for yourself. I merely see that they reap what they sow. That they get what they deserve."

"And what is that?" Leo asked, fearing he already knew the answer.

"Death."

Leo felt a chill snake down his spine and he shivered.

"The Empire sows death all the time. How many people have they killed? How many have they slaughtered? How many have they ruthlessly struck down without a shred of remorse? How can you look at what they've done—and continue to do—and not think they deserve to die?"

"But it's wrong," he protested weakly, but he could already feel his resolve crumbling.

They were just empty words, parroted after believing them for so long. A natural response, without any conviction.

"An eye for an eye, Leo. Is that so very wrong?"

"It's never right to do wrong in order to do right."

"Come now." The voice was soft, hypnotic even. It understood him. It did not judge him. *"You mean to tell me that when you heard that your mother and sister had been killed, you didn't wish to strike back at the Empire for what they'd done? I see your heart, Leo. I feel your anger, how it cries out for vengeance."*

He *did* want vengeance. He wanted them, all of them, to be punished. He wanted them to pay, to make them hurt and suffer, the way they had made him suffer. Where was the justice in this world if innocent people could be struck down and their killers walk free, without punishment, without consequence.

There is no justice in this world.

Again, his thoughts turned to Skye and something she had said. *They kill without consequence. So we speak the language they understand. We* become *their consequence.*

"Thought I might find you here."

Leo jerked, looking up to see Sheboleth walking toward him, picking her way through the rubble. Reaper's presence had vanished, leaving him alone with her. He glanced away, hoping that his eyes weren't too red and that they wouldn't betray him.

"Couldn't sleep," he mumbled.

"I guessed as much." She sat down beside him, among the stones.

Of course she had. She understood the weight balanced on his shoulders better than most. The majority of the Resistance didn't even know of Reaper's existence. The Triad had deemed it best to keep it quiet for the time being, not wanting to cause a panic. They had no idea what was coming or what he was being asked to do.

Another wave of emotion struck him and he clenched his chest, above where the stone lay, hating himself as he choked back another sob. He wanted to hit something, even the stone, despite the fact that it would probably break the bones in his hand.

"I can't do this, Sheboleth." *I can't be who you want me to be. I'm not some hero, I'm just…me.*

"Yes, you can."

"*I can't.*" He drew in a shaking breath, shielding his eyes with his hand so he didn't have to look at her. "I'm not the person you think I am. I'm not…good. I hate them. They deserve to be destroyed."

"You don't have to explain it to me," she said quietly. "I know. I fought for Anarsha, against the Empire for so long, only to watch it all crumble to pieces around us. I watched our king bring a demon back into the world and possibly doom us all. I tried to convince Chandra to leave with me, but…"

She trailed off and Leo didn't have to ask. "But you were still right, you know," she added. "We have to be better than they are, or else we're just as bad. How are we any different? How can we become the very thing we hate?"

"How else are we going to stop them? Nothing else gets anything done."

"They're not invincible, Leo. Every empire must fall, even this one."

But what about the cost? What about all the people that had died? That wouldn't magically be undone just because the Empire no longer existed.

"My family are dead," he choked out. "I can't put that right. I can't—" He broke off, feeling hot tears tracing their way down his face again. "I'm sorry."

"For what?" Sheboleth demanded. "For finding out you're only human after all?"

"It's too heavy."

"Then let me help you carry it. You cannot be strong all the time, Leo. You are flesh and blood; you are not made of steel. You are not like one of your mechs, unalive and unfeeling."

He lowered his hand and looked up at her, his tears still flowing openly, bared for her to see. Half of him expected her to judge him. The other half knew better.

He'd never had a friend, or perhaps anyone in his life, that he felt more comfortable simply *being* with than the dragon sitting beside him.

"And you're wrong, you know," she said. "You are one of the good ones."

He let out a disbelieving laugh. "I don't think so."

"You're stronger than you think. The Empire can take everything from you. They can take your family, your home, your freedom, even your life. But don't *ever* let them take your spirit. Don't let them change who you are."

He reached up, feeling the outline of the soul stone beneath his clothes. He supposed letting the Empire change him would be like handing them a victory, of sorts.

The Resistance could kill every soldier in the Empire, but it wouldn't bring his family back. It wouldn't restore to him what he'd lost. It wouldn't get rid of the pain. And it wouldn't be what his mother or Ana would have wanted.

Leo knew that, the same way he knew better than to listen to the whispers of serpents. He had lost his way for a moment, but Sheboleth had brought him back.

XXXII

Progress was frustratingly slow. The world could have ended several times over before the Triad ever deigned to lift a finger and Skye grew more restless with each passing day. Still, she acknowledged the truth that if they rushed, any chance they had might be over before it even began.

At last, after Sheboleth's return, with the promise that at least some dragons would answer their call for aid when the time came, the Triad put into motion the first of a series of assaults meant to weaken the Empire.

If the Resistance was to have any hope of maintaining a drawn-out siege, they would have to strike first and cut the Capitol off from the rest of the Empire. Skye wasn't sure that a siege was the right way to go, but they didn't know how long they had left before Reaper returned and would need to be able to hold out until they could get access to the emperor and his amulet. If they had to break the Empire in order to do that, then so be it.

When she received word of the first mission, Tristan summoned her to tell her directly. She thought she would very much enjoy the task the Triad had given her.

Tiachren had gathered the explosives they would need. He and Fae would accompany her and Sheboleth. It felt strange, knowing that Leo would sit this one out, when he had been by her side for the last few missions.

Of course, she had gone on far more missions without him, but in such a short amount of time, she had grown accustomed to his presence. And her heart still twinged painfully whenever she thought about how the last mission had gone, still not entirely able to absolve herself for her role in it.

He sought her out the evening before the mission. They would leave at nightfall, heading for Shemar. She was in her forge, sharpening her blades, though she shouldn't need them for this particular mission, if everything went as it should.

When does it ever?

Skye lifted the blade from the whetstone, the harsh sound cutting out as Leo walked in. Her hands had been shaking slightly anyway—though she hoped he hadn't seen—and she knew enough to stop before she hurt herself or worse, damaged a blade.

"How are you holding up?" he asked.

She looked up, wondering if she'd been that obvious. This would be the first time she set foot in Shemar since leaving it behind all those years ago. She hadn't expected to ever see it again and the thought of returning to a place that held such pain made her heart race.

"Fine," she answered.

She could do this. She could endure any amount of discomfort if it meant blowing up those damned mines.

He watched her, eyes dark, and she felt as though he could see through her, down to the lies she hid.

Though the days passed slowly, he looked more like his old self. Enough time had passed, spent concocting plans, that his hair had grown out and soon, it would be the same length as when they'd met.

"Is this really what you want?" he asked, coming closer.

"What do you mean?"

"If you blow up those mines, innocent people will die. *Real* innocents this time."

Skye frowned. As if she hadn't already thought of that herself. She knew the soul stone mines better than he did. And yet, she'd have thought he would have been all in support of the endeavor. If they failed to reach Reaper in time, it would fall to him to seal the demon away again and she wouldn't blame him if he didn't want that burden.

But instead of realizing the significance of what they were about to do, he criticized the plan.

"It's a necessary sacrifice."

"How can you say that? These are lives we're talking about. Doesn't that mean anything to you?"

"Those are the orders. That is the plan. We destroy the mines and there are no more soul stones or spirit shards or whatever the hell you want to call them. No more of those means no more mechs can be made. Fewer mechs makes our job easier when the time comes."

"What about the workers," he challenged, "the people who are only there because they don't have a choice? But for a twist of fate, you could still be one of them. How would you feel about some stranger arbitrarily deciding your fate?"

She glared at him, hating him for using her past against her. She wasn't one of those workers anymore and she never would be again.

"When I worked in those mines, I was so miserable, I would have welcomed it if someone came and blew the whole place up." She took a deep breath, brushing hair back from her face. "It's for the greater good."

Leo shook his head. "You care more about destroying the Empire than you do about helping its people."

"And what exactly are we supposed to do?" Skye demanded, stung by his accusation, though she didn't know why. Why should she give a damn what he thought of her? "We're facing down the impending end of the world, in case you haven't noticed. And I don't know about you, but I don't intend to give Reaper the chance to return if I have anything to say about it." She slipped her dagger back into its sheath. "You don't understand, do you? Every little thing we do is just a bandage slapped on a deep, hemorrhaging wound. It's never going to solve the real problem. It's never going to make things better. Don't you get it? The only way to help these people is to destroy Reaper and the Empire."

That was what had always frustrated her the most about everything she and the Resistance did. Every little victory was overshadowed, for her, by the fact that they hadn't really done anything. Even when they'd taken out the Minister and the Inquisitor both, it hadn't really changed anything.

It was a blow to the Empire, sure, or at least as much of one as they could deal. But the Empire would appoint someone else and replace both of them. Everything would go on much as it always had. Until the day the Empire came crashing down around them, nothing would ever really change.

It was never enough, anything they did. Until now. Now, it would have to be enough, because they wouldn't get another chance. They didn't have a seemingly endless timeline stretching out before them.

Leo looked at her and she saw pity in his eyes. She didn't want his pity. He understood better than most how much she hated the soul stone mines and why the Empire couldn't be allowed to continue its activities there.

Perhaps he merely resented that there was little for him to do. He couldn't even help Fae with the mech any longer and if they were right about the red spirit shards' purpose, the thing wouldn't even work without Reaper's influence. And the last thing they needed was to unleash a machine controlled by the very demon they sought to thwart.

"The ends don't justify the means," he sighed, but the fight had gone out of him, as though he didn't want to argue the point with her anymore.

"Yes," she said firmly, just as glad to bring an end to the conversation. "Sometimes they do."

She stalked out of the forge, trying to push his words out of her mind and focus on the task at hand, but that was easier said than done.

How could he not hate the Empire for what they had done to him? He had finally seen Akkadia for what it truly was and yet she couldn't fathom how he didn't feel compelled to do whatever it took to destroy it.

Skye began to despair of ever understanding him.

But none of that mattered now. She had a job to do and it was only the first of several. The train routes that linked the Capitol to Shemar and Elath would need to be destroyed so that the Capitol could not call for supplies or reinforcements. They would need to hijack shipments and destroy the Workhouses outside the city, the farms that supplied the Capitol with most of its food. Perhaps if they could free the workers there, they would join their cause and aid them in their task.

But first, the mines.

The soul stone mines glittered dimly below in the gathering dark from the collection of lanterns placed around the perimeter. Skye's breath caught as Sheboleth flew over the one place she had never expected or wanted to see again.

This place had claimed both her parents and would have claimed her too, if she hadn't found a way to escape. She only wished all three of them could have done it sooner.

The entrances to the mine yawned wide, pits in the ground that were even darker than the blackness around them. Women and children were especially favored, their smaller size allowing them to crawl into the dark, narrow spaces and ferret out the hidden gems.

Skye had spent most of her time creeping around in the dark, praying the earth above her wouldn't collapse and crush her. She'd emerged at the end of the day covered in dirt, her palms blistered from the pickaxes, hands scraped from trying to coax the gems out.

There was no need to be gentle with the stones. Nothing damaged them, not so much as a scratch, and now she knew why. But the same could not be said for her skin. Soul stones—and spirit shards, too, it seemed—were hard, unbreakable and sharp around the edges.

Surrounding the mines were the workers' cottages, ramshackle sheds pressed closely together. Each one had only one room that was barely big enough for a single person's bedroom, but somehow, they had made do. The floor was dirt and it was impossible to keep anything clean, though her mother had tried.

It was these houses that had been the source of Leo's concern. If the mine blew, there was no guarantee that the houses and workers inside would be spared. And yet, Skye knew that if they escaped unscathed, the foreman and guards would blame the workers for the explosion, never mind that it defied logic.

The workers couldn't possibly engineer such an explosion, but that wouldn't save them from being blamed and punished for it all the same. If they were going to die, she thought, better for the end to be quick.

They had already suffered enough.

The darkness would help hide the four of them from view, and the workers had retired for the night, so it was unlikely they would be spotted by one of them. But the guards patrolled the perimeter constantly.

Sheboleth dove downward, alighting nimbly on the edge of the tree line. The lights of Shemar winked in the distance, not too far away. When the mine blew, everyone in the town would hear it.

Skye slid off the dragon's back, clutching her pack's strap. She had left her crossbow behind in the ruins. It wouldn't do her much good here.

She glanced at the nearest entrance to the mine. In order for this to work, she, Tiachren, and Fae would have to climb down into the mines and place the explosives. This would hide them from view, but she shuddered at the thought of going back down there.

Some of the bends had been tight when she'd been twelve. How much tighter would they be now, eleven years later? What if she got stuck down there, so deep that no one would hear her cries for help? What if the mine finally gave way and collapsed? What if this was to be her grave after all, where she had always been meant to die, alone and in the dark?

She shook her head, shoving the thoughts away, breathing deeply. They had their comm devices. It would be all right. If something came up, they would be able to hear each other.

Unless the signal fails.

It didn't matter. The task was simply too big for a single person to accomplish. It would take all three of them.

By the time they were done, Skye didn't want there to be a single spirit shard remaining. They would all be buried under miles of earth, ideally lost forever.

Sheboleth would stand guard. If the unthinkable happened, and something went wrong, the dragon would warn them. If not all of them could get out on time, they had all agreed beforehand, that the rest of them should flee and blow the mine, even if someone remained behind.

The mines might claim her yet, but it would be worth it if they went up in flames.

Wordlessly, they set out, each taking a different entrance. Hopefully, they would meet somewhere in the middle, but there were many twisting paths and it was easy to get lost.

Skye's pack was heavy with all of the tiny, circular explosives crammed in there, each about the size of her palm. With one last farewell to the others, she steeled herself and ducked into the dark.

Immediately, she was aware of the sensation of a close space, folding out infinitely before her. The sounds of the night faded the deeper she went, bent nearly double to avoid the ceiling.

Once she was sure she was far enough away from the entrance that it would not be noticed, she reached up and turned on the small lamp attached to her headband. It did little to illuminate the space around her, and its charge would only last half an hour at most, but it was better than nothing.

The stones nearest to the surface had been picked over and so she was greeted by solid, uninterrupted stone. As she had feared, the signal, which could be unreliable at the best of times, was even worse underground. She thought one of the others might have tried to contact her at some point, but all she could make out was static.

She continued shuffling forward, pausing at regular intervals to press the explosives firmly against the wall. They flashed dimly in the darkness with two orange lights, pulsing to show they were armed. She carried the detonator in the pocket of her tunic, as did the others. If only one of them should make it out, they all had the ability to detonate the bombs.

Time passed at a crawl and with each step further, Skye felt the earth closing in around her, threatening to squeeze the air from her lungs. She gasped, drawing in shallow, rapid breaths. She couldn't get enough air. She couldn't get *any* in.

She had ventured deep enough to find the spirit shards. They sprouted from the stone in the darkness like crystalized flowers, their red color bright.

Suddenly, she thought they looked like blood that had been poured into a mold and frozen.

Somehow, she kept going, fighting the urge to throw the bombs further into the blackness and race back up to the surface. She needed to pace herself and not place them too closely together.

It was only when she reached into her pack and found one explosive remaining, placing it on the wall, that she allowed herself to turn and head back the way she'd come. She tried checking in on the others, to see how they were progressing, but received no answer. The signal likely couldn't penetrate the thick stone.

Skye moved more quickly now, no longer having to worry about stopping and placing each device, and yet it seemed to take longer to get out than it had to descend.

And then her light flickered and went out, plunging her into complete darkness.

She froze, hands on the walls on either side of her, breathing hard. In a blind panic, she rushed forward, scraping her hands and knees. The tunnel narrowed until she thought it would crush her, one of the stones scratching along her shoulder.

She sank down, motionless, the only sound her ragged breathing and the frantic beats of her heart. Her thoughts drifted to the others, wondering if they were waiting for her. Would the tunnels erupt at any moment behind her, a sudden flash of light and surge of fire rushing forth to engulf her?

Skye closed her eyes—or thought she did. There was no difference in the darkness. She thought of Leo and all the other things she would never get to see again if she died down here. The sun on her face, the wind in her hair.

Gritting her teeth, she surged back up and kept clawing, expecting at any moment to feel sudden stone against her outstretched hands. A dead end. Surely she had taken a wrong turn, remembered the way incorrectly, and become hopelessly lost.

When the opening came into view, the stars winking above, she let out a ragged sob of relief, collapsing onto the ground, limbs shaking.

But her relief was short-lived. Mindful of any guards that may be nearby, she scrambled to her feet and melted into the shadows.

Fae waited with Sheboleth, crouched down near the edge of the trees. Skye sank down beside them, listening to the blood roaring in her ears, the musty, earthy scent of the tunnels still clinging to her nostrils.

Only Tiachren was left now. She hoped he hadn't gotten lost. The minutes slipped by and still he did not emerge.

"Did he say anything to you?" Skye asked Fae.

She shook her head. "I didn't hear anything—and I didn't try to contact you guys either."

Oh, saints. The static she had heard must have been Tiachren. What if he'd been in trouble? What if he still was?

She reached up to activate her comm device. "Tiachren? Tia, come in. Tia!"

Nothing.

Should she go back after him? She didn't think she could bring herself to go back down there, but neither could she ask Fae to.

Skye squeezed her eyes shut. She was a Resistance member, a rebel, a thief, an assassin, a fighter. She had brought down government ministers and she would bring down the Empire yet. She was no longer the terrified little girl that had plunged a knife into a guard's neck and entered a darker world.

She was just about to stand and announce that she was going after him when she saw him emerge from the far entrance and hurry toward them.

"What happened? What took you so long?" she gasped as he reached them.

"I got turned around," he replied, sounding as breathy as she did. "I tried to tell you. But never mind. Are all the devices placed?"

Both Fae and Skye had empty bags. It was time for them to leave this place before they were spotted. Luckily, the patrolling guards carried lights of their own and were easy to track.

They let Tiachren have the honors, since this was technically his area of expertise. He waited until they were well above the mine, Sheboleth soaring in tight circles, before he pushed the button on the detonator.

Skye held her breath. For a moment, nothing happened. And then the ground erupted outward, chunks of stone hurled sky-high. One narrowly missed Sheboleth, Fae letting out a yelp of surprise, and Skye wondered if they should have gone even higher.

She had tried picturing what the exact moment would look like, when the explosives went off, but nothing could have prepared her for the sheer force on display.

The fireball that burst forth from the mine tunnels bathed the scene in a furious orange, painfully bright to look at. A wave of heat rolled over them. The entrances collapsed, new holes opening up in the ground, smoke billowing from them.

Skye stared, unable to look away.

The shockwave that radiated outward had flattened the nearest houses, sending debris flying through the air. She could hear cries ringing out from below as workers rushed toward the ruined homes. They tried desperately to shift rubble out of the way, but Skye knew it was hopeless. No one could have survived being that close to the blast.

You did this.

Skye had thought she would feel *something* at witnessing the destruction of the place that had made her life a living hell. Pride, a fierce sense of satisfaction, a sense of relief, of closure, a weight lifting from her chest. Something.

Instead, she felt empty.

Would her parents have been proud? Would they have cheered as their deaths were avenged? Or would they have wept, their faces burning with shame?

She tried to remind herself that it had to be done. They had to destroy the mines to ensure that the Empire could not make any more mechs. There would be enough of them to face within the city walls as it was. They could not afford any more. And when the Resistance attacks began, that would be the Empire's first thought—to produce more mechs in order to defend against further assault.

But it was cold comfort in the face of what they'd done.

Leo had warned her and she had not listened. She hadn't thought it would matter. Maybe she'd believed they would be further away and she wouldn't have to see the aftermath, how her actions affected the lives of those people. Maybe she had thought that she'd seen enough death that she would be numb to its impact, that it somehow could no longer touch her.

But she'd been wrong. These people were like her. She had *been* one of them once. Leo was right; it could have been her, under different circumstances. It could have been her and her family's lives snuffed out in an instant, by a callous, indifferent third party who viewed them as nothing more than a means to an end.

A necessary sacrifice.

Was that not how the Empire viewed its workers? Was that not the very reasoning they used to justify their own actions?

Bile rose in her throat and she forced it back down, burning as it went. She had finally gone too far. This was not the emperor or his guards. These people hadn't killed anyone. They had slaved away, perhaps hoping or dreaming for a better life one day. Maybe even some of them believed the Resistance could bring that future about, only for the very group they had foolishly put their faith in to take that dream away.

The Resistance was no different. They promised a better future, one where there would be peace and equality for all, and yet they spilled blood and took life as easily as the Empire did.

How easy it must be for the Triad, issuing their orders from afar, never having to lay eyes on the destruction they left in their wake.

Skye turned away, tears burning behind her eyelids, but she could not block out the cries from below. And in her mind, she saw the flash of the fire, seared into her memory.

She was glad when Sheboleth flew away and left it all behind.

But she would never be able to leave it behind. Not again. Not anymore.

XXXIII

There were no cheers upon her return this time, no one rushing up to her, eager to know how the mission had gone. It was still the middle of the night, the trip to Shemar taking far less time than all the way to the Capitol.

Fae and Tiachren, perhaps sensing the mood that had come over Skye, offered to brief the Triad for her. It was on the tip of her tongue to refuse. She had been a part of the mission and it wasn't in her nature to let others speak for her. She could give an account of herself; she wasn't weak.

But for once, she didn't have the strength to argue. Returning to the mines had affected her, more than she cared to admit, and the aftermath hadn't done her any favors.

Thankful for their offer and compassion, Skye retreated to her own quarters, but sleep wouldn't come. Each time she closed her eyes, she saw the fireball surge toward the sky again. She heard the cries of the workers, the words indiscernible, but the pain unmistakable.

The sense of victory she usually felt after a successful mission remained absent, refusing to come. It had been that way ever since the mission to the Capitol. Something had changed.

With a sigh, she stood, her bare feet cold against the stone floor. She had changed out of her usual tunic and leathers and into a long tunic that reached her knees, the air chill against her legs. For once, she had no weapons, no armor. They wouldn't help her now.

Silently, Skye walked through the caverns, wandering like a ghost with no destination in mind. It was eerily quiet, with most of the others having bedded down for the night, but what Skye wanted most at that moment was to hear another's voice.

She turned toward the war room, the light from the screens visible, outlining the curtains. But if Anyah were resting, she didn't want to wake her.

Instead, her steps moved toward Leo's new quarters. She knew where he'd gone, even though she'd never stepped inside herself. But she hesitated as the drapes came into view. He had enough of his own burdens without her adding to them.

Besides, what would he say when she admitted that he'd been right? That she should have listened to him.

She was about to turn away when she caught a glimpse of him through a gap in the curtains. He wasn't asleep, as she expected, but sitting on the edge of the bed, his head lowered. She froze. He hadn't seen her yet. She could still leave and no one would ever know she'd been there.

Skye stepped forward. Leo looked up, their eyes meeting.

"You're back," he said, as if they hadn't had an argument the last time they'd seen each other.

"Yes," Skye replied, her mouth feeling suddenly dry. "Did you wait up?"

"No, I—" He broke off. There was something haunted about his gaze, as though he were staring past her. "No." He cleared his throat. "How did it go?"

Now it was Skye's turn to be haunted, though she hadn't ceased to feel that way since the detonator had been activated.

Leo's brow furrowed when she didn't answer and he leaned forward slightly, as though to stand. "Skye?"

"It was horrible," she whispered. "You were right."

His shoulders slumped slightly. "Come here. No need to stand out there in the cold."

Feeling self-conscious, Skye slipped between the curtains. She was wearing nothing but her oversized tunic and underclothes. With the curtains surrounding them on all sides, blanketing them in darkness and silence, the setting suddenly felt more intimate, inviting.

Leo, who was barefoot himself—his shirt untucked, half of the buttons undone—leaned over to light the single candle on the nightstand. But unable to hold both the box and the match at the same time, the match refused to light, and she heard him swear under his breath.

Wordlessly, she reached over, gently taking the match from his fingers and lighting the candle for him. When she stepped back, shaking the match out, she was aware of how close they were to each other.

His dark eyes scanned her face for a moment before he sat back down on the edge of the bed.

"The mines," he said carefully. "Are they…?"

Skye let out a breath. "Destroyed."

She wanted to tell him how she really felt, how angry and empty and ashamed, unsure how one body could have room for all of those conflicting emotions.

But being so open, so vulnerable, didn't come easy to her. It felt like a weakness, giving someone else such power over you, telling them precisely what you thought or felt. And yet there Leo was, offering her the chance, if she wanted to take it.

She sank down beside him, the bed shifting beneath her weight. "I thought…seeing it all go up in flames would bring me some sort of peace, some closure, some measure of satisfaction, at least. But it didn't. When I try to close my eyes, I see them, burning. I hear them screaming. I don't think it will ever go away. Why won't it go away?" She squeezed her eyes shut, not wanting to cry in front of him.

"I ask myself the same question," Leo murmured, "about the things I can't forget. I can push it to the side when I'm awake, but the dreams still come."

Skye opened her eyes, glancing at him. She had given him a weapon with which to destroy her and in turn, he was giving her one right back.

"I had another one tonight," he went on. "Usually, they're slightly different, but tonight, I dreamed of my mother again—that she was still alive. It all feels so real, even though I know it's not. And when I wake up, any relief I might have felt vanishes because it's not the truth. It's like my mind is incapable of catching up with reality. The whiplash of emotion…it's exhausting."

Skye had experienced something similar herself, though the dreams had faded and become less frequent the more time passed. She knew what he meant about the whiplash of emotion, from devastation to fervent hope, to the crushing weight of reality, of *grief*, that always left one hollowed out.

"I know what you mean," she whispered. "I still have dreams of being trapped in the mines, either by cave-in or venturing too far down a tunnel and getting stuck." She shuddered. "Tonight, it wasn't a dream, afraid that I would die down there alone, in the dark, away from the sun, wondering if someone would find my bones down there some day. Maybe they would join me. To this day, I still hate the dark."

"This must be your least favorite time of day, then," Leo remarked. "Not that you can tell down here."

She shook her head. "No, not the night, the dark."

The night was intimate, a friend, that hid her from her enemies.

Leo turned to her. "Is it hard to live down here in the caverns, with both the dark and being underground?"

The reminder of the mines always hanging over her head.

"It was, at first. Still is, sometimes, if I'm honest. I like to go outside, whenever I can." She fought the urge to tuck her legs up on the edge of the bed and wrap her arms around them. "You were right," she said again. "I should have listened to you. All I could think about was my family—"

"I know. Saints, I know." At his side, his hand clenched into a fist, gripping the sheets.

Impulsively, she reached out and took his hand in her own, without thought or hesitation.

They had each had to come to terms with the loss of their family in their own way. They were both alone in the world, aside from each other and whatever friends and allies they managed to gain.

Skye's entire body felt hot. She wasn't used to being so vulnerable, to laying it all out there, holding nothing back. But she refused to let go, to back away. She felt scoured out herself, but not in a wholly bad way.

She drew in a shaky breath. "Can I stay with you? Not…like that. I just…don't want to be alone right now."

She waited for him to scoff, to mock her, to reject her, to send her back out into the cold, alone. But of course, despite her fear, he did none of those things.

"Of course."

Releasing her hand, he swung his legs back up onto the bed, settling back against the pillows, arguably a more comfortable position. The bed, which was larger than the standard cots, could hold more than one person.

Hesitantly, as if afraid at any moment of making the wrong move, Skye crawled over and laid down beside him, her legs tucked up as though to make herself small.

It was Leo who closed the remaining distance between them, as if to reassure her that it was all right, his arm around her, their bodies pressing together in the dark.

Skye laid her head on his shoulder, her hand on his chest, feeling his heat even through the thin cotton of his shirt. Slowly, she let herself relax.

She had never laid next to someone like that before. It was…nice. Even without a single dagger at her side, she felt safe in a way she couldn't remember experiencing before.

There was a sort of comfort in being with someone who also knew what it was to be broken. Broken things could be remade, but the pieces would never fit quite the same way again, if all the pieces were even still there in the end.

Skye closed her eyes, expecting to see the mines explode again, but no images came. She knew better than to think they were gone for good, but for now, it was enough, listening to Leo's quiet breathing, feeling his heart beating beneath her hand.

As ever, it was impossible to tell what time of day it was when Leo awoke, awareness slowly returning, but he thought it might be morning. He didn't remember falling asleep, and if he'd had any more dreams, he couldn't recall them either.

He blinked, turning to his left. Skye was curled up beside him, still asleep, lips parted slightly, her long lashes dark against her cheeks, black hair spread across his shoulder.

Leo swallowed and sat up, carefully disentangling himself. He stood slowly, easing his weight off the bed, not wanting to disturb her. With his back to her, he set about the task of buttoning his shirt. Not all of the buttons were undone, but it was still daunting.

Buttoning a shirt was never something he'd considered difficult, but he certainly did now that he had to do so with only one hand. He'd had to adapt over the months, growing accustomed to his new normal and new way of doing things, but buttons still gave him trouble.

He managed the first few and then inevitably came to one that must have been slightly larger—or else the hole was smaller.

No matter how hard he tried, his fingers simply refused to obey him, constantly slipping just when he thought he might have finally gotten it this time, if only he could push a little harder—

With a growl of frustration, Leo abandoned the effort, raking a hand through his hair, both embarrassed and angry. The ability to properly dress himself was just one more thing the Empire had taken from him.

Suddenly, Skye was there, moving to stand before him, and he jumped slightly, forgetting, for a moment, that she was there. He felt his face heat, that she had to witness his humiliation.

"Here." She reached out, her deft fingers making quick work of the remaining buttons.

"I can manage," Leo protested weakly. It felt like a lie, but pride was a terrible thing.

She looked up at him. "I know you can. But I'd offer to help regardless."

She turned and walked out, slipping between the drawn curtains, presumably to return to her own quarters and prepare for the day.

Leo watched her go, the drapes swinging shut behind her, pondering her words and the reason for them.

XXXIV

Lydia stood, surveying the destruction of the soul stone mines laid out before her, arms clasped behind her back. The smoke had faded, leaving behind chunks of stone and rubble. The houses nearest to the mine entrances had collapsed entirely and a few more had fallen when the mine tunnels shifted, collapsing in on themselves several hours after the initial explosion.

She'd been told that even more had perished then, trying to shift the rubble and search for survivors when the ground suddenly opened up beneath them.

The soul stones might be salvageable, but it would take time. Time they may not have. The rebels were growing bolder and she couldn't help but wonder if there was a reason for it. They hadn't targeted the mines before, so they must be planning something.

"The workers claim to have no knowledge of the bombing, Minister."

Lydia turned to the guard standing beside her. The other soldiers had rounded up the remaining workers while the foreman had been sent to report to her.

"And do you believe them?" she asked. She intended to find out for herself, but she wanted to know this man's opinion.

"Yes," he said simply. "The attack was too sophisticated for them to carry out on their own. If they did have something to do with it, they must have had help…" He trailed off, looking uncomfortable.

"The Resistance, you mean," she said, giving voice to the words he didn't want to utter.

She couldn't blame his discomfort. The emperor would be waiting for her report, but she was in no hurry to give it. Instead of going straight to the throne room upon her return to the palace, she sought out her brother and was relieved to find him in their quarters.

One of his eyes had been blackened and she didn't have to ask how it had happened. No doubt Desmond had lashed out at him, taking his anger at her out on Fabian instead. She felt anger spear through her, white-hot, but she tamped it down.

"How bad is it?" Fabian asked. He had heard the news and knew where she had gone. He sat on the edge of the sofa, but Lydia made no move to join him.

"Bad," she replied. "The emperor won't forgive this one."

He looked at her, green eyes full of concern. He knew what had happened to the last Minister of Defense and Lydia was reminded of what had nearly happened to her the last time she had reported to Desmond. He had wanted to kill her then, but something had held him back. She knew better than to expect the voice to save her a second time.

Desmond would most certainly try to kill her now.

She turned to leave but Fabian leapt up. "Don't go."

Lydia froze. "I have to. You know that."

Without turning, she left him then and made her way to the throne room, walking briskly. The time had finally come.

The throne room was suffused with light when she arrived. The heavy curtains had been pulled back from the windows, flooding the room. Lydia blinked as she entered, trying to make her eyes adjust more clearly. The emperor never had the windows open.

She did not slow her stride. She could make out Desmond, perched on his black throne, surrounded by his faithful hounds. Perhaps for the first time, Lydia felt no fear toward them. They would not hurt her. She knew it as certainly as she knew her own name.

Desmond tapped his nails on the arm of his throne. "Report."

And so Lydia did.

Desmond listened dispassionately as his Minister gave her report. It didn't matter what she had to say; he had already made his decision. He had been right that Lydia had an ambitious streak to her, but she wasn't reliable. She had been promoted beyond her capabilities and the whole Empire was suffering for it.

If she could not eliminate the threat of the dragons and crush the infernal Resistance, then she was of no use to him and he would have to replace her with someone more capable.

It was disappointing, really. When the last Minister had displeased him, he'd hoped that Lydia would prove herself, but she had failed even more miserably than her predecessor.

The soul stone mines were all but destroyed. Those gems were vital to the Empire's automata. Without them, how could they be expected to defend themselves against the rebels? They still had plenty of actual, human soldiers to call upon, that was true, but Desmond found them somehow distasteful.

Humans were imperfect. The mechs broke down, yes, but they were in every other respect the perfect soldiers. They did not grow weary. They did not feel pain or fear. They did not let their emotions get the better of them, because they had none.

"*Yes,*" the voice agreed. "*The perfect soldiers.*"

The Minister had finally stopped speaking. "Is that all?" Desmond asked.

"Not yet," Lydia replied.

She reached into her gray Minister robes, withdrawing a curved dagger, the blade glinting in the bright light.

Desmond did not move. Instead, he laughed. He'd known his Minister was incapable of carrying out her duties, in over her head, but he hadn't anticipated that she would take complete leave of her senses.

No matter. His dogs would protect him.

But they did not move either. Desmond felt a flicker of irritation, but remained unconcerned. The voice had always warned him of incoming danger and shielded him. This would be no different.

The fact that the voice's presence was just as nonchalant as he was could only mean that Lydia did not present any real threat.

He continued to think that, confident in his own security, right up until the moment Lydia lunged forward, plunging the dagger into his chest, burying it to the hilt.

Pain speared through Desmond's chest, both cold and warm at once, and he let out a gasp. He stared at his Minister with wide eyes, slowly glancing down to where the blade had struck. The silk of his robes was stained crimson, blood beginning to seep through the material.

The blade had pierced his heart, right where the amulet always hung, its weight familiar and reassuring. The stone was harder than steel and would have easily deflected the dagger's blow. But he could feel that the amulet had shifted to the side, leaving his heart wide open and vulnerable.

No.

Lydia watched his reaction implacably. She took a step back, her green eyes wild, and pushed a lock of hair out of her face.

"Did the voices in your head warn you about that?" she asked, tilting her head to once side.

Desmond gripped the armrests of his throne as the familiar voice she mentioned spoke, for a final time, in his mind.

"Only ever a pawn…"

Lydia watched in fascination as the emperor drew in a few more ragged breaths, choking on his own blood, and then went still. The dogs lay motionless at his feet. They had not moved once.

Hardly daring to believe what she'd done, she stepped forward and gently lifted the mask from the emperor's face, beholding his true appearance for the first time.

Fabian's description had been apt in every way except one. The emperor's eyes, if they had ever truly been golden, were now dark, so dark in fact that they looked black as they stared sightlessly to the side.

His face looked little older than her own, barely touched by the ravages of time.

Her gaze trailed over to the amulet, still hanging over his chest. The eye had opened, fixed on her, a beautiful but terrible mixture of amber and orange in color, the pupil dark as an abyss. There was no doubt that it saw her, but she did not feel the paralyzing, crushing terror that Fabian had experienced.

Slowly, moving as though not of her own volition, she reached out a hand toward the stone. She grasped the chain that hung around Desmond's neck, pulling it over his head.

The stone was surprisingly warm in her hand. This was the key to everything. This stone could cure Fabian. So long as it remained in their possession, neither of them would ever die. They would live out the passing centuries ageless, as Desmond had, ever since he took the stone from the last king of Anarsha.

Lydia knew it as certainly as she'd known the dogs would not attack. She let out a little chuckle. And to think she'd been relying on a scribe when the answer had been right here, all along.

She lifted the amulet, placing it around her own neck, and almost immediately she heard a voice speak in her mind, deep and resonant.

"Hello, empress."

XXXV

With his options limited, Leo tried to keep busy and make himself useful where he could, while waiting for news of the next mission, knowing all the while that he was their backup plan. It was impossible to forget how much was hinging on him, the soul stone around his neck serving as a constant reminder.

If the other members of the Resistance knew the truth, he had no doubt they would look at him whenever he appeared, but for now, he was grateful to be seen as just another member. They would likely find out the truth soon enough and Leo didn't really care to be the object of their attention.

Still, they knew *something* was going on, that the Resistance was planning something big.

Leo tried to remain out of sight, helping Anyah in the war room or retreating to Fae's workshop. There was little he could do to help her reassemble the mech directly, but he liked her company, the quiet intensity with which she worked.

He knew, however, that he was holding her back. She could work so much more quickly and efficiently if she didn't feel the need to accommodate him and find ways to include him. While he appreciated the efforts, it also reminded him of what had been lost.

Finally, one day, he made himself say the words out loud. "I'm afraid I'm not much use to you." *I'm not much use to anyone these days.*

Fae waved one hand. "Neither of us are, are we? So long as we're working on this." She gestured to the suspended mech, still motionless and incomplete. "Not much point now. It was never going to work and now we know why. The mechs aren't truly autonomous. They need a demon to control them." She gave a faint smile and then frowned. "Sorry, I shouldn't have—"

"No, it's all right." Fae was one of the few people who knew the truth. "No point in pretending otherwise, is there?"

No point in pretending I might not have to seal away an ancient demon.

"Actually, I have something that might help with that," Fae said tentatively. "I've been working on it in my spare time. I probably should have told you, but I wanted it to be a surprise..."

She trailed off, looking hesitant, and Leo realized she was self-conscious, worried what his reaction would be.

"What is it?"

"Through here." She jerked her head toward one of the covered doorways and led him further into the workshop.

The room was small and Leo stopped short, his eyes going at once to what she must have been referring to. There, resting atop a single table, was a mechanical arm, not dissimilar to the kind Leo had assembled as a doll maker in the Capitol.

"You don't have to use it," Fae said hurriedly, "if you don't want to. I should have asked first. I don't want to presume—"

"You made this?" Leo asked slowly, turning to her. "For me?"

She nodded. "I just wanted to help. I didn't want to imply that you….needed it or anything."

Leo stepped closer, running his fingers over the metal, admiring the intricacy of its collective parts. If he'd been making it himself, he might have made a few modifications, but that would be easy enough.

"It's impressive," he admitted.

"I had Anyah help me with the wiring," Fae said. "It can connect to the remaining nerve endings, giving you the ability to move it like a real arm. Or as close as we can get, anyway."

Leo sucked in a breath, his fingers stilling over the cool metal. Fae was offering him the chance to get a piece of his life back. A piece of himself, that he had thought gone for good. If he could move the fingers…if it could function like a real arm—

"I do have to warn you, though," she added. "Once it's done, it can't easily or painlessly be undone. It's more or less permanent. It will require maintenance and upkeep and if it's damaged, it will need to be repaired or replaced, which might involve yet more pain. I also tried to make it as light as I could, but it does have some weight to it— more than a real limb, at any rate—and I've been told that it may result in some muscle wear."

It wasn't perfect, but then, what about his situation was? He couldn't even button a shirt on his own anymore and he lived in near constant pain already. Sometimes, he could ignore it for a while, but then it would always come back, usually when he let his guard down.

This solution may do nothing to ease the pain, but Leo thought he could live with that. Saints knew he would have to learn to live with it anyway, one way or another, and he thought it a risk worth taking.

He turned to her. "Can you install it?"

Fae took a deep breath. "With a doctor's help, I think so."

"Do it."

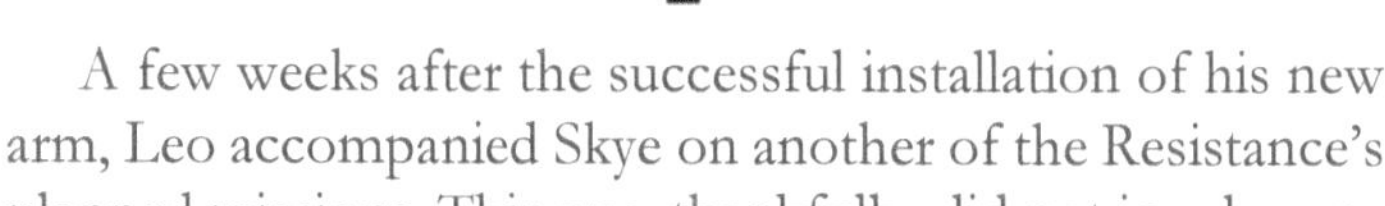

A few weeks after the successful installation of his new arm, Leo accompanied Skye on another of the Resistance's planned missions. This one, thankfully, did not involve any civilian targets.

They set out on foot, traveling without Sheboleth since she had a mission of her own to see to, though she had dropped them off along the way.

They each carried packs full of Tiachren's explosives and knew, on the other side of the forest, heading toward Shemar, there was another team, intent on the same goal.

They were to blow the railway lines, particularly any bridges, severing the Capitol from the outlying cities. The two of them walked along the tracks, which would take them to the closest bridge. Unlike his previous explosives, Tiachren had designed these bombs to go off after a certain interval once they'd been placed and activated. They needed to be a safe distance away when that happened.

Leo tilted his head back, savoring the feeling of the sun on his face. He hadn't been out in the field since before the disastrous mission to the Capitol and it felt good to be helping. To be *doing something*.

This mattered. It helped increase the chances that the Resistance's assault on the Capitol would be a success and they would need every advantage in order to stop Reaper before it was too late.

At his side, he clenched his right hand into a fist. He was still adjusting to its new capabilities and suddenly having two arms again. It wasn't perfect and could never make up for a real, flesh and blood limb. It was cold, unyielding steel, not soft or warm, and he couldn't feel anything with it, no sensations of any kind.

But it was better than nothing and Leo was immensely grateful for the gift Fae and Anyah both had given him. The sun glinted off of its surface as he walked, a multi-colored mixture of brown, brass, rust, and bronze, like the automatons.

As they neared their destination, the bridge looming ahead, Leo felt his pulse kick into a gallop. This wasn't a situation he'd expected to find himself in again, and he felt a rush of excitement and fear.

Wordlessly, Skye reached over, taking his hand in her own. He couldn't feel the warmth of her skin, but she didn't seem to mind.

Gently, he contracted the metal fingers, giving her hand a small squeeze in acknowledgement. He wasn't alone. She was there with him and it would be all right.

The two of them began to mount the bridge, the incline steep. The back of Leo's calves burned by the time they reached the peak and he desperately hoped no train approached from either direction. They had nowhere to go.

The bridge ascended to a dizzying height, rising above the tree line, stretching over the river that sliced through the forest. Leo could see the gleaming water down below, but there was no sign of the Capitol on the horizon. No sign of a train, either, as far as the eye could see, for which he was very grateful.

He couldn't help but wonder what it would be like to plummet from such a height. Sheboleth wasn't there to catch either of them if they should fall. Fortunately, the Empire kept such bridges in good condition, knowing how important they were to the transportation of goods from one city to the next.

Wordlessly, they set about their task, retrieving the small explosives from their packs and setting them at regular intervals, on each side of the bridge.

They had worked backward, starting at the opposite end of the bridge so that when they had finished, they simply retreated back the way they'd initially come, a bit more urgency to their pace now.

Leo was winded by the time they safely reached the bottom of the bridge and stepped back into the trees. He didn't see the exact moment the bombs went off, his view blocked by the thick foliage, but he certainly *heard* it.

The resounding explosion seemed to shake the limbs of the trees, sending flocks of birds scattering into the air. Leo pictured the bridge collapsing inward, plunging into the river below.

Skye turned to him with a wicked grin. "Let's hope the others did their jobs."

The Workhouses spread out below Sheboleth, stretching across the flat land that separated the Capitol from the edge of the Valderan rainforest. She had spied on its workers for years, but rarely had she seen them from this vantage point. No longer hidden within the safety of the forest tree line, she soared openly above, making no attempt at hiding herself now.

The workers were more like slaves, laboring beneath the unrelenting sun or pouring rain. They worked in all conditions, without exception, under the watchful gaze of the supervisors, and so there was no chance they would fail to notice her.

Her keen eyes took in their number at once, the groups of workers in the fields, the supervisors standing watch under covered pavilions, and the dogs.

Animals might not have been allowed within the city walls, with the exception of District I, but that did not apply outside of the Capitol. The Workhouses employed dogs to keep the workers in line and to discourage any of them from running off.

She had seen the hounds unleashed before, to track down a runaway worker and drag him back. She had heard their baying late at night. Sheboleth supposed the creatures were large when compared to humans, hairy things with pointed ears and lean, muscular bodies, but they offered no threat for her.

Her orders, from the Triad, were to destroy the farms so that the Capitol could not use the crops for food during the siege. She didn't expect the assault to last that long, truthfully, but it never hurt to prepare for the worst.

It was a lot of ground to burn on her own and she could feel the fire building in her chest already, fueled by her rage toward the Empire.

She had purposefully timed her departure from the ruins so that she would arrive during daylight hours, when the workers would be out. She wanted them to see her, panic, and flee. Ideally, they would be out of harm's way when the first flames arrived.

She had been ordered to destroy the farms. There was no need for the workers to die.

A few of the more attentive workers had already reacted to her presence, pointing and presumably shouting at the others. But for the others, who needed a little encouragement, Sheboleth let out a roar.

When it came to the Workhouses, dragon attacks were not unheard of. Sheboleth might have considered doing it sooner, if only to strike back at the Empire in one of the few ways she could.

Shaken from their initial shock, the workers scattered and Sheboleth could hear their cries of fear. But there was no organization, no rhyme or reason to the directions they scurried.

Roaring, she dove after them, swooping low, slowly herding them where she wanted them to go, and giving them the chance to be well out of the way before the flames began. As she did so, she couldn't help but feel a flicker of satisfaction. This was what dragons were supposed to be—powerful, feared, and unstoppable.

The first flames rained down onto fields already dry from a recent lack of rain, igniting the crops like dried tinder. Sheboleth swooped low, the wind from her wings fanning the flames, until every farm, every field was alight.

She soared overhead, surveying her work, listening to the crackling flames, bathed in their heat and furious orange glow. Smoke rose into the sky and she wondered if Leo and Skye could see it from their vantage point, deeper in the forest.

She turned, glancing across the open expanse toward the Capitol. The blaze would certainly be visible from the city. They would be able to see what she'd done.

Sheboleth let out one last defiant roar and banked back toward the forest. They had weakened the Empire as much as they possibly could. Now they could only hope it was enough.

The time for hiding in the shadows was over. Now, the Resistance would emerge, taking credit for each of the recent attacks on the Empire. To let the people know that the rebels not only remained, but were capable of dealing meaningful blows to the Empire that had oppressed its people for too long. They *could* take on the Empire and win.

Upon returning from detonating the bridge, Leo followed Skye deeper into the caverns, to a section he'd never been to before. Here, at last, was the source of the mechanical clanking and churning sounds he'd heard before.

Massive printing presses, powered by the limited electricity that he could now see was generated by large wheels churning through the underground streams. Hundreds of papers moved past, turned out as quickly as they could be made.

Stacks of finished copies lay on the floor beside the huge machines, the attendants adding to their numbers all the time. Leo picked up one of the finished copies, studying it. Propaganda, encouraging people to stand with the Resistance.

"We always produce them," Skye said, noticing his interest. "But we can't easily distribute them."

He wondered if these were some of the seditious materials the executed man had been caught with. His death now felt like a distant memory, from another life.

Leo knew what they had in mind for the pamphlets before they even carried it out and he helped them do it. Sheboleth carried a sack of fliers in her claws as she flew and he had his own smaller bundle.

Elath was their target, but other dragons, likewise laden with papers, had agreed to take care of Shemar and the Capitol itself. Leo tipped his bundle over the side as Sheboleth soared over the city, watching as they cascaded downward, fluttering, buffeted on the wind.

It was a strangely beautiful sight, but Leo couldn't ignore what it meant. The Resistance had never attempted anything like the scale of the recent attacks and they would need to move quickly. The Empire knew they were planning something, the increase in activity all the proof they needed.

The Resistance had announced their intentions and now it was time to act upon them. When all of the papers had been dropped, Sheboleth turned and headed back in the direction of the ruins. The ruins that none of them would likely see again after they set out for the Capitol.

If they succeeded, there would be no reason to return. No need to hide underground, in cold, drafty caverns any longer. They could finally be above ground, show themselves, and feel the sun on their faces.

They would finally be free.

If they failed, they would all be dead and it wouldn't matter anymore.

He tried not to think about what it would mean if they failed.

"What have you done?"

Fabian's voice seemed to echo across the throne room. It was only the two of them, he and his sister. And the motionless corpse, slumped over on the throne, that had once been Desmond.

It would be some time, he knew, before the emperor's body was discovered. Unless Desmond sent for one of his servants, he would be left alone, no one wanting to risk his wrath.

Except for Lydia, who had risked something far worse.

Still, it was only a matter of time until someone discovered what she had done.

His sister didn't answer his question. She didn't give the appearance of even having heard. She stood to the side of the throne, staring down at the amulet in her hand.

"Lydia, what did you do?" Fabian repeated, more forcefully this time.

She looked up. "What I had to. Desmond wasn't fit to rule. We both know that."

"And who's going to rule now?" Fabian demanded. "You?"

"Why not?" Lydia strode over to him. "We both could!"

"Lydia, now is not the time for a change in leadership! Not with the Resistance attacks growing bolder."

"Don't you get it? Now is our chance to crush the Resistance, once and for all. Unlike Desmond, I am not afraid to act. Nor am I mad."

Fabian stared at his sister, unable to escape the feeling creeping over him that he was looking at someone else. His sister was not reckless, not impulsive. He knew they had discussed Desmond's madness, his being unfit to rule. He knew she had mentioned that he needed to be removed from power, maybe even killed.

But now? Like this?

Perhaps some part of him hadn't thought she'd really do it. He knew Lydia had done things—sometimes awful things—in service to the Empire, following Desmond's orders, all of it to keep Fabian safe. But he'd never thought of her as a killer before.

"You sound like it," he muttered. "You certainly don't sound like yourself."

His eyes strayed to the amulet in her hand, clenched so tightly in her fingers, he might have thought she intended to crush it. He knew from Zak that the demon had whispered in Desmond's ear, at least partly to blame for his madness.

Was it whispering to his sister, even now?

She glared at him. "I thought you would have been relieved."

"Relieved?" Fabian repeated, incredulous.

"To no longer have to obey his every whim, no longer have to fear his wrath and unpredictable moods."

Now I have to fear yours. Fabian wasn't sure where the thought came from, but it felt like the truth.

He let out a breath. "And you think you can just take over? Announce yourself as empress and everyone will just be all right with that?"

"I'll make the announcement after the Resistance threat has been taken care of. No one will object once I've swooped in and saved them from certain destruction. They'll be so grateful, they'll eagerly accept me as empress."

Fabian shook his head. "Do you hear yourself right now? You can't just kill the emperor and get away with it."

"I can do whatever I want," Lydia murmured, her gaze once more resting upon the stone. "The voice will protect me."

"The voice? Is that what it told you? And you believed it?"

"It protected me once and it will do so again." She whirled on him, cradling the stone in her hands. "This is the answer we've been searching for, Fabian. It's right here, not in some dusty tome."

"What are you talking about?"

"How do you think Desmond lived for over a thousand years? The voice made it possible. It told me so. It can cure you, Fabian. You can live forever. You'll never have to die. Neither of us will."

There was a fervent light in her green eyes, almost zealous. Fabian felt an ache in his chest. His sister wanted to cure him, more than anything, and now she believed she'd finally found a way.

He glanced across at Desmond, still seated on his throne. A thousand years? Had he really lived that long? Had they been ruled by a single emperor all these years, faking his own death along the way, his life unnaturally extended by the demon trapped around his neck?

It all sounded insane, but everything Fabian had thought he'd known had been turned on its head the moment Zak revealed the truth about the demon. If that were true, why shouldn't this be also?

"You mean the demon? That's what the voice belongs to, don't forget. You can't trust a word it says. It not only drove Desmond mad, it allowed you to kill him! I don't think we can rely on its protection, or its false promises."

"It had no further use for Desmond," Lydia retorted. "He wasn't fit to rule. I am."

The ache in Fabian's chest grew, becoming painful, as he beheld what his sister had become. Or perhaps she'd always been this way and he'd just refused to see it.

He'd known his sister was ambitious and it seemed that ambition extended to a lust for power of her own. He wondered what else she might yet be willing to do—and what she had already done.

Suddenly, he thought of Zak, who had made them aware of the demon's existence in the first place. Fabian still didn't know what had been in those documents that the scribe had supposedly smuggled out of the palace and into the hands of the Resistance. He wasn't sure it mattered. And he wasn't sure if that story were even true.

The fact that he knew of the demon might have been enough to damn him. Lydia wouldn't want such information getting out. She would keep the amulet close to her chest—literally—the same way Desmond had.

If she could turn on Zak, a friend, what was to stop her from turning on him?

What might she yet do?

Lydia's expression suddenly softened and Fabian had to force himself not to flinch as she stepped up to him.

"I did this for us," she whispered, clasping her hand in his, the amulet pressed between them. "For both of us."

The warmth of the stone pressed against Fabian's skin and he sucked in a sharp breath as certainty flooded him. The same certainty Lydia had spoken of.

The amulet would indeed prevent his death. No one would ever hurt him again. No one's fickle whims would ever summon him, no matter how late the hour. No one would ever again strike him, hurt him, humiliate him, or make him feel small.

When Lydia pulled back, taking the amulet with her, the sudden absence of its warmth made Fabian feel cold.

And he found himself reluctant to let it go.

XXXVI

Leo sighed, staring up at the ruins and the blue sky beyond. The final preparations were underway inside the caverns and he knew he should join the others, helping to pack up anything that would need to be taken with them to the Capitol. They were setting out tomorrow morning regardless.

It was finally here, the moment he had both waited for and dreaded in equal measure. It was really happening.

There was no point in running from it or pretending otherwise. Soon, this would all end, one way or another.

Leo pondered the ruins. He'd felt drawn to them from the first moment he'd seen them. Would they succeed in their mission and finally avenge what had happened here, a thousand years ago? Would they put right the mistake that King Ulric had made? The folly of man? Or had that always been meant to be their undoing, the past millennia nothing more than a reprieve.

He winced, a throb of pain shooting through his arm. The soul stone, cold against his skin, felt heavier than normal, as if it could somehow sense that its time was near.

"Thought I might find you here."

Leo looked up to see Sheboleth making her way toward him.

"Are you ready for this?" he asked as she sat down beside him.

"I know you're not," she said wryly. "I haven't told you the spell yet, that you'll need if Reaper returns."

He sighed. "If everything goes wrong, you mean."

"It *won't*. We'll find that amulet and burn it."

"You've never lied to me, Sheboleth. Don't start now."

Her mouth twisted into a semblance of a frown. "Fine. We'll do everything possible to avoid that fate, but I can't make any promises."

"I know. Thank you." He shifted, turning toward her. "So what's this spell?"

"The same one used all those years ago by the saints to seal the demons away, if you believe such things."

The ancient Anarshan words felt clumsy on his tongue and he struggled with the pronunciation, repeating what she'd told him over and over, until the words were seared into his memory.

He doubted he could forget them even if he tried.

"So this is the language of the saints," he murmured. "Let's hope they're smiling down on us now."

The Resistance set out the next morning. They were joined, at the edge of the Badlands, by the dragons Sheboleth had summoned, who had agreed to help. There weren't as many as Skye would have liked—she'd have felt comfortable with more—but she hoped they would be enough. After all, Sheboleth was only one dragon and she had seen firsthand how much of a difference one dragon could make.

The other dragons mostly stayed off to the side, keeping to themselves, except for Sheboleth. She no longer seemed to belong in either group. She would never be a human, but she was also far too trusting of the humans for the other dragons to be comfortable with.

Every essential item had been packed and brought along with them. The armory had been emptied, weapons passed around to those who did not already have them. What little armor there was had also been distributed.

Skye had chosen not to wear any. She felt most capable in her black leathers. She had her knives and crossbow, with all her extra bolts. They would spare nothing in the assault.

There were too many people and supplies and not enough dragons willing to transport them, so they were forced to travel on foot. It would take several days to reach the Capitol and they all carried a canteen full of water and a pack of food.

Skye had made the trek to the Capitol plenty of times on foot, but the transportation Sheboleth provided had been a luxury she'd quickly grown used to. She'd forgotten how hard the trip was—and how long.

The sun had beat down fiercely across the Badlands. There was no shade or water to be found there and Skye was almost glad when they'd ducked beneath the shade of the rainforest, though the air here was muggy and heavy. The moisture seemed to cling to her clothes and skin.

Every now and then, a few of the dragons went to scout ahead and make sure there were no threats, no ambushes lying in wait. It didn't seem likely, but the Triad was taking no chances. But they encountered little trouble aside from a brief downpour.

At first, it was easy to distract herself, focusing on walking, each individual step, and ignoring the pain in her feet. But that soon became monotonous and Skye's mind drifted to the task that awaited them.

It really hit home the final night, as they camped near the edge of the forest. She couldn't see the Capitol through the trees, but she knew it was out there, along with the burned ruins of the Workhouses.

Closing her eyes, she could picture the great outer wall of the Capitol, her mind's eye lifting to each consecutive level, until it came to the tenth at the very top. The palace, where the emperor awaited, with the amulet they had come to destroy.

She sucked in a sharp breath. They would reach it tomorrow. Tomorrow, everything would end.

The camp sprawled around her, tents nestled between the trees. There were fewer fires, the Triad not wanting to risk as many as they had on previous nights, being so close to the city. Skye could hear the fires popping as logs shifted, voices carried on the gentle wind, the air filled with the smell of woodsmoke and roasting meat.

It was a relatively peaceful scene, but her limbs felt restless. And if she felt that way, she could only imagine how Leo must feel.

Turning, she picked her way through the camp until she came to where he'd pitched his tent. Unsurprisingly, it was empty. Skye straightened, glancing around. He could be anywhere, but she had a pretty good idea where he'd gone.

Putting her back to the camp, she walked toward its edge, the light from the fires and the sound of conversation fading behind her, the forest swallowing her. And then suddenly there he was, standing before her, staring off at nothing.

"How are you holding up?" she asked, her voice quiet, not wanting to startle him.

He turned, his eyes dark. "It's so close."

"I know," she whispered.

She had waited for this moment for eleven years, ever since she had fled the mines of Shemar and made her way to the Resistance.

It was the goal that had occupied each of her waking hours, the one she had fought and bled for, the one she would willingly die for. All those years, it had felt like the Resistance made no progress. That no matter what they did, no matter how many victories, it had never been enough. It had never brought them to this moment and Skye had begun to doubt if it would ever come at all.

And now it was finally here, closer than a kiss.

She had feared that the Empire would somehow reverse-trace Anyah's network signal and locate them. They would be forced to move, at best, or hunted down and eliminated at worst. Somehow, it had always seemed more likely that the Empire would destroy them before they could destroy it.

But it hadn't happened that way. They could still die, maybe tomorrow, maybe not. The Empire could still win, but for now...

"I've dreamed of this moment," she murmured, "so many times, and yet, I never pictured it quite like this."

Leo turned, facing her fully. "And what about after? When you picture that, what does it look like?"

Skye shook her head. "I don't know. That's just it. I'm afraid. Not of what happens if we fail; I know what will happen then. I'm afraid of the future, of what happens if we win. I never thought about my future and what lies ahead for me beyond this moment, beyond the Empire's defeat. To be honest, I...never expected to survive. Some part of me never really wanted to."

Tears suddenly stung her eyes, but she didn't brush them away. She didn't turn away from him.

"My family is gone. Revenge was the only thing that kept me going. But now…" She tilted her head, looking up at him. "Now I find myself caring about something else. Somone else. Something to fight for. To live for."

Leo inhaled sharply. "I'm terrified," he admitted. "It seems foolish, tempting fate, to imagine a future beyond tomorrow, beyond even this moment."

"Then let's figure that out when we get there," Skye said, feeling her skin flush at her own boldness. "For now, if this moment is all we have, let's make the most of it."

She felt her pulse thrumming in her veins, waiting to see what he would say. What he would do. She had opened herself up to him before, daring to be vulnerable, and trusting that he wouldn't use it to destroy her.

Instead, he had given her a weapon of her own to use. They were both armed, but the blades had remained sheathed. She knew he wouldn't draw it now. But did he feel the same vulnerability that she did, or was she merely making a fool of herself?

Leo swallowed and her eyes tracked the movement. "I can't deny what I feel for you, Skye," he admitted. "There's something between us, a connection that we've been dancing around the edge of. The question now is whether we want to fall over that edge or not."

Skye felt relief bloom in her chest, spreading like warmth, and her legs suddenly felt weak. He had said it, the words she wanted to hear.

Perhaps it was the fate waiting for them that made them bold. Such a confession seemed far less daunting when compared to facing down a demon. The thought made her feel slightly giddy, but whatever the reason, she didn't care.

Leo moved closer to her, the moonlight turning his hair silver. It had returned to the length it had been when she'd met him.

"We can take things slow. If you want to."

"I do," she whispered. "There was a time when I didn't need anyone. It seemed better that way. The Resistance was my family, my friends. I would die for them. I still don't need anyone." The collar of his shirt was undone and she reached out, touching his collarbone, fingers trailing down to rest upon the soul stone. "But I find myself wanting all the same."

Leo smiled. "It's nice, being wanted."

Skye smiled in return.

And then he leaned forward, closing the distance between them, and pressed his lips to hers.

XXXVII

It was still dark when Leo awoke. He could hear the sounds of the rest of the camp beginning to stir and he sighed, not yet willing to rise and face what awaited them. He doubted he could ever truly be ready.

Skye still slept, curled up beside him, blissfully oblivious. The two of them had retreated back to his tent the night before. Leo closed his eyes again, recalling what had passed between them, the pieces returning in flashes of sensation.

He remembered her hands in his hair, threaded through the thick curls. The small sighs Skye had made, her lips parting beneath his own. The kiss had been tender at first, almost hesitant, and then grew more urgent, a desperation to both of their movements, until Leo found himself kissing her with the hunger of a starved man.

Thinking back on it now, it had the unreality of a dream, one Leo would have happily stayed in a little longer. But they were out of time.

Skye stirred beside him, her blue eyes meeting his. There was a trace of fear there and the same regret that he felt himself. "It's time, isn't it? It's really happening."

Dawn had not yet broken by the time the camp had fully assembled, everyone rushing about to make final preparations. The darkness that still clung to the sky would help conceal those whose job it was to sneak into the city, but the main force outside the wall didn't intend to remain hidden. They would act as a distraction, meeting any forces that were sent out to stop them while the infiltrators carried out their tasks.

At least that was the plan, one of many pieces to the intricate puzzle. Leo accompanied Skye into the city. There had been some debate over whether this was the safest place for him, should they end up needing him to seal a demon. With the main force acting as a distraction, remaining there would hardly be safe. With fewer people sneaking into the city, there would be less defense should they be spotted, but that was the whole point—for the Empire not to realize they were even there until it was too late.

Leo wanted to stay by Skye's side, refusing to be separated, and in the end, he got his way.

Sheboleth, along with some of the other dragons, would fly up to the palace in the highest district. Part of Leo wanted to go with her, to witness the destruction of the amulet for himself, but there was nothing he could do to help with such a task and he would only be in the way.

Armed with some of Tiachren's explosives, he followed Skye along the bank of the River Charnel, to where it met the great wall surrounding the Capitol. Large drains opened up, allowing water and waste to exit the sewers. This, like so many times before, would be their entrance.

With Anyah having left her equipment back in the caverns, they couldn't track the locations of the guards within the city. They would have to be extra vigilant.

The foul odor of the sewers assaulted Leo's nose and he was momentarily transported back to the night he was forced to flee the Capitol. The sewers had been a lifeline then, as they were now. The ground was treacherous underfoot and he nearly slipped more than once, threatening to fall into the foul water slithering past.

He stuck close to Skye, her black clothing making her hard to see in the darkness. The only source of light was the lantern she carried, which would be abandoned the moment they exited the sewers. Tiachren trailed behind Leo, his feet sloshing through the water.

Even through the thick walls, Leo heard the sound of confrontation from up above. The rebels must have been spotted and now the guards were scrambling into position, carrying out their orders, manning the siege weapons, and preparing for the fight they suddenly had on their hands.

He shut his eyes for a moment, picturing the many trebuchets and ballistae that lined the city walls, and prayed that Sheboleth reached the palace unharmed.

Skye stopped before one of the ladders leading up into the city above. She hadn't consulted a map, but she didn't have to. They should have been directly under District I and when Leo clambered up after her, poking his head above street level, he saw that they were.

The familiar bars and run-down cafes and market stalls greeted him, smashed side by side with other less reputable places of business. There was no time for gawking. Moving quickly through the fading darkness, he followed after Skye, heading for the great wall that separated the Capitol from its enemies.

Other small teams were likewise carrying explosives and had been given instructions to target other sections of the wall. But the wall wasn't the only target. Far more dangerous were the guard barracks and the warehouses that held the mechs, but that, thankfully, fell to other teams.

Leo felt horribly exposed as they raced between buildings, bent low as they approached the wall. Any moment, he expected to hear a guard cry out, for them to be seen, for the feel of a crossbow bolt puncturing his flesh.

Leo shook the thought away and suddenly, the wall loomed before them. He'd never been so close to the Capitol's outermost defense before and was staggered at just how tall it was, rising over the rooftops of the highest buildings in District I. It almost reached the bottom of District II, surrounded, as all other districts were, by a smaller wall.

He craned his head back and could just make out the massive trebuchet directly above him. As he watched, the arm shot forward, hurling a stone at his allies beyond.

Skye already had her pack off and was placing the explosives. Leo hurried to do the same. Tiachren had instructed them to place the palm-sized devices six feet apart for maximum effectiveness, but there was no time to be precise. They couldn't stop and take measurements. Leo found himself guessing, but it would have to be enough.

The two of them had covered a decent section of the wall, but were by no means finished, when a far section of the wall suddenly exploded outward. Leo flinched, ducking instinctively, as dust filled the air, his heart hammering.

What had just happened? The bombs weren't supposed to go off yet.

"Tia!" He couldn't see Skye, but he could hear her voice, ringing through the dust-choked air. "Tiachren!"

There was no answer, not that Leo could hear. His throat tightened, dread coiling tightly around his stomach. Something had gone wrong. He took a step forward, wanting to find Skye, to reassure himself that she was all right, when the rest of the wall exploded in a screech of iron.

It had been a long time since Sheboleth had been shot at. She'd always been careful, even on missions to the Capitol, never to get close enough for one of the guards patrolling the wall to shoot at her. That all changed now.

Though she was hardly the only target, the other dragons accompanying her under fire as well. The bolts from the ballistae were faster than she had anticipated and one passed by too close for comfort.

She let out a hiss. These were hardly the same war machines of a thousand years ago. The distance made it difficult to judge just how close the bolts were before they struck and more than once, she rolled to the side in midair to avoid them, momentarily tilting her wings sharply.

A few of her companions were not so lucky. She heard more than one roar of pain as a bolt struck home and watched as a fellow dragon plummeted to the earth, wings slack. They were likely already dead before they hit the ground, but she hoped they landed on a guard or two.

The ballistae were effective weapons, but there were simply too many dragons. The palace loomed ahead, a great white building, the top floor lined with many windows. Sheboleth flew directly toward them, folding her wings at the last moment.

Glass shattered, the crescendo deafening as thousands of shards spiraled outward, glittering for a moment in the faint light as the sun struggled to rise. And then she was in, skidding across the black marble floor, her claws scrabbling and failing to find purchase, wings extended once more for balance.

Her momentum nearly carried her across the room to the windows on the other side. More glass shattered as her companions joined her. As she slowed to a halt, Sheboleth surveyed her surroundings.

The décor was overwhelmingly black and gold, the All-Seeing Eye of the Empire on full display behind the throne. But what she saw there gave her pause, her gaze lingering.

A man sat on the throne, slumped to the side, his head slightly bowed, one arm draped languidly over the armrest. Long white hair cascaded down his shoulders, partly obscuring his face. Though he now only vaguely resembled the man she remembered, she would have recognized him anywhere.

Snapping herself out of her stupor, Sheboleth lunged toward the throne, her claws slipping on the floor. The emperor. Desmond.

He'd clearly been dead for several days, at least. His hair had begun to dull, his skin shrunken and wrinkled, the long fingernails yellow and brittle. Blood stained the front of his robe. Someone had killed him.

Someone had gotten to him first.

Sheboleth could feel the others' eyes on her as they hung back. None of them had expected to find the emperor dead. They'd all been prepared to kill him, here and now, in order to get the amulet, but that was no longer necessary. The room seemed to hold its collective breath.

Sheboleth reached up with one hand, claws peeling back the emperor's robes. No chain hung around his neck. No amber soul stone dangled above his chest.

She froze. Someone had killed the emperor and taken the amulet. But who?

She stepped back, turning to the others. "It's gone."

"Gone?" one of them demanded, a note of panic entering his voice. "What do you mean *gone*?"

"I mean it's not here," Sheboleth snapped, desperation starting to tug at her as well. "Someone killed him and took it for themselves."

"We have to find it!"

Yes, but how? There were thousands of people living within the Capitol walls and any one of them might have taken it. There was no time to search every individual human, but they had to try.

They had to. Sheboleth had reassured Leo that he wouldn't need to use the spell she had taught him. That it wouldn't come to that.

And it still might not. They may have weeks left to search, before Reaper returned. Or they might have less than a minute. It might already be too late.

"Don't just stand there, look!" she heard herself growl. "Search everywhere. Do not stop until the amulet is found!"

An explosion sounded outside, the force rocking the floor beneath her feet. They must have succeeded in blowing a hole in the wall. Now, there was nothing stopping the rebels from pouring into the city and when they did, blood would spill. There were those among the rebels, Sheboleth knew, who would kill every Capitol citizen in their path, making the amulet all the harder to find.

But they had to try. Saints, they had to. They had no other choice.

But even as she turned to leave, Sheboleth couldn't stop the thought that crept into her mind, insidious and certain.

We've been outplayed.

Fabian stumbled as the floor trembled beneath him, the palace rocked by yet another explosion. When Lydia had first suggested leaving the palace, he had thought her mad. To him, it seemed as if they were running away and he said as much. But now, with the entire city under assault, he wasn't so sure.

"Not running away," Lydia insisted.

Some sort of fervor had come over her that he had never seen. She was excited, her eyes wild, her voice intense.

"Don't you see?" she went on, striding down the hall. "This is the first place the rebels will come. They've come to kill the old emperor, not knowing he's already dead. When they find him there and realize someone else has robbed them of that pleasure, they'll turn on us. It's not safe to stay here. We have to leave."

She insisted that they weren't fleeing the Capitol altogether, merely retreating someplace the rebels wouldn't think to look, where they could regroup and wait for their soldiers to subdue the rebels. They could go back once order had been restored.

But her previous confidence that she could deal with the threat of the rebels and become the city's savior appeared to have been shaken. Despite her assurance that they weren't running away, it felt precisely that.

Fabian couldn't necessarily blame her. The rebel force was larger than they'd expected and they had dragons with them. *Dragons.* Real ones, that could fly.

Fabian glanced up as they raced along the wall that separated District VI and VII, heading for the guard barracks. The dragons soared above his head, their movements far more graceful than any mech could ever be. He felt his footsteps slowing and had to force himself to keep up.

The siege weapons along the wall were firing at the beasts above, but Lydia passed them and the guards without so much as a glance. Fabian tore his gaze from the dragons and back to his sister, just in time to see the explosion.

A cloud of smoke billowed up as the iron wall buckled ahead, debris tossed into the air as if the metal weighed nothing at all. Lydia let out a shriek as she lost her footing and began to fall, vanishing from view into the smoke.

Fabian dashed forward, the smoke threatening to choke him. For a moment, he feared his sister had fallen, plunging down to the district below, and that he would glimpse her body lying broken. But instead, he saw pale hands gripping the ragged edge of the wall.

His sister dangled there, her hair disheveled, her Minister's uniform speckled with dust. Her feet hung out into open air with nothing to support them, swinging over the gaping chasm where the wall had stood only moments before. Her teeth were clenched, face contorted into a grimace.

Fabian threw himself onto his stomach and reached out, grasping her wrists, only to freeze. The amulet she had stolen from Desmond hung around her neck, the stone in plain view. For a moment, he caught a glimpse of the eye within before it vanished once more.

And he was seized with a sudden desire to have it, the temptation so great, he nearly gasped with the force of it. This was his salvation, the one thing that could save him, protect him, keep him safe. His sister couldn't save him, but the stone could.

Lydia had killed for this stone. She had killed for power. She had killed Zak.

Slowly, moving as if in a trance, Fabian released one of her wrists.

"What are you doing?" she gasped. "Pull me up!"

Fabian ignored her, reaching out toward the stone. He grasped it in his hand, feeling its warmth.

"What are you doing?" Lydia repeated, her voice rising in panic as the chain slipped over her head. "Fabian!"

"I know what you did." Fabian glared down at her. "I know about Zak."

The stone freed from her possession, Lydia stared at him, her green eyes wide, the zealous fervor fading, giving way to a dawning horror.

Fabian turned away then, leaving her dangling there, ignoring her cries, as he slipped the chain around his own neck.

Skye opened her eyes. She lay on the ground several feet from where she'd stood and she pushed herself into a sitting position. Her ears rang and her head spun as the ground shook beneath her, dust and debris raining down.

The wall, she thought dimly. *The wall exploded.*

Too soon. It had been too soon.

Wincing, she surged to her feet. The Capitol's great wall was simply gone.

"Tiachren!" she called again, coughing as the smoke stung her throat. "Tia!" He had been right in front of her when the explosion went off.

Stumbling forward, Skye approached the nearest pile of rubble, fearing he had been trapped beneath it. But that fear was quickly assuaged. He lay just beyond, motionless, his arms flung outward.

"Tiachren?"

Even as she spoke his name, Skye knew there was no point. She could see where the side of his skull had caved in, no doubt struck by a flying piece of debris.

Skye stared at his body in mute horror. One moment, he had been alive, and the next—

He'd always prided himself on his explosives, taking the utmost care with them. But here, now, something had finally gone wrong in the worst possible way.

Skye whirled, searching frantically. Tiachren might not have been the only one who'd been unable to escape the blast.

"Leo!" she called, jogging forward.

She found him lying a good distance behind, his eyes closed, covered in a thin layer of dust, and her heart seized in her chest. Quickly, she scanned his body for any sign of injury, but could see nothing.

"Leo." She shook him gently and he let out a moan, eyes flickering open. Dazed, not dead.

Skye sighed in relief, slumping down beside him.

His gaze fixed on her and he sat up, wincing. "What the hell happened?"

"The explosives—something went wrong." Her voice sounded hollow as she delivered her news. "Tiachren's dead."

Leo stared at her, expression mirroring her own shock. The dust was slowly beginning to settle and Skye glanced past him, freezing at the sight of two mechs. For a moment, she thought they would head for the gaping hole where the wall had once stood, expecting them to dash out and meet the rebels outside head on, in a last desperate attempt to keep them out of the city.

But they didn't. Their yellow eyes fixed on the two of them, as if the machines knew they were somehow responsible for the explosion.

This time, Sheboleth wasn't there to save them.

"Move!" Skye cried, grabbing Leo by the arm and hauling him up.

Her ears still rang and his probably weren't much better. But he scrambled up with her and followed as she ran in the opposite direction from the new opening in the wall.

The city was a picture of chaos. Fires raged in the upper districts. Skye could see the flames if she looked up and smell the smoke heavy on the air. Dragons swooped low, strafing the walls and buildings with flame.

Luckily, the metal ramps connecting the districts hadn't yet been raised and Skye darted toward one that would take them higher into the city, where they could hopefully lose the mechs.

She could hear the automata still behind them, Leo's footsteps mirroring her own. They raced up the metal ramp, boots clanging, pace momentarily flagging as they battled uphill. And then they were through, up onto District II, when another explosion went off.

Skye was thrown off her feet by the force, tossed sideways like a doll. She cried out as she struck the cobblestones, rolling. The air was so thick with smoke and dust that she couldn't see anything more than a few feet in any direction.

She coughed, blinking grit out of her eyes. She could no longer hear the mechs, or see their yellow lamp eyes cutting through the fog, which she took as a good sign. Perhaps they'd been obliterated by the explosion.

But neither could she see Leo. He was no longer beside her. Skye spun in a circle, calling for him, but there was no response. The only answering sound was that of the battle raging outside, now pouring further into the city.

Leo had been right behind her. Had he been caught in the blast? If the mechs had been blown to pieces, had the same thing happened to him? Should she stay in one place and wait for the smoke to clear or try and find him?

All of those questions raced through her mind, but no answers came.

Fabian wanted to get as far away from where he'd left Lydia as possible. Going back to the palace was out of the question. The thought filled him with fear, some deep-seated instinct telling him that he could not go back. To do so would mean certain death.

And so he went down, descending into the lower levels. Perhaps, in the confusion, he could slip out of the city entirely and then—well, he would figure the rest out later, once he reached safety.

Something made him stop dead when he saw the young man sprawled in the street before him. For a moment, he thought he might be dead, but then he struggled to his feet, wincing, one hand going to his ribs.

Fabian had never seen him before, his hair and clothes speckled with dust. His right arm was mechanical from the elbow down.

As if sensing Fabian's gaze, he looked up, their eyes locking, and the other man froze. He was a rebel, Fabian knew that with certainty now.

"*Kill him,*" whispered the voice. "*He will try to take me from you.*"

No. Fabian had just got his hands on the amulet. He wouldn't let anyone take it from him.

He reached for the dagger at his belt, his fingers fumbling. He wasn't strong enough to wield a sword and wouldn't have known how to use it anyway. The dagger was little better, but it would kill just as easily.

His shaking hand wrapped around the blade's handle and he ripped it free of its sheath.

Leo tried to back away, but the blond young man was too fast. There was a crazed look in his eyes, one of hate, as if Leo had personally wronged him somehow, even though he would have sworn they had never met.

He had only the dagger Skye had given him, all those months ago, and he felt woefully unprepared. He'd never drawn a blade against someone in a real fight before, only in practice.

But from the first slash, it became instantly clear that the young man wasn't skilled with a dagger. His strikes were quick, but wild. Leo tried to dodge as best he could, blocking where he had to. If he could maintain the defense long enough, his opponent might make a mistake, leaving himself too open and that would be his chance to strike.

He tried to think of what Skye would do, the advice she'd given him during their training sessions.

Skye… Where was she? What had happened to her? His chest spasmed suddenly, his concentration faltering. The young man took advantage, slashing at Leo's side.

Leo jerked his right arm down, cursing his foolishness. The blade glanced off his arm, the metal unharmed. He looked down at it and then cocked his arm back, his fist flying toward the other man's face.

The metal struck him in the jaw, the impact snapping his head back and knocking a few teeth loose, bouncing along the cobblestones.

Leo gasped, doubling over, as pain shot through his arm. He flexed his fist, examining the metal, but it remained undamaged.

Such a blow should have rendered the other man unconscious, but if he felt any pain, he seemed unfazed by it. He let out a growl, wiping his bleeding mouth on the back of his hand, and redoubled his efforts, movements unnaturally quick.

Leo yelped as he felt the dagger slice into his side. He couldn't spare a glance to assess the damage, but he could feel blood starting to run down his side, the sensation distracting.

He staggered back, trying to put some distance between himself and the man, but he tripped over a piece of debris and went down hard, his own blade slipping from his grasp. He glanced up, expecting the man to pounce and bury the blade in his heart, but he didn't.

He let the dagger fall to the ground. Leo's brow furrowed in confusion, but before he could react, the man was upon him, straddling him as his fists clenched around Leo's throat, grappling for the silver chain that hung there.

Leo tried to shove him away. The man was thin, wiry, and couldn't have weighed more than he did, but he fought with uncanny strength, a desperation to him that Leo didn't understand.

Suddenly, the man cried out and his grip lessened. Leo brought his boot up and kicked him in the stomach, throwing him off. A crossbow bolt protruded from the back of the man's knee. Skye stood behind him, lowering her crossbow and drawing a throwing knife.

Leo scrambled to his feet and his opponent did the same. Skye pulled her arm back, readying the throw, but stopped short.

They both stared at the man, at the amber stone that hung out of his shirt. At the eye that stared directly at them.

Terror overtook Leo, stronger than anything he'd ever felt before. He'd thought he'd known fear, but he was wrong. He couldn't move, couldn't think. He felt naked before that gaze, all his defenses stripped away, his worst fears laid bare.

And then one thought broke through as he realized what he was looking at.

Oh, saints.

The amulet hadn't been destroyed. Sheboleth and the others had failed to find it because the emperor didn't have it. This man did. Why did this man, whoever he was, have the emperor's amulet?

As Leo watched, the eye slowly blinked once.

And then the amulet exploded.

XXXVIII

The force threw Leo off his feet and he landed hard on his back, staring up at the sky, his vision darkening at the edges. His head had cracked against the cobblestones and he fought to stay conscious, grimacing as he sat up. He had thrown his arms up to shield his face and shards of crystal were now embedded in his left forearm like splinters. His right arm seemed fine, the metal holding once again.

A brief glance revealed what remained of the young man he had fought. His body had borne the brunt of the explosion, his flesh mangled, and Leo turned away from the sight, his gaze drawn instead to the shadow that had risen up above the body. It hovered in the air for a moment before darting upwards, rising over the far wall and vanishing from sight.

A moment later, Leo heard the first roar, the sound chilling his blood. And he knew, as certainly as he'd ever known anything, what it meant.

He's free.

Sheboleth froze the instant she heard the roar, her blood running cold. It was a sound she had heard once before and hoped never to hear again. She didn't need to launch herself into the air, rising above the rooftops and peering beyond what remained of the great wall, to know what she would see.

The Capitol itself was nearly in ruins. Embers flew through the air, mingling with the thick smoke as fire raged unchecked. Everywhere she looked, the citizens of the Capitol fled, scurrying for their lives, but unsure which way to go. Some of the rebels, as she'd feared, had taken out their vengeance on any civilian they could find. Their anger had simmered for years and at last had an outlet.

Wherever the amulet had been, whichever one of the humans had taken it, she and the other dragons hadn't found it in time.

"Where's Leo?" the dragon nearest Sheboleth demanded.

She didn't know the answer to that. She didn't even know if he was still alive.

"He probably fled," one of the others growled.

Sheboleth whirled on them with a snarl. "Say that again, and I'll give *you* a reason to flee."

"Enough!" Koal strode up to them, his steps confident despite his poor vision. "We must give him the benefit of the doubt. It's up to him now. We're needed out there. Hurry!"

There was no arguing with that. There was no changing what was done, no going back.

Sheboleth lunged for the great wall.

"Leo, get up!" Skye, suddenly appearing at his side, tugged at his arm.

"He's back," Leo said numbly, allowing Skye to help him to his feet. "Reaper's back."

"I know. We need to go."

Somehow, he forced himself to move, following after her. The stone's weight around his neck felt heavier than ever as they descended the levels, returning to District I and heading for one of the holes that had been blasted in the wall.

Leo tried to brace himself for what he would see, but he really had no idea. What did demons even look like? All the documents had mentioned was a beast. But no amount of preparation could have prepared him for the sight that greeted him.

The two of them stopped, standing in the gap in the wall, amidst the crumbled stone and iron. The bridge that led into the city stood just ahead of them, sloping downward to the open plain below. Leo could only stare in a mix of wonder and horror, unable to look away, a hot, dry wind ruffling his hair.

"Oh, saints," he whispered.

Downed automata lay strewn on the grass, some rent, others crushed. But for every one mech, there seemed to be a real dragon lying there, as well as two humans, both rebel and Imperial alike. Whether they were dead or dying, it was impossible to tell from such a distance.

Even when living in the Capitol or carrying out missions for the Resistance, Leo had never seen such death and he fought down a wave of nausea.

But none of that made his insides clench in fear or the color drain from his skin.

There, standing in the middle of it all, was Reaper.

The demon was indeed a beast, having taken the form of an enormous stone-gray dragon. The beast towered over the people, dragons and mechs below him. He must have been several hundred feet tall at least. The ground trembled beneath Leo's boots with every step the demon took.

He was covered from head to tail in gray scales. Darker gray armored plates shielded him from neck to tail tip, and from his toes to just above the middle of his legs. The armor plating was jagged and sharp. Dark gray wings spread wide, casting dark shadows on those below. His wingspan was absolutely massive, blotting out the rising sun.

Like Sheboleth, his front feet resembled hands, with long black claws. There were three black horns on his chin and five more behind his jaw. Two long horns protruded from the back of his head, connecting to the frills on his jaw. Two more horns sprouted from his nose and black spines ran down from his forehead, along his back, to the tip of his tail, which ended in two long spikes. The long black spines were connected by dark gray webbing that was jagged and torn. His wings were tattered on the edges.

As Leo watched, the beast opened his jaws, revealing long, curved, yellowed fangs, dripping with saliva. The demon let forth a roar. Leo cried out in pain, clamping his hands over his ears. Even when the sound had faded, his ears still rang with it and he half expected to find them bleeding.

Reaper raked the armies beneath him with bright, glowing amber eyes, the black outline surrounding them making them stand out starkly. The demon slammed one giant foot down on some unfortunate souls, tossing still more into the air with the other. Leo watched as humans, dragons, and mechs alike went flying like ragdolls, only to smash down to earth once more, their frames broken and crumpled.

This was the creature King Ulric had summoned. This was the beast who had devastated Akkadia's armies.

Skye squeezed Leo's hand and he turned to her. She had paled, but there was still a determined gleam in her blue eyes, sparking a sudden warmth within him.

"Let's go seal him away again."

Leo nodded and then they were running toward the fray, every instinct within him screaming to *flee*, to go the other way.

The battlefield was utter chaos. Despite Reaper's rampage, there were still automata clashing with dragons and rebels facing the Imperial soldiers that had swarmed out of the city to meet them.

But for the most part, they were scrambling, frantically trying to avoid the demon's vengeful wrath. A few brave dragons flew around him, attempting to distract him. Some humans hurled spears or fired arrows at the beast, to no avail.

No mortal could kill him. He had to be sealed away.

It was all Leo could do not to trip over the bodies littering the ground. Once or twice, he nearly slipped on the grass, slick with blood.

He jerked to a sudden halt as one of the Imperial soldiers stepped into their path, sword drawn. Without hesitation, Skye drew both her black daggers.

"Go. I can handle him."

Leo opened his mouth to argue, not wanting to leave her, but she glimpsed his expression out of the corner of her eye and cut him off. "Go! You have to seal him away."

He couldn't shake the feeling that this would be the last time he would see her. That if he stepped away, she would die here, on this battlefield, alone, and he wouldn't have been there for her in the only way he could.

Without waiting for a response, Skye sprang forward, bringing both daggers up to block, the blades colliding with a clang.

Leo let out a huff, knowing he would only distract her, and turned away. There was nothing the others could do—even if they'd known the spell, there was only one soul stone—and every moment that Reaper remained, more people would die.

As he drew near, he realized just how small he truly was compared to the demon. He stopped, daring to go no further. He was close, much closer than he would have liked, but not in immediate danger of being crushed.

Reaper seemed not to have noticed him and he prayed it stayed that way. The beast was still busy flinging people into the air, crushing the life out of them, or even bending down to snap them between his jaws.

Leo slipped the chain over his head, gripping the stone in one hand. All he had to do was recite the spell Sheboleth had given him and it would all be over. He took a deep breath, the ancient Anarshan words coming when he called them, and raised the stone toward the demon.

No sooner had he uttered the first word than Reaper's head snapped toward him, the amber eyes pinpointing him among the crowd. Leo faltered as he felt the burning eyes meet his, a chill lancing through him, stealing all the warmth from his blood, freezing his limbs.

It was far worse than beholding the eye that had peered out from within the amulet. If he looked close, Leo thought he could see flames burning in the demon's gaze, a glimpse of hell itself.

It was hopeless. Leo could feel his strength leaving him. Before he could continue the spell, Reaper slammed one of his front legs down, causing Leo to stagger and fall from the force.

And then, as the dragon took a step toward him, Reaper laughed.

Though the demon made no sound, his voice resounded in Leo's mind, deep and menacing, no longer a mere whisper.

"So they send a boy to fix the mess that men have made. Did you not think I would recognize the language of those who imprisoned me?"

Leo knew he should scramble back to his feet, but he couldn't seem to move.

"They sent you to face me alone."

The demon hadn't moved any closer to him. Leo gritted his teeth, snapping out of his shock, and forcing himself to his feet. "I'm not alone."

He spoke aloud, the sound of the battle raging around them drowning out his voice, but he knew the demon heard.

"Oh, but you are. Look around you, little saint. Yes, there are your friends and allies, fighting and dying around you, and yet, you are alone. They are all fighting their own battles. There is no one to help you. From the very beginning, all of them knew you would be alone in the end. And still, they willingly sent you out here to die." The demon chuckled. *"How little they must value your life."*

"You're a liar," Leo whispered, but it was too late. The doubt had begun to creep inside of him.

He looked around. At some point, his friends had all vanished. Skye had been held up. Tiachren had been killed. He didn't know where Fae or Anyah were or what had happened to them. He hadn't seen Sheboleth since she departed for the palace, but he knew her mission hadn't been successful.

His heart ached at the thought of her. More than anyone else, he wished she stood beside him now.

"Am I really?" Reaper hissed, lashing his tail slightly. *"Did they tell you your name would be praised in song and legend, written about in poems, remembered for centuries to come if you*

succeeded, little saint? Perhaps the more appropriate question would be—what did they fail to tell you?"

"What are you talking about?"

"Come now, it doesn't have to be this way. We are not so very different, you and I."

Appalled, Leo spat back, "I am nothing like you!"

"So certain, are you? Have you forgotten your revenge so easily? Do you not recall how your hatred for the Empire burned in your heart? I'm merely wreaking vengeance upon those whose forebearers imprisoned me for a thousand years. And here you are, bringing the Resistance with you, so that they, too, can finally claim the revenge they so desperately seek. Yet here you stand, acting all high and righteous, when you're no better."

Leo couldn't bring himself to say anything. He wasn't sure if that was because he had nothing to say—the demon *was* right—or if it was Reaper's influence affecting him.

The demon let out a hiss. *"The Anarshans wronged me. I helped them defeat their enemies and how did they repay me? A thousand years is a long time. The world changes, and yet, nothing really changes, does it? People are just as greedy, just as selfish, just as cruel as ever. They are more willing now than ever to destroy a fellow human being in order to get what they want. They are so self-consumed, they care not for the consequences, so long as they get what they want. They care for nothing and no one else."*

It reminded Leo of what Sheboleth had told him once, about humans and their propensity for wickedness. And it was true. Leo had seen the proof of it with his own eyes.

"Your world was already full of darkness, even without me in it. So, I am repaying those who have wronged me, as you have yearned to do, and I am ridding the world of its wickedness at the same time. Is that really so bad?"

The demon studied him. *"You have also done wrong in your life. Perhaps not as bad as some here, but still…what makes you worthy of being spared by me when others are not? We don't have to be enemies, little saint."*

"Wh—what do you mean?"

"Your family may have died needlessly, but your friends need not share the same fate. I know there is one friend whom you care greatly for. Perhaps even more than a friend? She cares deeply for you as well. I can sense it. She does not have to perish."

Leo stared at Reaper in alarm, the hand that held the amulet slowly sinking back down to his side. His mind was a whirlwind of emotion and questions he couldn't answer.

"How do you know this?"

The idea that the demon knew of his relationship with Skye, the feelings he had for her, and what they had shared together made him feel ill. It was private, precious, and not for the demon to know.

"I know everything. I know your fears, your weaknesses, secrets, thoughts, and your darkest desires. I know what your heart wants most, better than even you. But more than that, I can give it to you."

Leo looked down at the stone in his hand. "What do you want from me?"

The chaos from the battle continued to rage around them, but he barely noticed. It almost seemed to be unfolding in slow motion. His entire focus was on the dragon and the words he spoke.

"I will spare you. You will never again have to worry about what the future may hold. Your friends shall be well-treated and have all that they desire. No one shall stand up to you or harm you when I am your ally. All you have to do is kneel before me. Give me the stone and I shall grant your every desire. Shall I show you what I will do for you as your ally and not your enemy?"

Suddenly, smoke surrounded Leo, blocking out the sight and sounds of the battlefield. Even Reaper vanished from his view. He watched as images began to appear in the mist.

At first, he saw the Capitol, but unlike he'd ever seen it before. It wasn't separated by districts. Gone were the dingy lower levels with their hovels. The palace remained, but the Ministers' mansions he'd often seen now populated every level. The people were happy, smiling as they went about their daily tasks, dressed in fine clothes, every one of them appearing well-fed instead of starving.

The vision shifted to show Leo himself, slightly older than he was now. He was dressed in fine silk, his hair behaving for once, as he sat atop a gilded throne. Skye stepped into the room, wearing the loveliest gown he'd ever seen, flashing as the light caught it, her black hair pinned up.

Skye…who he had left behind.

Leo smiled as she walked up to him and he stood, taking one of her hands in his. She said something Leo couldn't hear and then she leaned in close to kiss him as the vision faded, the mist parting.

"I can give you all of it," Reaper whispered. *"Your friends don't have to die. You can save them, little saint."*

The life of royalty. That's what Reaper had promised him. Leo had worked hard every day in the hope that one day, he could give his mother and sister a better life. And his father had done the same. That was no longer possible now, but there were others whose lives could be made better.

He couldn't deny that Skye looked breathtaking in that dress, but that wasn't the Skye he knew. The Skye he knew would much rather wear her black leathers, a living shadow, fierce and deadly.

The details of the vision began to slip away, even as he grasped at them. None of it felt real, the whole thing hazy like a dream, and he couldn't have said what color her dress had been, even if his life depended on it.

And what about himself? He didn't wear such fine clothes. His usual appearance may not have been so elegant, but that was him.

And what of Sheboleth? She should have been there, too, in such a future, enjoying the best life had to offer.

The appeal of the vision faded. Reaper had tried to tempt him with the same offer he had made Desmond, the promise of a throne, of power, the ability to rule unchallenged. It might have appealed to some—and no doubt Reaper believed it something all humans would find appealing—but Leo saw it for what it was.

"You're a liar." He shook his head, taking a step back. He'd been a fool to even listen. "You would have me give this amulet to you. And then, once you have it, you would kill me and everyone else with no fear of retribution."

He expected the demon to be angered by his refusal, but instead, Reaper's eyes seemed to gleam with amusement. "*How can you be sure my words are false? After all, look at what I did for your emperor. The only reason the Empire became so great under his reign was because of me! The only reason his reign lasted so long was because of* me! *Without me, Desmond was nothing, just as you are now, little saint. He could never have accomplished any of that without my help.*"

"You only helped him because it suited your own interests," Leo growled. "It guaranteed you safety until you could be freed. You are no different from the humans you claim to despise. *Self-serving.*"

Reaper hissed audibly, his lip curling into a sneer, and he leaned his massive head down much closer to Leo than he would have liked. "*Of course. Your emperor was a perfect example of how your kind continues to allow themselves to be led astray by serpents. It would have been amusing were it not so pathetic. Very well, if you refuse to do what I ask of you, your friends will die. They will burn, wishing before the end that you had relented, but it*" *will be too late. Now watch, little saint, and know that all of this could have been prevented if you had but bowed to me."*

The demon turned back to the battle raging around them and parted his jaws, sending forth a column of flame at those before him. The fire roared as it shot toward its victims, engulfing them in a bright explosion of light. It was a quick death, leaving nothing behind.

"No!" Leo cried as he watched, helpless. The heat was so intense, he was afraid his own flesh would begin to melt, and he wasn't even in the path of the hellfire.

He gasped, terror and panic threatening to overtake him at the horror he had just witnessed. The fire gone, Reaper continued to crush or throw his victims high in the air, his long tail carving wide swaths. One such unfortunate victim landed a few feet from Leo, their eyes still wide open, neck bent at a sickening angle.

Clutching the amulet still in his hand, Leo felt as though those eyes were staring straight through him, accusing.

You did this, they seemed to say.

Voices began to cut through the clamor of the battle, calling out to him. He recognized Skye's voice and Anyah. His mother, even Ana, crying out to him. They all pleaded with him, accused him, their voices berating him, calling out for help or mercy that he could not bestow.

Leo cried out, covering his ears, but the voices only grew louder, rising to a scream, until he was screaming too.

And then one voice called out to him, clear and loud, cutting through the other voices and silencing them. "Leo!"

He opened his eyes as Sheboleth swooped down to land beside him. "The spell!" she reminded him.

Her presence comforted him, brought him back from the edge of whatever dark pit he stood upon. Whatever happened, he would not be alone at the end.

Leo raised the amulet once more and began the spell. His tongue tripped over words that hadn't been spoken in more than a thousand years.

Reaper whirled and lunged for him. Leo felt an instant's temptation to run, but he ignored it. Sheboleth stood beside him, resolute, staring down the approaching demon. He stood with her, despite the terror.

In a few more strides, Reaper would be upon them and one way or another, it would all be over. The demon's eyes were narrowed with hate, lips peeled back in a vicious snarl and he let out a short roar. Leo could see the blazing orange heat building at the back of his throat, the fire that would soon rush forward to engulf them.

He uttered the last word of the spell. It was over. He'd finished it.

For a breathless moment, nothing happened.

Then the soul stone in his hand began to glow blue and Leo looked away, shielding his eyes as a blinding light erupted from it, so bright he could see it through his eyelids. A sudden strong wind whipped at his hair and clothes, but he kept his head turned away, still gripping the stone.

"No!" Reaper roared aloud. "*No!*"

His roars of protest were abruptly silenced as the amulet emitted one last flash of light and then went dark.

Leo slumped to the ground, his energy gone, still clutching the soul stone. It was no longer cold, but warm against his skin.

Dimly, he heard Sheboleth say something to him, but he couldn't make out the words. He had never felt such exhaustion, life-draining and consuming. She hadn't mentioned anything about the spell resulting in one's own death, but in that moment, he could well believe it.

Perhaps she hadn't wanted to discourage or frighten him. It didn't matter now. Reaper was gone. Leo hadn't failed. When it mattered most, he had stood his ground and did what needed to be done.

He clung to that one fact, as the darkness took him.

The battle was beginning to dwindle by the time Skye found Leo. She skidded to a halt, kneeling beside him. He lay on his side, unmoving, the amulet laying in his open palm, his fingers curled gently around it.

"Is he dead?" she demanded.

Sheboleth shook her head. "I don't think so, but I don't know how much blood he's lost."

One side of his shirt was stained a deep scarlet, where the blond man's knife had struck him. Blood had also flowed over his forearm where shards of crystal had cut him. One cheek was streaked with dirt, his clothing coated in ash and dust. Skye cared about none of that, so long as he was still alive.

"Leo." She reached out, brushing hair back from his face.

His eyes fluttered open at the sound of her voice. "Skye…" His gaze moved past her to the dragon. "Sheboleth. It's over."

"Not quite," Sheboleth corrected. "But soon. Give me the amulet."

It was no longer blue, but a vibrant amber. Gingerly, Leo sat up, considering the stone, and then hesitated. Reaper may have been sealed away, but his influence remained and Skye sensed the demon, trying to sway him even now.

Not since the time of the saints had Reaper ever been so close to being once more sealed from this world. Everything hinged on Leo's decision.

His brow furrowed and he shook his head as if to clear it. He held his hand out. "Take it, Sheboleth. So that what happened today will never be repeated."

He tilted his hand, the stone sliding off of his open palm, landing on the grass with a muffled thump.

"With pleasure," Sheboleth growled.

Skye and Leo stepped back, allowing her room. The stone glittered in the morning light for a brief moment before it vanished in the torrent of flames Sheboleth sent forth.

In the end, there was nothing left, not even a trace, to suggest it had ever been there at all. There was just a blackened patch of scorched earth.

Leo sighed as if a great weight had been lifted from him.

"Now," Sheboleth said, "it's over."

XXXIX

The battle had ended shortly after Reaper vanished. The demon had so badly decimated the Empire's forces that those that remained soon surrendered to the Resistance rather than continue with the killing. Enough blood had been shed that day and no one much felt like spilling more.

Not that Leo remembered much of it. He didn't recall much after sealing the demon away. He had felt the tug of temptation, the demon making one last attempt to sway him, begging him to reconsider destroying the stone.

For a moment, Leo had wavered. And then the moment passed.

The demon was gone and the Akkadian Empire, which had stood for more than a thousand years, had fallen. Leo hardly dared believe it, in the days and weeks that followed, as he walked the streets of the Capitol he had once called home.

It seemed an eternity had passed since he'd first attended a Resistance meeting, but it really hadn't been that long ago.

The city itself had been heavily damaged during the siege and it would take some time to repair it. More than that, they needed to improve it. The living conditions in the lower districts were deplorable—but no more.

A week after the battle, the Triad appeared on the steps of the palace to address the people of the Capitol. All three Resistance leaders had survived the battle—something that Sheboleth had merely snorted at when she'd heard.

Leo stood in the back of the crowd, near Sheboleth. Being near a dragon made him more conspicuous—which he didn't care for—but she was more than willing to send any admirers away with a quick and scathing word or two.

Ever since the sealing, Leo had been hailed as something of a celebrity. He couldn't go anywhere without being recognized and waylaid, people wanting to offer their congratulations or admiration for what he had done, sealing the demon away. He'd tried to insist that he hadn't done anything, not really, but they didn't seem to listen.

His efforts had also been recognized by the Triad. With his old home destroyed during the siege, they had given him one of the mansions on the ninth district. Leo had tried to refuse, but in the end, it had been easier to accept.

Skye had also been given a nice house, for her loyalty and service to the Resistance, though she found herself at his place more often than not. Leo didn't mind in the least. The house was far too large for just one person. He spent most of his time there now, grateful to escape the attention.

The three Resistance leaders stood on the palace steps, triumphant yet subdued, their voices carrying easily over the hush of the crowd.

"We would like to express our condolences," Jemma said, "to those of you who have lost someone, whether to the Empire's oppressive rule or during the last battle for freedom. Their sacrifice will not be forgotten, nor was it in vain. Each and every one of you standing here today fought hard for freedom, for a better world, and those efforts at last have been rewarded."

Tristan took up the theme then. "The future begins today and it starts with all of us. We have worked hard to reach this day, but our efforts do not stop here. We must all work toward a more equitable and fair future, not just today, but every day moving forward. We must not forget where we came from or the struggles we overcame."

Rhaven spoke last. "Akkadia will be an Empire no longer and it will not have an emperor as its ruler. The three of us will do our utmost to be fair and just rulers, unlike our predecessor. We will form a council, but our rule will not be indefinite. We're still very much in discussion, but it is our intention that the people have a say in who will lead them. You will choose our successors, those who will serve on this council—and on every council moving forward."

Applause rang out, long and loud in the stillness. There was more to the speech, but Leo no longer bothered to listen. He turned, quietly slipping away.

Skye watched the speech from a nearby rooftop. The buildings in District IX and X had suffered far less damage than their lower counterparts. She was too far away to really hear what was being said, but she could see the faces of the people, turned toward the Triad, lit with hope, despite the fact that they stood in a city that had crumbled around them.

She sighed, glancing around. From here, at the pinnacle of the Capitol, she could see the rest of the city, sprawling out beneath her. It was hard to believe that she was really there. That this was really happening.

She had lived in the caverns beneath the ruins of Anarsha for the last eleven years—twelve now, she realized—and in its own way, it had become home. Now, she would live here with the rest of them.

She supposed she could have chosen to live in Shemar or Elath if she wished, but Shemar was out of the question and Elath smelled too much of fish for her liking.

Besides, there was something—some*one*—here that she would never part with. The city she had always despised, the city of her enemy, was now hers. Theirs.

The goal she had fought and bled for over the past twelve years had finally come to pass. *It's like being in a dream.* Nothing seemed quite real.

She glanced at the corner of the roof as Leo heaved himself up, slightly breathless.

"You make this look easy, you know that?" he remarked as he plopped down beside her.

She smiled. "What did you think of the speech?"

"I think it's what the people needed to hear."

She raised an eyebrow at him. It was an interesting answer.

She inhaled deeply. The air held a slight chill to it. Cold weather would be upon the Capitol soon enough and with the Workhouses destroyed, there was fear of a food shortage. That kind of unrest and turmoil was precisely what a fledgling republic did not need.

But that was a problem for the future. For now, the Empire had fallen and the city was theirs. She had watched the Empire collapse and had helped bring it about.

"We did it," she murmured. "We really did it."

"It doesn't quite feel real," Leo acknowledged, and she knew his thoughts had strayed back to the night before the battle. "None of it. Except for you." He nudged her gently with his shoulder, grinning at her. "You're real."

She returned the smile, but it felt wobbly. "I never thought…well, it's not that I never thought this day would come, but I never thought I'd be here to see it. So many others aren't. I just keep asking myself—why them and not me?"

Fae and Anyah both had made it, she'd later learned, much to her relief. But she couldn't help but think about Tiachren, Fitz, and all the others she had known throughout the years who had gone out on missions and hadn't made it back. Leo's fate had nearly been the same.

"I've been wondering the same thing," he admitted. "About most of what happened. And I don't have any answers. But one thing I do know is—" He took her hand in his. "—I thank the saints every day that I get to be here with you." He pressed his lips to her knuckles, their warmth burning against the cold.

Skye shivered. She smiled again, genuine this time, and pulled him to her. The cold faded away completely as she kissed him, her warm breath mingling with his.

Leo's cheeks were flushed when she pulled back, his eyes dark.

"Shall we go home?" she asked, eager to continue in a more comfortable setting.

"I'll meet you back there," Leo murmured, unable to resist stealing one last, lingering kiss. "There's something I want to speak to Sheboleth about."

"Fine," Skye conceded. "But don't keep me waiting too long."

Sheboleth was waiting for him when he climbed down from the roof and returned to the square where the crowd had gathered. It was beginning to break up now. The Triad's speech finished, they were eager to get home and out of the chill.

"You're too late," the dragon remarked. "It's over."

"Shame," Leo replied. "But actually, it's you I wanted to see. Will you walk with me?"

She rose to her feet and accompanied him down the street. Most of the people they passed parted for them without comment or incident. Sheboleth ignored the stares they gave her, most of them still not used to the idea of seeing a dragon strolling through the city streets.

But not everyone remained silent.

"Hail, demon-slayer!" one called out.

The shout only drew more attention and Leo heard more than a few murmurs calling him a saint. He winced. Luckily, no one had approached, kneeling before him, begging him to bless anything, but if they kept referring to him as a saint, he feared it was only a matter of time.

"I wish they wouldn't call me that," he muttered.

"Technically, that's what you are," Sheboleth pointed out. "You sealed a demon in a soul stone. You're the first saint there's been in more than a thousand years."

"*You're* the one who banished him, not me."

"Yes, well, what goes on behind the scenes isn't nearly as glamorous."

He sighed, wanting to change the subject. "So what happens now? Are you going to stay in the city?"

The two of them hadn't discussed any future plans and Leo suddenly felt a surge of anxiety at the thought that Sheboleth might leave. He had grown so used to her presence, to her being by his side, that if she were to leave, he would feel her absence like the loss of a limb.

Most of the other dragons had already left, still uneasy being in such close proximity to humans after years of being hunted. The mechs were out of commission, currently dormant in their warehouses and no longer a threat, but old habits died hard…if they died at all.

He wondered if Sheboleth wanted to join the others.

"I'll stay," she replied. "I can hardly return to my old life. There's nothing left to go back to."

Leo let out a breath of relief.

"I know what you mean. After I left it behind, I wasn't sure if I would ever set foot in this city again, much less call it home. But it's not the home I remember. Not anymore. And that's what I wanted to ask you." He slowed, looking at her. "Why me? Why did any of this happen?"

"Asking the easy questions, I see." Sheboleth huffed. "What happened all began over a thousand years ago, not with the greed of just one man, but many. We dragons may not be perfect, but it's a uniquely human failing to always want more. More land, more money, more power."

Leo frowned, dread curdling in his stomach. He had answered truthfully when he'd told Skye that he thought the Triad's speech was what the people needed to hear, but something about it hadn't sat well with him.

"Desmond is gone," he said. "We've replaced one human ruler with three others. The Triad may have good intentions, but they're still human." *Still susceptible to those failings.* "Does that mean we're doomed to repeat the past?"

Sheboleth sighed. "You should be celebrating, not asking me these things."

"Answer me, Sheboleth."

"You already know the answer. Yes, sooner or later, there will be another would-be tyrant who comes along."

Leo swallowed. "So what do we do?"

Sheboleth stopped walking, fixing him with her intense green stare. "Be vigilant and *remember*. Time will dull the memories, ease the pain. But you must remember what you fought for. What you fought against. And the cost that made it necessary. Fighting against the fading of memory is the hardest battle of all, but the most important, to ensure that this never happens again."

Skye was often gone in the days that followed, busy helping with repairs to the city and finding shelter for everyone, no small task with so much of the Capitol damaged. Leo hung back, wanting to be out of the public eye, but he knew sooner or later, he would have to step forth and face what had been done to his city.

One day, Skye returned earlier than expected, the door of the house they shared flying open, banging against the wall. The noise drew Leo, racing to the foyer from deeper in the house. Skye gasped for breath, doubled over, her hands braced on her knees.

"What is it?" Leo asked. "What's wrong?"

She shook her head. "Nothing's wrong. But there's something you should see."

Leo followed her out into the street, descending into the lower districts. The damage grew more severe the lower they went and it made him cringe to see how much they still needed to do, how far they still had to come.

"Where are we going?" he asked.

"To one of the orphanages. We've been checking them—seeing if any of the children got hurt and moving them into better living conditions. It's heartbreaking, really, what passes as an orphanage in this place—"

She was rambling in a way Leo had never seen before, fighting to contain nervous energy.

"Why are you taking me to an orphanage?" He had no doubt that the conditions were bad, but what did she expect him to do about it, this very instant?

Briefly, he wondered if she were about to suggest they take some of the children in. Saints knew there was more than enough room in the mansion, even with Sheboleth taking a liking to one wing of it.

Skye kept talking as if he hadn't spoken. "I wasn't sure at first." She turned, stepping through the open doorway of one of the buildings and into a dimly lit room. "But I recognized her from one of the pictures in your house…"

She broke off but Leo was no longer listening. He stopped in the middle of the floor, all sound seeming to fade away, leaving nothing but the blood rushing in his ears, as he stared at the sight before him.

The girl turned, her blonde curls bouncing slightly. Somehow, she looked older than the eleven years she must now be. But there was no mistaking those green eyes, widening in recognition.

"Leo!" She rushed forward, arms outstretched.

"Ana." He fell to his knees, scooping her up, wrapping his arms around her. Her curls brushed against his cheek, her arms wrapped tightly around his neck.

She seemed larger than he remembered, having grown in his absence. They had both changed.

Countless questions leapt to his mind, each competing with the next for dominance. Why was she here? How was she still alive? What had happened? Why had the Empire spared her? But it all mattered little now.

Leo felt tears prick his vision and squeezed his eyes shut, hardly daring to let himself believe this was real. All that time, he had believed her dead, never thinking he would get the chance to see her again, much less hold her as he was now.

He had believed his family gone, every last piece of his old life lost to him. Reaper had tried to convince him of that. In that, the demon had lied, as he had about so many things, but Leo had never been more grateful for a lie.

"I've got you," he whispered. "And I'll never let you go again."

Thank you for reading!

When I was twelve, I decided that my dream was to become a published author. I have since achieved that dream, but an author is nothing without their readers. So thank you, reader, for giving this book a chance.

If you enjoyed this book, it would mean the world to me if you would consider leaving a review on Amazon/Goodreads. Reviews are essential for authors. They help our books get seen, they help our books get promoted, and they can be the difference between whether or not another reader decides to take a chance on a book.

Thank you again for your support and happy reading!

ABOUT THE AUTHOR

Rachel Terry grew up in a small town where nothing much ever happened, dreaming of grand adventures and far-away places, which she found between the pages of books. When not writing, she can be found reading, making YouTube videos, gaming with friends, or indulging in her love of history. She currently resides in the Midwest with her family and a cat named Crinkles.

Visit her online at: rachel-terry.com

YouTube: RachelTerryAuthor

Instagram: rterrywriter

TikTok: rterrywriter

Facebook: rachelterryauthor

LIGHTBRINGER

LIGHTBRINGER
The Guardians Duology Book 1

When an old wrong leads to war, one girl finds herself in
the middle of it all.

THE PHOENIX AND THE CROWN

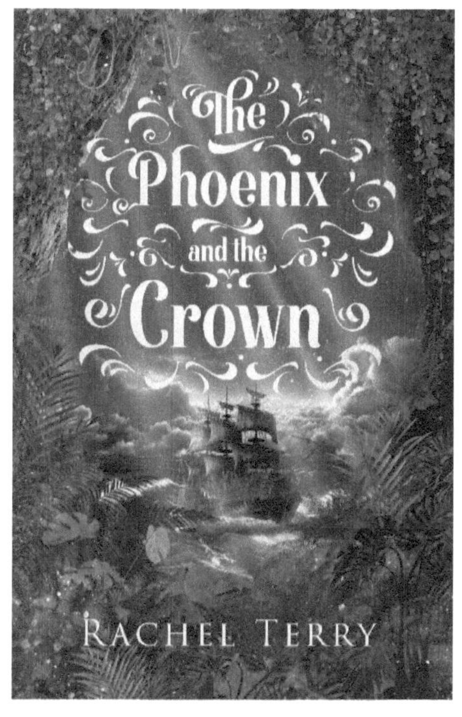

THE PHOENIX AND THE CROWN
Atlas Sea Book 1

A pirate with a deadly secret.
A princess desperate to save her dying kingdom.